Seal
of the
King

By
Ralph Smith

ACKNOWLEDGEMENTS

I would like to thank all of the people who helped make this story better by reading my early drafts and providing terrific input.

Lisa Alexander
Dennis Berube
Kim Brotherton
Mary Cilia
Anita Gillies
Tressa Janik (editing and input)
Peggy Meisch (final editing and input)
Deanna Roma
Sarah Scarborough – for her input, and Fantastic original cover art
William Smith (my son)
Martha Watson Stone

I would like to give particular thanks to my wife Martha, and my mother-in-law Alice, for all their hard work in helping me edit the early drafts and for all their input.

Visit us on the web at www.sealoftheking.com

TABLE OF CONTENTS

ACROSS THE DIVIDE

The flash of light was blinding. Raising his arms and ducking, he could feel the heat against his skin, and then it was gone. In that flash he had seen her again, her auburn hair swirling off her face as she turned, her dark eyes flashing that steely determination. He had seen her countless times before and knew her every detail. He looked around, but no one else appeared to have seen anything. Their curious looks told him they noticed his strange behavior. He was used to that. It had always been that way.

It started as far back as he could remember. When he was a child, it was his "imaginary friend". As he got older, though, he realized she wasn't like the childhood imaginings of others. She was something much more. There was a time when it confused him, and he felt alone because of his secret, but ultimately it became his strength. He knew without a doubt that she existed. He didn't understand it, but her strength was his strength.

In momentary glimpses, he watched her grow from a child to a woman, and she was always with him. The adorable little girl with flowers braided in her hair beaming up at her mother. The look of determination on her face as she fought her way up a tree, returning a hatchling to its nest; her tears of sadness at the sight of its lifeless body lying on the ground the following day. The countless images of her painted a picture of her innocence, her joy, her loving heart, and her passion for life.

As he watched her grow into a woman, he saw her suffer the pain of loss; he ached with the sense of her loneliness, witnessed the determined little girl become the fearless warrior. Yet what captivated him was that her pain had not turned to bitterness. It had molded her into a ferocious defender. Etched in his memory were scenes of her cradling a wounded child in the midst of battle, tenderly comforting a woman in front of the smoldering remains of a home, the look of joy on her face surrounded by young boys and girls playing, carefree under her watchful eyes. These scenes created a mosaic illustrating the beautiful spirit inside this amazing woman.

The affection he felt for her as a person frustrated him. How he wished he could ease her pain and loneliness and give her the comfort she so willingly gave to others. As much as her inner beauty captivated him, he also found the sight of her mesmerizing. Her long dark hair fell in waves down past her shoulders, her lean athletic frame was so strong and graceful. He had never seen a woman more beautiful.

At the behest of others, he had dated here and there, but to no avail, because she was there first. She was the standard that no other woman had ever come close to. He knew that to try to explain it to anyone was impossible. Either they would think him a fool or crazy. So he lived with his secret and the burden of carrying it. It was the thing that kept him separate from the rest of the world, living in the part of his heart no one else could see where he protected it willingly. There were times he thought she saw him too, looking at him with a warm smile or a longing gaze. She was his most precious possession, and yet he felt empty because of it. Like standing behind glass, seeing something so close, yet being unable to reach out to touch it.

He continued on his way down the busy streets, sliding unnoticed amongst the crowd, alone with his thoughts. It was times like this that being alone in a crowd was comforting. He didn't have to talk to anyone and he could hold that image in his mind; rolling it around like a precious jewel. Suddenly it occurred to him that this time was different from the others. He had felt the heat. It didn't register immediately because of his desire to get away from the looks of curiosity. He had never had an actual physical experience before. At first he dismissed the thought. Yes, it must have been his imagination. But no, he looked at his forearms and to his amazement saw some of the hairs on his arm were singed. How could that be? He considered it for a moment, and realized that, whatever the reason, things were going to change. He wasn't sure how, but he knew something was happening.

***

She had barely escaped the ball of fire; her skin still stinging from the intense heat. She glanced briefly at the tree it had smashed into, splintering it like a twig as it toppled away from her. She had moved out of their line of sight and allowed herself to pause and catch a few breaths, then headed off again. Making her way as quickly as possible while trying to maintain her cover, she knew she was in trouble. They were driving her towards the open plain where she would be exposed, but she had little choice. Her only hope was to make it to the gorge and lose them there.

Her endurance would be tested, but she was not about to give up. She pushed her thoughts of physical strain away and replaced them with what she had seen. He had been standing there looking at her, and had put his arms up to shield himself from the fire. She was all alone; separated from her team weeks ago, but knowing he was watching over her buoyed her strength.

Her whole life, the visions of him had given her strength and comfort. As a child, he was her friend when she was alone, smiling when she was happy, and sympathetic when she was sad. She reached out for her favorite memories of him, struggling with a horse twice his size, tending to a birthing calf, running with glee to his mother's welcoming embrace. He was unlike any boy she had known. She never saw him angry or mean. He always had a kind expression on his face.

She had endured a lot of teasing and looks of amusement when she spoke of him, but she didn't care. She knew he was real, and no one was going to convince her otherwise. When she was young, she was certain they would meet someday. But as she watched him grow into a man; tall and strong, so confident and self-assured, she had her doubts. His life, his world, was so different from hers. She saw things she never imagined even existed. She had no idea where he was or how to get there, and her life, her path, was set; she could never leave to find out.

She had no interest in marriage. She was a soldier, and would not rest in the fight against these wretched men as long as she could draw a breath. He was not in battle, and she had seen him with other boys and girls. She thought that with his rugged good looks, light brown hair, strong build, and penetrating eyes, he would have found a woman by now. Yes, she thought he was handsome, but her life followed a different path. She could not stand by as others suffered, and do nothing. She buried her thoughts of a normal life deep inside.

His life offered her a respite from her trials and eased the constant loneliness she felt. She saw him many times, his gritty determination to complete some task, or sitting staring off at nothing, his look of lonely melancholy inspiring a feeling of kinship with him. She thought that as different as his life was, he was just as alone as she was, but at least they had each other. She never told anyone about him anymore. As a child, her parents would give her an amused smile. And when she talked about him to the other children, they would tease her. Now he was her treasured secret; the precious thing she always had with her that no one could take away.

It had been nearly ten years now that she had been fighting in this war. She couldn't count all the missions and battles, but today for the first time she truly thought this one could be her last. Pushing that thought away, she reminded herself that she could not fail. She had to get "it" to the council; the tide of the war depended on it. She was being chased by well over fifty men; hard men who would fill her final moments of life with unimaginable torment if they caught her, and laugh while doing it.

She loathed all the killings, and felt the pain of it every time she dispatched even one of these wretched men. Long ago she had learned to live with it and let it go. She had no choice. If she hesitated, they would not. If she failed, someone else would pay the price. In spite of the overwhelming odds, she did not panic; panic was death. She needed her wits about her. She would fight to her last breath. With that in mind, she pulled forth her memories. She needed him now more than ever.

***

The next thing he knew, he was standing at his car door not quite sure how he had gotten there. Petersburg, a small city in northern Kentucky, sitting snugly on the bend in the river, was the epicenter for the larger farming community that surrounded it. David came into the city every Saturday and once a month during the week to take care of business matters. Because of its location on the river, it attracted tourists as well as serving as the distribution point for all the meat and produce for farmers like David. From here, ships and trains moved their goods off to other parts of the country, so the city was usually packed with people moving to and fro. The residents were friendly. Southern hospitality was alive and well here, but he was always ready to leave when the time came.

The countryside was where he felt at home. He had a strong connection to the outdoors. He longed for those days when he and his father had spent camping. In fact, he always kept camping gear in the car with him. He wasn't sure why. Perhaps a part of him wanted to be ready to go, just in case. Every excursion they went on was an adventure; climbing mountains, and building shelters. Hunting and fishing for food. It seemed his father knew everything about, well, everything. His father told stories day and night and captivated his imagination. Tales of kings and queens, monsters, rescues, ferocious beasts; it seemed there was no end, and every twist in the road or plant or tree reminded him of something else to share.

Often gone for days at a time, when they would arrive home, his mother would always hurry out to meet them as if they had been on a dangerous quest, possibly never to return. Her beautiful face would light with joy, and oh, her lovely embrace. He could close his eyes, see her face, smell her hair, and feel her holding him close as if never wanting to let him go.

Those years growing up on the farm were filled with long hard days, and yet he never wanted them to end. He got along well with just about anyone, but at the same time he always felt different and separate. Home was where he felt connected; there was something about being on his farm that renewed him. Even after his parents were gone, that was where he could find peace.

He was outside the city in no time and gazed out at the rolling fields separated by small forests. Life teamed around him, even though fall was setting in. He always enjoyed the sights of the animals grazing and the plowed fields lying dormant, waiting for spring. He was a farmer, like his father, because he loved it. His trip to the city today was farm business. He had managed the farm well these past six years, and had just paid off their last loan. He was proud of himself for being a good steward, and only wished his parents were there to see it.

The accident that took them from him was still a mystery. They were driving home late one night, and the car was found in a burning heap. His father was badly hurt, but not from the fire. His mother's body was never found. The authorities said that since the heat was so intense, they thought his mother must have been incinerated in the wreck. And now his father sat in a wheel chair staring off into space, unable to care for himself. It broke his heart seeing him that way, but he still went every week to visit.

His father had been so strong and could do anything. He made everything look easy. His father was the bravest man he had ever known. He never hesitated; when he was with him it always felt as if nothing bad could happen, yet as strong as he was, he had a gentle spirit. His father never belittled him, even when it came to his "imaginary friend". In fact, both his parents always accepted it as a matter of fact, and never tried to convince him that she wasn't real.

The drive home went by quickly, and the next thing he knew, he was turning off the road onto the driveway of the farm. As so often happens when he was remembering his parents, he lost all track of time. Feeling a bit melancholy as he drove up the dirt road to the farmhouse, it lifted his spirit to see Rusty, his chocolate lab, bounding out to meet him. Pulling to a stop, he hopped out of the Jeep, bracing for 100 pounds of furry love, and he wasn't disappointed.

"Hey boy, I missed you too. Have you been keeping an eye on things today?" He asked Rusty, as he rubbed behind his ears. The dog's paws pressed on his chest, while his hind quarters wagged in excitement. "Did anything happen while I was gone today? Come on, let's go inside, and get you something to eat." Rusty jumped down, and they walked up to the house.

He kept the house and yard just as it was when his parents were here. The plants in front of the porch were well tended and the grass neatly mowed. The front porch was inviting, even at dusk, with a swing and a few chairs to sit and relax on. They walked into the house, and everything was in the same place as the night his parents never came home. He didn't use the living room much, and hadn't had a fire in the hearth since then. He spent most of his time in the kitchen and den. He and Rusty made their way back to the kitchen, turning the lights on as they went.

The kitchen was warm, well worn, and large enough for a table and chairs. It was clearly made for cooking, canning, and preparing any other foods from the farm. Rusty was wagging his whole back end with the excitement of eating, as the bowl was placed on the floor. Looking out the window, while he filled the dog's water bowl, he noticed some strange lights off in the distance.

He absentmindedly put the bowl down as the dog ate steadily. Then he made his way to the rear door. The back porch was just large enough to escape the rain and clean your boots before coming inside. Standing there he had a clear view, and off in the distance he could see lights dancing in the trees. Standing there, he felt the hairs on the back of his neck stand on end, and a tingling sensation that began to run through him like static electricity. Something was going on, and he knew it couldn't wait until morning.

INTRODUCTIONS

He made his way back inside, "Rusty, you stay here. I'll be back in a while." He said to the dog, who was contentedly eating. It occurred to him that it was a bit strange that Rusty didn't seem to notice. The dog knew if a squirrel was in the garden while he slept, and yet, he seemed entirely unaware that anything was out of the ordinary.

He headed to the door, grabbing his coat and keys. In moments he was back in the Jeep, (the 4 wheel drive was a necessity on this property), and he headed out on the dirt road leading in the direction of the disturbance. The road was rough so he couldn't go too fast, but he was feeling a strange sense of urgency.

Unexpectedly his thoughts turned to her. It was many years ago. She was leading a team of men in the woods. She moved through the dense forest effortlessly while the others strained to keep up. They emerged from the forest and intercepted a group of enemy soldiers, with her in the lead. The fighting was fierce, and she was a blur of motion. A huge soldier was bearing down on her, while at the same time one of her team members was in trouble. With a look of complete calm, she sent an arrow to the defense of her compatriot first, leaving her only seconds to ward off her own attacker. Dispatching him with ease, she raced off to the aid of another of her fellows.

David, heading into the unknown, thinking of her, her strength, her courage, smiled.

***

She knew the soldiers were gaining on her, despite her grueling pace. She had led them to an area that was too rugged for them to take advantage of their horses, so they were pursuing her on foot now. Her strength was waning while the soldiers, having had the benefit of riding to catch up with her, were undaunted. The gorge was still far off, and at this rate they would overtake her before she got there. Her legs strained, managing the difficult terrain. But she was not one to panic, and as long as her heart beat, she had hope, but her hope was fading.

A memory of him floated to the surface. He couldn't have been more than ten or twelve years old. He found the calf injured, its leg stuck between two rocks. The area was remote, and it was near dusk. Freeing it, he tried to help it walk. The calf fell to the ground, so he picked it up. He struggled desperately to manage its weight. By the time he arrived back at the farm, it was pitch black. The frantic look of worry on his parent's faces, as he collapsed from the exertion, turned to joy at his smile of reassurance. He would never give up, and neither would she.

When she heard the whistle of the first arrow, it sent a chill through her. She knew better than to look back. She needed to focus on where she was going. A single misstep and they would have her. Even as tired as she was, her adrenalin kicked in. It gave her a small surge in her stride, but she still had a long way to go. Suddenly to her left, a massive flaming ball shattered a dying tree, sending sparks and debris flying. The acrid smell of the burning oil filled her nostrils. Her eyes stung slightly from the heat and ash. She dodged to her right just in time to avoid a few arrows. She quickly scanned the area, looking for anything that would give her an advantage, but she was exposed. There were some rock formations off to her left, but they were too far, and the lateral move would give them too much time to catch up with her. The reality of her situation hit her hard. Could this truly be the end for her? Unable to spare the breath to speak, she called out in her heart, and mind, Dear Lord save me!

**

He had gone as far as the road would take him. He would have to make the rest of the way on foot. The moon was out, so he had enough light to see. He had covered every inch of this ground countless times day and night, so the limited light didn't bother him. The crisp night air seemed to echo his senses. They were as sharp as could be. Every sight and sound caught his attention. He was moving through the woods as fast as he could, his sense of urgency rising. He knew he was getting close when he heard something.

The sounds were muffled like listening through water. It was the sounds of voices; the muted cries of an excited mob. As he moved towards a clearing he knew well, the sight before him took his breath away. What should have been a peaceful meadow was now a barren stretch of land filled with smoke. Small fires burned trees that were smashed, and splintered into kindling. A horde of men were making their way up the rise, brandishing swords, axes, spears, and bows. Shouting and screaming, their unkempt hair and beards gave them a barbaric appearance. Wearing dark cloaks and a variety of leather or chain mail armor, they were a fearsome sight to behold.

Out ahead of them, their quarry moved gracefully through the difficult terrain, her long legs dancing around obstacles as she evaded their arrows. Her dark hair floated off her shoulders, whipping to and fro with each of her evasive moves. She never looked back, but was always one step ahead of their attacks. In an instant, he knew who it was.

For a split second, he drank in her grace and beauty. She was strong and agile, and moved with an assuredness that was mesmerizing. She was not afraid. At least fifty men were clambering along behind her, but she showed no signs of panic. The small pack on her back, a bow, and quiver of arrows, were held fast against her slim yet muscular frame. She wore dark leather and tall boots that fit well and moved easily with her. His glimpses of her had always been fleeting. To see her like this was like finding water in the desert.

At once, he was filled with so many emotions that he couldn't move. The overwhelming joy at seeing her made him want to cry out. Then the terror of her predicament sent a wave of fear through him. There she was, all alone, trying to outrun death. He was barely able to breathe as a tear ran down his cheek, his heart breaking at the prospect of what was going to happen to her. With his next breath, all his emotions swirled into a rage-filled determination, propelling him to action.

His hesitation having lasted only a moment, he moved to intercept her, although he had no idea what he was going to do. He would not let these men lay a hand on her. No matter what the cost, he would try to save her. She did not see him coming, and he closed the gap between them quickly. Fortunately for him, her pursuers did not seem to notice him either. A few strides away and he saw it; a giant ball of fire heading directly towards her.

Having just dodged a barrage of arrows, she moved into its path. At a full sprint, he leapt towards her with his arms outstretched. As he grabbed her upper body, he twisted to pull her down on top of him so he would absorb the blow. He caught the look of shock on her face as she turned and saw the fireball pass just above, right where her head had been a split second earlier.

The moment she was in his arms, there was an explosion of sound and light. The magnitude of it was something he couldn't have conceived. The only thing he could think of is that it was like being inside a bolt of lightning when it struck, but even that seemed inadequate. Time suddenly stopped and lost all meaning. His only thought was to hold onto her, afraid that if he let go, she would be lost.

He hit the ground hard with her limp weight on top of him. He could feel her chest rise and fall against his. The brisk night air on his face, the return of the starry sky, and the sudden quiet told him that he was home again. The soft grass of the meadow was a far better place to land than the hard ground they had just left, but he was still momentarily stunned from the blow.

Looking from side to side, he could see enough to know they were alone. Then it hit him. He was there with her. All these years of seeing her, admiring her, believing in her, and now she was in his arms; a living, breathing person. He closed his eyes and soaked in the feel of her against him, the smell of her skin and hair. He was almost afraid to re-open them; afraid that if he did, she would be gone. He had been alone for so long, and she had been his only real comfort. Affection for her swelled inside him, after all she had done for him, helping to carry him through his loss and pain. To be there for her when she needed him filled him with joy to the point near giddiness. He felt her stir slightly, and instinctively reached up to touch the back of her head for comfort, to let her know she was all right.

At his touch, she sprang to her feet, and spun to take in the surroundings. In one fluid motion she drew her bow and nocked an arrow pointed straight at his heart. His eyes opened wide, but he didn't move a muscle. Amazed by everything about her, he just stared up into her deep dark eyes. That she could go from virtual unconsciousness to battle ready, in mere seconds with such grace and fluidity, demonstrated what he knew in his heart. She was no one to be trifled with.

Suddenly her eyes went wide and her bow lowered just a bit. She hesitated perhaps for the first time in her life. It only lasted a second, but it was just long enough to make him smile. She grimaced with annoyance at herself for letting her guard down, and quickly resumed her deadly stance. He couldn't help himself. His smile broadened, much to her annoyance.

"Why are you smiling? Do you think I won't kill you where you lie?" She asked with a forceful and commanding tone.

"I'm smiling because I've known you my whole life, and I never thought I would have the pleasure of your company. I'm smiling because just seeing you standing there is enough for me. And if I were to die in this moment, I have no regrets." He said. His smile gone now, replaced with the look of sincerity he felt in those words. She fidgeted uncomfortably, and he could see the turmoil building inside her. He knew she wasn't going to kill him, but wasn't sure what she was thinking.

**

Her head was spinning. She had almost given up all hope, had thought she was racing to her death, and now she found herself face-to-face with him. She swayed slightly trying to keep her balance. She had been reaching out for the strength he always gave her, and here he was instead. It was almost too much to comprehend. Out of thin air, he had clutched her from certain death; she had seen the fireball too late. She knew by all rights she should be dead.

He wore the kind expression she had seen countless times before. She knew in her heart who he was. He was strong, gentle, and caring. The one man, above all others, she felt she could trust, even though they had never met. He was the only one left who had been with her through her entire life. He was the only one who knew who she truly was. He knew her before everything changed, and knew the woman she had become.

Her instincts that had been forged during ten long years of fighting were colliding with her emotions in a way she had never experienced. She never let her guard down, and yet her heart told her she should. The conflict raging inside her overwhelmed her. It was all too much for her to understand.

***

He could see her chest rise and fall as she tried to take in calming breaths. Then the last thing he expected happened. She fell to her knees, dropped her bow, and began to weep. She lifted her hands to her face to hide her embarrassment.

He quickly got up and knelt beside her. He reached over to take her hands in his. "It's Ok, you're safe now," he said as she looked up into his eyes, her deep dark beautiful eyes full of tears running down her face. Now instead of the strong confident woman of purpose, he saw the vulnerable little girl who, no doubt, had been locked away for a long time. His heart ached for her, he wanted nothing more than to comfort her and take away her pain.

"Is it really you?" She asked, "I've seen you my whole life too, but never thought we would meet."

He smiled at her again, "I never dared to hope that we would meet either, yet you've always been with me." She began to sob, and he put his arms around her as she pressed her head to his chest to hide and find comfort. He sat there quietly stroking her head to calm her, waiting patiently for her to regain her composure. The truth was he felt as though he could sit there forever, feeling her against him, and it would be enough.

Finally, she pushed away from him, "I'm sorry. I haven't cried since I was a child. I don't know what came over me," she said, wiping the last of her tears from her face.

"It's all right. You were in a lot of trouble when I found you," he said. Standing up, he reached out his hand to help her to her feet. She hesitated a moment, then took his hand. Her skin felt warm and soft, yet her grip was strong and firm. Once on her feet, she gathered up her bow and arrow and replaced them on her back.

"I ... I thought it was the end for me," she said softly, looking down. "Those men have been chasing me for weeks, and they had me on the run all day."

"I see," he said, "that does explain some things."

"What do you mean?"

"The last time I saw you, there was a flash of light, and the hair on my arm was singed. As a matter of fact, that was earlier today."

She stood tall, and said, "Oh yes, I was almost more than a little singed that time."

He smiled at her, "I guess introductions are in order. My name is David."

She froze for a moment then said in a little more than a whisper "David?"

"Yes, does that mean anything to you?"

"Let's not talk about it here."

"Ok, my home isn't far, and I can get you something to eat while we talk," he said while smiling at her. "Although there is one thing I must know first."

"What's that?" She asked in surprise.

"What is your name?" He asked, smiling.

She gave a little laugh "Aurora. I guess I'm not used to meeting strangers with manners anymore."

"Well. Aurora, I just thank God I was there to find you."

"Where are we?" She said regaining her look of confidence.

"That, I think, is going to take some figuring out for both of us. Let's just say for now that you're on my farm, and you're safe."

As they started off, he could tell that she wasn't taking any chances and was on the lookout for anything unusual. Even though he was sure they were safe, he was also keeping a watchful eye. Walking together, his heart lifted. His fear of almost seeing her killed having abated, he felt like a schoolboy on a first date, and found himself grinning for no reason at all.

He led them through the woods back to where he parked his jeep. As they emerged from the woods and saw the car, she hesitated. Noticing her concern, he said, "It's Ok. That belongs to me. We'll use it to go the rest of the way back to the house."

"What is it?"

"It's an automobile, originally known as a horseless carriage." He smiled his reassurance.

"A carriage, without horses, how does that work?"

"It's probably easier if I show you," He replied. He walked her to the passenger side and opened the door. "Climb in and sit down." Once she was inside, he shut the door and made his way around to the driver's side. He opened the door and smiled as he watched her looking at everything with such curiosity. It had been so long since things like cars held such fascination for him, and to see her wide eyed wonder was endearing.

He put the keys in the ignition. When the car roared to life, she was startled a bit, and then smiled at him sheepishly. He turned the car around and started down the rough road to the house. As bumpy as it was, she was un-phased as she looked around and out the windows, taking it all in.

"This is the most comfortable carriage I've ever been in."

"On a better road it's even nicer."

"You have better roads than this?" She asked. "I've been on roads that were much worse."

"Since it's just me now, I don't get as much time to tend to the roads."

"You live here all alone?"

"Yes, just me, and Rusty, my dog. Other than the farm hands, it's just me."

She looked at him curiously but didn't say anything. He could tell she just didn't know what to make of the situation she found herself in. He was truly impressed by her, landing in a place so different, and not the slightest sign of fear or disorientation. Yes, she was fascinated by things, but still keenly aware of what was going on around her, and certainly she was no one to be underestimated. He could see her marking every movement he made; the turns on the road, the position of the moon. He was careful to take measured deliberate movements so as not to frighten her.

***

Aurora was sitting there amazed by everything. His world was so different from hers, and yet everything she saw felt so familiar too. She had seen him more times than she could count, and knew his world was different. Now she was able to inspect details that passed by too quickly in the glimpses she had over the years. She found it all fascinating.

It felt exhilarating and overwhelming all at the same time. She thought everything that had happened might be too much to cope with if not for his calming presence. He was her tether to reality. In her heart, she felt that he was everything she had imagined. All the visions she had of him throughout her entire life fit together seamlessly forming a picture. That picture was as clear in her mind as her own reflection, and it seemed to fit him perfectly.

She sat there taking it all in. She felt a nervous excitement, and at the same time she was afraid. She wasn't sure what frightened her. It wasn't the kind of fear she felt going into battle. This was something different, something she had never felt before. She had all but dismissed the idea they'd ever meet, and in the blink of an eye everything had changed.

***

As they pulled up to the house, Rusty had come running up to meet them. David looked over, and said, "It's all right; that's my dog Rusty. He'll watch over us while we're eating." She gave a small smile as if embarrassed that he read her thoughts. He hopped out of the car and gave Rusty a quick hello. "Rusty, we have a guest I want you to meet." He walked around to the passenger side and saw her trying to push the door open. "Allow me," he said, then opened the door and pointed to the inside handle. "You pull on this from the inside to open it". He made sure to keep any hint of amusement from his voice. He didn't want her to think he was mocking her ignorance. What he did find amusing was that clearly she wasn't used to anyone helping her with anything. He reached out his hand to help her down, and she hesitated once again before taking it.

When Rusty began sniffing her feet and legs, she looked at David for guidance. "It's Ok. That's his way of saying hello. He likes everyone." David reached down and scratched Rusty behind the ears. "Come on boy, lead the way into the house. This is Aurora, and I'm sure she's hungry." Aurora realized that she was, in fact, very hungry. Everything that had happened had kept her mind so busy that she hadn't realized it until he said it.

As they approached the house, Aurora looked around, and asked, "Did you build all this?"

David gave her a small sad smile, "No, my parents did, with some help. They moved here long before I was born, and built this place for our family."

Aurora gently touched his arm, and said, "It's lovely," then smiled. Her smile lifted his heart, and he smiled back. They walked up the front steps and into the house. Her eyes roaming over every square inch, taking in all the strange things she had never seen before.

David was surprised at his own calm. They had just experienced something so extraordinary, so unbelievable, but all he could think about was her. She needed him. She was the one who had almost been killed.

She was thrust into a strange place, and he was her only link to reality. There would be time to try to figure out what happened, but for now the only thing that mattered to him was her, and he couldn't let her down.

David knew better than to ask her to leave her pack at the door, so he walked her to the kitchen. "I'll be happy to show you around, but first you need something to eat," he volunteered, "and if you'd like to wash up, there's a bathroom here." Realizing she may not be familiar with how his world handled indoor plumbing, he thought he would spare her the embarrassment of asking. He opened the door and stepping inside, turned on the taps. "This one is cold water, this one is hot, and if you need to use the toilet, sit here, and when you're finished, push this lever. Here's the light switch, clean towels, and some soap. " She watched him intently, studying what he was showing her.

"Do you eat meat?"

She slowly turned her gaze from the taps and looked at him. "Yes, I eat meat." She said in a distant voice.

"Ok, I have some stew with meat and vegetables, some bread and cheese, and then we'll need something to drink. Do you prefer water, coffee, or tea? " She looked at him for a long moment. "Is everything all right?"

She broke his gaze, and looking down, said softly, "Life has been extremely hard for a long time, and I'm not used to such luxury. I'm also not used to strangers showing such generosity."

He gave her a small smile of understanding, "First, let me tell you that I expect nothing in return. Secondly, I was raised to show strangers hospitality, and to help those in need. And from what I saw tonight, you are undoubtedly in need." Her gaze softened, and she managed a small smile, too. She went into the bathroom and closed the door, taking her pack with her. David went to the kitchen sink and washed his face and hands. He didn't want to leave in case she came out before he got back, and might be unnerved finding herself suddenly alone in such a strange place.

He went to the refrigerator and got out the stew he had made the day before, checking to see if there was plenty for the two of them. He put it on the stove to heat and got out the bread and cheese. He realized that she never did say what she wanted to drink, so he poured a couple of glasses of ice water and put on a pot for tea. He thought that might help her relax. He set out the bowls and put the bread, cheese, some fresh fruit, and water on the table. As he was stirring the stew, she came out of the bathroom looking a bit refreshed, but tired.

He walked over to the table and pulled out a chair with its back to the wall, and held it for her to sit down. "Here, have a seat and help yourself to some food while I finish warming the stew." He noticed her surveying the room and his choice of seating for her. She seemed to approve and sat down, putting her pack on the chair next to her, easily within reach. "You never did answer my question, so I got you some cold water, and I'm making tea." She gave him a smile of approval and picked up the water, casually putting it under her nose. David pretended not to notice; then saw her take a long drink.

"Oh, this is so cold, and there's ice in it."

"I hope it isn't too cold for you. I can get you some without the ice."

"Oh no, it tastes good. I just didn't think it was cold enough for ice."

"This is a refrigerator and freezer." He opened the doors each in turn. "It keeps food cold or frozen, and we use it to make ice." She leaned over to peer inside and saw the variety of items on the shelves, most of which looked utterly foreign to her. Seeing her lean back, David closed the door and went back to stir the stew. Leaning over, he inhaled through his nose and proclaimed. "I think that's warm enough." She watched as he turned the dial on the stove, and the flame went out. He took the pot to the table and ladled some into each of their bowls, making sure he gave her plenty of meat. He set the pot back on the stove, and then joined her at the table.

Looking concerned she asked, "Who are you? Is this all a dream? Everything is so strange to me, yet at the same time familiar. Did I die tonight?"

He smiled, "You know me, just as I know you. I've spent my life seeing you day in and day out, and apparently you've seen me the same way too. There will be time for us to learn about each other, but for now I trust what I already know. You didn't die tonight. I suppose that after all these years it was finally time for our paths to cross. So eat and rest, and when you have your strength back, you can tell me everything. In the meantime, I hope my cooking doesn't disappoint you."

David heard the words coming out of his mouth and was surprised again by how calm he was. He was as shocked as she was, but somehow her dismay made it possible for him to be calm. He wanted so much for her to be ok; for her not to be afraid, that it made it easy for him to keep his own fears bottled up.

She slowly shook her head, picked up a spoon, and tasted the stew. It was warm and comforting, just as he was. "I've had worse," she said grinning, and with that, they both began to eat.

David did his best not to stare, but he could see the restraint she was using not to eat too fast. It was clear that she hadn't eaten recently, and under the circumstances, he wasn't at all surprised. He had no idea how long she had been on the run from the soldiers. He felt a swell of affection for her rise in him, and his desire to help her pushed aside all the confusion he felt over what had just happened. As much as he wanted to figure out what was going on, that seemed much less important than taking care of her.

***

Aurora sat there feeling so overwhelmed she became numb. She had been moments away from death, and suddenly she was in a strange place sitting at a table with him. It was all too much to comprehend. A million questions swirled at the edge of her thoughts, but after such a tremendous physical struggle, her intense fatigue and ravenous hunger prevented her from thinking clearly. She had no choice but to accept her circumstance until she regained her strength, and then she could try to make sense of it.

She savored each bite of food. It had been so long since she had enjoyed a proper meal, and with every mouthful she felt her mind clear a little more. One conclusion she had come to was that she was safe for now, and after these past few weeks constantly on the run, that was something. She still had her mission, but she would not be able to complete it until she figured out what was going on. Obviously, she wasn't in her land anymore, and she had no idea how she was going to get back. She needed to rest. As her hunger became satisfied, she became keenly aware of how tired she was.

After a bowl and a half of stew, two pieces of bread, some cheese and fruit, she took a breath, and said with a sheepish grin, "I have to admit I wasn't entirely truthful before. This may be the best meal I've ever had."

David chuckled, "Then you certainly have had a rough time of it. I'll be sure to make you something better next time."

She was meticulously eating every scrap of food he put out well after David had stopped eating. Seeing her slowing down, he spoke, "I have a guest room for you to sleep in tonight, and there's a private bath so you can soak in the tub or take a shower if you'd like."

He half expected her to ask what a shower was when she said, "I don't know if I should stay." Her face suddenly saddened.

"Why would you think that?"

She looked into his eyes, and he was surprised to see how sad she looked. "You've been remarkably kind to me, and I'm afraid I may be putting you in danger. All this is so grand, and no one since I was a young girl has served me like this. It's all so confusing, and I ..." She broke off, her words trailing into silence.

"Dear Aurora, I've already told you. I've known you my whole life. I've seen you in small glimpses through a window I couldn't open. I've seen you grow from a child to a woman. I don't understand it any more than you do. I'm just as confused and frightened, but there's one thing I'm certain of." He paused, "Everything in my life, and probably in yours, is going to change. In fact, it has already changed. From the moment I left this house and headed to that meadow where I found you, my life has been irrevocably altered, and I have embarked upon that path with no regrets. So you are going to stay here and get some much-needed sleep. I'll stand watch over you and not allow one hair on your head to be harmed."

She opened her mouth to speak, but her voice failed under his gaze. "Now that we have that settled, on to more important matters," he said. She closed her mouth and looked concerned. "Would you like some more to eat?" He smiled warmly at her.

"No, thank you, I've had quite enough."

David stood, and began clearing the table; "There are some clothes here that belonged to my mother, if you'd like something to sleep in. I think they'll fit you well enough. I'd imagine your leather might need a rest too. If you're ready, I'll be happy to show you your room, and we can pick out something for you to wear."

"Yes, I'd like that."

He reached out to take her hand, and without hesitation, she took his. As she rose from the table she wobbled unsteadily. David put his arm out to catch her as she staggered into him. "Are you all right?"

"Yes, I think so. It was a long day, and it has been two days since I ate anything more than a biscuit."

Standing there with her leaning against him, he could feel his heart pounding, and a tingling sensation ran up the back of his neck. Her outdoors scent filling his nose, her warm strong body against him, he could have stood there for hours. She looked up at him, and her face was close to his. Their eyes met, and he suddenly felt weak, too.

"Are you feeling better now?" He managed to ask in a soft voice.

"Yes, I'll be fine." She said. They slowly separated, and he gently held her arm as they walked back to the living room.

"This is the living room, although I don't spend much time in here since my parents.... I can make a fire while you change if you want to sit up. "

The room was filled with comfortable looking furniture; a couch, and some armchairs, the kind of room where a group of people could sit around and talk in front of the fire. "And back this way is the den where I usually sit and relax in the evening."

This room seemed to fit his personality better. It had a large overstuffed couch and chair, reading lamps, and a television. He thought she probably had not seen a TV either, but left that for another time. "Back here are the bedrooms. The guest room is over there to the left, and this room to the right is ... was my parents' room."

They walked in through the doorway. The décor was simple; a large bed, a couple of dressers, a door to some closets, and another to the bath. On the walls, the top of the dressers and the nightstands were pictures; lots of pictures. "This is my mother's dresser, and through here is her closet. You can pick out anything you need. I'll give you a minute while I finish cleaning the kitchen."

Looking a little lost she said, "Thank you. I don't know what to say."

David smiled "You don't have to say anything. I'm sure she wouldn't mind."

Aurora stood there as he left the room. She absent-mindedly set her pack down on the bed. Suddenly she felt a little silly that she was carrying it around, but she never let it out of her sight. Her survival often depended on it. She moved over to the dresser that he said was his mother's and opened the top drawer. Inside were undergarments like she had never seen before. They were so smooth and soft, and they shimmered in the light. She had never felt cloth like this. She also found some thick socks that would be warm and comfortable. In the next drawer were some long cotton nightshirts that would go all the way to her knees. She pulled one out and held it up to look at. Yes, this would be comfortable to sleep in. She wandered over to the closet. David had put the light on for her. One side was filled with beautiful dresses, and she couldn't help but run her hands over them. There was another rack of shirts and pants. Pants made of thick blue cotton she was sure would be extremely durable. She couldn't imagine having so much to wear. She only had what she could carry with her. This life, his life, was so foreign to her.

She walked back out to the dresser and looked for the first time at the pictures. Immediately she knew they were of his parent, and him. She recognized him as the boy; she too had watched him grow from a child to a man. Staring, without seeing, at one of the pictures, suddenly something in the back of her mind tugged at her. She stared intently, not at him, but at his mother. There was something she couldn't quite hold onto, floating at the edge of her memory.

"Hi, did you find something to wear?" David stood leaning against the doorway, the sound of his voice caused the thread of her memory to slip away.

"Yes, thank you," she replied. "I was looking at this picture, and there was something...." And her voice trailed off.

He walked over to her. "Oh, that's a picture of my parents and me. It was the day before the accident." He said in a soft voice.

She paused, not wanting to seem insensitive to his loss. "Something about her is familiar, but I can't quite place it." Her voice sounded a bit distant.

"In my mind, when I saw you over the years, I often saw you with other people. Perhaps you saw her with me at some point." He said reassuringly.

"Yes maybe that's it." She said, uncertainly.

"Perhaps, with a good night's sleep, it'll become clear in the morning." He said with a smile.

She slowly replaced the frame onto the dresser as if it were a delicate object that could shatter if set down too hard. "You put this here?"

"Yes, it was the last picture of us together, and I felt it belonged with the rest of them."

Not wanting to continue that conversation David said, "I took the liberty of starting a bath for you. Why don't you come this way, so you can soak for a while before you go to sleep?"

She grabbed her pack in one hand and the borrowed clothes in the other, turned to him, and said, "That does sound good."

She followed him out of the room and watched as he gently closed the door, as if trying not to wake a sleeping child. As he led her down the hallway to the guest room, something about the doorways began to tug at her memory, too. She dismissed it, and thought to herself that he was probably right that she had seen glimpses of this place over the years.

"Here you go," said David as he pushed open the door to the guest room. It wasn't as large as his parents', although she expected as much, but it was decorated with comforting earth tones, and had a warm cozy feel to it. As soon as she passed over the threshold, she felt at ease. She knew she was safe in here.

"The bed has a comforter on it, which should be enough to keep you warm tonight, but there are extra linens in the closet. You can put your things wherever you wish. Tomorrow we can wash your clothes to get the road dust out of them. In here is the bath, and it works the same as the other one. The tub is almost full, and I put some bath soap in the water for you. The lavender will help you relax."

She set her pack on the bed along with the clothes. She peered into the bathroom and could see the steam rising from the water. It looked extremely inviting. "Where do you get all of the hot water? Is there a hot spring nearby?"

David turned, "Oh no, we make it with a heater in the other room."

She smiled, "Things are just so different here than my home."

David went in, turned off the taps, and came out of the bathroom. Suddenly they were face to face again, and the smaller space made it more difficult to pass. David froze for a second and felt a wave of nervousness wash over him, a thrill that ran through him. He looked into her eyes, and they seemed to see right into him, not with the same penetrating stare as before, but a longing to see inside him. He wanted desperately to embrace her, to hold her close to him, and never let go. Before he succumbed to his feelings, he reached up and gently placed his hands on her arms and moved around her, increasing the space between them, with his back to the door.

"I'm going to make a fire in the living room so when you're finished if you want to sit before you sleep, you can warm yourself by the fire. I'll leave the door slightly ajar, so if you need me, just call out and I'll come. I won't come back until you tell me, so you can get dressed in private. Take your time. There's no rush." She nodded her understanding, and he left the room.

CONNECTIONS

She stood there staring at the doorway he had just passed through. It was all so much to take in. This place was so comfortable, he was so comfortable, and he made her feel safe. She had not felt safe since she was a young girl, and to accept all this was difficult. She had never met anyone like him. He was so gentle with her, and yet he had a quiet strength about him. She found herself in the bathroom with her pack and clothes, not quite remembering moving. The hot water looked enticing, so she closed the door and set her things down. She slowly began untying the bindings of her clothes. He was kind not to mention how dirty they were, and undoing the laces was a difficult task. As she slid her arms, then her legs out of her travel clothes, the leather sticking to her skin, she felt her body breathe in the fresh air. She reached down to touch the water, and found it to be as warm and soothing as it looked. She carefully placed one foot at a time into the tub, and could feel the hot soapy water enveloping her. The hard smooth bottom of the tub wasn't like anything she had felt before. She slowly lowered herself into the water, the warmth of it rising up her legs to her hips, and then to her stomach. She leaned back to let the water cover her all the way to her neck. Resting her head against the back of the tub she sighed, all of her muscles rejoicing in the comfort they were always denied. She could smell the lavender he put in the bath, and took deep long breaths through her nose to savor it. After a few moments, she allowed herself to slide down so her head went entirely under the water. She ran her hands through her hair to shake out any dirt, and rubbed them over her face. Sitting up, the cool air against her cheeks was refreshing.

The room was so quiet she could have heard a pin drop. Now, all alone with her thoughts, she considered the events of the day. It was hard to imagine that a few hours ago she was so close to death. Although death did not frighten her, she knew she still had work to do. She absent-mindedly looked over at her pack. She had to deliver "it"; that much was still true. Even as she considered her mission, the thought came to her. How she wished she could stay here. She felt childish for even thinking it. Her work was too important, but in this moment her life, her struggles all seemed so far away. She always put her needs second, and ever since she lost her parents, she had been single-minded of purpose. She would not; could not, fail in helping defeat the Dark One.

Yet somehow everything was different now. She heard David's words in her head, "My life has irrevocably changed." She knew that her life had changed too, and there was no going back. There were many people who fought with her; good people who stood tall against the Dark

One, and she felt a strong kinship with them. But this man, David, was somehow different. He had touched her in ways no one else had, and in such a short time. Although it really hadn't been a short time at all. She also had known him her whole life, known his determination, his strength, and his kindness. Somehow they were bound together, and somehow that bond was significant.

Then she thought of the prophecy, but that was too much to consider now. He was right. She needed some rest and to gather her thoughts. She was always one to act, but knew that to act without thinking was foolish. She needed to know more, to understand why she was here, who he was, and how she ended up here. At least that's where she would start. There was still time; not time to be wasted, but time enough to figure out what to do next.

***

He sat on the floor with his back against the couch, staring into the fire. He was finding it difficult to clear his mind. He was listening for her just in case. His senses were all on alert. He knew they were safe here, but just the same, he was not about to let his guard down. Rusty was curled up next to him asleep, breathing slowly. His hand rested on the dog, feeling his warm side rise and fall. He had thought about reading, but nothing seemed as intriguing as what had just happened. He thought about turning on the television, just for a distraction, but didn't want the sound to keep him from hearing her. So he sat there, trying to piece the day together. One thing was certain; he didn't have a clue what was going on, and that frustrated him. Then there was Aurora; she was a real live living person. After all these years, she was in the guest room of his home, not just a vision. If someone had asked him yesterday what he wanted, he would have said to meet her. Now she was here, and he had no idea what to do. For a brief moment, emotion overwhelmed him. He wasn't ready for this. He had no one to turn to for guidance. He longed for his father's advice and counsel. He felt a tear escape as it ran down his cheek. Then he remembered she needed him to be strong, and he couldn't let her down.

Finding her in that field was surreal. He had seen her world time and again, but today, he was there. How was that even possible, he asked himself? He knew she didn't have any idea what was going on either, and it was the fact that she needed him that allowed him to regain his composure.

He had seen her strength, her determination, and her fearlessness for years. Today, though, he saw her vulnerability, and to see her vulnerable changed everything. Any shred of doubt he had about the reality of her existence had been stripped away. It opened a floodgate of feelings he didn't know he had. He was always willing to stand up for what was right, to protect and defend people who needed it, but this was something so much more. He knew somehow that no one else saw that side of her and that letting her guard down with him was extraordinary. With that gift came an enormous responsibility, and the question was, is he up to the task? He wanted nothing more than for the two of them to stay here where he could keep her safe, but that was a foolish dream. These moments of respite were fleeting, and what was to come would test his limits. He knew without a doubt that this was the beginning, not the end. That what lay ahead of him was sure to be the most challenging events he had ever faced. He closed his eyes and longed for his parents, for their guidance and reassurance. He was never one to hesitate, never afraid to jump headlong into a situation, but this was different. It was more than just his fate; it was hers. For the first time in a long time, he was afraid. What if he failed? What would the consequences be?

A creak of wood snapped him back to reality. His eyes flew open to see her standing in the entrance from the hall. He hurried to his feet and took in the sight of her. There stood the leather-clad warrior in a cotton nightshirt that ran all the way down to her knees. It was light blue with a small floral pattern. It gently wrapped her beautiful figure, not too snugly, but enough to reveal her lovely shape. She had on a pair of white socks that came up over her ankles. Her hair had been neatly brushed out and fell down past her shoulders. Her face, hands, and the lower part of her forearms were lightly tanned from all the time she spent outdoors. Her calves were pale white from always being covered under her traveling pants. She held her hands together in front of her, looking like a young girl in need of approval.

She smiled a little and said, "I thought I might sneak up on you, but I guess I was wrong. Is this gown all right for sleeping?"

David swallowed his mouth suddenly dry, "Yes, you look lovely. Is it comfortable?"

She moved into the room, "Oh yes, it's very comfortable. I'm not used to wearing something so soft."

David looked at her hands, "Where's your pack?" He asked. A brief look of panic, and she took off back to the room. He heard her padded footsteps rushing in to retrieve her precious belongings. He stood motionless waiting for her return; in his mind's eye he could still see her standing there.

She returned a moment later, her pack dangling at her side with a sheepish grin. "Sorry, I'm sure it's safe here, I'm just not used to letting it out of my sight."

David smiled at her, "I understand, and I thought as much. Would you like to sit by the fire? I have some fresh tea." David asked.

"Yes, that would be nice." She replied.

He motioned for her to sit on the couch, and then pulled a small throw blanket from a chair next to it. He covered her lap as she curled her legs up under her. She leaned against the arm and back of the couch, facing him as he went to the small table to fetch the tea.

"Do you take any sugar or milk in your tea?" He asked.

"No, just plain would be fine, thank you." He handed her the cup, then sat at the opposite end of the sofa, leaning back to face her.

"How was your bath?" He asked.

She smiled, "I don't think I've ever had one better. I might not have come out if the water hadn't started to get cold."

He grinned, "I hope you're feeling relaxed and ready for a decent night's sleep. I have a feeling that tomorrow is the beginning of a long journey, but I have no idea where."

She looked sadly down at her legs, "Are you sending me away?"

David leaned towards her and put his hand gently under her chin, raising her head up to meet his eyes. "Never. I should have said we have a long journey ahead of us." He smiled at her, and she smiled back at him.

After a momentary pause, he pulled back his hand, and she said, "That was foolish of me. You've been terribly kind, and I have no right to expect you to do anything more for me. I should leave tomorrow, so I don't burden you anymore or put you in danger." Her expression had changed to the look of determination he so admired in her.

David stared into her eyes, holding her gaze until she faltered, then said in a calm commanding voice, "From the moment I pulled you out of the way of that fireball tonight, your life became my responsibility. Our fates are bound together. In fact, I believe they were set since before we were born. It's no coincidence that I was there tonight and that you're here right now. So you have my oath that no matter the cost, I will see through to the end whatever journey we must take. I realized tonight that this is the beginning of something far greater than our two lives, and that we must both play our part. I will only ask one thing of you." She gave him a small nod, looking at him with a mixture of admiration, surprise, and trepidation. "You must promise me that no matter what happens, you will never doubt my commitment and loyalty to you."

She managed to force out a small "Yes."

David went on, "In return, I commit to you the same. No matter what, I trust in you. Somehow, I know without a doubt that it is our bond, our unbreakable bond that will protect us more than anything else. Every instinct I have tells me that we will be tested, and that it is that test that we must not fail. It may seem crazy after a few short hours to make such a statement, and anyone who has not seen what we have seen our entire lives wouldn't understand. I hope you don't think me a fool acting on a whim, but somehow tonight, all the pieces seem to be falling into place, and I've never been more certain of anything." He paused, looking at her for some sign that she didn't think he was crazy.

She looked down again, and for a moment he thought she had her doubts. Then she raised her head strong, and proud, and met his eyes. In a steady voice filled with confidence she spoke "You're right, it does seem crazy. In fact, if it were anyone else who said those things to me, I would leave this moment, but something more than my own heart or my own head tells me that what you said is true." Relieved, David managed a smile, and Aurora smiled back at him. Then he saw her looking frightened for the first time, "I'm terrified that I'll fail. I've never admitted that before because the stakes are too high. I only hope you can forgive me if I do." A single tear ran down her cheek. David reached out, cupping her face with his hand, wiping away the tear with his thumb.

He spoke in a gentle voice "Don't borrow trouble from tomorrow, for today has trouble enough of its own. I'm afraid, too, but you're going to be fine, and together we won't fail."

She closed her eyes and rested her head in his hand. It was so comforting to feel his strength. She always had to be the strong one. This was the first time she felt it was ok to let go. For ten long years she had carried a heavy burden, and the weight of it was crushing at times, but it had suddenly lightened. After a few moments she opened her eyes and saw him sitting there, still holding her head in his hand, and drinking her face in with his eyes. She lifted her head, and he slowly recoiled his arm. Turning to look at the fire, she noticed it. She sat upright without a word.

"What is it?" David said. She was staring intently at the fireplace.

"Do you see that in the middle?"

He turned to look, "Do you mean in the fire?"

She shook her head, "No, in the middle above the opening. The circular design"

David looked back at her, "Yes, I'm not sure what it means, but my parents carved it into the house above every door and window."

Shocked, she turned to look, and to her surprise she saw it everywhere watching over them. "Do you have any idea what it is?" She asked her mind racing.

"No, they've always been here, and my parents never talked about them. I always liked the design and found it comforting to look at, but never thought to ask my parents what it meant." He said with his curiosity building. "Do you know what it means?" He asked.

"Yes, it's His mark, the mark of our Lord. That's why I feel so safe here; they cannot pass this seal. When his true servants place this seal, it creates a barrier that the Dark One and his servants cannot cross. Your parents must have been His servants."

"Yes, they were believers, they taught me everything about his word, and ... "

She cut him off "I'm sorry, I think you misunderstand me, it isn't just enough to believe. They must have been more than that."

He looked at her confused, "What do you mean?"

"Where I come from, there are followers. They are people who believe in the light. And then there are followers with gifts, like me. Then there are His servants. They are born that way. They stand in both worlds,

His and ours. They guide us in the fight against the dark. At least one of your parents had to be His servant"

David sat there silently, trying to understand the implications of what she was saying. Aurora stared at him waiting to see what he would say. Slowly, as if thinking out loud, he began to speak, "When I said my parents were gone, it wasn't an accurate way to describe it. It's just the phrase I've used because I don't normally like to explain it." She gently placed her hand on his to encourage him to go on. "It was the day before my 18th birthday. My parents had gone on a trip and were supposed to be coming home. There was an accident; their car hit a tree and burst into flames. My father was found on the road badly hurt, but without a burn on him, and they never found my mother's body. They assumed she was consumed in the fire because of the intense heat. My father survived, but he can't speak or move. He just sits staring off into nothing and nurses have to feed him and tend to his every need. I visit him every week, and after six years there hasn't been any change" his voice trailed off.

Aurora gently squeezed his hand, and when he looked at her she said, "Tomorrow we'll go see him." David nodded his head. "David, there's something else. I think I've seen your mother before."

His eyes wide, David asked "What?"

Aurora looked at him, and in a gentle voice said, "When I was looking at the picture in your parent's room and I saw your mother, I couldn't place it then, but I think I may have seen her before. I'm still not certain when or where, but she's extremely familiar to me."

David sat there staring at her, his head spinning, and after a few moments he regained himself. "Aurora, after today, as difficult as it may be to accept, I must admit that anything's possible." Seeing how tired she was, he added "But for tonight I think you need to get some sleep before you collapse from exhaustion." He gave her a smile, letting her know it was not a dismissal.

"Perhaps you're right. With some rest, my memory may become clear."

He stood and offered her his hand. She pushed the blanket off her lap, and he pulled her effortlessly to her feet. She turned and grabbed her pack. He followed her back to her room and pushed the door open, looking inside. All was as it should be, and he stayed at the threshold as she moved into the room. She turned to him with sleepy eyes. "I'm not sure how I'll sleep without the hard ground for my bed."

He smiled at her. "I'll be in the room next to you with the door open so I can hear you if you need me. Sleep well, and I'll see you in the morning."

She placed her hand on his chest, over his heart, and closed her eyes. Her touch sent a shiver through him. She looked up and opened her eyes again to see him gazing at her intently.

"You'll be safe here tonight."

"I know I will" she replied. "Good night, David."

"Good night, Aurora," then he pulled the door closed, but left a crack; just enough for her voice to carry through.

THE AWAKENING

Lost in thought, David made his way back to the living room. He gathered up the tea and cups, and laughed to himself as the dog slept on the rug in front of the fire. A dog had so few things to worry about, but his lighthearted moment was short lived. His mind began replaying the day's events again. Running through every moment, looking for anything he may have missed, considering her words. Before he realized it, he had finished cleaning the kitchen and made his way back to the fire that was burning brightly. He sat on the couch and stared at the seal on the mantle. He was finally getting tired, but it somehow held his gaze. The outer ring was a circle, and the inner markings were divided into three groups. He couldn't specifically tell what they were, but they gave the appearance of motion. As he stared at it in the dimming light, his eyes began to lose focus, and he thought he saw movement. Soon the inner markings began to swirl as if around a whirlpool in the center. Slowly at first, so he thought it was a trick of the light, and then suddenly it was a blur of speed. Beginning at the center, a small light started to emerge and began spreading until it filled the entire circle. The moment it reached the outer ring, he heard a bang.

He felt as if he was being propelled through the air, directly into the vortex of light. In an instant he was inside the light, and then he was surrounded by silence. He looked around. He couldn't tell if he had a physical form or not. While trying to sense something or gain some perspective on what was happening, a sound began to reach him. It was a voice floating in from a distance saying his name, "David". He called out "Yes, I'm here".

The voice responded, "You have acted wisely today. The time has come, the battle rages, and only through faith can you prevail. You have been given everything you need. Follow your heart and beware those who serve the Dark One."

David called out desperately, "What do I need to do?" As the voice began to drift out of his reach, he heard "You will know. Choose what is right and serve others."

David felt as if he fell back onto the couch or into his body; he wasn't sure which. His eyes popped open wide, and the room was filled with the morning sun. What felt like mere moments, had actually been hours. He was wide-awake, and stood up to look around the room. He felt different somehow, as if energy was coursing through him. It was something new that hadn't been there before. He stood, his eyes closed, trying to make sense of what it was, but the sensation was beyond his understanding.

He opened his eyes to see Rusty lift his head and yawn. David looked at the clock; it was six in the morning. He felt well rested and alert. "How about some breakfast, boy," he said to the dog. Wagging his tail, Rusty jumped up to follow him. David made his way to the kitchen and put on a pot of coffee. He gave Rusty a biscuit to tide him over while he got out his food. As the dog ate happily, David stared out the window, watching the sunlight shimmer on the grounds. While the coffee pot gurgled, he considered what he had heard. He still had no idea what he was supposed to do next. He was filled with a mixture of excitement and fear. What had happened to him last night was beyond words. He felt more alive, more connected to the world than ever before, yet the implications of it all were frightening to conceive.

Pouring himself some coffee, he lifted the cup to his nose and breathed in the aroma. The smell of fresh coffee in the morning was why he started drinking it in the first place. When he found himself living alone after the accident, he missed that smell and began making it for himself. Still dressed in his clothes from the night before, he decided to walk outside with his cup to get some fresh air. He went out the back door and the cold morning air felt refreshing. It was a bit brisk out, but he was a little stiff from being on the couch all night, and the fresh air was soothing. He wandered out into the yard and looked at the plantings, the trees, and the grasses. All the life around him seemed to touch him; it made him feel a part of it. As he stood there, he noticed something that never caught his attention before. The far edges of the garden had a curve to them. He made his way over to look at it. Why would the garden curve? All the fields were planted in rows. It was just more efficient that way. Once he reached the perimeter, he saw the edging that his parents had put there before he was born. He had never quite paid attention to it before, but for some reason it intrigued him. He began walking the perimeter, following the line. When he got to the end of the garden, he saw, for the first time that the edging continued on. He was surprised he never noticed it before. He had cut the grass here countless times. As he continued to follow it, he began to realize that everything looked different. Somehow the world seemed brighter more alive than it did before. He wondered to himself, was it because of what happened the night before, or was it just his imagination?

Making his way around the yard following the border, he quickly figured out that he was making a complete circle, and would end up right where he started. A circle. He thought about the circle of the seal. Was it possible that the house was a seal too? Picturing the seal in his mind, he tried to figure out a reference point to look for. He walked up onto the front porch, gazed out at the plantings, and there it was. The various shrubs and bushes in one of the beds had the same kind of elusive pattern in it. He had seen enough. It all made sense.

He made his way back inside. He decided to check on Aurora, so he quietly walked to her room, not wanting to wake her. He stood by the door and listened closely until he could hear her soft rhythmic breathing.

Satisfied she was resting peacefully, he made his way back to the kitchen. It was almost seven now, but he hoped she would sleep a while longer. She needed the rest. He went down the hall to his room, and thought he ought to clean up. The hot shower felt soothing after the cold morning air. He had been outside longer than he expected and felt chilled.

His mind was racing, trying to piece everything together, shifting between moments of clarity and confusion. What did it all mean? He wasn't exceptional in any way. Why was all of this happening to him? What was he supposed to do? Surely he must have been dreaming, but he knew he wasn't. Even after yesterday, and the impossibility of it, this was too much. He needed to try to figure out what was going on. He thought of her, and that calmed him. She was real, he knew that much, and as unsure as he was about anything else, she needed him.

He thought about her suggestion to see his father today, and felt that was the best place to start. So he pulled on some good jeans, his boots, and a decent shirt. His father hadn't spoken or even blinked anytime he went to visit during the past six years, but just the same, he felt going to see him was necessary.

He couldn't help but walk down and listen by her door one more time. Finding she was still asleep, he made his way back to the kitchen again. Rusty was lounging on the floor waiting and got up to meet him. He reached down and rubbed him behind the ears. It was comforting to have company. "How are you? Did you get enough to eat this morning?" he asked the dog. Rusty stood there panting, and when David went to the sink to wash his hands, the dog flopped back down on the floor.

The smell of the bacon cooking on the stove top made him hungry, so he fixed himself some toast to tide him over. Relaxing at the table with the dog at his feet, he periodically got up and flipped the bacon. Between the shower and some more coffee, he had warmed up again, and sat patiently waiting for Aurora to wake up. Instead of trying to think about things, he worked on clearing his thoughts. He often found he did his best thinking when he didn't think at all.

By the time 9 a.m. rolled around, he was getting restless. He needed to keep busy, so he decided to make some breakfast potatoes. He busied himself slicing the potatoes, cutting some onion, and while the potatoes were cooking, he cut up some apples and some bread for toast. He was relieved when he heard the soft patter of her feet entering the room. He was afraid he might cook everything in the house if she hadn't awoken soon. His thoughts were spinning, and he needed these mindless tasks to keep him focused.

"Good morning," he said without turning around, as he finished turning the last of the potatoes.

"Good Morning." she replied, "Do you have eyes in the back of your head?"

He let out a small chuckle, and said, "No. I heard you coming." Then as he turned to face her, he asked, "Did you sleep well?" The sight of her almost made him drop the plate of fruit he was taking to the table. She was still wearing the nightshirt and socks. Her hair was pulled back into a braid, fully exposing her face. He had been so distracted by other thoughts that it was like seeing her in person again for the first time. She was more radiant than he had seen her ever before, and her smile was captivating. Unlike the night before, she was perfectly at ease leaning against the doorframe, exuding confidence. The nightdress, hanging loosely, outlined her exquisite frame. Her eyes were looking at him with a different intensity than he had seen before; a longing, she was taking him all in, inside and out. He stood frozen in place.

"Yes, it may have been the best night's sleep I've ever had."

"I'm so glad" he managed in a smaller voice than normal. Clearing his throat to regain himself, he said, "Why don't you sit down? I've made some breakfast."

She had moved too, and met him at the table, standing just inches away. He set the plate down without even realizing it. She was only a couple of inches shorter than he was, but his boots added to his height. She tipped her head up to look him in the eyes and placed her hands on his chest. They felt warm and strong, and at her touch, a shiver ran through his entire body.

"I feel I haven't properly thanked you for all you've done for me," she said as she slid her hand up behind his neck, pulling him closer to kiss his cheek. Her lips, lingering, pressed firmly against his skin. He was rooted to the spot unable to move. When she broke the kiss, she wrapped her arms around him and pulled him into a tight embrace. Suddenly he had control of himself again, and he hugged her too. Every inch of her was pressed against him. She had turned her head to the side, and laid it down against his shoulder and chest, her arms firmly around his back. He could feel the subtle curves of her body against him, and he felt unusually warm. His heart was pounding, and he breathed in her scent. Instinctively his hand went up and gently caressed the side of her head. She moved slightly and nuzzled a little closer under his touch.

He couldn't have been sure how long they stood there; time had lost all meaning. When she finally lifted her head and leaned back in his arms, she looked up and said, smiling, "The food smells good."

David smiled back and said, "I'm starving."

She sat down at the table, and he turned again to the stove. He had completely forgotten about the food and was thankful he had turned off the burner.

"Would you like some eggs?"

"Yes, that would be lovely."

He had been ready, so he grabbed some eggs and cracked them in a bowl. "Do you prefer the yokes broken or runny?"

"I'm used to them broken."

He whipped the eggs and poured them into the pan. They cooked quickly while he put bacon, potatoes, and toast on their plates. He tipped the frying pan up and divided the eggs between them. Turning to the table, he saw her enjoying a piece of apple while watching him intently.

"Here we go. I don't want anyone accusing me of not feeding you enough."

She smiled, and said, "I don't think that will be a problem."

He looked at her, then clasped his hands. Closing his eyes, he said a prayer. When he finished, he turned to her. "I have some things to tell you while we eat."

He began telling her about the seal, what happened, and what the Lord told him. He had to keep reminding her to eat, as she was lost in his words. Then he went on to tell her about the ring around the house, and how the house itself was somehow part of a seal. She drank in every word he said, and when he was finished telling her what had happened, he asked, "Do you have any idea what it all means?"

"Not really. Where I come from, we're in a terrible battle with the Dark One, and what you did, looking into the seal and having the Lord speak to you, was extraordinary. Only powerful servants can do that."

"But I'm not a servant, I didn't even know what that was until you told me last night. I'm not a warrior, and I've never even fought in a battle."

"That may be true, but you said it yourself yesterday. The course of our lives has changed, and now it may be time for you to follow a different path," she said kindly.

David sat there considering her words, then said, "I've been mulling things over, and I think you're right. The first thing we need to do is go see my father. It's not far, and he hasn't spoken in six years, but something tells me that's where we need to start."

Her expression of determination back, she nodded with agreement. "We have to be careful. We've been safe here because of the seal, but once we venture out beyond its protection, we're vulnerable."

David placed a reassuring hand on hers, "I won't let anything happen to you. Unfortunately, you can't take your bow where we're going. You'll have to leave it in the car and borrow some more of my mother's clothes. I don't think we want to attract the kind of attention your leather armor would bring."

She frowned at him as though she didn't like this idea too much. "I won't go anywhere without my pack," she stated, leaving no room for argument.

He laughed, "I had no doubt about that." She gave him a sheepish grin, having asserted herself so strongly only to end up unopposed.

"When you're finished eating, you can pick out some clothes to wear. I would suggest some pants made of this type of cloth," he said pointing to his jeans, "and any top you like. She should have some boots or other shoes in there, and as soon as you're ready, we'll head out." Aurora nodded her understanding. The moment she was done, he quickly began cleaning up. It didn't take long, and he went back to his room so that he could be prepared too.

Aurora stood looking at the photos of his mother. Again that nagging feeling of an elusive memory tugged at her, but it would have to wait. She had no trouble finding the pants, and was pleased to find they fit well. She didn't want to look like his mother, but she was looking to get ideas of what to wear. She had been around men her entire life, but no one had affected her the way he did. He always reacted to her differently than she expected; he disarmed her. It was frightening, but at the same time, drew her to him. She also never had a man comfort her except for her father. Men had tried to court her, asked her to become their wife, but she had no interest, and was not about to become someone's trophy to sit at home. He was different though. He hadn't acted the fool boasting and trying to win her affections. He treated her with respect as an equal, and the way he looked at her was different. Most men looked at her shape with hungry eyes. He looked into her eyes, trying to see inside her.

She had never been with a man, and in war she had seen too many women who had fallen victim to gangs of soldiers. She had seen their empty gazes, the bruises and broken skin, not to mention what she couldn't see. She had little opportunity to see firsthand what a marriage of love was like, except her parents, and by the time she could start to understand, they had been taken from her. She had been alone ever since, and the few men who did try to have their way with her against her wishes, regretted that decision for the few remaining moments of their lives. She knew he would never treat her that way, even when she was vulnerable, and in his arms he only offered her the comfort she was seeking, and nothing more. Even though when they touched she became weak and felt a nervous excitement she didn't quite understand, she felt safe.

Now she stood looking at her reflection, feeling silly for worrying about her appearance, perhaps for the first time in her life. She had found a lovely light colored top and a short leather jacket that reached to just above her waist. She had a trim, well-toned athletic figure born of a hard life travelling on foot and fighting in the war. She knew rich woman were voluptuous, and she was anything but rich. She found some boots that came all the way up her calf and laced snuggly around her pants. She knew it wasn't important, but felt the need to look nice. She liked these clothes. They were comfortable and allowed her to move freely. She inspected herself one more time all the way around, and when she was satisfied, she headed to her room. Her pack lay on the bed. Seeing it there, she realized that she had let it out of her sight. She couldn't believe she would have done that, but everything was so different here, and most importantly she felt safe. Even so, there were some chances she would not take.

She opened her pack, and began sorting through her things. He had said no bow, but she still wanted to be prepared, so she slid a small knife into each boot for easy access. She pulled out her pendant and placed it around her neck, dropping it inside her shirt. Then there was the box; it was about a foot long, a few inches tall, and a few inches wide, tied with a string. She considered it, staring at it, wondering what she should do. She was in an unknown land. Was it safer to leave it here under the protection of the seal? Or should she take it with her? Turning it over in her hands, she finally decided there were too many unknowns out there, and the seal had never failed. She looked around and decided to slip it under the mattresses of her bed. She took out her clothes and looked at them. They were worn and tattered from her hard life too. So she laid them on the bed to be tended to later. She removed her cooking items and some dried biscuits. Now all that was left were things she would not be without. There was a small throw blanket on a chair, and she packed it on top of her things to keep them hidden. She stood up and headed to the door. She was ready for whatever they would face.

***

David was waiting patiently near the door, looking out the window. He was keenly aware that, in some ways, he was seeing this place for the first time. Something had happened to him last night that made him see everything differently. Everything seemed so much more alive than ever before. He wasn't sure what to make of it, but felt that somehow it was significant. He heard Aurora trying to sneak up on him, and smiled. "Hello," he said, and he could hear her sigh with amused frustration.

"I'm starting to think you do have eyes in the back of your head," she said. He turned to look at her. She stood tall and confident before him, and for a moment he had no words. His silence caused her to falter slightly. "Do I look alright? I wasn't sure if these clothes were right for me." She asked, feeling self-conscious.

He grinned, "You're nothing short of perfect," he said. She flushed and looked around for some way to change the subject. "Are you ready to go, then?" He asked her.

Regaining herself she said confidently "Yes."

He reached out for her hand "Then we should be off."

FIRST BLOOD

David held Aurora's hand as she climbed into the Jeep. He chuckled to himself when he noticed the slight bulge in her boots. She may have agreed to leave her bow, but he assumed she would be prepared. Little did she know he had a few things up his sleeve too. Everything about her captured his imagination. He knew she was not someone to be underestimated, but there was so much more. Considering the enormity of everything that he was discovering in such a short period of time, he thought it was only because of her that he was not sitting in a corner asking, why me? He had been on autopilot for the past six years, going through the motions, wandering aimlessly, doing what he had always done without a sense of purpose. She lit a fire in him. He wanted to be worthy of her presence in his life. If he had been forthright, he would have had to admit that this woman of his dreams was all he ever wanted. Now that she was here, he couldn't bear the thought of losing her, of not getting to know her fully, not just what the small glimpses of her told him. So far, he was not disappointed. In fact, every minute they spent together made him want more.

He climbed into the seat next to her, took her hand, looked at her, and said, "And so it begins." She nodded her agreement, and they set off. It wasn't far to the facility where his father was. Aurora asked him about the roads, buildings; all the things he took for granted that she had never seen before. It felt as if they had barely started when they were pulling into the drive.

Massive grounds in the middle of a lonely stretch of road surrounded the facility. It offered the peace and quiet its residences needed to recover, or in more severe cases like his father, exist undisturbed. There were only a few vehicles there, and David guessed they had arrived between shifts prior to the noontime meals. He hadn't planned it that way, but was glad. He didn't want to have to answer a lot of questions.

"They're rather strict about visitors," David said, "so follow my lead. I know most of the staff so they may not say anything, but just in case I have to make something up, try not to act surprised."

Aurora replied, "I'll play along."

David added, "One more thing, no matter what, stay with me. Please make sure we don't get separated." He gave her a serious look to drive his point home.

"You can count on it." She said.

David opened her door and took her hand, helping her out of the car. They turned and headed up the walk, neither one of them letting go. It felt natural walking with her, holding her hand, but it was also their silent affirmation of solidarity. They both knew that these were the first steps on a long road ahead; that no matter the outcome today, it was significant.

Entering the building, David made his way directly to the reception area just as he had countless times before. "Hello Eleanor. I see you're looking as lovely as ever," he said in a slightly sugary voice to the woman behind the desk. "How are they treating you today?"

She looked up from her work, flashing a skeptical smile at him. "Don't think you can smooth talk me, David. They are treating me as badly as ever. How are you?"

David leaned against the counter "I'm OK. Overworked as usual, but I carved out some time to come see my father."

She peered up at him, "but it isn't Thursday," she said. Then David saw the sinister shadow behind her eyes. It sent a cold chill through him. He saw for the first time who this woman that he had seen every week for the past six years, truly was. He could feel the darkness in her, the hatred and anger that burned inside. Being this close to her made his skin crawl, and it took all of his self-control not to recoil in horror. "I see you have a guest today, and who is this young lady?" She said without her usual friendly tone.

David, realizing this was trouble, felt that he had to do something bold to assuage her suspicions. David said, "Eleanor if anyone beside you were asking, I wouldn't risk spoiling the surprise." Eleanor raised her eyebrows, "But if you promise not to tell." He added.

"David, how long have you known me? I'm not one to gossip." She stated firmly.

"This is Sarah. We're getting married, and I couldn't wait to come and tell dad."

Aurora gripped his hand tightly to steady herself. She had been prepared for a charade but had not expected this. She felt a flutter inside, her face suddenly hot, and realized she was smiling.

"Oh my, David, that is wonderful news," Eleanor said, her voice at ease again. "I had no idea you were seeing anyone. You never mentioned anything."

David pushed back from the counter and put his arm around Aurora. "We met last season at a livestock auction. Her father is a farmer too, and I proposed to her this weekend. Can you believe she accepted?" He said with a smile.

"How lovely, Sarah you are a lucky girl. This young man is extremely kind, and I have never seen anyone as attentive to a patient here as he is to his father. I'm sure he will take excellent care of you."

"Thank you. It was all so sudden, but I couldn't resist him." Aurora said putting her arm around him and squeezing. Then she looked up at him and smiled.

Not wanting to risk any unnecessary conversation that might uncover their charade, David said. "We're going to head up. I can't wait to tell Dad."

Eleanor stood unexpectedly, and asked, "Excuse me, but I have to ask, what is in your bag dear? It's rather large for a purse." She had a cold gaze on her face, and again he saw the shadow rage in her eyes.

"I made him a throw for his lap. I thought, sitting all day, he might get cold from time to time." Aurora reached into her pack, and pulled out the corner of a knitted throw from his mother's things to show her.

Eleanor looked at it for a moment and then gave a small smile. "As thoughtful as he is, I see. You two should be quite happy together. Enjoy your visit." Eleanor said. Then she sat back down in her chair.

"Thank you Eleanor. We'll be sure to say goodbye on our way out." David said as they walked off. He marveled at Aurora's quick thinking.

Once on the elevator, he pulled Aurora to him, and she fell into his arms. Aurora was unsure what he was doing, and was still unsteady from his talk of marriage, but once in his embrace, she didn't care. He placed his cheek next to hers and whispered into her ear. "I hope I didn't offend you with my talk of marriage."

She managed a small "No, I was just surprised."

He whispered back to her "I felt we needed something big to distract her, and you were brilliant." Her face flushed at his compliment, and she was glad he couldn't see it. "There's something wrong here. I saw a shadow behind her eyes twice. I think we're in danger. Remember what I said, and stay close to me. Whatever happens, we must not be separated." At those words, she regained her composure. She nodded her head against his, letting him know she understood.

He let go of her, and they turned to face the doors, instinctively clasping hands again. Since they were only going to the second floor, the elevator stopped a moment later, and the doors opened. With the slightest apprehension, they moved into the hallway. He knew they were in danger, but didn't know how much. He was uncertain whether or not his ruse was going to work. He only hoped it would get them in and out without any trouble. He walked down to the recreation room where the patients were this time of day. The door was open, and as they approached the room, they saw the giant orderly, Gordon. Gordon was a mountain of a man. He stood a full head taller than David, and had to weigh 200 pounds more. He was mostly muscle, just the kind of person to help keep a crowd in line.

"Hello there Gordon, how are you doing today?" David asked in a jovial tone.

Gordon stood and looked at the two of them. "Eleanor said you were on your way up." Gordon said in a low gruff voice. He looked the two of them up and down, and David felt a twinge of annoyance as he lingered on Aurora. "Your father's over by the window."

He made eye contact with David, and the shadow was there behind his eyes, too. David put his hand on Aurora's back and gently prodded her into the room. He scanned the room to see if he could spot anything else out of the ordinary, and he noticed the other two doors. They were undoubtedly locked, but there, nonetheless. As they made their way to the window, he spotted his father with his back to them. Seeing him sitting there, a shell of the man he was, always made him feel a pang of pain at his core. This time was no different. He walked up to his father, and moved around in front of him "Hi Dad. How are you today?" He asked even though he knew he would not get an answer. "I brought someone to meet you." David looked at Aurora and saw that her eyes were bright, and she gave him a sad smile. She moved around in front of his father and knelt down to look at him.

David had his hand on his father's as Aurora looked up into his face. "David, look," she said urgently.

He saw a single tear running down his father's cheek. David knelt down to look into his father's eyes. He was shocked to see a battle raging between darkness and light, and his father's light was fading. David sat frozen for a moment, then stood abruptly. Reaching down for Aurora's hand, he helped her to her feet.

"Sarah, why don't you show Dad the throw you made him?" Unsure what he was doing, Aurora reached into her pack without hesitation and pulled out the throw. She gently placed it on his lap, and after she had arranged it to her satisfaction, David said, "Sweetheart, let's take dad out for a stroll in the fresh air. With your new throw on his lap and the sun shining, it's a perfect day for it."

She looked at him for a clue, but he offered nothing. "That sounds like a wonderful idea," she said. David reached down, unlocked the wheels of the chair, and then turned it towards the door with Aurora close by his side.

When Gordon saw them coming, he stood up. "What are you doing?" He asked in a gruff voice.

"I'm going to take my dad outside for a little stroll so we can talk in private. Perhaps Eleanor didn't tell you, but Sarah and I are getting married, and I want to tell him all about her, but a little privacy would be nice."

Gordon stood there looking at him. David knew he wasn't a rocket scientist, and he could see that Gordon wasn't sure what he should do. Deciding to press on while he had the advantage, David pushed the chair forward past Gordon, Aurora right at his side. As the elevator doors closed, he saw Gordon heading their way. David leaned over as if to kiss Aurora, and whispered in her ear. "We have to hurry."

When the elevator doors opened, he strode straight for the exit. Then he heard Eleanor call after him. "David, what do you think you are doing?"

David stopped and turned, keeping one hand on the chair. "I'm just taking Dad outside for some fresh air so I can tell him all about our plans."

Eleanor moved out from behind her desk and made a beeline straight to them. "David, I don't think it is a good idea for you to take him outside. We don't want him to get sick now, do we?" Not only did he see the darkness swell in her, but he saw her face, as if for the first time. Her skin was like a sickly mask covering something hideous and evil underneath.

David was thinking fast. He knew they needed to get outside as soon as possible. "He has the throw that Sarah made for him. That should be enough." David said in as casual a tone as he could muster.

"Why don't we check with one of the doctors?" Eleanor spluttered trying to stall him.

"Eleanor, I have come to this facility every week for the past 6 years. I signed my father into this facility so he could have the best care, and I pay for him to stay here. Are you suggesting that I would do anything that would jeopardize him?" Eleanor was at a loss for words. David pressed on "I know everyone here has his best interest in mind, but this is the most significant part of my adult life, and I want to share it with him. Now we are going outside for a brief walk on a beautiful sunny day, and if you delay me any further, I will have to reconsider if he belongs here." Eleanor stood there fuming. She knew she couldn't stop him by herself. David turned and moved quickly to the door. As he, Aurora, and his father stepped outside, he could sense them coming. Gordon, Eleanor, and a second orderly were rushing to catch them.

For a moment, David was terrified. He didn't know how he was going to save his father from these beasts. He had promised to protect Aurora, and instead he had brought her here, placing not only her life at risk, but her very soul. He had acted foolishly, and they may have to pay the price. Then his fear turned to anger at those who were threatening them. As his fury grew, it drew power into him from all around them. It felt like a charge of static electricity coursing through him, and his mind became clear. He heard the door open behind them as their pursuers hurried to catch up.

David paused and bent down as if checking the wheel. As the three of them began closing in on them, in one fluid motion, David, pulling one of the daggers from Aurora's boot, turned and plunged it into Gordon's chest. He let out a horrible howl like a wild beast, and suddenly began convulsing where he stood. The other two stopped dead in their tracks, looking at him. Gordon began writhing, his arms flailing as he seemed to be deflating in front of them. Without hesitation, David turned to the other orderly, and, seeing the same shadowy rage in his eyes, grabbed his head and pulled it down, bringing his knee up to meet it.

Eleanor moved towards David, raising what was now a claw like hand, preparing to strike. Aurora did not waste a moment and followed David's example, thrusting her other dagger into Eleanor's chest. Her scream was even worse. If it had continued, they thought their ears might have bled. The other orderly was reeling from the blow that would have deprived any normal person of consciousness, but he began to regain his senses. David reached inside his jacket, retrieving another knife, and plunged it into the beast's heart.

In a matter of moments, all three of them had shriveled into hideous creatures wailing in torment, and then they exploded into fragments of shadow and disappeared. Aurora stood, poised to strike, scanning for any more attackers. David reached down, grabbed the knives, handing her two back, and sheathed his own.

"We have to hurry. Let's get to the car quickly." His hands shaking, he pushed his father as fast as he dared, and once at the car, opened the passenger door. "Please sit in the back behind me." He said to Aurora, who did not question him, but climbed quickly into the car. David easily lifted his father's frail body and set him in the seat, fastening the belt to keep him in place. He rushed back around, and in moments they were on the road. His fear for his father and adrenaline were the only things keeping him going.

"How did you know they were demons?"

"I'll explain when we arrive. We can't talk now. We have to hurry."
Aurora didn't argue. After what just happened, she realized he knew
something she didn't. She put her hands on his shoulders, and her comfort
steadied him. She was a hardened warrior while David had never
experienced real battle before. If not for her touch he thought he might
vomit, but he had to hold it together for his father's sake.

David was driving as fast as he dared without risking attention or
getting them into an accident. They couldn't afford a moment's delay.
They finally saw the road to the farm, and when he turned onto it, his
father began twitching.

"Hold on Dad, we're almost there."

Suddenly his father's head turned towards him. A hideous growling
hissing voice came out of his mouth. "You are too late, boy. You will not
make it. I will finish him."

David shouted, "No!" He placed his hand on his father's chest. It was
agony. The pain was threatening to knock him unconscious, but he had to
hold on. The voice screamed and howled as his father's hands clutched at
his arm, trying to pull his hand away while struggling against the seatbelt.
It took every ounce of his strength and will power to hold on. It was all he
could do to guide the car where he needed it to go. He could see it just
moments away, the perimeter of the seal. He braced himself as they
crossed it. He barely noticed Aurora, still clutching his shoulders, as an
explosion of light and sound filled the vehicle. He could see a wall of light

passing through the car as they crossed over the line. As it washed over his father, the beast was thrown back out of him screeching, as it exploded into fragments. He jammed on the brakes, and the car skidded to a halt. His hand fell as the car stalled. He just barely made out the sound of Aurora's voice as he slipped into unconsciousness.

***

Aurora fumbled with the door, trying to get it open, until she figured out how to pull the right lever. She did not panic; she never panicked, but she was frightened. Getting out of the car and pulling open the driver's door, she quickly pushed David's head back and put her head on his chest. She could hear the steady beating of his heart, his chest rising and falling, and she knew he would be all right. She quickly went around to the other side and opened the door. David's father was pale and looked terrible. Again she placed her head on his chest. His heartbeat was extremely faint and his breathing was weak. She stood up placed a hand on his chest and forehead and closed her eyes. Shutting off all thought and slowing her breathing, she reached out for her gift. She could feel it fill her as it had done so many times before. Then she released some of her power into him. Almost instantly he began to moan. She withdrew her hands and in a soft voice said, "You're going to be all right."

His eyes still closed, in barely a whisper he breathed out, "David."

She leaned in and said, "He's all right. Try to relax. We're safe now. I'll be right back."

She rushed up to the house, passing Rusty, who was standing nearby and appeared to be surveying the perimeter. She opened the front door and dashed back to his parents' room. She went in and pulled down the covers on the bed. She knew that it would be difficult to get him inside and didn't want any unnecessary obstacles.

Hurrying back to the car, she unbuckled David's father. She grabbed his left arm and pulled him out onto her shoulder. Because he had been so sick for so long, he wasn't as heavy as he could have been, but it was still a struggle for her. She carefully made her way up the steps of the porch and was cautiously moving through the doorways, trying not to bump him against the jamb. As gently as possible, she laid him down on the bed and let out a sigh. He moaned slightly, and his eyes opened just enough to see her. He breathed out weakly, "Thank you." Then he drifted back into unconsciousness. She placed her hands on his heart and head and reached out again for her gift. It told her that he was all right; now he only needed rest and food.

Already winded, Aurora wondered how she was going to get David inside. Scrambling to the door, she was amazed to see him stumbling out of the car and grabbing the door for support. She darted to him and grabbed his arm.

"Hold on," she said pushing her shoulder up under him for support.

"I can't see," he said with a hint of desperation in his voice.

"It's alright. You're safe now. It is going to be all right. Just hold on until I get you inside." She pleaded.

"My father," He croaked, "I couldn't find him."

She struggled against his weight "He's fine. He's inside resting now. Just a little further," she said as they made it to the steps of the porch. She had to use her free arm to pull on the railing for support, and with some difficulty they managed to make it up. Stumbling forward, she barely made it through the door. When she reached the sofa, she tried her best to slow his fall. Once he was down, she rolled him onto his back and got his legs up so he wouldn't fall off.

"Lie still now, you need some rest. I'll be here watching over you." She placed her hands on his head and chest, and with the little strength he had, he moved his hand to hers. Calling her gift, she released some power into him and felt his muscles slack. She leaned forward and pressed her lips to his forehead. He was going to be fine.

She pushed herself to her feet and slumped into a nearby chair, taking deep rhythmic breaths to slow her pounding heart. She knew the seal would protect them. She had seen what it would do to any threat that tried to cross it. She sat there staring at him, watching his chest rise and fall. She had been fighting this battle for 10 years now and would have been caught entirely unaware, yet he saw things she hadn't. He knew what to do in the face of things she was sure he had never seen before. No longer alone, and with someone who could, and would at any cost protect her, caused a swell of emotion inside her. She reached up and wiped a single tear from her face. She needed something to do while she waited; something to keep the feeling of helplessness at bay. She decided they would need some food when they woke, and she wanted to be ready.

Rusty had come inside and was lying on the floor watching over David. Seeing the dog there was somehow comforting. She made her way to the kitchen and realized finding what she needed would probably be half the battle. She only ever cooked for herself with a single pot, and over a campfire. So she decided that she should start with something simple. Yes, he had some fruit and cheese in this box that kept things cold. She pulled on the handle, and saw a puff of smoke like hot breath on a cold day come out of it. She knelt down to look inside and was amazed at how cold it was. There were all sorts of things in there that she didn't recognize, but then she saw some apples. Looking further, she found a block of cheese, and decided that was a decent start. She placed them on the counter and shut the door. She was about to pull her knife out of her boot when she noticed a wooden block filled with knives. She inspected a few until she found a shape she liked. Then she remembered that he had some dishes to put it on, and started opening doors and drawers until she found them. She also found some glasses, and realized how thirsty she was. Drawing a glass of water from the tap and taking a long drink, she thought that of everything she had seen in the house, water in the tap was the best. A canteen or basin was warm and not usually fresh.

She cut up the apple and some slices of cheese. Then she found the

bread and carved off several chunks. She felt that this would be enough to

take the edge off when they woke. Then she saw the teapot and a glass jar

with the bags in it he had used. She took the pot, put some water in it, and

placed it on the stove where he had warmed it. Looking at the dials on the

stove, she wasn't quite sure what to do. She inspected the dial and saw Hi,

Med, and Low. Then she thought to herself that they must indicate how

much fire comes out. She turned it to Hi, and heard a low hissing sound,

but there was no flame. Curious, she looked a little closer. She could smell

something like perfume. It was unpleasant, so she leaned back. Wondering

what she was supposed to do, she was startled when she heard,

"You'll blow the house up if you do it that way." David said from the

doorway. Unsteady on his feet, he walked over, turned the dial until she

heard a clicking sound, and a whoosh as the flames lit under the kettle.

"What are you doing up?" She said sternly, "You need some rest."

"Clearly I'm keeping you from blowing us all up." He said with a

smile.

"You know what I mean," she said disapprovingly at his attempt at

humor.

He reached over and lifted her chin with his fingers to look into her

eyes. "I'm fine," he said in a gentle voice. "Thank you for taking care of

my father and me."

Suddenly she wrapped her arms around him, burying her face against his chest and shoulder. He hugged her back and began gently stroking her hair.

"You gave me a good scare," she said, "I... Well for a moment..." She stammered.

"It is alright," he said in a soothing voice. "We're alright now."

She straightened up "I should go check on your father."

David held her arm and said, "I just did. He's still sleeping. We'll check on him in a little while. In the meantime, that tea you were about to make sounds perfect."

They sat down at the table with their tea and the food she had prepared. David said their prayer, and then turned to her. "Thank you for making this. That was very thoughtful of you."

She smiled brightly and said, "Oh it wasn't any trouble. The hardest part was finding everything." She enjoyed his praise and marveled at how at ease he made her feel, in spite of what they just went through. "Tell me what happened today," she said, taking on a serious tone. "I was there, and I'm still confused. How did you know they were demons?"

"I think something happened to me the other night when I looked into the seal. Somehow I can see and sense things I couldn't before. I feel connected to the world in a way I can't put into words," David said. Then he went on to explain how, when he saw the shadows behind their eyes, he could sense the evil, and had guessed what it meant. When they saw his father, and he looked into his eyes, he could see the struggle between the dark and light. He could see that a demon was trying to possess his father, and he was losing the fight after all these years. He told her how as the demons pursued them, he felt power flow into him, and then he knew what had to be done. These demons had assumed a human form, and if he did not act quickly and take advantage of the element of surprise, the two of them would have been no match for them.

After that, he remembered what she had said about them not being able to cross the seal. He came up with the idea that if they could get his dad across the seal, the demon in him would be forced to let go. He told her he didn't want to say anything so the demon wouldn't know what he was planning. It was only in those few moments before they arrived that he realized that he had to help his father hold on so the demon could not take him. The problem was that they were locked in battle, so the only choice was to hold onto both of them. He explained that he was somehow able to draw the demon partially into himself, so that when they hit the barrier, all three of them would be forced to pass. He told her that the pain was excruciating and that the explosion of light had temporarily blinded him. In his last moments of consciousness, he was able to let some of his power leave him and go into his father, helping to keep him alive.

She looked at him, mesmerized by what he was saying. She was moved by the fact that he had so willingly risked his life to save them both. Because what he did not say but she knew, was that he made her sit behind him, knowing full well the risks he was going to take. When she was holding his shoulders during those final moments, she felt his power envelope her, too, and it was his protection that prevented the demon from latching onto her when it was ripped from his father. If it had, she wasn't sure what would have happened when it exploded as they crossed the seal.

"David, over the past 10 years I have been in many battles and seen many miraculous things. What you did today was truly astounding. I think there's much more going on than we know, and I hope your father can help us understand."

David looked a little uncomfortable at her praise. "I only did what had to be done, and I'm thankful that my guess was right. I'm so sorry that I put you at such risk. I was a fool and could have gotten both of you killed or worse today. If you hadn't been there, Eleanor might have finished me off. I hope you can forgive me."

Aurora looked at him kindly, and said, "You saved my life yesterday. I suppose that makes us even then."

David smiled at her and said, "Thank you," then reached out to take her hand. "I hope my father can help us understand too. I think we can go and talk to him now." He stood up and gathered a plate of food, and she poured him a glass of water. They headed to his room and slowly pushed open the door. His father was lying there, frail and thin. It broke David's heart to see him this way. He knelt down beside him, setting the plate on the end table. Aurora put her hand on his shoulder for comfort. She was afraid it was too soon, and could sense the pain it caused David to see him this way.

David gently placed a hand on his father's shoulder and in a soft voice asked, "Dad can you hear me?" His father began to stir slightly. "Dad, it's me, David. I'm here with you. We're at home." David's voice cracked as his father's lips moved a little. They were clearly parched. David took the glass from Aurora, and gently lifting his head, tipped it up to his lips. He poured a little water into his mouth and could see his father swallow.

After several small sips, his father said in barely a whisper "David," as his eyes opened slightly. "Oh, my son, I never thought I'd see you again."

David's eyes filled with tears, but mustering a confident tone he said, "Dad, I'm here now, and you're going to be alright."

His father stirred slightly, "David, you need to call Molly."

David repeated, "Molly. Aunt Molly?"

His father's strength failing, he said, "Yes. Tell her the hour is at hand." He was slipping back into unconsciousness.

"Dad, I will. I love you, and I need you. Please don't leave me again", he said pleading to him.

His father rallied slightly and said in barely a whisper "I know, son, and I love you too." Then he was still again.

Aurora gently pushed David aside, placing her hands on his father again. Closing her eyes she could feel that he was just too weak, but that it was not over for him yet. "David, he's alright," she said gently, "it's just too soon after such a long struggle. We need to give him time."

He looked at her, a single tear running down his face. "I was afraid I failed him."

She took his hand, pulled him to his feet, and said, "No, David, you saved him. Whether or not he survives, you saved him from a horrible fate. But don't give up hope yet. He may still recover."

This time he reached out for her and rested his head on her shoulder. She held him tightly. He took a deep breath and then stood tall, rallying himself, "It seems we have work to do, let's go call Aunt Molly."

She smiled at him encouragingly, "Lead the way," she said.

He was pacing the floor waiting for her to answer as the phone rang. Aunt Molly was old fashioned. She only had one extension, and it was still a rotary phone. David didn't call her regularly because talking to her on the phone was a challenge. She tended to shout into the receiver so you could hear her.

Seething with frustration after several minutes he looked at Aurora "if she doesn't answer soon I'm just going to go there." Aurora stepped closer, smiling and put a calming hand on his arm, when suddenly, sound came blasting out of the phone.

"Hello, who's calling?"

Aurora was startled at the sound, and David rolled his eyes. He didn't understand why his father wanted him to call Aunt Molly, but he wasn't about to argue.

"Aunt Molly, it's me David." He said, with as much patience as he could muster.

"OHHHHH, David dear, how are you? It's been a while since you called me. I was beginning to think you had a new favorite Aunt. How have you been dear? Are there any new girls in your life?"

Aurora snickered at David's look of exasperation "Aunt Molly, something's happened"

She cut him off "Oh! Really! Are you getting married? It's about time you settle down dear. You need a woman in your life. You can't live in that house all alone forever you know."

David, getting more impatient, raised his voice to be heard "My father's at home."

Molly stammered, "What do you mean, your father's at home. What are you saying, David? You know how fond I am of you, dear, but please spit it out."

David said louder this time, "He said to tell you the hour is at hand. Do you know what that means?" For the first time David could remember, Aunt Molly was silent. "Aunt Molly, are you there?" He asked urgently.

In a somber tone, David had never heard before, she said, "David, would you please repeat what you just said?"

David, looking puzzled, said slowly "My father is home, and he asked me to call you and tell you that the hour is at hand."

There was a momentary pause, and Aunt Molly asked, "Can he come to the phone?"

"I went to visit him today and we were attacked, so I felt the safest thing was to bring him home. After he rested a little while, he spoke to me," his voice unexpectedly cracked, "and he told me to call you and give you that message. He's asleep now, but he's extremely ill. Please Aunt Molly, can you help me?" As much as he tried, he couldn't keep the desperation out of his voice.

Suddenly Aunt Molly spoke to him with complete authority, and in such a commanding tone it shook his confidence. "David, do not leave the house under any circumstances. Do you understand me?"

"But I don't ..."

She cut him off "David. Please do not make me repeat myself; do you understand me? "

Realizing she must have an idea what is going on, he agreed, "Yes, Aunt Molly."

She continued "Thank you. Now I need to know. Are there any people out in front of the house, and is there any chance you were followed home today?"

David walked to the window "I don't see anyone out front, and no, we weren't followed home exactly."

"David, this is not time to be coy, spit it out. What happened?"

David replied, preparing for a million questions, "OK, Dad was possessed by a demon, and when I forced it across the seal, the demon exploded. Other than that, no one followed us."

After a slight pause, she said, "Good enough then. Is there anyone else with you at the house?"

Surprised at her reaction, and more so at her question, he replied, "There's a woman here. Her name is Aurora, and it's a long story."

Aunt Molly lost her newly found composure, "What! Aurora's already there! Dear Lord, we haven't much time."

David interjected, "How did you know about Aurora?" David looked at Aurora, her eyes going wide at the mention of her name.

Aunt Molly, in a sympathetic tone, said, "I'm sorry dear. I don't have time to explain now. In fact, we have terribly little time at all. Please follow my instructions, and I'll be there shortly. When we hang up, go to the hearth in the living room and light a fire. Make sure it's good and hot, and made of hard wood. Do you understand?"

He agreed, "Yes, I will."

Aunt Molly continued "I'll be bringing others with me, but under no circumstances should you invite anyone else in. If they cannot enter on their own, they are not one of us. Do you understand, dear?"

"Yes I do. Will you be able to help my father?"

"We'll do everything we can. I must go right away, but I'll explain everything when I arrive."

He heard the receiver click as she hung up the line. He stood there silent for a moment, unsure what it all meant.

THE PROPHECY

Aurora looked at him, anxiously waiting to hear what was said. He looked up from the phone, turned to her, and said, "She knew you were coming. She just didn't think you'd be here yet."

"How did she know I was coming? We didn't know I was coming. Who is she?"

David answered in a perplexed tone, "She's my aunt, my father's sister, my strange goofy aunt, who is always more worried about whether or not I meet a nice girl, or if I'm eating enough. She's always been good to me but never interested in anything… meaningful." David paused for a moment looking confused then said, "Oh, that's right. She told me to make a fire. We better get to it."

While they were getting the fire going, he told her word for word everything she said. Once the fire was burning hot, he said, "I want to check on my Dad again."

She nodded then said, "I'm going to get us some water."

David walked back to his father's room and quietly pushed open the door. He watched him, and seeing that he was breathing steadily and still sound asleep, backed out of the room, and pulled the door most of the way shut. He returned to the living room to find Aurora sitting on the couch with two glasses of ice water on the table. As he sat next to her, she handed him a glass.

"Aurora, does any of this make sense to you?"

Pausing a moment to gather her thoughts, she answered, "I told you that only a true servant can create a real seal. My thought was that at least one of your parents, probably your father, is a servant. That may mean that your aunt is one too. Servants are not of this world, yet they live in it doing our Lord's bidding."

David was about to speak when they both were startled by a knock on the door.

David sprang to his feet with Aurora hot on his heels. He positioned himself in front of her, prepared to meet whatever was at the door first.

"Who is it?" He called to the door.

"It's me, Molly. I'm going to come in now even though you haven't invited me, so that you know I crossed the seal on my own."

David stepped back, frantically looking around trying to come up with a plan in the event this was a trick. The door opened slowly, and to his relief Molly stood in the threshold. She was a tall, attractive woman who had aged well. Even as goofy as she was, David was always surprised she had never married. "Molly, it's really you." He said. Stepping forward, he placed his hands on her arms and looked into her eyes. Behind them, he saw her light, and with a sigh of relief, pulled her into a hug. "I'm so glad to see you."

Squeezing him hard, she said, "I'm delighted to see you too, dear, but please take me to your father. After I see him, we can talk."

David said, "Of course, Aunt Molly. This is Aurora. She helped me rescue him."

Molly moved over to her and gave her a warm hug, too. "Dear one, it's so nice to meet you after all this time, but please excuse me, I must tend to his father."

Aurora, slightly embarrassed by the display of affection from someone she just met, said, "I understand."

Without waiting, Molly headed to the bedroom. David reached out and took Aurora's hand and led her back to his dad's room. As they entered, Molly was already kneeling by the bed with her hands on his head and chest, her eyes closed. Neither of them said a word, but watched, waiting for Molly to speak.

After a few moments, Molly said, "You used your gift, Aurora, and gave him some of your power." It was a statement, not a question.

"Yes, I wasn't sure what to do. I'd never seen anything like that before." David pulled Aurora close to him, putting an arm around her, and she leaned her head against his shoulder.

"Your gift is what has kept him alive until now."

David felt his affection for her rise in him. He turned and kissed her gently on the head. He felt the tension in her body ease as she pressed closely against him. "Aunt Molly, is he going to be alright?"

In answer to his question, he heard his father speak in a soft voice "Molly, you sure took your time in getting here." David's heart lifted at the words.

"Oh be quiet, Gabe, I'm trying to concentrate."

After several long moments, while David fought the urge to ask the barrage of questions racing through his head, Molly finally pushed herself to her feet. "David, dear, please come over here and help me sit him up to take an elixir I brought."

David hurried over, placed a pillow against the headboard and reached down, lifting his father gently upright.

Through dry lips, he managed to say "I used to be the one taking care of you when you were sick."

David smiled at him "I guess it's my turn, then." Once he was satisfied his father was comfortable and not going to flop over off the bed, he stepped out of the way. Molly had retrieved a jar from her bag and measured out some unpleasant looking liquid into a glass.

Molly looked at him sternly. Gabe begrudgingly let her tip it to his lips, and drank it down. "Ugh that stuff is awful."

Molly set the glass down on the table and said with mock impatience, "Don't give me a hard time, Gabe. You know you are going to have to drink every drop." Then she smiled at him "Now, I'm going to check in with the council while you talk to your son here. Wait until you hear what he and young Aurora did.

His eyes going a little wide, he said, "Aurora, really? Well that makes sense."

Molly said solemnly "You better get your strength back, Gabe. Things are much farther along than I would have imagined." With that, she turned and left the room. David walked over, grabbed a chair from the corner, and pulled it up to the bedside for Aurora to sit. Then he sat on the edge of the bed next to his father.

"Dad, I can't tell you how overwhelming it is to see you here; to hear your voice again." David said, his eyes welling up with tears he was trying desperately to hold back. The elixir was working quickly. His father lifted his bony hand, and although he was weak from all he had been through, reached out and grabbed David's hand. Feeling him squeeze his hand lifted the sadness David was feeling. "Dad, I'd like you to meet Aurora."

Gabe gave her a kind smile "Yes, Aurora, I have waited a long time to meet you, young lady." He peered into her eyes, looking inside her just like David did. "And I have to say, you're even lovelier than I had imagined."

Aurora went flush. "I see where David gets it from," Aurora said. "How am I going to manage with two of you around?"

David spoke, "Don't let her fool you, Dad; she can handle herself. I've never seen anyone else like her."

"David, as I recall you've seen her for a very long time." He said knowingly.

"Dad, just since yesterday, so many things have happened, and I - we're so confused. Can you please tell us what's going on?" David said in a somber tone.

"I will, Son, but it would help me if you told me everything that happened first. I've been out of touch, as you know, for quite some time." David nodded, and just then Molly entered the room.

"How's the patient?" She asked.

"I've been better, but I'll live. David was just about to fill me in on everything that happened."

Molly nodded, "An excellent idea, I'd like to sit in if you don't mind. A few of the others have already arrived and are watching the perimeter." Molly walked around to sit on the other side of the bed "and I think we need to have you start at the very beginning, both of you, from the time you first saw one another."

The two of them sat there telling their stories. When Aurora talked about how her parents were killed by soldiers' right in front of her eyes, David reached out to take her hand for comfort. Then she talked of so many horrors of the war she was fighting, it broke David's heart to hear how hard her life had been. When they reached the events of the day before, Molly and Gabe fidgeted and leaned in closer, hanging on every word. When they finally finished, Molly and Gabe looked impressed.

The elixir appeared to have done a lot for Gabe, and he was the first to speak, "I'm so proud of you my son."

David beamed, "Thank you, Dad."

Molly spoke, "Yes, dear, you both did splendidly. We've been trying to figure out for six years how to get your father out of that place. It's crawling with those beasts. They would have known the minute one of us had shown up, and it would have been an all-out war. I'm guessing they could not see that you were a threat. That may prove extremely useful to you in the times to come." Molly sighed, "Of course, it's a miracle you both didn't get killed, but we can't argue with the results. Time for another dose, Gabe." She concluded with a stern look at him.

While Molly measured out some more of the wretched drink for Gabe, David asked, "Please tell us what it all means?"

After forcing down the elixir, Gabe looked up at Molly, and they shared a look of uncertainty. Then Gabe said, "Where to start?" Gabe turned to face the two of them, and, seeing their anxious looks of anticipation, he sighed, and then went on. "As you know, since the dawn of man there has been a struggle between dark and light. The balance between dark and light ebbs and flows. There are times when each one advances against the other, but the balance must be maintained. Darkness only consumes and destroys, where light nurtures and creates. What those of the dark, the evil one, don't understand is that this battle makes the light stronger. That by drawing those to it who have evil in their hearts, it purifies the light and strengthens it. They also do not realize that because the dark only consumes; that if they were ever to defeat the light, they would consume even each other until there was nothing left. This is clearly evidenced by how easily they turn on one another, and in stark contrast to the way those of the light defend and protect one another."

"During these ebbs and flows, events will culminate to a tipping point. This tipping point shapes what is to come next; a period of more dark or more light. We are on the brink of crossing a tipping point into an era of terrible darkness if we fail. The world that Aurora lives in has suffered immensely, and is on the verge of losing the battle. Her world exists here and now, but is separated by a force I cannot explain. If her world were to fall, it would open pathways between these two worlds, allowing the war that wages there to come here. That would be the tipping point. Only a select few of the most powerful servants can travel between

these two worlds without dire consequences, yet somehow you two did."
He paused, allowing them to consider what he said.

"Dad, what are you trying to tell us?"

"A single grain of sand added to a cart can be the one to cause it to
break. The two of you are the ones who can change the tide of this battle." ·

"Dad, I know Aurora's a skilled warrior, but I've never been in a war
before. What makes you think I can make a difference? Aunt Molly said
we were just lucky today." He said feebly.

Aurora leaned towards him, placed her hand on his leg, and looked
up to him. "No, it was only because of you today that we succeeded. You
saw things I didn't; you knew what to do, and I didn't." She said looking
at him with affection, and at the same time, certainty.

"I know, David, because I know you, and because of the prophecy."
Gabe said. David and Aurora turned to look at him with wide eyes.

Aurora speaking first, "It's true then? When we first met and he told
me his name, I thought perhaps, but I … I just couldn't… well…"

"Yes, dear, it's true. We've always believed it was him, and I think
after today, Molly would agree, we're certain."

Molly added in a somber tone "Yes, Gabe, I agree."

With a slight hint of panic in his voice, David asked, "What
prophecy?"

"As you know, prophecies are a tricky matter. They never say on this day at this time some specific thing will happen. If they did, people, good and evil, would try to interfere to affect the outcome." Molly said. "As for this prophecy, well, it is a tricky one to interpret. The Bible tells us of the final battle, which will occur at the time of the second coming. It does not tell us about the many battles in between. This is one of those battles. The prophecy of which we speak was not written down, so that it would only be passed between those of the light." David noticed Aurora looking somber, so he reached out to take her hand again. Molly continued, as if she was teaching a group of students. "Before we get to the prophecy, there are a couple of noteworthy points to consider. First, do you know what the word Messiah means, the literal translation?" She pressed on, not waiting for them to answer, "It means anointed one; a person who was chosen by God to lead his people." She paused a moment for them to consider this. "Yes, we refer to Jesus as the Messiah because he is our Lord and Master. However, there have been others who were anointed to lead Israel. Do you recall any?"

David looked at her, and in little more than a whisper, said, "Do you mean King David?" She raised her eyebrows, and David said with more force "You can't be suggesting that I'm him?"

She shook her head "No, dear boy, I'm not. He is with our Lord. But you have two crucial things in common with him. You are a descendant of the house of David. Your Mother comes from his line." At the mention of his mother, he felt a pang of pain. Molly went on "And possibly more importantly, you are faithful and have a pure heart. Do you remember what it says in Isaiah? There shall come forth a shoot from the stump of Jesse, and a branch shall grow out of his roots. And the Spirit of the LORD shall rest upon him, the spirit of wisdom, and understanding, the spirit of counsel, and might, the spirit of knowledge, and the fear of the LORD."

"It tells us, in addition to the coming of Jesus that, in times of great need, the house of David will rise up to lead." She added.

David looked down, his face a little flushed, and said in a low voice, "I don't think I'm that special."

Molly clicked her tongue "Your humility is a lovely quality, but we don't have time to debate the facts right now. There is one more thing I want you to consider." David looked up at her again. "Do you remember what the stumbling block was for the Jews? Why they would not accept Jesus as the true Messiah?"

David nodded, and answered "Yes, it was because they thought the Messiah would be a king, who would lead them in the battle to vanquish their enemies, and restore the glory of the house of David." He stopped abruptly at his own words.

Molly went on. "As I said, prophecy is a tricky matter and is often misinterpreted. Men typically think in worldly terms and how prophecy applies to them, not necessarily the larger struggle between good and evil, dark and light. That is why this prophecy was not written down, but carried through the ages until it would come to pass. This prophecy speaks of both worlds, not just this one, so only those who know of their existence can understand what it means."

"What does the prophecy say?"

Molly closed her eyes with a look of reading something that wasn't there, and said, "When the hour of darkness is at hand, a son of David will be anointed to lead his people, and he will find favor with the Lord. A child of equal measure from the house of Roktah will rise up to awaken the Lion, and together they will face the Evil One. They will be bound at birth by our Father, separated until the time of fulfillment, when they will unite in his cause." Molly opened her eyes, "You child are from the house of Roktah." She said looking at Aurora.

Aurora blinked, "Yes, but there's something I must show you." She stood and hurried from the room. The three of them shared a questioning look. In mere moments, she returned with the small box tied with a string in her hand. She held it out and said, "I was on a mission to bring this back to our council." She carefully opened the box and pulled out an aged piece of parchment. "The prophecy WAS written down." Unrolling it, she took a nervous breath and swallowed before she read it to them. "When the hour of darkness is at hand, a son of David will be anointed to lead his people, and he will find favor with the Lord. A child of equal measure from the house of Roktah will rise up to awaken the Lion, and together they will face the Evil One. They will be bound at birth by our Father, separated until the time of fulfillment when they will unite in his cause." She paused, and said, "But there's more. Together they will face the evil one, and through their sacrifice, both houses can be saved."

She rolled up the parchment, and they sat in silence for a moment. Then David spoke. "This is all too much. Just yesterday I was a simple farmer, and today you are telling me I'm supposed to face the evil one? You know I love you both with all my heart, and I would do anything for you. I just don't know what to think, I..."

"Son," Gabe said gently placing a hand on his arm "I know this is all difficult to accept, and I had always planned on telling you long before now. I had always hoped to give you time to prepare, but as you know, we were denied that opportunity. Now you need to know what we're up against. The night your mother was taken from us, we were being followed." David sat up straight eyes wide. "You see we weren't the only ones who thought you were the one in the prophecy. Unfortunately, the Dark One can corrupt even servants, and we were betrayed by someone we trusted. Your mother and I left you here in the hopes of preventing them from finding you. We were traveling to see the man we believed was going to divulge your identity. We had hoped we could bring him back to the light before it was too late. What we didn't know was that he had already sealed his fate. As soon as we were on the road, we realized we were being followed. I tried to lose them, but eventually they forced us off of the road." You could have heard a pin drop as they sat silent hanging on Gabe's every word. "I was shaken badly when the car hit the tree, but managed to get out and face them. Unfortunately there were too many of them, and they overpowered me. They beat me severely, and before I lost consciousness, I could hear your mother's frantic screams for help. "He choked slightly on the words" I saw the car burst into flames. I called out desperately for your mother, and they laughed with glee at my anguish over losing her. Then one of them grabbed me, and I was wracked with pain as the demon latched onto my soul. It was unbearable, and I passed out. The next thing I could remember was seeing you looking at me, crying. I wanted to scream and call out to you, but I was locked in a deadly battle with that beast and couldn't muster the strength even to blink." David, Molly, and Aurora all had tears in their eyes, and Gabe went on, "The loss of your mother, and the constant torment were almost too much for me to bear. If it hadn't been for you, your strength, you coming to see me every week, I just don't think I could have held on."

"Dad I... I don't know what to say. What if I'm not strong enough, what if ... What if I fail?" David said as he looked away, feeling ashamed.

"Son, I know you, I know how remarkable you are. You saved me, not just today, but every day for the past six years. I can only guess that because they could not see the light in you, they were waiting to see if someone else was the one in the prophecy. They knew about Aurora, too. That's why they went to take her and killed her parents. Make no mistake

David; I would give anything to lift this burden from you. But what they did to me, what they did to you, Aurora, and her parents, and what they did to your mother is nothing compared to what they will do if we fail." Gabe finished, tears in his eyes now, too.

David sat quietly for a moment considering what his father said as Aurora held his hand tightly to let him know she was with him. From somewhere deep inside him or from outside him, he wasn't sure, he felt his courage swell. He sat up with a look of determination, and said, "We won't fail." They all looked at him and nodded. His resolve was unshakable.

"We best get out to the others then, and you, Gabe, have one last dose to take." Molly said. Gabe grimaced but didn't argue.

"I'd like a moment alone with you, Aurora, please. Allow me to help my father into the other room first." David said. Aurora gave him a small smile and a nod, indicating her agreement. David went over to his father, who was pursing his lips after having finished the last of the elixir.

"That is some nasty tasting stuff."

"Here, Dad, let me help you up." David put his father's arm around his shoulder and helped him up to his feet. He was again struck by how thin he was. It pained him that his father, who had been such a strong man, could be so frail now.

"Don't worry, son," Gabe said as if sensing David's mood. "I'm going to be alright."

David said earnestly, "Dad, I can't tell you how much I missed you. Please, as soon as we can, there are some other things I want to ask you."

Gabe reached around with his other arm, and David pulled him into a tight embrace. Speaking softly into David's ear, Gabe said, "I love you so much, and I can't tell you how proud I'm of the man you've become." Then he said, as if he was reading David's thoughts "Don't be afraid. I have faith in you." With that, his father patted him on the back, and in silence they turned and made their way into the living room.

David was surprised to see so many people there. Some he knew and others he didn't. Helping his father into an armchair that would support him, he turned and said, "Excuse me. I'll be back in a minute."

David stood in the doorway of his parents' room looking at Aurora, who was lost in thought again, gazing at the photo of him and his parents. Just seeing her standing there warmed his heart. She was so beautiful and strong, and in spite of all she had been through, she was still full of life. The pain of her loss and the horrors she had seen had not damaged her spirit. He wanted nothing more than to tell her it was all over, and they could stay here where it was safe. He could have sat there soaking her in for hours, but he didn't have that choice.

"Hi" he said, and she was startled a bit.

"I didn't hear you come back." She replied, looking at him a bit flustered.

"I'm sorry. I didn't mean to startle you." He walked over to her and took the frame setting it down on the dresser. He reached out and took her hands gently in his. "Are you alright?" He asked, "I know it must have been difficult for you, recounting what happened, especially to your parents." he said kindly.

She looked down at their clasped hands. What was it about him that affected her so, she wondered. It was as if he could see inside her. All these years she had taught herself to be strong, to lock her weaknesses away, and yet he exposed them with no effort at all. "I'm afraid, and ashamed," she said. He lifted a hand to her chin and gently raised her face to look up into his eyes. He placed his warm hand on her cheek, his fingers gently touching the side of her neck, and his thumb wiped the tear running down her face.

"Why?" he asked tenderly. Her emotions were welling up inside her, threatening to overtake her. She had bottled up her feelings for so long to protect herself, so she could be strong in the face of so much danger. She had never known anyone she felt safe enough with to let them out, and now they were rising up against her will. It was madness that, after spending so little time together, she felt she could trust him, and in truth she had no choice because she could not contain them any longer.

She said, "I didn't tell the whole story before. The day my parents died there was something else." He waited patiently, not rushing her. "The day the soldiers came, my parents made me hide inside a wardrobe with a fake back. I could see what was going on through a small hole, and I could hear everything. Before I got in there, they made me promise that no matter what happened, I was to stay hidden. They made me swear it." She added as if pleading with him to understand. "When the soldiers burst into our home, the first thing they asked was where I was. My parents lied, and said I had left the day before. Enraged, the commander hit my father hard across his face with a club. I could hear his bone crack and saw blood burst from his mouth. My mother was screaming, begging them not to hurt him. But still my father kept saying I had left. The commander motioned to one of the other soldiers, and he grabbed my mother, putting a knife to her throat. He said he would kill my mother if my father didn't tell him where I was. And when my father said he didn't know, the soldier slit her throat, and she dropped to the floor choking on her own blood. As she lay there dying, my father wailed a horrible scream of pain. Then the commander grabbed his hair, pulled his head up, and drove a short sword into his heart." Aurora was sobbing now. David put his arms around her and pulled her close. She grabbed onto him, holding him tight, feeling as if she let go the pain would overwhelm her.

He placed his hand on her head for comfort. "It's not your fault," he said, trying to comfort her. She heaved an enormous sob and looked up at him, the pain on the verge of tearing her apart.

"Yes it is. All they wanted was me. I stood there frozen in fear. I could've come out and let them take me."

David looked into her eyes and in a firm voice said, "No!" She was startled by his commanding tone, "They would have killed them anyway. If they had gotten you as well, your parents' sacrifice would have been for nothing. They thought that you were the one mentioned in the prophecy, so they probably would have just killed you too. Instead, you have honored your parents with your life. You have taken their gift and used it to help others and to fight against the evil that made them suffer."

She blinked. She knew he was right, but having relived it was like a fresh wound. That simple statement of fact did little to ease the pain she was feeling. She pressed her head against his chest as he continued to hold her. She could feel his warmth radiating through her. After several long minutes her breathing slowed, and when she regained her composure enough to speak, she said, "The prophecy".

David still stroking her head, and holding her close asked gently, "What about the prophecy?"

Aurora took a steadying breath then said, "It says our sacrifice will save our people. What if when the time comes, I don't have the strength to do what must be done?"

He leaned back just slightly, enough that she knew he wanted her to look at him. She peered up into his eyes. His gaze was full of compassion, not a hint of judgment or doubt, and then he said, "I promise I'm not going to let anything happen to you. Do you remember what Aunt Molly said? Prophecies are tricky business, and you can't be sure what the outcome is. But whatever comes, remember one thing, we'll be in it together, and no matter what, I'll be by your side."

Staring up into his eyes, wrapped in his strong embrace, she suddenly felt the weight on her heart lift. She managed a smile and pressed her head against him again, squeezing him tighter. They stood there in silence for a little while when David finally spoke, "I guess we'd better get inside with the others. We can find some time to talk later." With that, they let go of each other, and David asked, "Would you like to wash your face before we go?" She nodded, and went into the bath. After splashing some cold water on her face, she stood looking in the mirror and smiled to herself. She knew without him saying it that he would still be waiting for her when she returned. She was glad she still had her hair pulled back in a braid. Otherwise it would be a mess, and she wanted to look pretty for him. She dried her face and turned to the door. As she reentered the room, her smile broadened, seeing him standing patiently waiting. As she headed towards him, something caught her eye. There on the wall in front of her was a large close up of his mother. She froze in her tracks.

"What's wrong?" David asked.

"Your mother," she managed in a distant voice.

"Yes," He said, walking to meet her.

Suddenly her memory came to the surface. She said desperately, "I saw her, a few weeks ago, I saw her!"

David looked astonished and asked, "Where?"

"I remember now! I was traveling with a small group of fighters, and we were headed to disrupt a supply line. We unexpectedly ran into a much larger group of soldiers transporting a small group of prisoners. Each one was chained behind a wagon, made to walk in shackles. Before we could get away, they saw us, so we had to stand and fight. The battle was fierce, and because we were so outnumbered I became separated from the rest of my team. Trying to gain a better position, I ducked under one of the wagons, and the prisoner standing there saw me. A soldier came running up before I could move on, so I had to stay hidden. He shouted at the woman and asked her if she had seen someone. She said she didn't know, and he hit her hard, knocking her to the ground. She held her hands up and begged him, saying 'please, she went that way', and pointed in the other direction. When the soldier ran off, she turned to me, and said 'go child, quickly before they return'. I thanked her, and she smiled at me through her bloodied lips saying 'it's alright, but please hurry'. That woman was your mother, and she saved my life. That's why I was alone when you found me. I've been on the run ever since," she added trying to offer an explanation why she hadn't gone back for her.

David stood for a moment in stunned silence, a mixture of joy and horror swirling inside him. His mother was alive, but she was a prisoner.

He saw Aurora looking at him nervously, then reached out and pulled her into his arms. He could feel her melt with relief. He spoke in little more than a whisper, "Thank you." She held him tight as if to thank him for not blaming her. "We better tell the others," he said. She nodded in agreement then they headed for the door.

THE COUNCIL

They walked into the living room and saw no less than 20 people, most of whom David did not recognize, sitting in a semicircle around the fire. One man in the center sat facing the fire, staring at the seal as David had done. He appeared to be in some sort of trance and unaffected by the conversation around him. They had brought chairs from all over the house, and he could hear voices coming from other rooms. There were two empty seats next to his father, so he made his way to them.

"Ah, David and Aurora, we are all happy to meet you." said, a tall handsome looking older man.

The others all acknowledged their agreement with nods and smiles of encouragement. He stood and walked to meet them at the chairs they had reserved for their use.

"Please do sit down. Molly has briefed us on your harrowing ordeal, and there is so much for us to talk about." His air of authority was absolute. David saw his father give him a smile of encouragement, so the two of them sat without saying a word. "My name is Michael, and we are all members of the council of servants. We have come to help you."

David cleared his throat to steady his voice, "Thank you." He said. "We have just discovered something important." He turned to his father, placed a hand on his arm, and in a consoling tone said, "Dad, Mom's alive. Aurora saw her just a few weeks ago. She was being held prisoner, and they were taking her somewhere."

Gabe lowered his head slightly, and then looked up at his son, with an expression of controlled pain on his face, "As much as I would give to see your mother here again, we may not be able to save her." With tears welling up in his eyes at seeing the look of complete disbelief on David's face, he said, "What you have to do is more important than anyone of us. You must remember that." His voice failed him.

Michael added, with a touch of sympathy, "Your father is right. All of the world could be lost. What would be gained if you saved her, only to deliver her to a living hell?"

David's mind was racing, and without realizing it said, "It sounds like she's already in a living hell."

David's thoughts were spinning. Were these the kinds of sacrifices he would face? Sacrificing himself wouldn't be easy, but his mother, his father, Aurora? He wasn't sure he had the strength for that. If he succeeded and ended up losing everything he cherished in the process, what kind of victory would that be? "Maybe I'm not the person of the prophecy then." He said, "I wouldn't be willing to sacrifice anyone of you given the choice, and I don't even know most of you. How am I going to succeed?"

Michael said to him in a reassuring voice, "You were chosen to be anointed for this task. Your heart and your faithfulness will be the strengths that enable you to succeed. None of us here know what lies before you, only that when the time comes, you will have to choose the right path. The path that you choose will determine the outcome. We only seek to prepare you for what may lie ahead. What you do when faced with those difficult choices, we cannot predict."

David looked at him thoughtfully, "You're saying I might be able to save her, and fulfill the prophecy?"

Michael said, "I'm saying that there is no way any of us can answer that one way or the other. But you need to be forewarned that what you decide will have far-reaching consequences, and that you may have to pick between your own desires and the fate of everyone else."

Aurora reached over and put a hand on his arm. He turned to her and gave her a weak smile. She gave his arm a gentle squeeze to let him know she understood and to tell him that he wasn't alone. He put his other hand on top of hers so she knew he understood. Looking up, he saw Michael watching them with a somber expression of satisfaction.

"So what's next?" David asked.

Michael smiled just the slightest bit, and said, "Yes, he is the one." There was a collective look of relief amongst the entire group at these words. "And this young lady is not to be underestimated, young man."

Not quite sure what just happened, David said, "I know she isn't. I only hope I can keep up with her." Aurora beamed with pride.

"Now to answer your question, we have assembled here to anoint the two of you in fulfillment of the prophecy. We have watched you both for many years to determine if you truly were the ones it referred to. Your father," Michael said to David, "told us of your visions of a young girl from a distant land. One of our council members searched for her, and we have watched from a distance. But it was not until tonight that we were certain you were the ones."

"Like your namesake, King David, you do not seek glory for yourself, you are faithful, and your heart is true. Although you are not to be anointed King, you are to lead our people in battle. This battle will be more fearsome in many ways, and the outcome will affect us all. You must remember the lessons of King David. It was his faith and loyalty to the Lord that brought him victory. But you must also remember how even David was tempted with power, and in a moment of weakness, was tricked into betrayal."

"Aurora." Michael turned to her, and said, "You have also demonstrated your pure heart and faithfulness. Even after the loss and pain you suffered, you did not turn away. You remained true. That is why the

Lord has blessed you with many gifts. But you too must beware of the tricks of the evil one. He knows your fears and will use them against you."

"Now I ask you both to bow your heads," Michael said as he drew a small vial from his pocket. "In the name of our Lord and Father, I anoint you both his chosen ones, that his spirit would rest upon you and strengthen you." He poured a drop of oil on each of their heads. They could feel the warmth spreading through them as they were filled with the Spirit. They lifted their heads and looked at each other, understanding passing between them. There was no turning back now. They would see this through, together, to the end.

The group stood and faced them. Solemnly they all bowed their heads, acknowledging their commitment, except for the man who was fixed on the seal. He had remained seated, and without warning he spoke, "It is done." Everyone turned to him, waiting for more. He shook his head slightly, and said, "That is the only message I have."

A slight look of surprise came over the group. Then Michael spoke again, "I see." He turned back to David and Aurora. "I would suggest you eat and get some rest so you can begin your journey tomorrow. We will prepare some things for you so that you may set out first thing."

Unable to hide his disappointment, David asked, "Is that it? I don't mean to be rude, but don't you have any idea of what we need to do? Where we start?"

Michael looked at him with a hint of sadness, "I'm sorry, I honestly don't know. We were hoping for some guidance, but this message tells us that it is entirely up to you. Only you will know what to do, and the Spirit and your heart will guide you."

David sighed; then turned to Aurora, "I don't know about you, but I'm starving. And for all I know, this will be the last meal we get, so would you like to join me for dinner?" He smiled at her, and she couldn't help but smile back.

"I think that sounds like a great idea." She said.

David turned to his father, "Dad would you like to stay here and eat, or go into the kitchen?" The others began leaving the room and chatting amongst themselves.

David's father, looking tired, said, "I think I need to rest here for a while longer. You go eat."

David gave him a 'don't be silly' look. "Dad, I'll bring some food to you, and we'll sit here together if that's alright with you, Aurora?"

She said, "Of course. Let me give you a hand." They got up and made their way to the kitchen.

With all the people in the house, David was suddenly reminded that the last time it was this crowded, it was his mother's funeral. It hit him again that she was alive, and he could be faced with a terrible choice. He pushed the thought away. There was no use tormenting himself over the unknown. When the time came, he would save her if possible.

David was happy to see that his guests had prepared food already, and plenty of it. They hadn't eaten much since breakfast, and after a day like today, he was famished. He could see the hunger in Aurora's eyes too. They fixed 3 plates of food and headed back to the living room. His father was talking with Michael and Aunt Molly.

"Did we miss anything?" David asked.

"As any good father, he is concerned for his son." Michael said, "We were discussing the possibility of sending one of our members with you. There are a few of us who can travel between the worlds. Having one of us with you would offer some protection, but it would also attract attention to you. Young Aurora here has been quite a thorn in their side, but they would not recognize you there. We know that they are aware of the prophecy, but they are not certain whom it is about. That may be your best protection."

David turned to Aurora, "What do you think?"

She looked pleased that he asked her opinion first, and then taking on her confident warrior demeanor that he knew so well she said, "I think you're right. I've learned to travel unseen through my land, and it will be difficult enough for the two of us alone."

Michael seemed satisfied, and David looked at her reassuringly. David's father tried to raise an objection. "But don't you think" he started, and David put a comforting hand on his shoulder and said,

"Dad, I agree too. The enormity of this task is overwhelming, and the added responsibility of another person's life is more than I think I can bear."

His father looked at him with a slight pleading in his eyes, but conceded. "David, I know this is a terrible burden, and I only wish ..." Gabe's voice trailed off.

David replied "Remember Dad, you told me God's will does not take us where his grace cannot sustain us."

Gabe looked up at him, managed a smile, and said, "Great! Now he's using my own words against me." The welcome levity made them all chuckle a little.

"I will let you have some time alone then." Michael said as he turned to leave.

"Michael?" David said, and Michael turned back to face him, "How do we get back to the other world?"

Michael said, "Ah, that is a problem. Honestly, I don't know. Those of us who can, do it using our gift. How the two of you accomplished it, we have no idea. You will have to figure it out, and I'm sure you will. The only thing I can tell you, which may be helpful, is in some places the divide between the two worlds is smaller. You may need to find such a place."

David stepped close to him, looking directly into his eyes, and said, "One more thing please?"

Michael looking curious asked, "Yes?"

David replied, in a thoughtful yet serious tone, "Please give me your word that you'll do everything you can to protect my father while I'm gone. I need to know that he's safe."

Michael reached up, clasped David's arms, and said, "I will protect his life as if it were my own." Then Michael turned and left.

Gabe looked at his son with pride, and said, "Now don't you worry about me, son. Molly is going to stay with me until I'm fully recovered. She may drive me crazy, but she's a fantastic cook."

Molly pointed a finger at him and said, "Don't you start with me, Gabe."

They all chuckled again and sat down to eat. Gabe regaled them with one story after another, Molly often interjecting to accuse him of exaggerating. It was a welcome diversion from the serious matter at hand. Aurora smiled and laughed, and David's heart lifted to see his father so full of life again.

After a while, Molly stood up, and said, "Alright Gabe, you need to get some rest now." He gave her a sour look. "You'll have some time in the morning to see your son off."

David stood and said, "Come on Dad, I'll help you back to your room. Aunt Molly, will you please keep Aurora company until I get back?"

Molly smiled, and responded, "I'd be delighted to." Aurora placed a hand on him and smiled, appreciating his thought for her.

David called Rusty, who trotted over happily. David helped his father to his feet, and together they walked back to his room with Rusty in tow. "I like her," his father said.

David smiled, "Yes, I like her too, dad."

Gabe added, "And she's quite pretty, don't you think?"

David shook his head, and replied, "Dad, I thought that was Aunt Molly's job."

Gabe laughed a little "Son, you wouldn't deny me a little fun now, would you?"

Once inside the room, Gabe turned to his son, having regained enough strength to stand on his own, and said, "David, come see me in the morning. I have something I want to give you for your journey." Then he pulled him into a hug. "I'm so very proud of you."

David squeezed him tightly "Thank you Dad. I had you as an example to follow."

Gabe let go of him and said, "Now go look after that young lady. I can manage from here."

David replied, "Alright, goodnight Dad. Rusty you stay here, and keep an eye on him."

Gabe responded, "Good night, my son."

As David approached Aurora and Molly, he overheard Molly saying, "So dear, you don't have any special man in your life?"

"Thank you, Aunt Molly, I'll take it from here."

Molly gave him a sheepish smile, and retorted, "Well dear, old habits are hard to break. I'll leave you two to enjoy each other's company," and she bustled off.

David sat next to Aurora, and said, "Sorry about that. Aunt Molly has always been a bit obsessed with matchmaking."

Aurora smiled "It's alright, I found her charming, and your father's quite a character."

David laughed a little. "You could say that again. He drove my mother up the wall sometimes."

There were still a number of people milling around giving them glances here and there. David, noticing the prying eyes all around, turned to Aurora and asked, "Would you like to sit outside for a little while so we can be alone?"

She smiled broadly, "Yes, I would."

They stood and made their way to the front door. A couple of people gave them a quick introduction, but they soon found themselves outside in the crisp night air. David led her to the porch swing with its back to the house, facing the yard. Even though they could still hear muffled voices, the semi quiet and darkness was relaxing. She sat down on his right and pressed up against him, laying her head on his shoulder. He reached his arm around her, and she lifted her hand to hold his.

"Are you warm enough?" he asked.

"Yes, it feels good to be out in the fresh air."

They sat in silence. David couldn't remember ever feeling so at peace. He wondered how he could be so content at this moment when in a few short hours they would embark on a terrible journey.

***

Aurora could hardly believe what she was feeling. She had never before let a man even hold her hand, and here she sat, David with his arm around her, and it felt as natural as using her bow. The past ten years had been filled with loneliness, struggle, the burden of responsibility, and worst of all, seemingly endless death. She had killed more men than she could count, seen too many of her fellows fall, and her protection had been to build an impenetrable wall around her heart. The weight of it all too often felt as if it would crush her. It was only through sheer force of will and determination that she persevered. Somehow just as he was able to walk through the divide, he effortlessly breached her defenses. It frightened her. She didn't like being vulnerable, but at the same time it was a relief. She was tired and alone. The emptiness she felt was suffocating, and yet when she was with him, all those feelings washed away. She actually felt happy, and it had been so long she almost didn't recognize it. The idea that she wasn't alone anymore, not simple companionship, but something more, lifted her heart. As she thought about it, she realized he hadn't truly broken through her defenses, because he had already been inside them. He had been one of the precious things she had been guarding her whole life. Her visions of him had been her comfort and her strength so many times. Since the moment they finally met he had, without hesitation, proven himself to be everything she had imagined, and much more. For the first time, in so long she couldn't remember, she felt safe, not just physically, but her heart and soul too.

***

As if she were reading his thoughts, she said, "I wish we could just stay here forever," and nuzzled a little closer to him.

David answered, "I would love that too." Then he added with hesitation in his voice, "Do you think, maybe someday when all this is over, we could come back here together?"

She let go of his hand and looked up to meet his eyes. She reached up and put her hand on the side of his face. His heart started racing as she looked into his eyes. Then in a soft but sure voice, she said, "I would love that."

Time seemed to have frozen. He couldn't move. He felt her skin on his. The smell of lavender from her bath long gone, her natural scent filled his breath. She was moving ever so slowly towards him. Suddenly all his senses were alert; he heard a sound off in the distance. Out of the corner of his eye he saw it fly through the air. Everything seemed to happen in slow motion. His left arm lifted, and he pulled her hard with his right arm, twisting around onto his feet as he reached out and grabbed an arrow that had been speeding directly at her heart. Pulling her down onto the floor on top of him, he immediately rolled over and jumped to his feet. He leapt from the porch and ran towards the place where the sound had originated. Reaching the edge of the seal, he stopped and scanned the area. He heard her footsteps coming up behind him.

"Go back," he shouted, but she ignored his warning. He turned and held up the arrow, walking to meet her. David said, "Someone tried to kill you. Now please come inside."

She exclaimed, "What! Here!"

David gently turned her towards the house, and replied, "Yes, I guess someone knows where you are." He followed closely, keeping himself between her and the perimeter.

As soon as they entered the house, David spotted Michael, and they went directly to him. "Michael, someone tried to kill Aurora," he said, holding up the arrow. "We were sitting on the front porch when they shot this at her from beyond the seal. I went out to check, but they were gone."

Michael, looking grave, said, "Time is running out. I will alert everyone. You two get some sleep. You'll be safe inside. They cannot pass the seal. We'll keep watch during the night, and in the morning come up with a plan to facilitate your escape."

David in a somber tone asked, "Michael, how did they know?"

The two passed a knowing look. "I'll see if I can find out." Michael said.

David walked over to Molly. "Aunt Molly, will you please come with me?" Sensing the urgency in his voice, she didn't say a word, but followed them to the bedrooms. "Aunt Molly, someone just tried to kill Aurora while we were sitting on the front porch." She raised her hand to her mouth in a gasp. "Michael is going to alert everyone, and they're going to organize a watch tonight. Will you please stay in my father's room and keep an eye on him? I'm going to watch over Aurora." He leaned in and whispered. "I'm going to move her into the room next to my parents'. If anything should happen, bang on the wall, and I'll hear it."

Molly looked at him with a trace of shock on her face, and in an equally quiet voice asked, "Are you suggesting that someone here has betrayed us?"

David replied, "I'm not taking any chances." She nodded and slipped into his father's room.

He and Aurora walked down to her room, and once inside he started arranging the bedding to give the impression of someone under the covers. "Is there anything you need in here, besides your pack, of course?" He smiled at her, attempting to put her at ease.

"Just the night shirt," she said picking it up.

"Ok then let's go."

They walked down the hall and ducked into the room beside his father's. "Don't you think someone might have seen us come in here? That door is visible from the other room." Aurora asked.

David gave her a determined look, and said, "I'm counting on it." She nodded in understanding. David moved the furniture around so that anyone who came in and went over to the bed would be trapped. Then he organized the bed to look like the two of them were lying down under the covers. In the closet, he found more linen, and fashioned a spot where they could settle in, out of the line of sight of the open door.

"I'm sorry it won't be as comfortable as the bed." David said.

Aurora smiled, "It's a lot better than sleeping on a jagged rock in the rain."

David shot her a mischievous grin, "In that case, what are you complaining about?"

She hit him lightly on the arm, "I wasn't complaining" she said, and he laughed.

"OK let's get settled in. The bathroom is in there." She went in, washed up, and came out in the nightshirt. David half wished she had kept her jeans on; the sight of her made his heart skip a beat. After he washed too, they settled down on the makeshift bed.

***

She sat there resting in his arms, comforted by his warmth as he gently stroked her head. Ever since she lost her parents, her life had been in danger. She never let her guard down, and yet here she sat feeling perfectly safe. Someone had just tried to kill her, and he had saved her. She knew she should be afraid, but somehow she couldn't be. Somehow with him there she knew everything would be all right, that he would not let anyone hurt her. She thought about coming back here when all of this was over. It was something to look forward to. She never imagined an end to it all, and now it seemed possible. Even though the possibility was remote, and they might not live long enough to attempt it, that thought comforted her. Considering what it would be like to have a normal life, she drifted off to sleep.

It was pitch black when she started to stir. Something had disturbed her. Suddenly a hand was over her mouth, and she heard David whisper into her ear "Sh." She froze as he slipped his leg out from under her. There was the slightest sound as the door unlatched. Very slowly a low light outlined its frame. Little by little the light grew wider as it reached out to the bed where the decoy of pillows and blankets lay. In the opening, she caught a flash of steel. She was too experienced to panic. Instead, her mind raced with the possibilities of how she would defend herself. David had silently moved into a crouching position, waiting to strike.

Time moved slowly as she watched the figure enter the room. He was a squat, powerfully built man, but he was still counting on the element of surprise. As he approached the bed, she held her breath, not wanting to give any indication that he was being watched. Drawing up the dagger, he plunged it into the pile where one of their hearts should have been. When his hand hit the soft pillow instead of muscle and bone, he was momentarily stunned, and David leapt. As Aurora jumped to her feet, she saw David knock the man onto the bed, grabbing his hand with the knife and pulling it back at an odd angle, so he dropped it. Kneeling on his back pulling his arm up and twisting it, David spoke,

"Hello there, are you looking for us?" The man grunted with pain, David was clearly twisting his arm near its breaking point. David reached down and grabbed the dagger. "Aurora, would you please call for

Michael?" David asked. She walked to the door and called out his name. She saw him hurrying in from the other room.

"What is it, child?" He asked a look of concern on his face with several others in tow.

"A man tried to attack us, and David has him pinned down in here."

As Michael and the others entered the room, David put the knife to the man's throat and told him to roll over slowly. Someone switched on the lights, and they saw the man lying on his back with David standing over him, held in place by the threat of the knife.

"Dear Lord Artemis, how can it be you?" Michael asked in disbelief.

"Michael, you're a fool, we've already lost. He made me an offer. He said if I helped him I would have a place of honor when he rules. He... he ... he told me the prophecy would fail," Artemis ended, weakly looking up at David standing over him. His eyes went wide as David looked at him, not with anger or hatred, but with pity and sadness. "Oh dear Lord, what have I done? How could I have been such a fool?" Artemis wailed. Then he reached up, grabbing David's arms, and said, "Please forgive me. He knows you're coming." Then he pulled the dagger into his throat.

David screamed in anguish "No! No! I didn't want to…. I…. Please don't die" Then with a look of torment on his face, he leapt off of him and turned to the others asking, "What can we do?"

Michael rushed over. Artemis gurgled, then his eyes turned dark. "It's too late." Michael said sadly.

Grief stricken, David looked at Michael. "I wasn't going to kill him, I wouldn't have…"

Michael placed a hand on his shoulder to stop him. "David, it wasn't your fault. He was already lost. He killed himself so that he could no longer betray us. In the end, it was the only thing left he could do to try to redeem himself. Once you turn yourself over to the Dark One, his hold is nearly impossible to break. Come, let's get you two out of here." Michael said to David and Aurora. Silently they left the room. "Do you need anything?"

"No, thank you," David said in a daze. He turned to Aurora, and she shook her head. "We'll head back to get some sleep." David added woodenly, the enormity of having killed someone weighing on him.

They turned and headed to Aurora's room. She pulled down the blankets and fixed the pillows so they could lie down. They climbed into the bed, and this time he rested his head on her shoulder. Her arm around him, she gently stroked his head and lightly kissed his forehead. She could feel his pain as he sought comfort in her arms. Whether Artemis killed himself or not, David felt responsible. Then he said to her in barely more than a whisper, "I didn't mean to."

She said in a tender voice "I know." Laying there in silence, it wasn't long until they were both asleep.

AND SO IT BEGINS

Aurora awoke slightly stunned. The room was filled with daylight, and she was alone. She got up and went to the bathroom to freshen up. She came out and stood looking at the clothes lying on the dresser. Her leather traveling clothes looked so worn and unladylike next to the clothes she had borrowed from his mother. She stood there feeling foolish. She knew where they were going, ladylike would not serve her well. She liked looking nice for him, but she knew things were about to change. The brief respite she had enjoyed, as tumultuous as it was, would soon be at an end. Suddenly there was a soft knock at the door.

"Aurora, are you awake?" She heard David's voice.

She felt warm inside at the thought that he would not leave her alone for long and that he was her protector just as she would be his. She also marveled at how much respect he showed her. He had stayed in bed with her all night and just held her. Now, here he was in his own home, asking her permission to enter the room.

"Come in. I'm awake." She said to the door.

David walked in with a tray holding two plates of food, some coffee, and juice. "I thought I'd bring you some breakfast." He said with a smile. "Our keepers are cooking up a storm in the kitchen. I'm afraid we won't have a moment's peace if we go in there to eat". He set the tray down on the dresser and turned to her. She walked over to him, and without hesitation threw her arms around him and kissed him full on the lips. He wrapped his arms around her in return. She melted in his embrace, and then buried her face in his chest.

"Good morning," he said, "I guess I should bring you breakfast every day."

She looked up at him her face flush "I'm sorry…. I don't know…. I" she stammered.

"Sh." He said softly. "I can't imagine a better way to start the day." Standing there holding each other, they were surprised by a voice at the door.

"Um, excuse me." Aunt Molly said, with a cat that ate the canary grin on her face. Both of them now red in the face, she went on "when you two are finished getting…. Um ready. We were hoping to talk to you."

David grimaced, "We'll be there shortly. Thank you, Aunt Molly." Turning to Aurora, he added, "Now she'll be insufferable." They both laughed.

They ate their breakfast and talked about what they wanted to bring with them. When they were finished, David left her to get dressed. She decided to wear the borrowed clothes a little longer. Then she headed out to find him. She strode confidentially into the room, surveying the group, and saw David wasn't there. "Excuse me, where's David?" She asked.

"He's in the back with his father. Can you please tell him we're all waiting?" Asked Molly.

"I'll be happy to." She replied. She approached the room and saw the door was shut. Hesitantly she knocked softly and asked, "David are you in there?"

From behind the door, she heard him say, "Yes, please come in, Aurora."

She walked in, and David and his father were sitting on the bed next to each other. They both stood as she entered.

"Come sit down here with David. I have something for the two of you." Gabe said to her. The two of them sat down. Aurora looked at David questioningly, and he raised his eyebrows to say he had no idea.

Gabe went to the dresser and was rummaging around in one of the drawers, then said to himself, "Ah, here you are." He turned to the two of them and smiled. "The night my wife, your mother, was taken, we didn't take anything with us that would identify our connection to the council." Gabe held out his hand and in it were two beautiful matching crosses. He reached down and picked up the first by the chain. "These crosses were mine and your mother's. We left them here that day. I want the two of you to have them for protection, and as a reminder; a reminder that even in your darkest hour, you are never alone." He took the first cross and held the chain wide so he could place it on David's head.

Then he took the second one, and reached towards Aurora, her eyes on the verge of tears she said, "Oh, it's too much for you to give me something so precious."

Gabe smiled and said, "I'm willing to give you the most precious thing I have, my son. What is a necklace compared to that?"

Then he placed the chain around her neck as a tear ran down her cheek. Gabe reached out his hands, and placed one on each of their shoulders, and spoke, "If I have found any small favor with my Lord, may He bestow his blessing upon you both. May He protect you always in the face of evil, may He grant you success in all your endeavors, may He bless you with wisdom and courage, and fill you with His spirit." He lifted his hands from them, and David and Aurora stood.

"Thank you, Dad," David said. Then Aurora reached out and embraced Gabe.

"Oh yes, thank you for showing me such kindness." Aurora said.

Gabe leaned back to look at her. "You are welcome, my child. Now God's speed on your journey. We better get out there before Molly and Michael come storming in here."

David and Aurora smiled, and with that they headed to the living room. Everyone was waiting, Molly giving them a reproachful look. Molly opened her mouth to speak, but was cut off by Gabe before she started. "Molly, you wouldn't deny me a moment alone with my son at such a time as this? Would you?"

Molly, looking disarmed, replied, "No, of course not, Gabe. But we better get started. Time is not on our side."

The three of them moved in and took the empty places left for them, then Michael spoke, "As it is written, when two or more gather in his name He is with them." Michael paused as everyone joined hands with those around them. David and Aurora felt a charge ripple through them like static electricity filling the air. "Lord, we seek Your blessings. In this late hour we ask You to guide us to Your will. We stand against the evil one in Your name. Glory to You and Your kingdom forever. AMEN."

They all stood, and when they released their hands, the air went still again. Michael spoke "You all know what you have to do. May the Lord be with you."

The group began to scatter, and many of them headed to the door to leave. Michael came over to David and Aurora, and asked, "Are you ready?"

They looked at each other, then David spoke, "Almost. We just need to change into some traveling clothes, collect our packs, and we'll head out."

"We've prepared some food, dried meat, biscuits, and other assorted items for you to take. Is there anything else you can think of?"

"How did Artemis get past the seal?"

"He was not possessed yet. Sadly what he was about to do, he was doing of his own free will. It would have sealed his fate, and bound him to the Dark One forever."

"Will you be staying here?"

"Of course. I gave you my word. A group of us will remain here not only to help look after your father, but, God willing, to see you return."

Michael gave him a smile, and David asked, "You mean this isn't a one-way trip?"

Michael reached out and placed a hand on David and Aurora's shoulders, and said, "I truly hope not."

David turned to his father, and said, "Dad, we're going to go to your room and get some clothes for Aurora, if you don't mind?"

"Of course, Son."

The two of them headed back to the room, and Aurora said a little sheepishly, "You don't like my traveling clothes?"

David, giving her a warm smile said, "I love seeing you in your traveling clothes. Although, I'm afraid you'd be more recognizable wearing them, don't you?"

Aurora, slightly embarrassed, flipped her hair back nervously, and said, "I guess you're right."

David asked "What would a woman who isn't as exceptional as you wear?" He smiled a little mischievously at her, knowing he was pressing a small advantage.

Aurora hit him lightly on the arm, "stop teasing me. You need to be serious now." David laughed.

After looking through drawers and the closet, Aurora seemed satisfied. David left her to change while he went to find some clothes to complement hers. David found some dark pants he wore on the farm, and a black shirt. He knew, from what she told him, that if his clothes were too well kept, they would stand out. He chose the dark colors thinking they would be less visible traveling at night, allowing them to avoid as many people as possible. He had also gotten out his and his mother's long leather traveling coats. They came down below the knees, and not only offered protection from wind and rain, but also had a lot of inside pockets for keeping things safe. He had a weathered leather backpack that would do well for supplies, extra clothing, and a few other items. He would have liked to take a regular camping pack, but thought it would draw unwanted attention.

They both entered the hallway at the same time. Aurora was wearing a simple pale blue dress that laced up its front and ran down below her knees. She had on his mother's tall boots that ran up under the bottom of the dress. Her hair hanging free now, falling over her shoulders, caught the little light in the hallway and shimmered slightly. The sleeves of the dress came down just below her elbows. In her hand she held her pack and the traveling coat. He walked up to her and slid his arm around her waist. She put her hand to his chest, looking flustered.

He leaned in as if to kiss her, then shifted his head to whisper in her ear, "I feel leather under your dress. Your traveling clothes, perhaps?"

He leaned back, and she looked up at him confidently "You didn't think I was going to go out there unprepared did you?"

"Never."

They walked out to the living room together to find David's father, Aunt Molly, and Michael sitting together talking. All of the others had gone or were busy elsewhere.

David spoke first. "I think we're as ready as we're going to be, so I guess it's time for us to head out."

Gabe asked, "Do you have an idea where to start?"

"I'm going to go to the clearing up on the northeast ridge where I found Aurora. You said there are places where the divide between the worlds is smaller. Perhaps that's one of them. When we get there we'll see what we find."

Gabe smiled at him, and then Michael stood and said, "I hope to see you again soon, young man."

Aunt Molly got up as well and gave him a loving hug saying, "You be careful out there." Then she hugged Aurora, saying, "please try, and keep him out of trouble."

"I will."

Gabe standing now, hugged his son without saying a word; afraid he would betray his fear of losing him. Then he hugged Aurora, and said, "Goodbye Dear. I truly hope to see you again."

Afraid if they waited too long it might be impossible to leave, David took Aurora by the hand and led her to the door. Taking one last look back at the three of them standing there, he smiled reassuringly, turned, and left. He walked to the door of his Jeep, still parked where it landed just after their narrow escape, and opened the passenger door for Aurora. He held out a hand to help her up, and said to her, "Are you ready?" She nodded, and he closed the door. They drove in silence up the road towards the clearing, both lost in thought. David pulled the car to a stop, and left the keys in the ignition. He wouldn't need them where they were going. He turned to Aurora, and reached out a hand. She took his in hers, "There's no turning back now."

"I don't think there ever really was."

He nodded slightly, and said, mustering a cheery voice "and, so it begins."

She didn't wait for him this time. They climbed out of the car, shut the doors, and headed up the trail. As they approached the edge of the clearing, he heard the whistle. He pushed Aurora gently away from him, and the arrow sliced through the air between them. Aurora's expression, after seeing the arrow pass by, turned from dismay at being pushed, to her warrior gaze. Being back in her element, wearing her traveling clothes, covered as they were, created a transformation inside her, and she became fluid motion. David turned to spot her would be attacker. He marveled at how in a seamless movement Aurora had unsheathed her bow, nocked an arrow, and spun to aim and fire. Her arrow hit its mark with astonishing speed, catching her would be assassin dead center in the chest. They ran over to him, keeping an eye on the surroundings, wary of any other assailants. David had knelt down to check his pulse when suddenly there was an unearthly scream as the demon inside this form escaped and shattered in front of them.

Looking at his arrows lying on the ground David said, "These are the same ones used last night. I'm guessing he was the one who tried to kill you then too."

Aurora, still scanning the area, said, "I believe you're right. I don't think there's anyone else around."

David agreed, "I don't think so either, but we should get going." She nodded in agreement. They headed back to the clearing, and before they stepped into the open, David stopped, placing a hand on her. "I sense something about this place, I'm not sure what's going to happen, but take my hand, and no matter what, don't let go."

Aurora sheathed her bow, checked to see if her dagger was in reach of her free hand, and took David's hand in the other. They shared a silent look, and then stepped out together, moving steadily forward. They began to feel a static electric charge running through them. David felt drawn to a spot towards the middle of the clearing, and as they headed to it there was a crackle in the air, and they could feel the hairs on their arms standing on end. "Hold on," David reminded her, and when they reached the spot, there was an eruption of sound and light. David could feel Aurora being pulled from him He swung his other arm around to get a better hold of her, and she did the same. It felt as if they were inside a tornado of sound and light, then with a bang, they hit the ground. The impact was so hard it almost knocked them over. Then there was silence.

They were standing on the barren hillside where he had seen her just days before. The shattered stumps of trees battered and burned, the parched earth, and the rocky landscape were clearly the result of a fierce battle.

Aurora spoke, "It's even worse here than when I left." She said, looking at the still smoldering remains of a once giant tree, "I imagine when I disappeared in front of them they destroyed everything trying to find me."

"They were remarkably thorough too. Which way should we go? We probably shouldn't stay here too long."

Aurora gestured with her hand, "Lets head this way. We need to get to the council so we can tell them about the prophecy. It may take us a couple of days, but we should be able to manage it safely."

"That sounds like a good plan to me. It looks like we have about six hours of daylight left before we need to find some shelter."

They started down the rocky slope, climbing over the debris from the attack. He admired how graceful she was under such difficult conditions, and her stamina was impressive. He was used to long days on the farm, but she didn't even seem to be breaking a sweat. They stopped to take a drink of water a few times, but she was determined that they get to cover before they do more than that.

They reached a tree line as dusk was setting in, and found an area of heavy brush they could use to rest for a few hours before continuing. They both agreed that traveling at night would give them some advantage. The long traveling coat David brought for Aurora covered the blue dress in dark leather so the two of them would be hard to spot. Still feeling vulnerable, they decided not to make a fire. David was rummaging through the food, picking out some things that would be good cold.

Aurora said, "I'll be right back."

"Where are you going?"

A little embarrassed, she said, looking away from his eyes, "I have to relieve myself."

"Oh … don't go too far. I promise I won't listen."

She waved her hand as if to brush him off. A few minutes later, waiting for her to return, David had that sense that something was wrong again. He headed off in the direction that Aurora went until he heard some voices, and a wave of terror filled him. As quietly as possible he made his way towards the sound and caught a glimpse of the flickering light of a fire. As he approached, he heard the men talking in a gruff angry tone, "Who are you? What are you doing out here? Tell us or we'll have to make you tell us." Moving closer, his heart fell. There stood Aurora, held by two men with 3 others standing in front of her. Their apparent leader was threatening her with a knife. He was amazed to see her face filled with anger, not fear, and it filled him with courage.

Without thought, he stepped into the small clearing, and said fearlessly, "Let her go."

The men were slightly shocked, but these were not the sorts to be easily intimidated. Realizing too late what a fool-hearty move he had made, he started thinking quickly. He saw a pleading look of panic on Aurora's face telling him to run, but he couldn't; he wouldn't do that.

"My wife and I are traveling to her sick parents," and in a feigned tone of pleading added, "Please, we are no threat to you. We mean you no harm. Please let us be on our way."

Like a shark smelling blood in the water, this only encouraged the men.

The leader said, "Grab him."

The other two came to David, but he decided this was not the moment for action. The knife was now at Aurora's throat held tight by one of the two men holding her. He could not risk provoking them. The other two men were large and strong, but loped like dumb beasts towards him. Once they flanked him, each one grabbed an arm and pressed it to his side. They held his hands in front of him, so they could see them.

"A compelling story," growled the leader, "but what of her bow? What woman on the way to tend to her sick parents carries such a weapon? We're looking out for a woman with a bow. We lost her not far from here a few days back." He strode over to Aurora, then reached out, and pulled open her coat. The blue dress was bright in the firelight. Seeing something so womanly surprised the man. "Hmm, perhaps you are just travelers. Even if you are, you still have to pay for passage. I don't suppose you have any gold, but such a lovely shape might be worth the price."

The men all snickered, and David felt his fear turn to rage building like a wild beast within him. David spoke, requiring all of his effort to control his voice. "Please, you don't have to do this."

The leader looked at him, and laughed, "No, but I want to." He said, annunciating every syllable, mocking David's foolish statement.

As the man reached out to touch her, David felt something rise in him, an explosion of fury like nothing he had ever experienced before. The air began to sizzle with the same electric charge they felt earlier, and he let out a roar of sound with such force it momentarily stunned the men. That moment was all they needed. David saw the man holding the knife to Aurora with wide eyes lowering the blade enough for her to act. As she reached up and grabbed his hand, twisting the knife away from her throat, David made his move. The two men holding him had slackened their grip just enough for David to push his arms down, and swing them up behind the men. Then with a surge of strength that poured in from outside of him, he pulled the two together in front of him, their faces smashing together so hard he heard the breaking of bones and saw a gush of blood as they hit. As they staggered back, they released him entirely to grab their broken faces, trying to get the blood out of their eyes.

David reached into his coat and pulled out 2 knives, throwing them directly into the hearts of the men holding Aurora. They fell to the ground, writhing in pain with horrible screeches as the dark shadows burst forth from them and splintered in the light.

The leader of the group was recovering from the shock, seeing what David had done. An evil grin passing over his face, he raised his knife, and began to turn to Aurora. The smile still on his face, thinking he had outmaneuvered David, turned to wide-eyed shock as Aurora plunged a knife deep into his chest. The unearthly scream that exploded from the man was deafening as he fell. They all watched as the dark spirit rose from him and burst into fragments.

David, standing tall, the air still alive around him, turned to the two men bleeding profusely. In a powerful commanding voice, he said to them "Decide now, you can choose life or death, light or dark, but make no mistake. Lie to me, and you will suffer the consequences."

The first man turned to him, and said, "I will give you my answer." Then he tried to lunge at David staggering a little. David easily evaded him, and as he came around, David took hold of him and snapped his neck.

The second man, fear showing on his blood spattered face, looked up at him and asked, "How can I go back after all that I have done..."

David looked at the man and spoke without the harsh tone in his voice. "There is only one way. You must ask for forgiveness."

"You would forgive me?"

"Yes I would, but it is not my forgiveness you must seek. But heed my warning. If you leave this place with treachery in your heart, you will not make it ten paces."

The man nodded and slowly got to his feet. He turned and walked off, David and Aurora standing, silently watching him. Nine paces out the man turned to look at them, then with his next step, he fell dead to the ground.

David turned to Aurora and asked, "Are you alright?"

She walked up and started hitting him on his chest, yelling, "You could've gotten yourself killed! What were you thinking? I made a foolish mistake and risked everything."

David pulled her into his arms, and she went slack against him. "It's alright," he said, "it's alright."

Aurora, resting her head against him, said, "I'm so sorry I was being stupid, going off so far just because I was embarrassed. You could've gotten killed."

David said tenderly, "Just be prepared to forgive me the next time I make a mistake, and we can call it even."

Aurora just couldn't understand, how after what just happened, he could so easily lift her mood. He had not diminished her, he had kept them as equals. A lesser man would have chastised her to assert his superiority, but not him. Affection for him welling up inside her, she looked up and kissed him on the cheek.

He smiled, and said, "We'd better get back to our supplies before any animals get into the food. Not to mention we don't want to find out if these thugs have any friends around." She nodded her head in agreement; they picked up their weapons, and headed back.

***

David was still tormented by Artemis's death; he understood it wasn't his fault, but he still felt responsible. Even though he had intended to harm them, they weren't in any real danger then, and David would have let him go, given the choice. This time was different. These men were certainly evil; not the same kind of demons as the ones holding his father, but they surely would have killed him and Aurora, or far worse for that matter. He didn't like the fact that he had to kill them, but he also felt he had no choice.

He considered the way he had become filled with power. His rage at them for what they intended for Aurora had somehow allowed him to draw the power in. He didn't understand it yet, but he knew something had changed in him the other night while he was drawn into the seal. Somehow he had been plugged into the world around him, connected to the 'light' in a tangible way. What happened today made it clear to him what they were facing. These men had willingly given their souls to the Dark One, and there was nothing he could do for them. They had chosen their path, and whether he liked it or not, he would have to do whatever was necessary to protect himself and Aurora, or they would fail.

***

Back inside their hiding place, they were happy to find their things untouched. They had a meal of some dried meat and biscuits. As hungry as they were now, it was like a feast. They agreed they would be safe to rest there for a little while. They packed up their gear just in case they had to move in a hurry, and gathered some brush to pull over them for cover. Once securely hidden, Aurora pulled David's arm tight around her as she lay on her side, enjoying his warm body against hers. She rested her head on his hand, comforted by the feel of his skin on her face.

In little more than a whisper Aurora asked "David?"

"Yes Aurora?"

"Do you have a woman in your world?" She waited for him to answer, and for a moment she was afraid her question had bothered him.

"No, I don't"

After a few moments, she asked, "Why?"

"I dated a few girls when I was younger, but I always had someone else in my heart."

Aurora's heart sank. There was someone else who had his heart, and she asked, "Oh, is she very special?"

"Yes she's extraordinary. I've never met anyone like her, and no one else has been able to take her place."

Aurora was starting to feel a burning in her stomach, she knew it was foolish since they had just met, but she somehow had thought maybe they had something. Unable to hold back she asked, "Will you marry her some day?" Afraid to hear the answer, she closed her eyes.

"I don't know. I only met her a couple of days ago, and I haven't asked her."

Aurora a bit bewildered, "What do you mean?"

"Aurora, you have been in my heart and mind my whole life. There has never been any room for anyone else, and I've never met anyone who could compare to you."

A flood of relief washed over her, and feeling a little giddy, she said, "I hope I don't disappoint you," as she pressed closer to him, wrapping herself in the comfort of his presence.

"From what I've seen so far, there's more to you than I ever dreamed." He gave her a small squeeze. "Now rest your head. We'll need our strength to survive this ordeal so that I may bring you home again someday."

"Yes." She said, in answer to both statements. Feeling as though the rest of the world did not exist, she drifted off to sleep.

FRIENDS AND FOES

David awoke and considered his situation. It was still dark, so he wasn't sure if he had been asleep for hours or minutes. Aurora was still fast asleep in his arms, so he didn't want to move and risk waking her. He considered the events from earlier and thought of his father. From a very young age, his dad had always taken him into the woods camping, hunting, and teaching him survival skills. Together they had studied martial arts, and his father was always testing him. It seemed all in fun at the time, but now he thought he had always been preparing him for this possibility.

Ever since the other night though, after gazing into the seal above the mantel, something inside him had changed. He felt his connection to the world around him as he lay there in the dark. This was the first time he had a chance to be totally alone with his thoughts. He reached out with his senses to feel his surroundings. So many scents and sounds, yet he was easily able to pick them apart and put them back together to form a picture without seeing. He knew they were safe for the moment and relaxed in the comfort of her touch. Aurora, her scent like the fresh outdoors, her strong body, was more vibrant than anyone he had ever known. He breathed her in and basked in the warmth of her presence. In spite of her hardships, she was pure, her spirit was undamaged, and he would do anything to protect that. He knew it was the prospect of her violation that had unleashed the rage he felt earlier. And yet, it was more than just his rage; it was something outside of him that joined with his rage, amplified it, and turned it into something palpable he could have forged into a weapon.

He lay there as long as he could, then he managed to disentangle himself without waking her. He carefully slipped out from under the brush, and making sure she was hidden, walked a short distance so he could spy the moon through the trees. He saw it was still high in the sky on the receding side of its path. It was after midnight, so he decided he should wake her. Back at their shelter he removed the brush cover, being careful not to startle her, then knelt down beside her. Placing a hand on her shoulder he said softly "Aurora." Gently stroking her arm, her head turned towards the sound of his voice, and she slowly opened her eyes. Seeing him there she suddenly sat up. "Nothing's wrong. I'm sorry I had to wake you, but we only have a few hours before daylight, so I think we should get going."

She nodded sleepily, and he offered her some water. She took a drink, and her head started to clear. They picked up their packs and stepped out into the night.

Aurora turned to him. "I've lost my bearing now that it's dark. I'm not sure which way to head."

David said, "I think we'll be safe if we go back to the tree line where we can walk in the open for a while."

She didn't like the idea, but nodded in agreement, feeling they had no other choice. As they emerged from the forest, the plain before them was bathed in moonlight. Getting her bearings, Aurora indicated the direction, and they set off with her a few steps ahead leading the way. They kept up a brisk pace until the scorched earth started to show signs of life. First some grasses, then eventually it became a meadow rich with life, and a sprinkling of trees with patches of fall flowers. He could smell the fragrance on the breeze, and off in the distance heard the sound of water.

"Can we get some water here? We're almost out." David said softly.

"Yes there's a place not too far where we won't be exposed."

Making their way through a patch of trees and down a difficult slope, they found a stream of fresh water. Before they left his farm, David hadn't thought much about what this land would be like. He was encouraged to see this beautiful place in contrast to the war zone they had entered. Aurora knelt down at the water and began filling her canteen, and David did the same.

"Where are we?"

"We're near a farming village on the outskirts of the city of Kahn. I have friends there where we can seek shelter and gain news of the war. We'll follow this stream down to the village, and by then it will be daylight. His forces haven't come east this far yet. But we're afraid it won't be long until the fighting gets here." Aurora explained.

"How much of the land does he control?"

With sadness in her voice, she said, "He's been gaining every year since I can remember. I would say that seven in ten cities have fallen, and they roam free in the wild lands. We're losing the fight. The only advantage we have is they don't attack in winter, which allows us time to regroup."

"Do you know how it started?"

"Only a little. The war was raging when I was a child, but we lived in an area untouched by the fighting until the day my parents were killed." She paused unintentionally, then went on, "I was told that many years ago the Dark One and his forces were contained in the land of Tartaros. It is a foul and evil place where no one would dare go. There are many stories of travelers passing the land and accidentally straying into its borders, where monstrous beasts attacked them. Then an evil ruler desperate for more power somehow formed an unholy alliance with the Dark One. In doing so, he opened a pathway for his army to attack. The foolish king was killed in a most brutal fashion, and his lands were seized. From there, they began to spread out like a plague taking one city at a time and subjugating all the people into slavery. Many vile men joined with his forces, and, in exchange for their souls, were given free rein to do as they wished with the spoils of victory. Many decent men were slaughtered, their wives and children raped and tortured. They destroy everything in their path. Those who are willing to stand and fight have been retreating further and further, and soon there will be nowhere to go."

"It sounds desperate."

"That's why the prophecy was so vital to us. My mission was to deliver it to our council so that we could try to figure out what it meant. A member of an ancient order of prophets gave it to me. They told me it was our only salvation. Little did I know that it was about me."

"Yes, no pressure there, save the world or everyone suffers or is killed." He said in a distant voice.

She stopped and turned to face him, her face set with the look of determination he so admired. "I know this task seems impossible, but for what it is worth, I believe in you, and I'll stand with you until my last breath."

David lifted a hand to her face "That," he said, "is worth everything to me."

She blushed, and said, "We better get on with it then", turned, and headed off.

He matched her pace and smiled to himself. Thinking this all seemed so impossible, that a few short days ago he was just someone living on a farm, and now here he was on a fantastic, dangerous, and deadly serious journey. Everything that happened during the past few days would be too much for him to handle, if not for her. Foolish as it was, he felt that just having her believe in him was enough. If he failed, having her standing by his side would make it tolerable. But for her as much as for everyone else, he was determined not to fail. Every minute he spent with her made him long to return home so they could have a chance at a life together. He imagined that anyone looking at him from the outside would find it unbelievable that he could feel this way. That didn't matter to him, because he had never been more certain about anything else in his life.

As they followed the stream, the rocky bottom began to smooth out, and the water slowed as they came to a bend that wove around to the right alongside a dense forest. They followed the river-bend as the water became deeper, and he could see just past the tree line as it opened up into a small lake. Off in the distance, grey smoke rose from a fireplace.

"We're almost there."

"I look forward to sitting down and resting my legs. You keep up quite a pace."

She looked back, giving him a satisfied grin "I'll remember that next time you suggest I need a rest. Maybe that's your way of telling me you need to rest?"

David laughed, "I'm sure you will."

Just to be on the safe side, they stayed close to the tree line. Dawn was breaking, but their dark clothes would still make it hard for them to be seen. Once the farmhouse was in view, they could see candle light flickering through the window where the fireplace was burning. David assumed it might be the kitchen, and that someone was up early starting breakfast.

"Everything looks normal to me. What do you think?" Aurora asked him. Her question was an acknowledgment of the fact that several times, he had heard things and sensed danger she had not.

"It seems safe to me," David replied. With that, they moved into the open and headed to the house. Aurora stopped about 20 feet from the door and whistled, once, twice, three times. Watching carefully for any movement, she waited a few minutes then did it again. Then they saw the light moving about inside the house.

"I didn't want to frighten anyone. This is early for some of them, especially the children, who may be asleep."

David saw the slightest movement of a curtain, and then a few moments later the door opened. A woman peered out cautiously. "Who's there?"

"Jasmine, it's me, Aurora." Aurora said.

The door swung wide, and the woman stepped out, candle in hand. She was older than the two of them but still had her looks. She also had dark hair, but her eyes were a lighter brown and did not have the intensity that Aurora's did. She had a strong, yet feminine appearance. David was struck by her presence. She had an air of authority about her.

"Aurora. Is it actually you? Oh dear girl. We thought the worst." Then she hurried up the path to meet them, and gave Aurora a long hug.

"Jasmine, it's fantastic to see you. I almost didn't make it back, several times, but David here has been my protector." She said as she turned to face him, gently placing a hand on his arm.

David smiled, and said, "It's a pleasure to meet you Jasmine."

Jasmine looked at him, scrutinizing his face, and everything about him. Her face was fixed in a smile that masked her thoughts. David stood patiently watching her make her assessment as Aurora fidgeted a little in silence.

"May I please have your hands?" Jasmine asked David. She gave Aurora the candle then held her hands out to take his. Without hesitation, David placed his hands in hers. They both felt that tingling sensation that was becoming familiar to him. Now Jasmine offered a real smile.

"It's so nice to meet you, young man. Please do come in. Aurora is like family to us. You must tell us everything. The Council has been desperately hoping you would come back soon." Jasmine said.

Aurora hurried to take his arm, and briefly placed her head on his shoulder as they followed Jasmine to the house. He knew it was her way of saying thank you for respecting Jasmine's test. David turned his head and kissed her on top of her head. She squeezed his arm a little, then stood straight before Jasmine could notice.

As they entered the house, Jasmine said in a hushed voice "everyone else is asleep so please come back with me to the kitchen so we can talk." They nodded their agreement in silence.

The house was warm and felt cozy after the long night of traveling in the cold. They could smell the bread baking, and it made them both feel quite hungry. Once in the kitchen, they removed their traveling coats, and Jasmine let out a gasp.

"Aurora. Where did you get that dress? Were you married?" Jasmine exclaimed.

Aurora, blushing a deep shade of red, said, "Oh no," as she lifted the dress to expose her traveling leather underneath. "It was David's mother's. I borrowed it to disguise myself on our journey."

Jasmine turned her gaze on David, and in a stern voice asked, "You haven't taken advantage of her, have you?"

Even more embarrassed now, Aurora exclaimed, "Jasmine!"

In a calm reassuring tone, David said, "No, Ma'am, I wouldn't dishonor her in any way." She looked into his eyes as if daring him to blink.

Satisfied, Jasmine said, "As I said, she's like family to us. You can't blame me for being concerned."

David said, "I don't blame you one bit, Jasmine. I'm happy to see her so well loved."

Jasmine, a little flustered after preparing for a fight that didn't happen, said, "How about some fresh bread then? I just took it out of the oven."

David said, "That sounds wonderful! It smelled intoxicating when we walked in."

Aurora added, "Yes. And last night's meal was in the woods without a fire, so we're a little chilled."

Jasmine, regaining her composure, said, "Then sit down. I'm sure I can come up with a good breakfast, and while I'm getting it together, I want you to tell me what happened since you left. We've been worried sick over you."

Aurora said, "You might not believe me if I do. I'm still finding a lot of it hard to believe."

Jasmine looked at her reproachfully, "Aurora, I've known you almost your entire adult life. Nothing you could tell me would surprise me. I've always known how remarkable you are."

Just then a man walked in, rubbing the sleep from his eyes, "Aurora! I thought I heard voices." Aurora and David both stood. Aurora gave the man a warm hug.

"Miles, it's wonderful to see you. I hope we didn't wake you." Aurora said, "This is David."

David reached out to shake Miles' hand, Miles looked at him, confused. "OH… I'm sorry. Where I come from we shake hands as a greeting." He pulled his hand back. "It's a pleasure to meet you Miles."

"Thank you, young man," Miles said, then he gave his wife a sideways glance. She nodded and smiled, and in a cheery voice he added, "It's a pleasure to meet you too. A friend of Aurora's is a friend of ours. Please sit."

"Aurora was just about to tell me everything that happened to her since we last saw her. "With a tone of encouragement, she added "including how she met David here."

Miles said with a smile "sounds like my timing is perfect. Breakfast and a good story."

David smiled encouragingly at Aurora to tell the story. She took a deep breath and said, "I guess I should start at the beginning then.

Jasmine, do you remember me telling you about the boy I've seen my whole life and watched grow into a man?"

Jasmine said, "Of course, Dear. You used to talk about him all the time when you were younger and..." She froze in midsentence.

"This is him. David is the man I've seen my whole life, and he's watched me in the same way."

Jasmine, finding her voice, said, "That's incredible. But how did you find him? Where does he come from?"

Aurora, reaching over to take David's hand for strength and to reaffirm their bond, continued, "As you may recall, my last mission was to retrieve the scroll from the temple. The team I was traveling with made it there without incident, and after retrieving the scroll headed back. On our way, we were alerted to a supply convoy for the Dark One's forces. While heading to disrupt the convoy, we accidentally ran into a larger force of the Tartaros Guard. During the fighting, I became separated from the others."

"Yes, we heard about that from them when they returned." Miles said.

With a hint of excitement in her voice, Aurora asked "oh! Then they're alright?"

"We lost Akron and Elan." Miles replied sadly. "They said the fighting was fierce, and we feared we'd lost you too. I'm sure there was nothing more you could have done."

Aurora looked down and said, "I understand. We were caught totally by surprise. It was a miracle that any of us survived."

Jasmine spoke kindly, "You can't save everyone, Aurora. Remember that. Now, go on and tell us the rest."

Aurora nodded sadly, and then taking a small breath said, "Once I was separated, I was under siege from a group of soldiers, and had no choice but to escape. I doubled back trying to find the others but couldn't, and since they were hunting me still, I had to move on. I didn't want to take a chance on leading them here, so I headed for the high country near the plain of Azura. I evaded them for a long time, but they were relentless, and they were gaining on me. A few days ago they caught up to me, and I was leading them into the crags at the western end of the plain. I was hoping I could lose them once I made it over the top inside the gorge. I was desperate as they were right behind me. They had even managed to get some catapults in close and were sending fire rocks and arrows at me."

Jasmine brought food to the table said, "Oh dear, it's a miracle you escaped. How did you ever manage to get away?" She continued serving everyone, then sat to join them.

Chewing quickly, Aurora swallowed her bite of bread. "That's when David showed up. He appeared out of thin air and knocked me out of the way of a fire rock that surely would have killed me. But when he did, the two of us somehow passed through a hole in the world and landed in his world." Aurora paused to allow them to consider what she had just said.

"What do you mean his world?" Jasmine asked.

Aurora looked to David for help, and he said, "I don't know much. But the way it was explained to us is that our two worlds exist in the same place and time. An invisible divide separates them, which is narrower in places. Our two worlds work in unison to help maintain the balance between dark and light, good and evil. It was one of those narrow spots where we were able to cross over."

Miles and Jasmine sat fixed in rapt attention waiting for Aurora to continue. "Once back in his world, David took me to his home and cared for me. While we were there we discovered his home was protected by "Seals", and thought that his father may be a servant. That night David, staring into a seal while I slept, had a vision." Miles and Jasmine looked impressed but said nothing. "The next day we went to rescue his father, who was held captive by demons. And after we got him home, David called his aunt, who assembled a council of servants to meet with us. They told us many things, and we learned that David and I are the ones referred to by the Prophecy."

Jasmine gasped, and Miles looked grim, asking, "Are you sure?"

Aurora said, "Yes we're sure. The scroll I retrieved was a copy of 'the prophecy', and the council knew it too. After that, we made our way back and came here."

Jasmine put her hand on Aurora's, and giving her a warm smile said, "Oh child. We always knew you were meant for extraordinary things. I only wish…." Her voice trailed off as her eyes began to fill with tears.

Aurora, giving her a look of confidence and determination, said, "Jasmine, you have always been so kind to me, but you mustn't be afraid. I know we face a terrible challenge, but together, and with the help of our Savior, nothing's impossible. If it's His will that we're all delivered, then it will be so. If it's His will that David and I do not return, then we'll stand tall and faithful to Him to the very end."

David looked at her with a smile of admiration; even with the prospect of such a daunting task, his heart rose, knowing that someone such as this would be by his side. In fact, if not for her, he thought his courage might fail. Without realizing it, he had reached out his hand, cupping the side of her face. His heart rose as she broke into a smile of contentment, leaning her head into his hand and looking affectionately into his eyes.

Jasmine, a tear running down her face said, "To see you happy even under the weight of such responsibility. Oh, how I wish you had a simpler life. I've always feared something would happen to you before you ever found someone who cared about you so much."

Miles stood and said, "You two should get some rest after travelling all night. I must go immediately to alert the council so that we can assemble today. Clearly time isn't on our side, so we must act quickly."

David stood, and said, "Thank you. Is there anything I can do?"

"No, just get some rest. It sounds as if you'll have more than enough to do, and you'll need to be ready." Miles answered. The two men shared a nod of agreement. Miles walked around to his wife and kissed her on the forehead. "I'll be back soon."

Jasmine stood and said, "We'd better get the two of you somewhere to sleep. Come. We have an empty room in the back."

Jasmine led them out of the kitchen and quietly to the back of the house. She opened the door to a small room with a bed, table, and basin. Then she said, "Aurora has stayed here many times. The children are still asleep, and our room is a mess, so I hope you won't mind. The bed is rather small."

David turned to her and said, "It's more than enough, thank you. We slept in the woods last night." He smiled then added, "Remember that I said I would never dishonor her in any way. I'll sleep on the floor."

Aurora said sternly, "You will not! You can lie next to me on the bed."

Jasmine patted David on the chest gently and smiled as if to say she wasn't worried about it anymore, and said, "I wouldn't argue with her, Dear, as she can be very stubborn."

David laughed. "No doubt."

Aurora said, "All right you two. We aren't going to get any sleep if you stand there picking on me all morning."

Jasmine gave a small wave of her hand and shut the door. Aurora and David set down their coats and packs, pulled off their boots, and lay down on the bed. It was small, but Aurora, lying on her side, pulled David's arm tight around her, wanting him as close as possible. Lost in the warmth of his embrace, she was asleep in moments.

David, lying still, feeling her rise and fall with each peaceful breath, considered what was ahead of them. He realized that he truly had no idea what to expect. Wondering to himself would their mission take days, weeks, months or more? No, he thought everyone had said time was short. Events were culminating to an inevitable showdown that could not be avoided. The only question is what would happen along the way, and would he be ready.

Holding her in his arms was bliss he had never known. He could have let himself feel cheated that it had taken so long to get here, to meet her, and that there was a distinct chance it would be over too soon. But he would not give in to that temptation. He was given a precious gift, and he was not going to waste a minute of the time they had together thinking about what might not be. He was going to savor every moment they spent together. He breathed her in and let the scent of her fill his nostrils, the fragrance of the soap she used long since gone. She smelled like the fresh outdoors on a fall day full of life. Lying there with her soft hair against his cheek, he drifted off to sleep.

David woke to the sounds of voices in the house. The room was bright with sunlight, and he thought it had to be afternoon. Gently slipping his arm out from under Aurora, she stirred slightly. He pulled a blanket over her and went out into the hallway. Making his way to the kitchen he found Jasmine, Miles, and two other men sitting at the table deep in discussion.

"Hello. I hope I'm not interrupting." David said cheerfully.

Jasmine quickly got to her feet and said, "No, no, please come and sit down with us. This is Aaron, the leader of our council, and this is Edwin one of our council members, and a longtime friend."

"It's good to meet you both," David said.

"It's good to meet you too. We have been praying for help in this accursed war. Things have gotten worse for many years now, and we fear we can't stand much longer." Aaron said.

"Yes, one more season may be our last." Edwin added grimly.

David sat there a moment, feeling the intensity of their gazes. Once more he was reminded of the enormity of the situation. Who did they think he was? He had no military training, and he was not a seasoned warrior; why did they think he could do what they had been unable to accomplish after so many years?

"I have to be honest with you. I have no idea what I'm supposed to do. I have no idea if I can succeed where so many others have failed. I'm just a farmer. I'm not a warrior; I only found out about your struggle a few days ago. I must admit I'm afraid that I might fail." David said solemnly.

Aaron looked at him thoughtfully and said, "All those things you said may be true, and yet here you are. Most men, given the choice, would not have come. You were chosen for a reason. It is not for us to question the will of our Lord, only to follow it, and trust in Him."

"I can't argue with that, but I can make you a promise. Regardless of the outcome, I'll see it through to the end. I too put my faith and trust in the Lord, and that's all I need to know. In the meantime, I would appreciate anything you can tell me that may help," David said with confidence.

"That's all we could ask, and of course we'll try to help you in any way we can." Aaron said.

"Can you please tell me where the *Dark One* is? And how I can get there?" David asked. "As I've pondered over the prophecy, I believe there's only one conclusion I can draw. I have to face *him*, and somehow when that happens, the events will unfold as they are meant to, and if I make the right choices, then we will prevail."

"Unfortunately I don't see any other way either." Aaron said. "*He* dwells in the heart of Tartaros, an evil and dangerous place. The journey there will be extremely difficult. You could travel around *his* forces through desolate lands and mountains, but it will take you months to arrive, or you can attempt the most direct route, which will take you a few weeks. The direct route is through lands *he* already controls, and they are swarming with *his* armies. I would not suggest it, but we have reason to believe that *he* will be most vulnerable at the winter solstice."

David spoke half to himself, "The winter solstice is just over a month away."

Aaron said, "Yes it is. This year there are certain alignments that are taking place at the winter solstice, and we believe that may give you an advantage."

Aaron went on to explain how certain celestial bodies were positioned, and that it coincided with the North Star's position as it did over 2000 years ago when Christ was born. He also discussed genealogical cycles and numeric patterns that suggested a confluence of events pointing to that date. David was listening politely, but it was far too much information for him to absorb or make sense of. So he was satisfied to accept the conclusion that this was the deadline. That made sense. Everyone had told him that time was short, and in his heart he knew they didn't have months to travel.

After Aaron finished his explanation, David spoke. "I'm in no position to question your analysis. Quite frankly, I believe we have to act quickly. I don't think we can wait months for us to travel around the armies, so I think we need to come up with a plan to pass through them."

Edwin said, "That will be very difficult."

David agreed, "Yes, I'm sure it will be. Perhaps we can disguise ourselves as two people who would be allowed to pass. Can you offer any suggestions?"

Aaron said thoughtfully, "That may be possible. However, there is a problem if you are questioned too closely."

"What is that?"

"There are essentially three types of men and beasts that you will encounter. There are vile, evil men who are just that, and would be no more dangerous to you than anyone else. Then there are those who bargained their souls for power. They are comparable to our gifted and can see the light in someone and would attempt to kill you on sight. Lastly there are demons who are his spawn; soulless creatures that feed on fear. They too can see the light, and despise it."

"Do the men who bargained their souls for power appear like regular people? And when they die, does their spirit cry out?"

"Yes, that's right. They can be difficult to kill. You need to either stab them in the heart or cut off their heads."

"I've had several encounters with that kind. I could see the shadow of darkness behind their eyes, yet they could not see that I was of the light."

Aaron, mildly surprised, said, "Really? That could be extremely helpful to you. That could give us more options in coming up with a disguise. If you were traveling as an emissary, and they could not see you were of the light, you may be able to pass through unharmed. But they would be able to see Aurora was."

"I was thinking about that too. When she and I went to see my father and rescued him, they did not recognize her. Do you think that somehow my protection could have extended to her?"

"Jasmine has told us some of your story; how the two of you have been connected since you were children. Normally a gift does not extend in that way, but it may be that the bond you share makes the two of you different. The question is, will it be strong enough under such difficult conditions with so many adversaries? Of course, the bond you have comes from our Lord, and it is said, what the Lord has wrought, let no man tear asunder. And as we know, even demons and beasts are subject to His authority."

David said, distractedly, "Yes, Jesus drove out evil spirits and demons with a single command." Something was nagging at him, and he couldn't place it. Deciding he needed to think away from them, he asked, "How soon do you think the rest of the council should be here? I think I need to wake Aurora and give her something to eat before they arrive."

Aaron answered, "It shouldn't be too long now, perhaps another hour."

David asked, "Jasmine, would you mind if I took some food to her?"

Jasmine answered "No, of course not. Let me get something together for you."

David turned back to Aaron again, "One more thing. What do you know of where the *Dark One* dwells?"

Aaron said darkly, "Exceedingly little, only rumor actually. No one has ever gone there and returned."

David said softly, "I guessed as much." Then in a clear voice, "I like the idea of posing as an emissary. Would you please work on that while I attend to Aurora? I'm planning to leave in the morning. Will that be enough time for you to prepare?"

Aaron looked at David, giving him that penetrating stare he had gotten so many times in the past few days. Then with an air of surprised satisfaction, said, "Yes, I will make sure everything is prepared, and we will be ready by morning."

David stood as Jasmine brought him some food and water, and said, "Thank you, Jasmine." Then, turning to Aaron, said, "thank you."

Aaron asked, "For what?"

David said, "For being forthright and allowing me to consider my own fate instead of trying to tell me what to do. It's clear you're used to being in charge, and I appreciate the respect you've shown me."

Aaron smiled. "Young man, we are all headed down a path that has no map. I'm old enough to know that I don't know everything, and that you were chosen for a reason."

David nodded and said, "I'd better go get Aurora." He turned and left, feeling the enormity of it all again. He went from feeling like he had no idea what he was doing to moments of clarity, but he couldn't see more than one step ahead. In many ways, he wished he could go home, but there was a part of him that would never give up like that. As he walked back to the room, he shook off his feeling of doubt and thought back to Aurora. They were in it together, they both had their fears and doubts, and at the same time they believed in each other. They were bound to one another, and that bond was their strength and protection. They were bound to one another before they were born. Aaron had said it. "What God has brought together, let no man tear asunder." The only way their bond could break was if they broke it, but he knew neither one of them would betray the other. He only hoped their bond was strong enough for his protection to extend to her.

He listened by the door and could hear her soft rhythmic breathing, telling him she was still asleep. He quietly pushed it open and set the food down on the table. He stood for a long moment, looking at her. Just seeing her there warmed his heart. He sat down on the edge of the bed and gently pushed the hair off of her face. She stirred slightly at his touch, then in a soft voice he said, "Aurora."

She rolled onto her back, opening her eyes, looked up at him, and smiled.

"Hi there," David said in a soft voice.

"Hi" She replied, "What time is it?"

"I think it's about 3 in the afternoon. I'm sorry to wake you, but the council will be assembled soon. I thought you might like a chance to eat and clear your head before they get here."

"Oh, I didn't realize it was so late."

David got up and brought her some water. She sat up to take a drink. Looking out the window, he saw a pleasant spot to sit where she could eat in the fresh air and enjoy a view of the lake.

"Would you like to sit outside for a little bit? It's warm and sunny, and we could have some quiet time together while you eat?"

She smiled and put her arms around him, laying her head on his shoulder. He wrapped his arms around her too and sighed.

After a few moments of just sitting there, she said, "I suppose if we're going to see the council, some fresh air would be good to help me wake up."

David said, "Then let's get you up, put your boots on, and I'll grab a blanket for us to sit on."

They went outside and sat down under a tall strong oak. The branches were high enough to let the afternoon sun in to warm their skin. It was a beautiful day, and the light danced on the lake in front of them. He sat with his back to the tree. Aurora sat so she could lie back across his leg and into his arm, looking up at him as she ate. She noticed the surroundings just enough to add to her sense of peace. But she was more interested in his company than anything else.

He sat there absent-mindedly stroking her hair as he told her about his conversation with Aaron and the plan he thought of. "What do you think? Does that sound like a good idea to you?" David asked.

Again it warmed her heart the way he sincerely asked her opinion. Many had feared her, but the kind of respect he showed her was not like anyone else.

"Normally I'd say the plan was suicide, but I think you're right. They don't 'see' you the way they see the rest of us. It was only when we were separated in the forest yesterday, and those men found me that they knew who and what I was. But when we went to get your father and we were side by side, they couldn't. Remember that the lady we first met believed your story about getting married?" Aurora said blushing slightly.

"Yes." David answered.

"Well it must have been our bond, as he said, that extended your protection to me."

"We just don't know how far that protection extends. I'd be a lot happier if the distance between us didn't matter. With all the perils of this journey, if we were separated, you'd be in even greater risk."

Aurora looked at him affectionately. She put her arm around him and said, "I don't know how our bond could be any stronger than it already is."

David smiled at her, and then it hit him. "Aurora," his voice a little weak and his mouth suddenly extremely dry. "I think I may know a way." He said.

Aurora asked "How?"

David looked at her with his trepidation showing in his face, as he said, "We could marry." Her eyes widened, and her face could not hide her surprise. "I know it sounds crazy, and I hope you don't think I'm being forward. I mean I wouldn't expect you to be intimate with me or...." His voice failed him.

She sat bolt upright, and he began to panic, thinking he had ruined everything. Then she threw her arms around him and said, "Yes!"

A wave of relief washed over him. He felt a mixture of jubilation and exhaustion. For the few seconds she stared at him in disbelief. He thought he might have crossed a line that would damage the feelings she had for him. That would be a loss he was not prepared to recover from.

Suddenly Aurora began to giggle. Leaning back to look at him she said, "I believe that's the first time I've seen you afraid."

He laughed too. "You have no idea. I was afraid you might think the worst of me."

She pulled him close again, resting her head against his. "I've lived for so long with the possibility of each day being my last. I never thought I could dream of a life that was more than fighting the war. Somehow, finally meeting you changed that. As impossible as it seems, you've made me believe I could have more."

"I only hope we can."

Aurora leaned back to look at him again, and tenderly placing her hand on his face said, "If it's our fate that we don't survive this final battle, even the short time we'll have together will be more than I ever dreamed, and I'll be satisfied."

David smiled at her. "I've felt so empty for a long time, and you've filled that emptiness. I want to have every moment we can together. But if today is my last, just having you in my life will have been enough. You are more than I ever dreamed of, and I'm humbled by your presence."

Her eyes held his gaze as she moved closer to him. Her soft full lips parted slightly. He could feel his heart racing as she closed her eyes. Slowly their lips met as her hand slid around behind his head, pulling him to her. She pressed her lips hard against his, and he pulled her close to him. His heart was pounding against his chest, each beat drumming in his ears. He felt the curves of her firm body melting against his, and he was entirely lost in her touch.

It could have been hours or minutes. It didn't matter. What passed between them with just this one kiss was almost overwhelming.

***

She leaned back, gazing affectionately at him. She had felt it too. Her heart still pounding, she mused that pleasure had become a foreign concept to her, but this was more. It wasn't just their bodies that had touched and embraced; it was as if their souls had momentarily passed through one another, and in that moment they were one. She slid down, resting her head on his chest with his arms wrapped around her; she could have stayed there for eternity. As they sat quietly, she closed her eyes, savoring the memory of being lost in him.

Finally, with a touch of sadness, he said, "We have to leave in the morning. I'll talk to the elders and see if they can perform the ceremony for us tonight."

Tonight, she thought, and pushed herself up against him more closely. Yes, she didn't want to wait any longer than they had to.

"At least I have your mother's dress to wear." She said, "My leather travel clothes wouldn't be fitting for a bride."

"I wouldn't care what you wear. No clothing can hide your beauty." David said, then added reluctantly, "I hate to say it, but we'd better get back. They should be gathering now, and they'll be looking for us."

She nodded and sat up. They gathered their things and headed back to the house. Holding hands, both of them had contented smiles and were lost in their thoughts.

When they arrived at the house, Jasmine came to meet them and looked at them curiously. She could see a difference but couldn't put it into words. "I was just about to come looking for you. The council is meeting in the back building."

"We went down to the lake to sit while Aurora was eating." David said.

"I see," said Jasmine. "We should get over there as soon as possible. Leave these things. We can put them away when we return."

The three of them hurried off towards a building in the back. David thought it looked more like a barn than a meeting hall, and as they entered he saw that he was right. They had benches and some tables arranged with chairs, but it was clear that it was used as a barn under normal circumstances.

David turned to Jasmine and said, "Can you please excuse us for a minute", and he and Aurora went straight to Aaron.

Aaron saw them coming, and said, "Good. We can get started now."

David asked, "Can we please see you in private for a moment first?"

Aaron, looking a little unsure, said, "Yes, we can talk over here."

The three of them walked off to a stable area, where some horses were enjoying an evening feeding.

"Aaron, I was considering what we discussed earlier about how our bond gave Aurora certain protections when we were close. When Aurora and I talked about it, I remembered something you said, 'What God has brought together, let no man tear asunder.' Then I recalled that phrase is part of the wedding vows. It occurred to me that if we were to wed, it would strengthen our bond, and she might be better protected."

Aaron looked at him thoughtfully, then said, "That may well be true, but a marriage of convenience is not the same and would not have the strong bond you seek. Now if you two loved each other that would come from God."

David looked at him and without hesitation said, "I do love her; I've always loved her." He felt Aurora sway a little holding onto him; he only hoped it was for the right reason, and he dared not look at her.

Aurora stood there, hit with a wave of emotions so strong she could hardly stand. Hearing him say it out loud like that without doubt, with such certainty, shook her to her core. She had felt it but tried to deny it in case it wasn't true, and at his words she knew that she was just as much in love with him.

Aaron looked at her uncertainly "Aurora, do you feel the same way?"

David couldn't look at her; he was paralyzed with fear at the prospect of her saying no.

Aurora struggled to find her voice, then blurted out with such force it startled Aaron and David, "Yes, oh yes, I do." She began to cry, but they were tears of joy. Then she threw herself into David's arms with such force it knocked him back a step.

Aaron, smiling, said, "Then it's settled; you shall be wed. And as fortune would have it, I have been ordained and can perform the ceremony if you would allow it."

David, looking at him over Aurora's shoulder, said, "That would be perfect."

They made their way back to the group, and David and Aurora sat with Miles and Jasmine. Aaron went over to the apparent leaders of the council, and they moved close to hear what he was saying. David and Aurora sat holding hands, unsure of what was going to happen. After a few moments, Aaron stood to address the group.

"As most, if not all of you already know, we have gathered tonight because the time of the prophecy is at hand. We approach the final hour that will decide our fates. Aurora was sent to the temple to retrieve the scroll that detailed the prophecy so that we would be able to work towards its fulfillment. Her journey back was most difficult, but by the grace of Our Father, she was delivered into the hands of this man David. David, whose lineage is that of King David himself, is the one about which the prophecy speaks." He paused briefly, as some members whispered to each other. "As it turns out, the other person the prophecy refers to is none other than Aurora." This time there was even more chatter amongst the group. "These two have shared a remarkable bond their entire lives that only a few have known about. This is no ordinary bond; it has linked them between two worlds. It is the strength of this bond that allows them the ability to stand before the *Dark One* with any hope of victory. I'm pleased to say, to strengthen their bond even more, they have decided to marry this very night." This time there was no holding back. The group burst into conversation. Jasmine almost leapt out of her seat to hug Aurora, who was thoroughly embarrassed. "Please, everyone, I'm almost finished." The group quieted down. "Thank you, yes, this is excellent news, and more importantly they are to marry, not out of obligation, but because they love each other. I have known Aurora for many years, and in the brief time I have spent with David today, I have come to believe with certainty that they are two halves of the whole. I also believe that together they will be much more formidable than either one alone. Now, since time is working against us, unless there are any objections, I will marry them."

Aaron stood looking around the room to see if anyone offered their dissent, but there was none given.

"As we are all in agreement, I would ask David and Aurora to come forward and kneel before me."

David looked at Aurora, and she smiled encouragingly. They walked forward, and holding hands, knelt facing Aaron and looked up at his kind expression.

Aaron began speaking the moment they were still. "David and Aurora, as a servant of the most high God, it is my honor to affirm your bond of marriage today. He has brought you together at this place and time, and as such His blessing will be upon you. I will ask you now to acknowledge the covenants of this union. Do you two take each other to be husband and wife in sickness and in health?"

Together they said, "We do."

"In feast or famine?"

"We do."

"That you will not allow anyone to come between you?"

"We won't."

"That you will remain joined together until death do you part?"

"We will."

"Please rise, that we may all give you our blessing." They all spoke in unison, saying, "Lord, please bestow your blessings on these two humble servants. Lord, we lift them up to You that their life together brings glory to your kingdom."

"In the name of the Lord our Father, I bind you together as man and wife. What God has brought together, let no one tear asunder."

They stood facing each other. David looked at her, mesmerized at how radiant she was.

"You may now kiss the bride."

***

David reached up and tenderly cupping Aurora's face, pulled her slowly towards him. Her wet eyes reflecting the candlelight, her full lips enticing him to kiss her, he barely noticed her reaching up to place her hands on his arms. As their lips met, just as by the lake, he felt his heart pounding as they each wrapped their arms around one another. He became lost in her touch and felt as though they were one. He couldn't hear a sound. He only felt her presence, in him, through him, all around him. When their lips parted, he looked into her eyes and could see she had felt the same. Suddenly they both realized where they were and looked around as sound began to flood back into their ears. Everyone in the room was saying something, and as they looked at Aaron, they saw the look of surprise on his face.

"What is it?" David asked, "Did we do something wrong?"

Aaron hesitated a moment, and said, "I have never seen anything like it. None of us has."

Aurora asked, "What do you mean?" She was slightly embarrassed; perhaps it was their behavior that had shocked everyone.

"Didn't you notice anything?"

"Well, I mean we were... our eyes were closed." He said a little embarrassed.

"When you kissed, sealing your vows, a bright light surrounded you both. It was beautiful, as if we could see the light of your souls as they were joined in holy union. Truly God has blessed you both."

Now David and Aurora were even more embarrassed. Everyone there was coming up and telling them how they had never seen anything like what had happened. They were encouraging them, saying that surely God was with them, and they wished them their blessing on their journey.

Food had been brought into the room, and the two of them were thankful for the distraction. More than anything right now, they just wanted to be alone, but they knew they would have to wait a while longer. They sat with Jasmine and Miles while they ate. David was entertained, watching Jasmine interrogating Aurora for all the information about him she could get. Aurora kept flashing little smiles his way as he pretended not to hear any of what they were talking about. Jasmine was acting like a big sister, and Aurora was enjoying every moment of it.

As they sat there, David began to get an uneasy feeling when he noticed a commotion at the door. Someone had arrived, and several others were busy greeting him, including Aaron. David casually watched out of the corner of his eye as they appeared to be telling him about the day's events. Aurora looked at him with a sheepish grin after Jasmine said something about David, when she caught his look. With a slight flicker of his eyes, he directed her attention to the new arrival. She immediately recognized what he was telling her. Turning to Jasmine, she excused herself and got up from the table. David watched her closely as she stealthily made her way around the perimeter of the room. Meanwhile, Aaron and the visitor made their way towards David.

David remained seated, not wanting to alert the man to his suspicions. Jasmine had moved next to him and was talking to him about Aurora. She told him how she had begun to lose hope she would ever meet someone. It didn't take long before Aaron and the man were standing in front of him. David stood as Aaron said, "David, I would like you to meet Lucas. He was delayed in getting here, but has come to meet you and Aurora. He has been on our council for many years."

"It's a pleasure to meet you, Lucas. Thank you for coming. I'm humbled that so many council members have traveled so far just to meet me."

In a jovial voice, Lucas attempted to put David at ease, and said, "Oh no, not at all. It is my honor to meet you. Where is Aurora? I haven't seen her in years."

David said casually, "She's around here somewhere."

Lucas said with forced humor in his voice, "Just married, and you have lost track of her already?"

David grinned and said, "If you know Aurora, then you know she can take care of herself."

"Yes I do, young man, yes I do. I must say it's quite something to meet a man who could tame her."

Aaron was looking at David and getting the sense that something was wrong.

David could feel his anger rising, but kept a tight hold on it so when the timing was right it would be at his fingertips. "Lucas, I would never try to tame her. She is perfect just as she is."

Aaron interrupted "Lucas, such talk on their wedding day."

Before Lucas had a chance to answer, David spoke, "It's alright Aaron, Lucas doesn't mean to be disrespectful. He's only doing *his master*'s bidding."

Lucas stammered a little, "I don't know what you mean by that, but I certainly didn't come all this way to be insulted."

David said with absolute authority, "Lucas, don't try to pretend with me. You serve the *Dark One*, and he sent you to spy on us, or worse. Now if you confess, I will spare your life."

Aaron, aghast, looked at the two of them, not knowing what to do.

Lucas began looking around uncomfortably, unable to look David in the eyes, and said, "well I … I just don't know what you are talking about… I …" Then he reached around his back for something, and a look of shock and terror appeared on his face.

Standing behind him, Aurora said, "Looking for this?" She held up a large dagger.

Aaron, finding his voice, said, "Lucas, how could you?"

Lucas, in full-fledged panic, now raged at them. "You fools! You're all doomed. You can't win; these two will fail. You have no idea what you're up against. *He* knows everything, and *he* will prevail. Join *him* or suffer for all eternity." Then with a mixture of pain and fury, he turned to David and lunged.

David almost effortlessly lifted his arm and thrust it into the center of Lucas's chest. On impact, he released the rage into him like a controlled explosion. Lucas was thrown more than 20 feet, as if he was hit with a cannon, and crashed into the wall. Before anyone else could react, David was standing over him with Aurora at his side.

As Lucas was gasping for breath, David stood over him, and spoke. "Tell us why you came here tonight."

Lucas, coughing up blood, managed to say, "*He* wants to know your plans."

David said, "You can tell *him* not to worry. I'm coming to face *him*. You can tell *him* that I will be there soon enough, and then we can finish it."

Lucas spluttered, "*He* will punish me severely for my failure."

David said, "If you don't want to go back, you can ask for forgiveness."

Lucas looked at him perplexed. "Forgiveness? You want me to ask you for forgiveness?"

David said, "Not me, I cannot forgive sins against the Father, only He can. But you are running out of time so you must decide."

Lucas looked at him for a minute, then said, seething with anger, Who do you think you are to talk to me that way?"

David looked at him sadly, and said, "Goodbye Lucas, and remember my message while you are being punished. Perhaps it will help spare you some pain."

Lucas looked at him, filled with hate, and when David turned, his eyes went blank and he was gone.

David turned to Aurora, his rage gone. "I'm sorry, but I think we have to leave tonight. If we stay, we'll bring unnecessary danger here."

Aurora said, "I agree. As soon as you're ready, I will be too."

David turned to Aaron "Were you able to make our preparations for the disguise? It may not matter, but any trouble we can avoid would be a blessing."

Aaron, still reeling from the shock of what just happened, looked at David and gathered himself. "Oh, yes, we found that the ruler of Southaven has been planning to send an emissary to *him* to negotiate a treaty. Miles has a carriage with some horses he will give you to take, and we have some robes that should help sell the deception for the regular troops at least. We have been preparing some food and other stores for the journey. Although I must say, after Lucas, I'm terribly concerned for you both."

"*He* wants us to come, so I don't think they'll be trying to stop us, but there could be men who don't know to let us pass."

"What do you mean *he* wants you to come?"

"Before we left my world, a man tried to kill Aurora. He told us that the *Dark One* knew we were coming. I believe *he* knows about the prophecy. Lucas wasn't here to try to kill us. He only tried to attack me because he was cornered. I think the *Dark One* still believes that *he'll* prevail when we get there. The problem I see is that, like that gang we met on our way here, not all of his men will know to leave us alone."

"You may be right. I'll double check on the preparations so you can be off as soon as possible." He turned and left.

Aurora was talking to Jasmine and Miles now. David walked over to them and said, "I'm so sorry that we brought you trouble. You've been so kind to us, and I don't want to put you or your family in any more danger."

Jasmine spoke "David, it's not your fault. We've been a part of the war for a long time. Just promise me something."

"What's that?"

"Please bring Aurora back to us some day."

"I'll do everything I possibly can to fulfill that promise." David said, giving her a small smile. Then he turned to Aurora, and took her hand "Are you ready?"

Aurora nodded and gave Jasmine a parting hug. Then they headed back to the house. It only took a few minutes to check their packs, gather their things, and then they went out to meet Aaron. Once outside, they saw Aaron leading the horses pulling the carriage heading towards them.

The carriage was well built but not ornate, with a bench in the front for a driver and his companion. It was high enough to see well over the horses, but still kept the driver below the top of the carriage. David thought that could prove useful if they were approached from behind. The top was loaded with their supplies, and the main cabin appeared to be large enough for the two of them to sleep in. There were a number of windows to allow them to look out in any direction with thick curtains that could keep out the night air. The back was tapered in towards the wheels, which would make climbing up difficult, if not impossible, for would-be assailants. Considering the circumstances, he thought it would serve them well for as far as they could take it. The horses were large quarter horses, strong and well-built for a long journey. In the event the carriage couldn't take them all the way, these horses would.

They walked over to Aaron, and he gave them a sad smile.

"Not much of a wedding night for the two of you."

At that, Aurora, standing there keeping a watchful eye, fidgeted slightly, and David said, "Aaron, thank you for all of your help."

"It is my honor. I only wish that we could do more for you. There are stores of provisions, the garments we spoke of, some additional weapons behind the seat, and some blankets for you and the horses."

"You've done more for us than you know." He put his arm around Aurora. "Whatever happens, you've given us a gift that no one can take away."

Aaron smiled "Like you, I'm but a humble servant. May God watch over you, always."

"Thank you, Aaron." Aurora said.

Aurora and David climbed up onto the bench. David took the reins, and they set out. The moon was high in the sky, so there was just enough light to see the road. They had to travel slowly, and when he looked back, he could see Aaron watching them leave. They had been through so much already, and yet they knew it paled in comparison to what lay ahead.

Aurora nestled up next to David. He held the reins in one hand and had an arm around her. Thankfully the horses were well trained and knew the road, so there was little for him to do. Once the house was fading into the distance Aurora spoke.

"He was right."

"Who was right?"

"It wasn't much of a wedding night. I hope you aren't too disappointed."

"Aurora, just sitting here with you, holding you close, is a gift, and I cherish every moment of it. If we are to have a proper honeymoon I'm willing to wait for a time and place that will honor how precious you are to me."

She pressed up close to him in that way that was becoming familiar, and he welcomed it, never wanting to let go.

An unwelcome bump on the road disrupted their embrace. "Oh!" She exclaimed, "It's not like the roads we traveled on in your world."

"I suppose not." He smiled.

The lightheartedness gone from her voice, she asked "What do you think is going to happen to us?"

David turned and kissed her on the forehead, then said, "Honestly I don't know."

"It sounded as if you had some idea about our journey to Tartaros."

"Do you remember Artemis?"

"Of course. He did try to kill me."

"I think he alerted the assassin we killed in the woods near my house. Yet he only tried to kill you. He knew about the prophecy, but he only knew about the first part. I think the *Dark One* also knows about the prophecy, and that *he* wants me to come because *he* believes *he* can defeat me. I think they only tried to kill you so the 'Lion' would not awaken. *He* knows that together we are stronger. That's why *he* tried to keep us apart."

"Do you have any idea why *he* thinks *he* can defeat you?

"Because of what you told me, I believe *he* has my mother." David said somberly.

"Oh David, I'm so sorry."

"The last part of the prophecy says that we will stand together before *him* and that because of our sacrifices, both houses can be saved."

"Do you think you'll have to sacrifice your mother?"

"I'm holding hope on what my father and Molly said that prophecies are tricky business, and that they are not always clear."

"That's true, I only hope..." Her voice trailed off.

"What is it?"

"That my sacrifice isn't you." She said through a choked voice.

David pulled her closer, and she rested her head on him. "Remember, don't borrow trouble from tomorrow. If there's a way, we'll find it. Besides, don't think you are getting out of that honeymoon so easily."

Blushing, a little, she smiled and said, "You can count on it." She reached up and kissed him on the check, lingering a moment as her soft full lips pressed against his cool skin, "and you'd better not try to get out of it either."

"I wouldn't miss it for anything."

"How do you do it?"

"How do I do what?"

"One minute I feel fear or despair, and the next you have me laughing or flirting with you. You always make me feel as if there's hope for us. Hope that we can have a life together."

David said in a thoughtful voice, "I guess it's because I love you." She felt weak again as her heart rose at the words. "I know I only said it for the first time today, but I think I've always known it. My life before this week was empty except for the small moments I saw you. Knowing that you're here with me, I don't feel empty anymore. I feel that anything is possible as long as we're together. In spite of everything, I have hope that we'll prevail. We must prevail because a life without you would be empty again, and nothing else could fill that void. So instead of worrying about tomorrow, I'll savor every moment we spend together."

She turned and grabbed him, almost knocking the reins from his hand, and said, "I love you too. I was afraid to admit it to myself, afraid that you wouldn't feel the same way. Promise you'll never leave me, promise we can be together always." She looked up at him with a few tears of happiness running down her cheeks, realizing she asked something that may not be up to him.

He smiled at her and said, "I promise, my life is yours, and with every breath I have, I'll fight for the chance at a future together."

"I guess that'll have to do then." She said smiling back at him. She was in no hurry to move. She held onto him, her head against his chest. Listening to his heartbeat as she reveled in how alive she felt.

"Tell me all about your life growing up. I want to know everything about you." David said. "Remember, we have a long trip ahead of us so no need to rush."

They spent the next several hours sharing stories of their childhood, and could have kept talking all night, but guessing it was around 2 in the morning they decided to sleep for a few hours before setting off again.

They found a small clearing off the road to pull the carriage out of the way behind some trees. David unhooked the horses from the carriage and tied them to a tree so they could rest and graze. He pulled a couple of the blankets out to cover them for the night. According to Aurora, they were still in relatively safe territory, far from the enemy lines. David found some water and gave the horses a drink to tide them over until the morning. He made his way to the door of the carriage to find Aurora had gotten some blankets organized into a makeshift bed.

"Ah, our new home," David said cheerfully, "it's even nicer than in the woods."

Aurora chuckled, "It's a little small, so it is a good thing I like you."

"I planned it that way so you couldn't get away from me."

"Hmm I'm not going anywhere."

"I like the sound of that."

They pulled off their boots and travelling coats, and climbed under the blanket, curling up next to each other. It was small so that they couldn't fully stretch out, but under the blanket they were warm, and more importantly they were together.

David gave her an affectionate kiss on the cheek and said, "Good night, my love."

Aurora cooed, "Mmm, say it again."

"Good night," David said teasingly.

Aurora gave him a light tap on the arm saying, "You ... don't tease me."

David chuckled, then in a soft voice said, "Good night, my love."

Aurora said, "Good night. I love you too."

In no time at all, and they were asleep.

***

They found themselves standing together. They were holding hands. He liked feeling her hand in his, and she liked it too. They didn't know where they were, but that didn't trouble them; they were together. The surroundings were hard to make out; the only thing they could see was each other. They smiled at one another. They knew they were safe, in fact they felt at peace. Off in the distance they heard a sound and turned to look, but didn't see anything. The sound was moving towards them like a warm breeze off the water. They welcomed its embrace. When it reached them it was comforting and strong, and filled their hearts with joy.

"My children, you have done well. Your faithfulness and purity pleases me. Travel to the valley of Roktah, then north to Tartaros. I will watch over you on your journey. Seek My will in all things, and I will be with you always."

"Lord, what of my mother?" David asked.

"She is one of my faithful children and awaits your arrival."

"What will we have to sacrifice?" David asked.

"At the appointed time all will be revealed. Be wary of fear and temptation. Those are *his* most dangerous weapons."

"Lord, what of my parents?" asked Aurora.

As His voice began to fade, they heard "They watch over you filled with pride and joy."

They woke, still lying next to each other, stiff from not moving during the night. They sat up and looked at one another.

Aurora asked, "Were you there too or was it just a dream?"

"It was just like when I stared into the Seal."

Aurora's eyes were glistening with emotion. David could imagine how much it meant to her to hear what He said about her parents. He put his arms around her, and she welcomed his embrace. The sun was up and bathed the inside of the coach. It was warm and comforting after the cool night. They sat in silence for a little while, listening to the sounds of the morning, the birds, crickets, and the slight rustling of the trees from the breeze.

"I guess we should get up. I need to check on the horses. They're bound to be hungry after such a long night."

Aurora squeezed him a little, then let go. "I'll see what we have for breakfast."

David busied himself feeding and watering the horses while Aurora put the bedding away and found some bread and fruit for them to eat. They decided not to bother with a fire for coffee so they could get moving sooner. Once the horses were bridled to the carriage and everything was packed back into place, they set off. It was a beautiful day. The warm sun was keeping them comfortable, and the clear blue sky filled them with a feeling of hope.

"Would you like breakfast?" Aurora asked.

"That sounds good. What did you find?"

"Well there's some fresh bread, cheese, and some apple I cut up for us."

"Sounds perfect."

They began eating. Aurora handed David small pieces so he could manage the reins while he ate.

"What do you think it all means, what we were told last night?" Aurora asked a little hesitantly.

"I'm not entirely sure, but I have a feeling there's more to come."

"I was thinking the same thing. Roktah is not on the direct route. We will be going further east before we head north. Perhaps there's something there we need to do?"

"Please, tell me about Roktah."

"As you know I'm from Roktah, and the valley is where our forefathers settled. It's a small city surrounded by farming communities. My parents and I lived well outside the city until it was overrun. I fled the area after that, and it's been under their control ever since."

"What's in the city?"

"I remember a marketplace where people from all around would come and sell their crops and other goods, a town square, a meeting hall, all kinds of shops for everything you could need. I didn't travel to the city often. I spent most of my time in our village."

"Is your village south of the city?"

"Yes it is. How did you know that?"

"Just a hunch. I have a feeling we need to go there first."

"I don't know what we'll find. Many of the houses were burned. It was..... horrible." She said sadly.

"How many days do you think it will take us to get there?"

"We should cross into their territory in another day or so. Then it's another day or two, depending on what kind of trouble we have." She gave him a slight look of concern.

"Us have trouble? Every day since we met has been a picnic."

She laughed a little. "If all of our adventures so far have been a picnic, I have to wonder what your idea of trouble is."

David laughed, "Getting on your bad side. Now that sounds like trouble."

"And don't forget it. I've been taking it easy on you so far," she said with a smile.

"Since we don't expect to see much today, would you like to get some rest inside the carriage while we travel?"

"No, I feel fine," she said as she laid herself across him, looking up at the sky. "Why don't you tell me more about what your life was like growing up? I'm sure you caused all sorts of trouble."

David said teasingly, "No more than you, I suppose."

David went on to tell her all about his life on the farm, school, tractors, all sorts of things, and she asked questions about everything. His life compared to hers was much simpler and a whole lot less scary. She was fascinated by everything he told her about his world, and told him about how different hers was. They effortlessly talked for hours, and after a short break for the horses around midday, they continued on. Late in the day, the air started to cool as the sun set.

"A little way ahead there's a small village. It's the only one between here and the border. Do you think we should stop there for the night? I found a small supply of gold so we could pay to stable the horses and get a room."

"Do you think it's far enough away to be safe?"

"I've stayed there in the past. Occasionally they get some thugs passing through, but troops haven't ventured this far yet."

"I guess it won't hurt to check it out. Once we cross the border, I'm guessing the four of us won't get a lot of rest."

At dusk, they approached the village where there were a handful of shops all closed for the day. Only the Inn had lights on; they could hear the sounds of guests coming from inside. Out front there were a number of horses tethered to the rail. Based on the gear, these riders hadn't traveled a long distance, but they weren't farmers either. Since they were in friendly territory, they decided not to bother with the dress clothes Aaron had packed for their trek through the dark lands. Wearing her travelling coat, Aurora put the gold she found in her pocket. David tethered the horses to a post, and grabbing their packs, they headed inside.

They opened the door and felt a blast of warm air carrying the smells of food, ale, and sweat. They walked in to see a group of 6 men off to the right sitting around the table eating, laughing, and talking. They looked like hard men, and David immediately took note of their weapons, a mixture of short swords, knives, a mace, and crossbow. There were few other patrons; a couple keeping to themselves, and a lone man sitting in the shadows. Seeing them enter, a man with a leather apron approached, smiling at the arrival of new guests.

"Good evening, good evening, I'm Horatio. Welcome to my inn. How may I help you tonight?" He said preoccupied, but in a jovial voice as he shot a quick glance at the group of men.

"I'm David, and this is Aurora." David said, noticing Aurora dissecting the room with her eyes.

"Oh Aurora dear, I almost didn't recognize you. Not in your usual attire, are you?"

"Hello Horatio, how have you been?"

In a softer voice, he said, "Well, things are getting a bit tenuous these days. I fear what the spring will bring." Then he shot another quick glance at the men.

"Horatio, we'll try not to add to your troubles. Is Andrew handy to stable the horses?"

"Oh yes dear, I'll go get him. Please have a seat over here." Horatio guided them to a table near the other couple, but away from the men. As they sat, he stood patiently watching them.

Aurora reached into her pocket and pulled out a gold piece "Can we please get some dinner and a drink, as well? We'd also like to see about a room." Horatio's eyes wide seeing the gold, looked at her and David.

"My dear, why of course. I would never pry, but is this man your husband?" Horatio asked in disbelief.

Aurora, staring at him with penetrating eyes in her no nonsense voice said, "Yes, that's right. We were married yesterday."

Horatio, a little flustered at the news, said, "Well dear, that's terrific news! I have to say I thought it might never happen. Um, I mean not that you aren't lovely dear … um… yes, you young man, must be quite…. Well…. Um special, to have won this young ladies' heart; my, my, that is something." Horatio was withering under Aurora's gaze.

"Thank you, Horatio. I guess that's a compliment."

"Oh yes, yes dear. I'll be back with your food shortly. Which horses are yours, so I can tell Andrew?"

"There's a carriage out front with two large quarter horses. Can you please stable, feed, and water them, and bring the carriage around back out of sight?" asked David.

"Why yes, I certainly will." Then still mumbling to himself as he walked off, they heard him saying, "Aurora married... I still can't believe it."

David looked at Aurora and broke out in a big smile, and she flushed brightly.

"Not a word." She glowered at him.

David laughed, "I wouldn't dream of it. I told you being on your bad side isn't my idea of a good time."

Aurora gave a small laugh. "I have a reputation to protect, you know."

"I noticed. Horatio was so nervous I thought he might forget why we were here."

"Ugh, wait until he tells Matilda." As the words escaped her lips, they heard her.

"AURORA!! Oh my dear, Horatio just told me the news." A stout woman with a broad smile came scrambling up from the back, her arms waving. "Oh dear, is it true?"

They both stood to greet her, and Aurora said, "Hello Matilda, it's great to see you too. Yes, it's true, Horatio hasn't drunk all the ale yet tonight."

Matilda gave her a quick hug, then turned to David "Let me look at you," she said as she gave him a quick look up and down. "You are a nice looking young man, but if I know Aurora, you must be very stubborn too."

"I don't know about that, but it's a pleasure to meet you. I'm David."

"Oh dear, it's delightful to meet you too. Young Aurora here has been our guest many times, and she has helped us out on a few occasions. I'm terribly fond of her, and so glad she has finally met a man that she didn't want to knock his front teeth out. You do have all your teeth still?"

"So far I have managed to avoid having her knock out my teeth." Then he said in a quiet voice leaning in so Matilda and Aurora could hear "But I always have my guard up because you never know. She might just want to show me who's in charge." Then he gave her a sly grin.

Aurora hit him on the arm and Matilda laughed, "Oh dear, you may have met your match, Aurora." Matilda said, chuckling. "He's the first man I've met who wasn't afraid of you. How about I get the two of you something to eat?"

"That would be lovely Matilda." Aurora said.

"Yes, please, thank you very much Matilda." David added.

"Oh dear, and manners too. You two sit. I'll be back shortly," Matilda said as she bustled off.

Matilda's boisterous visit had caught the attention of the group of men, but David could see they weren't getting up anytime soon. He just made sure to sit so he could keep an eye on everyone in the room, and so did Aurora.

"So it seems you do have quite a reputation." David chided her.

"Oh stop it, I'm embarrassed enough." Aurora said playfully, now that they were alone.

"They seem nice enough."

"Oh yes they are, but it's a hard life this close to the border, and if it ever came down to it, I think they'd probably sell us out."

David considered that for a moment filed it away, and then asked, "Do you recognize anyone else in here?"

"No, but I'm keeping an eye on those drunk men over there."

"So am I. Tell me what kind of trouble have you helped them with in the past?"

"Mostly the occasional unruly patron who didn't want to pay for their meal. One time a man got a little too friendly with Matilda, and when

Horatio said something to him, the man hit him. I showed the man the error of his ways." Aurora said with an air of satisfaction.

"Did you now, and how did you do that may I ask?"

"I put a dagger in between his legs, and told him if he ever stepped foot in here again that I would find him and finish the job."

"I'm sure he found your offer quite persuasive," David said grinning at her.

"I do have a reputation of keeping my word," she said confidently.

The next thing they knew, Matilda and Horatio where there with steaming stew, some hard bread, a couple of tankards of ale, water, and hot tea.

"This looks like a feast." David said cheerily.

"Oh dear, you flatter me. I didn't want to keep you waiting while I made something else, and the stew is fresh," Matilda said.

"It smells delicious," Aurora said.

"Andrew has taken the horses and carriage around back as you asked. He doesn't think anyone saw him either, so we'll be discreet about it. I'm assuming you don't want to attract a lot of attention?" Horatio said as he flashed another look at the men. They both nodded at him. "Very well, Matilda and I will prepare an upstairs room for you. We'll give you the nicest one we have, although it isn't quite a honeymoon suite," he said with a bit of a smirk.

David said, "Not to worry, I'm sure it'll be fine. We're leaving at first light, and won't be up late," in an attempt to spare Aurora some mischievous looks from their host.

"Oh, that's too bad. If there's anything else we can do for you, please let us know," Matilda said.

"We will. Thank you again for such kind hospitality."

"Oh, it's our pleasure, dear," Matilda said with a wave, as they headed off.

They hadn't realized how hungry they were until they started eating. They agreed, having a warm meal after travelling all day felt good. They didn't have any ale, as they were afraid it would dull their senses, and they weren't prepared to take anything for granted. The other couple had left, and only the table of six men and the lone diner were still in the room with them. After having had several rounds of ale, the men began getting louder.

"Should we go upstairs?" Aurora asked.

"I don't think so just yet. I'd rather not have to wonder who might be coming up the stairs. Let's stay until these men leave."

"Yes, ale can make men do stupid things."

"Women too," David replied giving her a sly grin.

"And what do you mean by that? Women don't go bothering innocent travelers after they've had one too many tankards," she said, defying him to contradict her.

"I suppose you're right about that one," he said, smiling at her.

She looked at him, her mouth half open, prepared to defend what she said, only to be thwarted by him again. Now a little flustered she said, "Well then…. Hopefully they don't stay all night."

"I second that."

As Aurora was about to speak, David turned and was on his feet in the blink of an eye. The lone man, who had been sitting in the shadows, standing now, was startled by David's sudden appearance, and took a step back.

Aurora, having learned to trust his instincts, immediately got to her feet too. Then remembering she was wearing the delicate blue dress over her traveling clothes wanted to swear, but held her tongue.

"Hello there," David said to the man in a causal voice.

He was about David's height and had on a cloak with a hood pulled up partially covering his face. Hidden by the cloak, it was hard to see his build, but for the moment David had the element of surprise on his side.

"Hello," The man said in a gruff voice.

"I thought perhaps we knew each other."

"No, I don't think so."

"Why don't you lower your hood so I can see if I recognize you?"

"I'm on my way out."

"Really, it's too hot in here to wear a hood. It will only take a moment. I have an excellent memory for faces."

Aurora could see the man was nervous. David had him trapped in between two tables.

"I just want to pass, please. I'm not making any trouble," the man said with rising anxiety in his voice.

Then to Aurora's surprise, David said in a kind voice, "I understand, but perhaps I can help."

The man stood frozen for a minute, not knowing what to think, when suddenly he said, "Fine, you want to see under my hood -- here."

He pulled his hood back to expose his face. It was scarred with burns and his bones were disfigured from having been broken. The hair on the right side of his face was all gone, his scalp looking as if it had been dragged over gravel. Aurora flinched. It was not at all what she had expected. David did not flinch. He stood there looking at the man calmly gazing at him, his facial expression unchanged.

David spoke first, "Who did this to you?"

The man had puffed up, expecting anything but that, and with those words, seemed to deflate in front of them.

"There was a gang of men. They came to our home, raped my wife, beat me badly, and set fire to our house. I went inside, barely able to see, trying to save her, but in the fire and smoke I couldn't find her." At these words, he began to weep and his legs gave out.

David grabbed the man and helped him to sit at their table. They sat quietly for a moment, giving him a chance to regain himself. They gave him some tea. The man sipped it, giving himself something to focus on until he could think clearly again.

"I'm sorry. I should go."

"No. I said I would help." David said, "Are those the men that did that to you and your wife? Is that why you're following them?"

"How did you know?"

David felt Aurora's anger build, so he gently placed a hand on her, asking for patience.

"It's enough that I know. What would you do to these six men? They are heavily armed, and you've been hurt."

"It doesn't matter what happens to me. They need to pay for what they did to my wife."

"I understand, but your wife would not want you to jump off of a cliff, and attacking these men by yourself is as sure a death as that."

"Are you telling me that I should do nothing? I should just let them get away with it? How can I dishonor her like that?"

"When did this happen?" David asked him ignoring the man's question.

"It was a little over a month ago. I've only recently been well enough to come find them. They're so vile they don't even hide after such a crime," the man said, his anger rising again.

"Where did it happen?"

"Just over Grey Ridge on the other side of the river where we have..... had our home."

David stood and looked at the man with such authority that he froze. "Stay here."

Aurora sprang to her feet. She had no idea what he was going to do. She was furious for what they did to this man, but she was frightened for David.

David marched over to the table where the men sat and fearlessly looked them in the eyes. Before they could speak, he said in a casual voice "Excuse me gentlemen, but were you on the other side of Grey Ridge across the river about a month or so ago?"

One of the men turned to him and said, "What business is it of yours?"

Through a mask of total calm David said, "My friend over there said six men, who looked like you, came by his home a month or so ago, and took something from him. I told him he must be mistaken because you do not look like the kind of men who would take something that doesn't belong to you."

A couple of the men were eyeing Aurora, and she returned an icy glare. Then the boldest one of them stood.

"Are you accusing us of taking something from that freak over there? You can't prove anything, and neither can he." He stood facing David, trying to intimidate him.

David, the fury in him building, spoke in a tone of absolute authority without a trace of fear. "That man's wife was raped then she was burned alive inside their home. He was beaten badly, and burned trying to save her from the fire. You tell me who the freak is, him or the men who did that to him?"

The other men began to rise while their apparent leader said to David, "Now you listen to me. You'd better get your hide out of here before you end up looking worse than him. And just to show you what gentlemen we are, leave your woman here, and we'll show her a good time, and what a real man is."

The men began to laugh, and as one of them took a half step toward Aurora, David exploded into action. The air cracked with the energy coursing through him. He hit the man in front of him so hard in the chest that it lifted him off his feet, sending him sailing over the table into two of the others. In an instant, David spun around and grabbed the man who had moved towards Aurora, pulling his arm so hard they heard it break as he fell to the floor. The remaining men stopped dead in their tracks.

David motioned to the lone man to come over now. Then he turned to the men standing before him saying, "Now let's try this again. Do you remember this man? Do you remember what you did to his wife?"

One of the men fell to his knees and said, "Please. Yes, it was us, please forgive me."

"It isn't for me to forgive you. What about the rest of you?"

One by one they started getting down on their knees. As the man on David's right's, knees were just about to touch the ground, he pushed up and lunged at David. Another on his left started to move around the table. In one fluid motion Aurora spun, pulling out her dagger and slit the man's throat before he made it two steps. David turned to the side, and as the man came up from the ground reaching out for him, David grabbed his head and snapped his neck. Neither of the other two men moved.

"Now you two, it is not my forgiveness you must seek, it is that of this man, and our Lord and Father. I say to you right here and now, if you are truly remorseful, you will live, but your life belongs to this man. You must serve him as payment for a debt you can never satisfy. If you are not truly remorseful, you will fall before you reach the door. What is your answer?"

The first man to fall to his knees said, "I will serve him. Lord, please forgive me."

The second man said, "Yes I'll serve him too."

David, still filled with the power he drew in, turned to the lone man, placed his hands on his face, and let the energy flow into him. As the power moved from one to the other, the light was too bright for them to see. When it stopped, it revealed the man's face healed and whole again.

The man stood looking at David in astonishment. David looked at him kindly and said, "I'm truly sorry for what has happened to you. Please do not dishonor your wife and your Lord by becoming what these men were."

"I won't. Thank you for what you've done for me."

"Don't thank me, but give your prayer of thanks to the Lord, for I can do nothing against His will."

"I will," the man said. "You never told me your name."

"I'm David. Perhaps we'll meet again someday."

The two men stood and picked up their comrade with the broken arm. As they made their way to the door, the second man fell to the floor, causing the man with the broken arm to fall to the ground. The first man reached down to check them and said, "They're dead."

David looked at him and said, "Remember the gift you have been given here today, and do not squander it."

"I won't," he said. Then he turned and hurried out after his new master.

Horatio and Matilda peered out from around the rear door. Horatio asked, "Is it alright to come out now?"

"I'm so sorry for the mess. Can I help you clean up?"

Horatio answered, "I can't believe what I saw here today. I… I … have never seen anything like it. Who are you?"

"I'm just a man like you, Horatio. I hope that we haven't caused you any trouble by stopping here. Let me help you straighten up, and if you prefer that we leave, we'll be on our way."

Matilda said, "Don't even think about it. We are blessed to have you two here. I'll get Andrew and we'll move these men out back so they don't attract any attention until after you leave tomorrow." She turned and hurried off.

Horatio bolted the door. In a few minutes, Andrew was there. He was a scrawny young man in his mid to late teens, and when he came in, he looked over at Aurora. Blushing, he said, "Hello Aurora. It's good to see you again." Then seeing the carnage said, "Oh my, what happened here?"

Matilda said, "Come on, Andrew let's get this sorted out, and we can talk about it later. You are going to have to go out when we are done and see if any of their horses are still out front."

They all worked together, and in no time the inn was cleaned up. Andrew went out front and found the others had taken four of the horses and left two behind. He brought them around to the stables.

***

David looked at the dead men. They were not possessed like the others they had encountered, just wicked men who had become like animals preying on the weak. David had slaughtered animals before, so the sight of blood didn't bother him, but this was different. He felt a bit queasy as they hauled the bodies out back and sopped up the blood. He noticed the others seemed somewhat unaffected, and it struck him that their lives were so much harder than his had been that death was too commonplace. His heart ached for them all, and especially Aurora; he only hoped he could help put a stop to it all.

Once they were all finished, they sat down to share some tea. David was amused by the puppy dog expression Andrew had on his face looking at Aurora. He figured she probably never noticed before.

"Aurora, I think we should give these fine people some extra money for all the trouble we caused, don't you?"

Horatio said, "No, you have paid us handsomely, and after what I saw tonight, I know you are doing the Lord's work. Besides, we got two horses out of it already."

David and Aurora laughed a little, and David said, "Fair enough. Thank you. Is it safe for you if we stay here tonight?"

Matilda said, "We have thieves and murderers pass through here every day, and you think the two of you put us in danger? Don't be silly. Tomorrow we'll contact the constable about the bodies. He won't ask too many questions once he gets a look at them. They were an awful lot."

Andrew said, "I can stand watch tonight down here, so you're safe," looking for Aurora's approval.

She smiled at him and said, "Thank you, Andrew. You're a dear friend."

Andrew was so red that he was almost purple. He said, "Well, I want to do the right thing too."

David looked at him and said, "That is very kind of you, Andrew, but be sure to come get us if anything happens. I know you're brave, but it would break our hearts if anything happened to you."

Andrew said, happy for the approval, "I will, Sir."

"Please call me David. If you don't need anything else from us, I think we should get some sleep. We want to be off at sunrise. What do you think, Aurora?"

"I'm ready for some sleep." she said with a smile.

They all said goodnight, and Matilda escorted them upstairs. They were in the room at the farthest end of the hallway. When she opened the door, they could see a full size bed with warm looking blankets, a washbasin, chair, and table. Matilda had put some fresh flowers on the table, and some fruit.

"I hope this is alright. It isn't particularly fancy, but I'm guessing you truly are going to sleep tonight," Matilda said with a sly grin to Aurora.

"Matilda!" Aurora said, blushing slightly, then added "You never put flowers in a room for me before. You don't have your eye on my husband do you?"

Now Matilda was blushing, "You're such a sassy young girl. Goodnight. I'll wake you at sunrise."

"Thank you, Matilda," David said.

"Yes, thank you," Aurora said, with an affectionate smile for her.

She waved them off and left. They sat on the edge of the bed next to one another to pull off their boots.

"Never a dull day."

"Not with you around," Aurora said to him cheekily.

David gave a little laugh. "I guess I have to take some of the blame. Well, I guess for tonight, all of the blame." In a sad voice, looking down, he said, "I'm sorry. What I did tonight was foolish. I put everyone in jeopardy. I don't know what I was thinking."

Aurora reached over, placed her hand on his face, and encouraged him to look at her. In a tender voice, she said, "No, you saved that poor man. No one can give him his life back, but you kept him from throwing it away foolishly. I've never known anyone as compassionate and caring as you, and I wouldn't have it any other way."

He gave her a small smile. "What would I do without you?"

"Probably get lost on your way to Roktah."

"No doubt. Should we get some sleep?"

"I think so. Daylight will come quick enough."

"I don't think we're going to have any trouble tonight, but I'm going to sleep in my clothes just in case. If you're uncomfortable in your leather under your dress, I can step out so you can change if you'd like."

Aurora looked at him for a moment as her emotions swirled around inside her. She hadn't thought about things like changing her clothes or him seeing her without clothes on. All of a sudden the prospect was frightening. What if he didn't find her attractive? Her head was spinning with the thoughts of seeing him with no clothes on, especially at the thought of them being together. It was frightening and at the same time exhilarating, and dear Lord, she thought she had no idea what to do. What if it was terrible? Would he regret marrying her?

All of a sudden she thought she was going to cry, and she blurted out "What if I'm a terrible wife?"

David looked at her, his face full of compassion, and asked tenderly "Why would you think that?"

"I don't know anything about being a wife, I don't know how to care for a husband, and I ... I ... don't know what to do... well as a woman....
"

David, starting to understand, said, "Aurora, you are everything I could ever want in a woman. You'll be the perfect wife just as you are. I love your heart and your mind. I love who you are, and you could never disappoint me."

"But I've never been with a man, and what if I'm terrible?"

"Please remember I've never been with a woman either, so I don't know what to do exactly ..." David felt himself getting red this time. "I only hope that I won't disappoint you either, and that is why I don't want us to rush because well... when the time comes, I want it to be special for both of us."

"What if you don't find me attractive?"

David smiled. "Aurora, I have never seen a woman as beautiful as you are. And as I have come to know your heart and your spirit, I find you more and more beautiful each day."

"Really?" she said, feeling silly about asking the question.

"Really. Every time I hold you close and feel your body next to mine, I want nothing more than to run away with you. To go somewhere that we can be alone, without all the worries and responsibilities we face now and get lost in your embrace."

"I feel the same way too. I just never thought I'd have these feelings."

"Neither did I. So let's have an agreement."

"Alright. What is it?"

"Let's agree that we'll wait until all of this is over and that we'll learn together how to be a husband and wife. For now, we are soldiers, and when we win this fight, then we can help each other win that fight too."

"That sounds good to me." She smiled and hugged him.

Pulling her close to him, he said softly in her ear, "I love you with all my heart."

She squeezed him tightly, and said, "Oh, and I love you with all my heart too."

David pulled down the cover and let Aurora climb into the bed, then he lay down on his back as she put her head on his chest, and an arm around him.

"Aurora, in spite of all the danger and hardship we face, lying here with you, I feel like the luckiest man in the world."

Pressing herself closer to him, she said, "I could stay right here forever."

He kissed her on the head and said, "Goodnight."

"Goodnight."

In moments, they were asleep.

ROKTAH

The next morning Matilda got them up just before dawn. Andrew had already gotten the horses and carriage ready to go. Matilda gave them some warm food to eat as they traveled. They all said their goodbyes, and David and Aurora headed out by first light to avoid any attention.

Once they were safely outside of town, they opened Matilda's care package. The bread was still warm, and they enjoyed the food she had sent with them.

"You have to give Matilda credit. She can cook."

"She sure can. Every time I pass this way, I stop there."

"Andrew sure does like you," he said teasingly.

Aurora, going red, chided him, "Don't start first thing in the morning, you."

He chuckled a little. "Ok, I'll wait until after lunch."

"You better watch it, or you won't get any lunch," she said, teasing him back.

As they were talking, they came around a bend and found themselves in clear view of a small group of border sentries.

David grumbled, "How foolish of me, not paying attention to what we're doing. We haven't put on the clothes Aaron gave us."

"They've already seen us. We can't do it now."

"I agree. We're just going to have to hope we can still pull it off. Be ready for anything."

"You know I will."

David slipped his hand behind the bench, and true to his word, Aaron had indeed put some extra weapons there. He felt the hilt of a short sword. David and Aurora were wearing their traveling cloaks, so they still had a few surprises in there too. As he looked at the men, he saw two of them had bows at the ready. Not wanting to raise any suspicion, he kept the steady pace they had been on as they rounded the bend, then slowed as they approached them.

"Stay up here while I go down to talk to them. Your height may give you an advantage. Please give me a couple of gold pieces too," David said to Aurora.

Aurora handed him a few pieces of gold that he put into his pocket. Pulling the carriage to a stop some twenty feet or so back, David climbed down as one of the men walked over to him, saying, "Where do you think you're going?"

The men had the same rough unkempt appearance as the soldiers that had been chasing Aurora the first time they met.

In a formal tone, David said, "Good morning Captain. My wife and I are emissaries from Southaven. We are on our way to Tartaros, to discuss an alliance."

The man flinched at the name, then said, "I'm no captain."

"Really? I would have thought with such an important post, they would at least have made you a captain. I will be sure to tell your commander. If Southaven is going to forge an alliance, we need to know loyal soldiers like you are well compensated."

The man eyed him a little suspiciously. "You don't look much like an official."

"We just traveled two weeks through hostile territory. We're trying to maintain a low profile."

"I guess that makes sense."

"Good then. I thank you for your time today. We have a long way to travel before nightfall." He turned to head back to the wagon.

"Wait a minute."

"Oh yes, how foolish of me. I almost forgot." He reached into his pocket with the man closely watching him, and pulled out the gold Aurora gave him. The man's eyes going a little wide, David handed him two gold pieces saying, "Here you go, my good man. Keep up the good work."

The man stood there for a minute looking at David, feeling the coins in his hand. David gazed back at him calmly, unblinking, waiting for the man to decide what he was going to do.

Then the man said, "Very good. Safe travel to you." Then he turned and walked off, as the others parted for them to pass.

David climbed back onto the carriage, giving no indication he was concerned, and with a flick of the reins they were off. The two of them sat quietly until the men were out of sight.

"That was a close one, and it only cost us two gold coins."

"Why didn't we just kill them? Not that I like killing, but we are at war."

"For starters, if we leave a trail of dead bodies, we might attract some unwanted attention."

"That's a good point."

"Also it was an unnecessary risk. I don't want to take any chances with your safety if I don't have to."

"Last night you could have easily killed all six of those men. There were only four here. I wasn't worried about that."

"Last night was different. I was able to draw on the power of the Spirit. I was saving that man's life, like the time when you were in trouble, in the woods. Those men were attempting to harm us and would have killed that man last night. These men today, yes they were thugs, and no doubt had done terrible things, but they weren't trying to kill us. They will be judged for their lives, but I don't think I'm supposed to do that. In a way, I think this was a test or a reminder that we have to be on guard so that we don't become what we're fighting against."

"One thing is for sure. We knew this wasn't going to be easy."

"That's one thing I'm certain of. How far is it to Roktah from here?"

"We could reach it tomorrow if we don't run into any troops. They're supposed to be extremely active in this area."

"Are there any more towns between here and there?"

"There's one inn that we can probably make by nightfall, but from what I've heard, it's not a place that decent people go to anymore. It mostly caters to troops."

"Perhaps we should try to pass it at night, to see if we can't get by unnoticed."

"That sounds like a good idea to me. There are some woods we should come to after midday. We might be able to find a place to pull off and hide the carriage behind the trees and wait. It would also give the horses some rest."

"Perfect."

They rode until midafternoon, when they found a clearing that was large enough to turn the carriage around in and well hidden behind a wall of trees. By this time, the breakfast Matilda had sent with them was long gone, and they were hungry. David busied himself taking the harnesses off the horses and giving them food and water. He wanted them well rested, since they would be riding late tonight.

Aurora got some supplies out of their stores, and set out a blanket for them to sit on in the sun while they ate. They were both stiff from sitting on the driver's bench for so long, so it felt good to move around and stretch their legs. Once the horses were settled, they sat down to enjoy a quiet lunch together. The sun was shining, warming them under the crisp fall breeze. They were lying on the blanket, Aurora resting her head on David's arm and shoulder, gazing up at the clear blue sky.

"I could just lie here all day," Aurora said with a sigh.

"It is hard to imagine we're in the middle of a war zone, isn't it?"

"You had to remind me, didn't you?"

Chuckling a little, David said, "Sorry about that."

"Maybe we can just pretend we're normal people on a picnic, and we don't have anywhere to go."

"I like that idea."

"When I was a little girl I used to love to dance. Some nights there would be gatherings and musicians would play, and everyone would dance and sing. We all sat outside on blankets like this. We had so much fun. Do you think we can go dancing someday?"

"I would love to go dancing with you, but I have to warn you, I'm not very good at it."

"Just the idea of doing something, other than fighting and planning, sounds good. I was starting to think that was all my life would be, but now I have hope that it can be so much more."

"Then that's the first thing we'll do when this is all over." He pulled her closer, kissing the top of her head, and he could feel her smiling.

After a couple hours of enjoying doing nothing, they decided it was time to be on their way. Packing up the carriage and harnessing the horses, they set off again, feeling refreshed. The air had cooled, and it wasn't long before the sun started to set. Fortunately the moon was still up enough for them to see the road. It did slow their progress, but they felt passing the inn late would attract less attention.

They meandered slowly along. They did not want to push the horses too hard, just in case they had to attempt a quick getaway. It was well past dusk by the time they came upon the inn. They could see light coming out of the windows and hear the raucous sounds of the men eating and drinking. Keeping a steady pace, they were relieved not to see anyone outside. They had stopped talking, trying to be quiet and on alert for any movement around them. They were sure there was no way anyone could hear them over all the racket emanating from inside. But it sounded like such a large group of men that they didn't want to find out.

Before they knew it, the inn was well behind them, and they both let out a heavy breath, as if they had held it the entire time.

"That went well," David said.

"Yes, it sounded like at least 20 or 30 men inside there," Aurora said.

"What do you think? Should we travel for a couple more hours before we stop for the night?"

"That should put us near the top of the ridge. I think we may be able to find somewhere to hide the carriage, and then in the morning we can head down into the valley of Roktah."

"Sounds like a plan. I think I should stop for just a minute to water the horses."

"Alright, I'll watch for any unexpected guests."

David pulled the carriage to a stop, then hopped down and fetched water. While the horses were drinking, he checked their harnesses, making sure they didn't have any sores and that they weren't too hot. He climbed back into the driver's bench. Aurora took her seat next to him, and they set out again.

"The horses seem healthy. They're exceptionally strong. The harnesses are padded, so they don't have any sores. We can easily go for another couple of hours."

"I think I can make it that long too," Aurora gave him a tired smile.

"Do you want to lie down inside the carriage?"

"No, I want to stay up here with you. Besides, someone has to keep an eye on you, so you don't get us into trouble."

David chuckled a little. "Who better for the job than you? At least lie back here so you can rest a little."

Aurora laid down across the bench, resting her head on his leg, looking up at him. He put his hand on the side of her head and gently stroked her cheek with his thumb.

"Go ahead and rest. I'll let you know when we get to the ridge."

"I won't fall asleep. I'm enjoying looking up at the stars. I love the way, during fall, the night sky is clearer; the stars seem brighter."

David sat quietly, listening to her, and in a few minutes she was still. He tried to avoid ruts in the road as best he could in the dark, but Aurora was fast asleep. He looked down at her periodically, and it warmed his heart seeing how peaceful she looked. He thought he would give anything to spare her the difficulties he was sure would come. But he knew, prophecy or not, he needed her, and that she would never leave his side even if he tried to convince her to.

He still felt shocked that just a few short days ago he was living a normal life, and how quickly everything had changed. He mused over the idea that if he told anyone he knew what had transpired, they would think he was crazy. And yet as fantastic as everything that he had learned was, he had no trouble accepting it all now. He realized that, in a way, he already knew life wasn't only what he had grown up with. All the times he had seen her throughout his life, he knew her world was not like his, but he knew without a doubt that it existed. It was that knowledge that made it possible for him to accept it all, because he had been prepared, even if he thought it might never come.

He could see the top of the plateau she told him about, so he began looking for cover. Seeing a large group of trees, he veered off the road so he could check the area to make sure they could get back out.

Gently moving her head, he said, "Aurora, we're here."

She stirred slightly and slowly opened her eyes. "I guess I dozed off a little."

Smiling at her, he said, "Yes, a little. I'm going to check out this area behind the trees to see if we can take cover there. I'll be right back."

She sat up, surprisingly alert. "Ok I'll stand watch."

David got down and went over to see if they could pull behind them and easily get out the other side when it was time to leave. He went back to the carriage and climbed back up.

"We should be fine," he said, as he encouraged the horses forward. Once they were well hidden, he got down, took the harnesses off the horses, and tied the horses to a tree. He gave them some feed and water and covered them with the blankets, then headed back to the carriage.

He climbed inside and found that Aurora had lit a small lantern. It provided just enough light to cast a warm glow. She had laid out their makeshift bedding and gotten out a small snack, since they traveled through dinner. A few pieces of fruit, some bread and water would take the edge off. It was too late for much more. Tomorrow they would arrive in Roktah, so they needed to get some rest.

"I see you cooked a late supper for us."

"Oh yes, I have several delicacies; cut fruit and bread," Aurora flashed him a mischievous grin.

"One of my favorites," he said, as he sat down next to her on the floor.

"Here, take a taste, but be careful. It might be hot, as I just took it off the fire," Aurora smiled broadly as she took a piece of apple and held it up. She placed the apple to his mouth, and he took a bite. It was fresh and crisp.

"Oh, that is delicious. Is it your own recipe?" he asked teasingly.

"It has been handed down for generations in my family," she said. Then reaching up and turning his face towards her, "You got some on your chin." She wiped the juice off his chin with her thumb, then with a sly grin she put her thumb into her mouth, and said, "Mm that's good."

David suddenly felt extremely warm, as his heart began to beat faster.

"Here, would you like another bite," her face now impassive.

"Yes," David said looking into her eyes, lost in her gaze.

She took the piece and placed it in his mouth, along with the tip of her finger, gently pulling it across his lips as she pulled her hand back.

Her gaze more intense now, she asked, in a husky voice, "How did that taste?"

David swallowed the half chewed piece and forced out the word "delicious."

"Did you get any on your chin this time?"

David, unable to move, managed to say in a soft voice, "I don't know."

"Let me look," Aurora said as she leaned closer to him.

His heart was pounding so hard; he could hear every beat in his ears. He was getting extremely warm, and the nervousness he felt was like waves crashing on the shore. She placed her mouth on his chin as her soft wet lips, then her tongue moved across his skin. The touch of her seemed to travel through his entire body like a charge of electricity.

She looked at him directly in the eyes, and said in barely more than a whisper, "I think I see some more." She closed her eyes as her lips met his. His mouth opened slightly as her tongue reached out to taste him and then withdrew, as their lips held each other in a gentle embrace. He was totally lost in her kiss, and he couldn't tell if it lasted for seconds or hours.

***

Aurora sat there feeling his warmth. She hadn't planned on kissing him, but she was drawn to him. She could taste the apple juice and feel his soft full lips on hers. She felt more alive in that moment than she ever had before. Being this close was electrifying. His strength seemed to reach into her through his touch. His fingers found her neck and gently moved around to the back of her head, pulling her close to him.

Without thought, she found herself turning to face him, her legs straddling his lap. Then his hands found her waist. His large strong hands were firmly pressing against her as their tongues rolled around one another and sent a wave of passion through her. Passion she never knew she had inside her, like nothing she had ever felt before. She was his to do with as he pleased. She couldn't stop him; wouldn't stop him.

***

David felt her exquisite body under his hands as he slowly moved them up her side, taking in every inch of her perfection. Nothing existed outside of the feel of her against him. The longing in her kiss was consuming him with an unquenchable desire for her. His hands reaching her shoulders, he pulled her closer.

Their mouths parted as they pressed close against each other, and he whispered in her ear, "I love you."

She said in a breathy voice, "I love you too." She leaned back to look at him, her eyes bright beaming with happiness.

He smiled at her and reached up to hold the side of her face. She leaned into his touch, and he said, "There's nothing I want more in the world than to be with you; but not here, not now. This time and this place could not possibly do justice to how precious our first time will be. You are perfect, and I would wait a lifetime if I had to so that we could share this treasured gift together and savor every moment for as long as we want."

They put their arms around one another and held each other close, resting their heads together. They sat in silence for a while when Aurora finally leaned back.

"I guess we should get some sleep then."

"I guess we should."

They lay down in their makeshift bed, holding each other close, and David said, "Good night, my love."

Aurora cooed a little, "Good night, my love. Sleep well."

"You too."

***

Aurora was lying there, savoring all the emotions she had just experienced. From what she had heard and seen of men, she knew that not many would have waited. It filled her heart with joy that he loved her so much that being together was too precious to be rushed. And she knew that when the time came, the passion would be there, and with every moment they spent together, it would grow just the way the love they have for each other continued to grow.

***

David could still taste her on his lips; resting his head against hers, he breathed her in. Feeling her back pressed up against him, he thought he could lie there forever. He marveled at her. She was perfect; perfect for him. He had never dreamed he could be this happy. It didn't matter why they were together or what they had to do. As long as she was with him, anything was bearable.

The sunlight shining into the carriage woke them. It felt warm and inviting on their faces, and even though they were stiff from sleeping in such tight quarters, they felt well rested. They decided to eat while they traveled. For some reason, they both had the sense that time was of the essence. David fed and watered the horses, then hooked them to the harnesses while Aurora put up the bedding, organized their meal, and checked their weapons.

They set off. It wasn't long until they crested the plateau and were headed down the road into the valley. The road was flanked on either side by patches of tree lines separated by grazing meadows and fields of crops. A small stream was on their left, and they decided that when they stopped they would replenish their water supplies.

After a couple of hours, they entered a heavily wooded section of road that took a sweeping turn to the east. Although they could not see far ahead, they kept up a steady pace as their sense of urgency increased. As they broke through the tree line, they saw a farmhouse up ahead. In front of it had to be at least a dozen armed men.

The gang was kicking a man on the ground. David, with a flick of the reins, sent the horses into a gallop. The men didn't hear them yet over the hooting, yelling and cries for mercy from the man on the ground. As they got nearer, three more men emerged from the house, dragging a woman, 2 young girls who couldn't have been more than 10 or 12 years old, and a young boy by their hair.

The screams were horrifying. David and Aurora shared a look. She had on her warrior face, and David was the picture of fury.

"Get your bow and climb on top of the carriage," David said to Aurora. She nodded and moved quickly into place. He shouted back to her, "Hold on."

Over all the commotion, the men still had not heard them approaching. They were close now, and Aurora was taking aim. David turned the carriage so that they would arrive in parallel to the men, and as Aurora started to let her arrows fly, he pulled back hard on the reins. As the horses began slowing, he reached behind the seat and withdrew the short sword.

Aurora's shots were true. She dropped the two men who were holding the young girls with arrows to the heart. As David leapt from the carriage, he saw a third arrow hit the man dragging the woman. The men turned at seeing their comrades' fall.

David flew towards the men with such force that the first man he hit with the sword was practically cut in two. The rest of the men were momentarily surprised by their sudden appearance, but it didn't last long. They began to move towards David while Aurora let arrows fly at the men headed her way.

The air around David was crackling with the same electric charge as before, his fury palpable like a thunderstorm. Almost immediately the men went on the attack. He was constantly moving; spinning as soldiers came at him from the left and right. He thrust the sword into the man on the left while delivering a side-kick to the man on the right; so powerfully, it threw him off his feet, cracking his chest plate.

Aurora had dropped the man holding the boy, and 2 more that were coming her way.

David pulled the sword out of the soldier only to spin around and decapitate another one coming up behind him. Two men were heading for him, and David spun into a roundhouse kick, catching both of them in the head, each in turn, with such strength that he could hear their jaws break as blood gushed from their mouths.

Aurora had jumped down from the carriage, and 3 men were headed towards her. She reached into her coat and pulled out a dagger, throwing it into one man's heart. The other two were almost upon her, one raising his sword. Aurora ducked under it as he swung, coming up to drive an arrow up under his chin into his skull. The third man got a hand on her arm and pulled up a dagger to stab her.

David turned to the three men coming at him and threw 2 knives. The first hit one of the men so hard it went in through his face and stuck out the back of his skull. The second appeared to miss, but landed in the back of the man who had grabbed Aurora. As he yelled, she shoved the palm of her hand up into his nose so hard that she shattered the bone, and he dropped to the ground.

The last two men were upon David now, both with swords and clubs drawn. David stepped back and turned to his left, missing the swing of one sword, but caught the tip of the second blade with his left arm. His right arm swung around with the momentum of his turn, and caught the man on the back of his neck, severing his spine. The other man caught David hard in the back with a club, dropping him to his knees. David turned to look up at the last man; his sword risen to strike, when an arrow hit the soldier in the back and pushed its way out through his stomach. He toppled over, a look of shock on his face.

They were all dead.

David, still pulsing with the energy he had drawn in, went over to the man who was badly beaten; bent down, and placing his hands on him, released the healing energy into him.

Instantly Aurora was at his side and said urgently, "You're hurt."

"I'm Ok. Let's check on these people first," David said, then turned to the man on the ground, and asked, "Are you alright?"

The man, in shock at what just happened, said, "Yes, I ... who are you?"

"I'm David, and this is Aurora. Let's check on your family."

Aurora was already checking them as David and the man got there. She looked at David and said, "Other than some scrapes, they seem fine."

The family was hugging each other, crying. David put his arm around Aurora. She returned the gesture and said, "You need to let me look at your arm."

"In a minute," he said softly, looking at the relief on the faces of the family in front of them.

After a few moments, the husband and wife turned, he stepped forward, and said, "Dear God, thank you for saving us from those men. What they would have done to us if you hadn't arrived, I can't bear the thought."

"We're happy that we could help you," David said.

"I would ask you to come in and let us prepare a meal for you, but they've already taken all that we had. They came today, and when they found nothing, they decided they would take us instead." The man's eyes fell to the ground in the hope of not seeing what might have been.

"We have food. Come let us share a meal together," Aurora said.

David suddenly realized how thin they were; these people were on the verge of starvation.

"Yes," David said, "we have more than enough."

The woman and her children's eyes brightened, and she asked, "How can we ever thank you?"

Aurora stepped forward, "No thanks are necessary. Take your family and clean up, and we'll prepare the food."

The man and the woman turned and ushered their children to the house as David and Aurora walked off to the wagon, their hearts aching for the suffering of this family.

"We have to help these people," Aurora said with a trace of anguish in her voice.

"I know," David said, gently putting his arm around her.

David brought the carriage around to the front of the house and tethered the horses to a post. Then he and Aurora began unloading supplies from the roof. They had enough food for a long journey, so they had plenty to give these people a decent meal. They picked out some of the best food they had; the fresh bread, dried meats, fruit, cheese, and carrots. They decided these people were too hungry to wait for them to cook anything. Bringing it inside, they found a table in the front room to set everything out, and began cutting it up for them to share.

The family entered the room looking much better with freshly washed faces and clean clothes. They looked extremely hungry, and David saw the children's eyes fixed longingly on the food before them.

"I apologize for not introducing myself." The man said, "I'm Jotham, this is my wife Aida, my oldest Daughter Serena, my other daughter Ruth, and my son, Samuel."

David looked at him with a warm smile, and said, "Please, there's no need to apologize. We're honored to meet you. Now let us give you some food, and then we can talk." The children, who were showing such restraint waiting for permission to eat, impressed David. They looked up at their father, he gave them a small nod and a smile, and they rushed forward.

As David and Aurora quickly handed them pieces of everything, the children gave them a small "thank you." The three of them retreated to some chairs and began eating, looking at each other, smiling. Just the act of eating brought color back to their faces.

Jotham and Aida came forward and sat at the table. David and Aurora placed large helpings in front of them, and then joined them. They sat quietly for a moment, allowing the couple to eat. They were so hungry that it took all of their self-control not to stuff their mouths full. David took Aurora's hand in his, and looked to see her with a single tear running down her face. He knew the significance of having saved these people from suffering her loss.

Once David saw the couple begin to relax, he asked them "Can you tell us what's been happening to you?"

Jotham looked at him for a moment, gathering his thoughts, then he spoke. "After the siege, any of the able-bodied men left alive were put to work as slaves. We farmers were allowed to stay on our land as long as we continued to work it and provide food for the troops whenever they came.

Each year the demands for food grew and grew as more of their armies moved south. They steadily took all of our livestock, and our crop yield failed to keep pace with their demands. A few weeks ago they came and took everything we had left, leaving us without a single piece of grain. We've been foraging in the woods and fishing to survive, but had barely been able to hang on. We've been praying night and day for our Lord to deliver us. Then today they came, and when they found we had nothing to give," he paused, "they did not believe us, and would have surely killed me and a far worse fate for my wife and children, if you had not come."

"What of the other farmers in the surrounding area?" Aurora asked.

"Some of them have already suffered terribly, and others are not far behind. We've been gathering, in secret, to worship our Lord and beg for His mercy. Thankfully He has heard our prayers and sent you to us," Jotham said.

David and Aurora looked at each other with a questioning glance. Was this why they were sent to Roktah?

David said, "Please tell me about the men who were forced into slavery. Where are they?"

"They are being held in the city at night and brought out each day to work on the roads and other projects," Jotham answered.

"How many troops are there in the city?"

"Approximately 200. Most of the troops have moved south in preparation for the spring offensive. They are building a vast force in the hopes of tipping the scales and completing their conquest."

"How many slaves are being held there?" David asked, as Aurora shot him an inquisitive look.

"Several hundred men. They have been treated badly, and many are sick."

David sat, quietly considering what he had been told. Aurora was looking at him as if trying to read his mind. When she finally spoke, she asked, "Do you think if we release the prisoners, they may be able to retake the city?"

"Maybe," David said, "I'm just not sure yet. We've been sent here for a reason, and until we know what it is, we aren't going anywhere. Jotham, you said that you all meet in secret. How many of you are there?"

"Our numbers are down to about 50 now."

"How quickly can you arrange a meeting?"

"Normally 2-daystime." Jotham said. "We have a farming community on the eastern side of the city where we have found a safe place to meet."

Aurora's eyes went wide, and she asked, "Is it where the twin river meets?"

"Yes, do you know of this place?"

"It's where I grew up." Aurora said in a distant voice. David gave her hand a gentle squeeze.

David asked, "Is it possible to arrange the meeting for tonight?"

"It's possible if I leave right away."

David gave Aurora a quick look of reassurance, then turned to Jotham and said, "You and your family take our carriage. None of you will be safe here if anyone comes looking for these men. We will take some of their horses and meet you there at dusk. There's plenty of food and supplies. Take whatever you need."

Jotham, with a look of sudden determination, said, "I will not fail. Truly the Lord has answered our prayers." He stood, and David and Aurora joined him.

David said, "I'll tend to the horses, and you can leave shortly."

The oldest daughter, in a meek voice, said, "Father, I'm frightened." That seemed to take Jotham's breath away for a moment.

David walked over to her and knelt down, looking up into her eyes. He took her hands and said, "Serena, you have been so brave, but don't be afraid, the Lord is with us. Put your faith in Him, and He will not fail you." She nodded, her smile brightening.

David stood and turned to Aurora, a tear running down her cheek. He walked over and reached up, gently wiping it away. "Can you please bring the men's horses around? We'll take four with us and tether the rest to the back of the wagon," David asked her in a tender voice. She gave him a small nod and headed out the door, followed by Jotham.

Aida turned to David and said, "I just don't know what to say."

David said kindly "You don't have to say anything. Please gather up only what you have to, and bring the children out front as quickly as possible." David smiled at her, then turned and walked out. He got some feed and water for the horses, checked their harnesses and hooves, and grabbed his and Aurora's packs, along with a few choice weapons.

Aurora and Jotham came around from the back of the house with all 14 horses in tow. They tethered 4 of them to a post and brought the other 10 around behind the carriage. After fashioning some rope into a lead, they attached it to the rear of the carriage.

"Jotham, please be careful, and avoid running into anyone on your way. If you are stopped, perhaps you could tell them you are delivering these horses to some other group of soldiers. These are strong horses if you don't push them too hard. Should you need to get away, they'll have the strength for it," David said.

"I know a route that will keep us safe. I'll see you at the village later."

"We'll be there by dusk. Aurora knows the way. God's speed to you."

His family safely aboard, Jotham replied, "Thank you, we'll be there."

Aurora waved to the children, Jotham climbed up onto the bench, and then they were off.

Watching them leave, David turned to Aurora, and asked, "Are you alright? I know this was hard on you in more ways than one."

She smiled and said, "Yes, I'm fine. I was a little unsettled earlier, but knowing they're safe now makes me feel better." She smiled at him, then put on a stern look and added, "Now no more arguments. Let me see that arm."

They walked inside and David took off his shirt to expose the cut on his arm. Aurora looked at him for a moment, taking him in. This was the first time she had seen him without a shirt. She had felt his muscular body against hers, but somehow this was different. It hit her for the first time how handsome he was, his strong chin and penetrating brown eyes. He had short brown hair, exposing his neck and broad shoulders. He was well-built and trim. His arm, chest, and stomach muscles were all chiseled from hard work. She felt the desire to reach out and touch him, something she had never felt before.

"Is something wrong?" David asked.

"Uh, no," she said, gathering herself. Then looking at the cut she said in a playful voice "Oh my, this is nothing. I can't believe you made such a stink about it."

David let out a hearty laugh and said, "I know, I do go on, don't I?"

She chuckled as she pulled some things out of her bag. She put some salve on it, then a bandage, and said, "Now let me look at your back. That was quite a blow you took." Inspecting the area, she added, "You are going to have a good bruise, but I think you'll live."

David put his shirt back on. He turned to see her looking at him again, and she quickly looked away, and said, "I guess we'd better go."

After gathering their packs and putting on their traveling coats, they went outside and mounted the horses.

"Where are we going?" Aurora asked.

"I want to scout the city. We need to know what we're up against," David said.

"What are you thinking we're going to do?"

"I have no idea," He said with a smile, "but I'm guessing we'll figure it out together."

Aurora gave him a sly smile, "Unless you jump into something before I have a say in it."

David laughed, "I have done that on occasion, haven't I?"

Aurora, now in a serious tone, "Yes, and look at your arm. We need to be careful. This time there will be far too many men for us to handle."

"I promise. Far be it for me to argue with you."

Aurora said, smiling again, "Remember that. Now let's get going."

"Lead the way."

She gave her horse a gentle kick, and David followed. They left at a trot, heading to the northeast. The road they were traveling wound its way through farmland that showed signs of neglect and unhealthy crops. It was as if a plague had covered the land and was slowly destroying everything.

***

David considered the battle they had just had, and it occurred to him he did not have the queasy feeling of their previous encounter. He knew what these men were going to do and felt no mercy for them. These men were not possessed. They were willingly destroying the lives of people like Jotham and his family. David thought catching them in the act, unlike their encounter at the tavern, had changed everything. Hearing of the atrocities and witnessing them were two different things. Any unresolved doubts had been stripped away. Seeing what they were fighting to prevent filled him with clarity and steely determination. It was no longer theoretical; now it was personal.

After a couple of hours they came to a forest, and upon entering it, when they were safely out of sight, Aurora pulled her horse to a stop. David stopped next to her and she said, "When we get through the forest, we'll be close to the outskirts of the city. Why don't we give the horses some water and let them rest, so we're all fresh just in case."

"Will we be very exposed when we leave the woods?"

"Not too badly. There is a tree line that runs around the west and north sides of the city. We should be able to circle around it and get a close look at what's going on."

The two of them, having gotten off of the horses, tied them to some trees and busied themselves giving them water and a little feed. They sat down and leaned against a large oak to stretch their legs. The tree canopy allowed a fair amount of sunlight in, so by this time of the day it was warm enough to be comfortable. Everything was quiet except for the sounds of the birds and rustling of small animals nearby.

It felt comforting sitting there taking in the sights of the forest. Seeing how alive it still was in spite of the desolation that surrounded it. The smell of pine and cedar, the damp earth preparing for winter's cold with a blanket of leaves and pine needles. All these things reminded him that even during a harsh winter, life was there waiting for the rebirth of spring. They were heading into a cold, unforgiving winter, but they too could emerge into the spring. Hope was alive even when they couldn't see it.

They sat quietly for a short while, and when it appeared the horses had finished their food, Aurora stood.

"I guess we have to go. We shouldn't stay in one place too long anyway," she said, then reached out a hand to him this time. "I long for the days we can just sit together," she added as he stood, then put her arms around him.

"Now that is something worth fighting for," David said, then gently kissed her on the head. She squeezed him tightly before letting go.

In minutes, they were back on the horses heading down the trail. Up ahead they could see where the trees opened up to a well-worn field, so they slowed their approach.

"We should be able to ride the western tree line without being too noticeable. We will be pretty far from the city."

"We should probably slow to a walk so if we are seen, we might look less interesting."

"Yes, but I don't like being out in the open any longer than we have to."

"We won't," David said as they broke from the tree line.

In the open now, the road they were on veered to the right, leading down into the valley. They headed to the left to follow the tree line. The hillside was rocky with sporadic patches of grasses, wildflowers, and brush. They could see the city sitting at the bottom. It wasn't particularly large, but clearly at one time it had been grand. The north side of the city had a large 6-story building with a once grass-covered square in front of it. There were smaller two story buildings in rows to the south, separated by narrow stone streets with alleyways interspersed between them periodically. On the east, west, and south sides of the city were groups of buildings that appeared to be residences that were three and four stories high. There was one main road that led up to the city from the south that passed through a large stone archway.

The valley sloped down to the city from the north, east, and west. There was a small river running along the eastern edge of the city. They could see hundreds of people moving around, and off to the south, a makeshift garrison with troops milling about. The garrison was a blight even on this dying landscape. David imagined that the slaves and prisoners were held there. The eastern side of the valley was steep and rocky, running up the side of a small mountain. Its barren grey appearance seemed to echo the feeling of the city, cold and unwelcoming.

"This used to be a beautiful place. I remember coming several times as a child. It was alive with shopkeepers and merchants all selling their wares. Shoppers would come from all around and children ran free in the streets. Now it looks like a tomb for people who haven't died yet."

David sat quietly, taking it all in. Even in the sunshine it looked dark and uninviting. The people he could see were hurrying from place-to-place, like rats hiding from their prey.

They were nearing the northern tree line when Aurora said, "Look, there's an opening. Perhaps there's somewhere we can hide the horses."

"Good. Let's check it out. Then we can get to the east side through the forest. The tree line is a lot closer over there, and we'll have a much better chance of being spotted if we stay on the horses."

They made their way into the woods and found a small clearing that was well hidden. After securing the horses, they grabbed their packs and weapons and headed through the trees towards the city. Once they caught a glimpse of it, they forged their way through the forest and kept hidden as much as possible.

They reached the eastern side and moved to the edge of the trees, crouching down to get a better look. From their vantage point, they could see all the way to the southern gate.

"I've only seen two patrols of four men each so far. What about you?" David asked Aurora.

"Me too, and they don't appear to be paying close attention, either."

"I thought the same thing. They look as if they're going through the motions. I didn't see them glance this way once."

"I guess, after all these years, they don't think they need to worry about an attack."

"I suppose so," David said. "It looks like most of the troops are inside buildings; the garrison perhaps?"

"It could be, or they may have a good-sized force inside the council building."

"Look over there," David said, pointing to the northeastern corner of the city.

They saw a young woman, with a bundle in her arms, slip around the corner of a building. She looked around nervously. Seeing the coast was clear, she made a dash for the trees. She was maybe a hundred feet from their position.

"I wonder what she's doing." Aurora said.

"It looks like she's trying to run away."

The woman had gotten about half way across the open area when four soldiers came running out from around the corner of the building. One of them shouted at her, "Hey you! Stop! Where are you going?"

The woman turned and froze for a second, then realizing she was caught, took off at a sprint. The men followed quickly and were easily gaining on her.

"So much for avoiding any contact," Aurora said, as the two of them got to their feet.

Staying inside the trees so the men wouldn't see them coming, they ran as fast as possible, weaving around the dense foliage. They didn't worry about being quiet. The shouts of the men covered the sounds of snapping twigs and scraping brush. They were all shouting vile curses at the woman and promises of unspeakable things when they caught her. Suddenly they heard a scream of unbridled terror. The sound of it seemed to pull them even faster, igniting a fire within them. Moments later they caught a glimpse of the men and their quarry through the trees. The woman was on the ground with one man holding her hair; pulling it so savagely she had dropped her bundle. She was clutching at her head for some small relief. Another was on the ground grabbing at her legs, making clear his intentions, while the remaining two laughed at her torment.

They were close now. David could see Aurora out of the corner of his eye. She was running at full speed, dodging brush and trees, pulling out her bow, and drawing an arrow with the grace of a practiced dance move. Without missing a beat, she leapt over a branch, came to a complete stop, and fired as David kept running forward. He heard the arrow fly past him, seconds later followed by another. He watched as the first arrow hit the man on the ground dead center in the neck. The force, at this close range, snapped his head to the side before he toppled over. Then the second arrow caught the man pulling the woman's hair in the chest. The evil grin still on his face as he fell back, pulling her with him.

The other two men were momentarily stunned, looking at their fallen fellows, as David leapt into their midst. They turned to see him, a look of shock on their faces. David drove the short sword into the chest of one of them up to the hilt. Then he turned and slashed the throat of the second soldier with his dagger, so deeply that it almost severed his head. They fell to the ground with a thud.

He turned to the woman who was crying, curled up in a ball on the ground, and said, "It's alright. You're safe now."

She looked up at him with terror in her eyes as Aurora burst into their midst. As her fear turned to relief, the girl started to sob.

"I thought... they... were going to kill me... or... worse."

David and Aurora knelt down in front of her. Aurora put a comforting hand on her. "They aren't going to hurt you now. I'm Aurora, and this is David. Please tell us what happened?"

The woman said, "I'm June. My parents and I live on a small farm to the north. The soldiers came and took all of the food we had, and my parents are ill. They need something to eat, or they'll surely die. So I came here to the city and managed to get in unnoticed. I stole some food, and was trying to escape when they spotted me."

David got up and went over to the bundle on the ground, and began gathering up its spilled contents.

Aurora said to her, "I don't blame you. That was a very brave and dangerous thing to do."

June said, "I didn't have any choice. My parents won't last much longer. I just hope I can get back in time."

David turned to her, the bundle in one hand, and reached out with the other hand to help her to her feet. "How far is it?"

June said, "It's a 2 day journey on foot. They took all our horses' ages ago. I had to walk the whole way."

David turned to Aurora and said, "I think we can help."

June asked, "How?"

Aurora looked at her and said, "We have an extra horse. You can take it to get home to your parents."

David said, "First, let me cover these men. If anyone comes looking for them, then we'll have more time to get away from here."

They quickly pulled the men into a thicket and covered them with brush and branches. Anyone looking hard enough would find them, but it should buy them enough time to get away unnoticed.

As they walked back to the horses, June told them everything she saw in the city. Many of the men were eating and drinking, and while hiding in alleyways, she noticed a number of them stumbling from too much ale. David asked her about the council building, and she told them that it only had a few men out front and did not appear to have anyone coming and going. They moved quickly through the woods and were pleased to see the horses were undisturbed where they left them.

"How long a ride do you have?" he asked June.

"It's less than a day on horseback. There's a family I should be able to reach by nightfall who are friends where I can stay tonight," June answered, "I can't thank you both enough for what you've done for me."

"You can thank us by getting home safely," Aurora said.

"I will. There aren't any patrols this way. They always take the open roads."

David gave her one of the spare horses, thinking it would be better rested. He said to her, "Be careful, and do not lose faith. Perhaps we'll see you again someday." He handed her some of their dried meat and a couple of biscuits. "Here is some food to eat while you ride. You need your strength too."

She smiled at him. "I hope I do meet you both again, and surely our Lord sent you to protect me."

David and Aurora gave her a smile, and Aurora said, "Now go quickly." June turned and headed up a small trail. They stood there watching until she was out of sight.

"I guess that's our cue. We'd better get a move on too. We need to get back to your village before it gets dark."

Aurora, looking apprehensive, said, "Yes, we should get going."

David reached out, taking hold of her arm. He gently pulled her into a hug, and said, "I'll be with you." She squeezed him tight.

They only allowed themselves a few moments to shut out the world and get lost in each other's arms. Then they mounted their horses and set off. They moved as quickly as possible while still trying to remain inconspicuous. Once inside the cover of the forest, they pushed the horses into a gallop. Soon they were on the other side of the city and heading towards Aurora's home. Seeing there was no one in sight, they sped on their way, only stopping once to give the horses some rest. As dusk was approaching, they could see the village ahead of them. It was small, made up of a number of brick and mud homes with low roofs. There were a few barns, and what appeared to be a small square in the center with a well. They could see a number of people, horses, and their carriage out by the largest barn. Surrounded by fields with only a few clusters of trees, this place wouldn't have been David's choice for a secret meeting. As they approached, a few people came out to meet them, and then suddenly they saw Jotham come running from the barn, waving.

Jotham shouted, "David and Aurora, I was starting to worry about you." Turning to the other men, as David and Aurora pulled their horses to a stop, he said, "These are the two people who saved us this morning."

The men's faces changed from looks of concern to happiness at the new arrivals. David and Aurora dismounted their horses, and one of the men walked over to introduce himself. "I'm Eustus. Jotham has told us a little about you, and we have called a meeting of the council of elders to hear what you have to say."

"Thank you. We're looking forward to meeting everyone."

Aurora asked, "Do Miles and Solidad still live here?"

Eustus answered, "Yes they do. They are inside with the others."

Aurora instinctively grabbed David's hand, and he gave hers a gentle squeeze, letting her know he understood.

David said, "Perhaps we can water the horses before we go in. They've been ridden hard today."

Jotham interjected, "Please. I'll take care of it, and come in to join you the moment they are settled."

David and Aurora followed Eustus towards the barn. As they crossed the square, David stopped at the well.

"Eustus, do you mind if we take a drink and wash our faces?" David asked.

"No, of course not. I have been preoccupied with your arrival and forgot my basic manners."

"No apologies necessary," David said with a smile. "We're all preoccupied these days."

He and Aurora knelt at the well and scooped up water to drink and rinse the traveling dust off their faces. The water felt refreshing. David stood, enjoying the cold breeze against his wet skin, surveying the village.

Suddenly something stirred in him, and he spoke. "Have you changed this place since the siege?"

Eustus asked, "What do you mean?"

David turned to look at him and asked, "Have you added buildings and plantings since the siege?"

Eustus looked at him curiously, "Yes we have. How would you know that?"

David looked Eustus in the eyes with a penetrating stare. Eustus met his gaze with a patient calm expression.

"Eustus, you are a servant, and you turned this place into a seal."

Now Eustus was examining David, looking past his eyes, and after a moment of silence said, "My, my, that is interesting. Yes, young man you are correct. I think there is more to you than Jotham realized. He said you did miraculous things, but there is something more, I think."

"My father is a servant, and our home is part of a seal. It struck me that this village is out in the open, and seemed like a strange place to have secret meetings. I guess the seal protects you now, but when it was raided years ago, it did not have that protection."

Aurora took hold of David's arm to steady herself. He moved closer and put an arm around her. He saw Eustus give her the same penetrating gaze, then smiled at them knowingly, and said, "It seems there may be more to both of you. Come inside. We have some food. It isn't much, but you must be hungry after this long day."

"Thank you. We would appreciate that."

They entered the barn, and David and Aurora were taken aback by the number of people. It was far more than the 50 they expected. It looked as though everyone's entire family was there, men, women, and children of all ages. Jotham had clearly convinced them all that this was a significant event.

The barn was tall and thankfully large enough to accommodate everyone, even if the quarters were a little close. The dark hand-hewn wood had a warm feel, and the massive timbers gave the place a look of simple grandeur.

Eustus led them to the opposite side of the room where there was a table with some food set out. It was simple fare; some bread, cheese, and a random assortment of items from a few carrots to a couple of apples. It struck David that these people had brought what little extra they had, and it wasn't much. He felt overwhelmed with compassion for them, touched by their generosity.

Aurora leaned close to him, and said, "These people must be starving."

"I know."

Eustus said, "Please help yourselves. We have all brought what we were able to."

David, "I don't know what to say. Thank you."

Aurora added, "Yes, thank you. You're too generous."

Eustus said, "It is our privilege to serve." Then he walked off.

If David and Aurora hadn't been so hungry, they probably would have felt too guilty to eat at all, but after the rigors of the day and not having eaten since the morning, they each took a piece of bread and a small piece of cheese. They thought about the supplies in the carriage, but did not want to offend these people by refusing their generosity. David, taking a bite, turned to see a small girl looking up at them.

He knelt down and said, "Hello, young lady, and who might you be?"

"My name is Sarah."

"I'm David. It's nice to meet you, Sarah. Do you live here in the village?"

"We live on the other side of the river, my mommy, my brother, and me. The soldiers took my daddy away," Sarah said as she stared longingly at the cheese in David's hand.

David, noticing, asked her, "Would you like some cheese, Sarah?"

Her eyes going wide, she nodded her head. "Oh yes, please. I'm awful hungry. We haven't eaten today."

David handed her his cheese as she began to grin from ear to ear. Then David said, "Why don't you have a piece of bread too, and go share it with your brother?"

Sarah said, very enthusiastically, "Oh yes, David, I will. Thank you very much." Then she ran over to a little boy sitting by the wall and turned, pointing at David as she was talking to her brother.

David stood to find Aurora looking at him, smiling, when she said, "Here have some of mine."

He smiled back at her and said gently, "You eat it. I'm suddenly not very hungry." Then his grin faded, and she could see a fire burning in his eyes as he said, "God willing, we're going to put an end to this."

Aurora looked at him with that fierce determination in her eyes. "Yes we will."

Eustus returned, and seeing the intensity of their expressions asked, "Is everything all right?"

David turned to him and said, "We were sent here by the Lord, and we don't know why, but what you people are enduring is intolerable, and if there's anything we can do about it, we will."

Eustus said, "That is very kind of you to say, but the *Dark One* has a vast army, and as brave as the two of you might be, I'm not sure that it would be enough."

David suddenly felt that sensation again; only it was not driven by rage. It was like energy washing through him, imbuing him with that sense of clarity and certainty he had during their previous council meeting.

"Where I come from there's a story about a man named Gideon. The Lord asked him to lead an army against a vastly superior force. Gideon asked the angel of the Lord, 'How can I defeat this vast army?' The angel told him that the Lord would defeat them. Gideon had to have faith. Then he told Gideon to take his small force to the edge of the city and to blow his horn, alerting the enemy to his presence. When he did, the enemy went into such a panic that they slaughtered each other to a man. It is not for us to defeat *his* army. The Lord has asked us to be faithful, and He will deliver us."

Eustus, listening to David attentively, suddenly went wide-eyed and said, "In the city council hall, there is a secret chamber protected by a seal. Inside the chamber is a blade said to be forged from the horn of an Angel, a horn that was said to have defeated an entire army with a single blast. The men at the time were told to forge the horn into a blade, and that when the hour of darkness was at hand, the Lord's anointed one would come to retrieve it."

David and Aurora looked at each other, understanding now that this was the reason they were sent to Roktah. David turned back to Eustus and asked, "Do you know the prophecy?"

Eustus asked, "Which prophecy?"

Even though David had only heard it spoken once, he knew it by heart, and said, "When the hour of darkness is at hand, a son of David will be anointed to lead his people, and he will find favor with the Lord. A child of equal measure from the house of Roktah will rise-up to awaken the Lion, and together they will face the *Evil One*. They will be bound at birth by our Father, separated until the time of fulfillment when they will unite in his cause."

Aurora gave him a quick glance. She knew he left off the last line.

Eustus asked, "What are you saying?"

"The hour of darkness is at hand. I'm from the house of David, and Aurora is from the house of Roktah. In fact, she comes from this very village. We have been anointed to lead the battle against the evil one. It is time for us to act. It is time for the people of Roktah to stand."

Eustus looked at him, stunned by his words. Then his face became resolved, and he said, "It is time to talk to our people." David nodded in agreement.

Eustus led them around to a platform where they could stand above the crowd, and then he spoke. "Brothers and sisters," he paused for the crowd to quiet, "Brothers and sisters, we have come here often for many years to pray for our deliverance. The time has come. We are in the final hours. This is David, and our own daughter Aurora. I ask you to listen to them."

David stepped forward. He wasn't sure what he was going to say but knew the words would come. He looked out at the crowd. Many faces held a look of rapt attention, and others looked uncertain. He had never spoken before a crowd before. He was a simple farmer, but all that had changed. Everything that had happened to him during the past week, everything he had seen, and all he had done, humbled him. Who was he that the Lord should find such favor in him?

Without thinking David spoke. "Brothers and sisters of Roktah, I stand before you today, your humble servant. The Lord came to us," he looked at Aurora standing tall and confident by his side, "He told us to come to Roktah and seek His will. He has filled our hearts with compassion for your plight and determination to end your suffering. Tomorrow together we will retake the city and purge it of His enemies."

The crowd burst into chatter. Aurora took hold of his arm, indicating her surprise. David looked at her reassuringly, then turned back to the crowd, and spoke. "Brothers and sisters," he paused for a moment allowing them to quiet, then went on "the hour of darkness is at hand. If we do not stand now, the suffering you have seen will pale in comparison to what lies ahead."

A man in the crowd spoke, "How can the few of us and the two of you defeat this vast army?"

David answered, "It is not for us to defeat the enemy. The Lord will, if we stand faithful to Him. Anyone who has any doubts must not come. I tell you that as long as one man or woman amongst you has unwavering faith, you will be delivered. But any man or woman who is afraid or has doubts must not come."

Jotham, standing in the back of the room, said in a loud clear voice, "I have seen the power of the Spirit in these two, and I will stand with them in the name of our Lord." Then he made his way to the front of the room. The silence was deafening. When Jotham reached the platform, David extended his hand, helping him stand up next to him. Jotham turned to face the crowd, standing tall with an expression of fearless determination. At that, six more men made their way to the front and stood before David.

One of the men looked side to side at the others who had joined him, then said, "We will stand with you too."

David looked out at the crowd and said, "So it is clear our victory tomorrow is by the Lord's hand and not our own, let no one else join us. I ask all of you to stay here in this village where you will be safe inside the seal. When we return, it will affirm for you the truth of the prophecy. 'When the hour of darkness is at hand, a son of David will be anointed to lead his people, and he will find favor with the Lord. A child of equal measure from the house of Roktah will rise-up to awaken the Lion, and together they will face the *Evil One*. They will be bound at birth by our Father, separated until the time of fulfillment when they will unite in his cause'. Once the prophecy has been affirmed to you, the people of Roktah will inspire all the other cities to unite against our enemy and drive them out of their homes."

David turned to Eustus and asked, "Is there somewhere we can go to discuss our plans for tomorrow?" gesturing to the men standing with him.

"Yes, come this way."

As they all began to walk off, a man and a woman approached, and the woman said, "Aurora, is it really you?"

Aurora turned and exclaimed "Solidad, Miles, I'm so glad to see you! I was looking for you in the crowd but didn't see you." She rushed to them and hugged Solidad.

David turned to meet them, and Aurora said, "David, these are the people who saved me after my parents..." She still had trouble saying the words. "They helped me escape to the south."

"It's an honor to meet you."

Miles said, "We always knew she was exceptional. Now tell us, Aurora, what is this young man to you besides the fearsome warrior Jotham has described?" He added with a knowing look.

Aurora blushed, taking David's arm, and said, "We were married a couple of days ago. He's my husband."

She looked at David, beaming, and he returned the look with a loving smile of his own.

Solidad, nearly in tears, said, "Oh, that's wonderful! To see you happy again fills my heart with such joy." Then she leaned in and asked with quiet excitement, looking at her dress, "Are you with child?"

Aurora and David, both blushing fiercely, stammered until David finally found his voice "no, she isn't. We haven't had a honeymoon."

Solidad said, "I apologize for prying. I feared the worse for her when she left, all those years ago. I'm so happy to see her well again. The boys will want to see you too."

Miles said with a sly grin, "Yes, although I'm afraid they'll be quite disappointed to know you are married." Then he chuckled.

Aurora was blushing so brightly that David thought she might explode, so he put his arm around her, and said, "Perhaps we can come visit you tomorrow. Unfortunately, tonight we need to talk with Eustus and the others."

Solidad said, "Oh that would be lovely! We'll see you tomorrow then, dear." And with that they gave a small wave as they turned and left.

They departed through a side door, and Eustus led them to one of the houses. They walked in to find a table and some chairs in front of a large hearth. The room was dark. Eustus went over to light a lantern, and Jotham and another man began setting a fire in the hearth.

David said quietly, so no one else could hear, "I didn't know I had competition for your hand? Do I need to be worried about visiting the boys tomorrow?"

Aurora turned and punched him in the arm, "Oh you stop it, or I'll …" She cut short what she was going to do to him for teasing her as Eustus approached.

Eustus said, "Excuse me. May I talk to you in private for a moment?"

David said, "Of course." He turned to the men, and said, "Excuse us for a moment, we'll be right back. We need to speak to Eustus about something." They all nodded at him as the three of them headed into a back room.

This room appeared to be the kitchen of the house. It was relatively small, had a large fireplace with a brick oven and a table in it. Eustus lit an oil lamp, and they sat at the table.

Eustus started talking in a low voice. "I must first apologize, but I overheard your conversation with Miles and Solidad. I'm very familiar with the prophecy you spoke of, but did not want to put any ideas into your heads. I was waiting to hear it from you, so I could tell if you truly are the ones named."

Aurora said, "We didn't name ourselves. A group of servants has been watching us since we were children because they believed we were the ones. They are the ones who anointed us. We only met within this past week, although we have seen each other in visions our whole lives."

Eustus quickly said, "Please do not misunderstand what I'm saying. I do believe you are the ones. In fact, I'm certain of it. What you have said and done are more convincing to me than your birthrights. The true anointed are the ones who serve, not seek their own glory."

"Thank you, but what does that have to do with Miles and Solidad?" David asked.

Eustus answered, "Ah yes, well," looking a little embarrassed, he asked, "Did I understand correctly that you two were just married?"

In unison, David and Aurora said, "Yes." Then they exchanged a small smile at each other's lack of hesitation.

Eustus then asked, a little hesitantly, "Did I understand correctly that the two of you have not consummated your marriage?"

David and Aurora, both blushing again, looked at each other. Then David said, "No, we haven't."

Eustus asked, "Please forgive my questions, but I assure you they are for a good reason. Why did you marry?"

David explained how the evil spirits could not see the light in him, and that because of the bond he and Aurora share, that when they were close, she had the same protection. He told him that they got married in an effort to strengthen their bond so his protection for her would be stronger.

Eustus, looking a little disappointed, said, "I see. I thought it was something more."

Aurora asked, "What do you mean?"

"You see, the strongest bond you could have formed would have been if you loved each other, not simply a vow of marriage."

Again in unison with such enthusiasm, Eustus sat back and they said, "But we do love each other!"

Eustus, smiling broadly said, "You do. Why, that is outstanding."

Aurora said, "I have loved him my entire life, but was always too afraid to admit it until I heard him say it too."

Eustus asked curiously, "Then why haven't you consummated your marriage?"

David answered, a little embarrassed, "I have loved her my whole life too. But neither of us has been with another, and we don't want to squander such a precious gift as that in a cramped carriage or on the run from murderers. I love her too much for that. I love her for who she is, not just her physical form. If I were to die tomorrow never having experienced the beauty of her flesh, it wouldn't matter because I have experienced the beauty of her spirit, and everything else pales in comparison." David finished strong and confidently.

Eustus asked Aurora, "Do you feel the same?"

Aurora, holding David's arm, smiled broadly at his profession of love for her, and said, "Yes, I do."

"I'm humbled by such love. I must tell you that beyond everything you have told me that will be your greatest protection in the final battle."

David asked, "What do you mean?"

"The *Evil One* thrives on fear, temptation, envy, all of our worst traits, and everything *he* touches is tainted. *He* despises love and cannot stand in the light of our Lord. Your love, your purity, your physical purity, will be like fire on his skin. *He* would not be able to bear to touch you."

"That's good to know."

Eustus said gravely, "Yes it is, but do not underestimate *him*. *His* evil knows no bounds. *He* will try everything to break your bond because it is your only protection, and I pray it is enough."

"I appreciate your candidness. Would you please give us a moment alone? Then we'll join you and the other men."

"By all means," then Eustus stood and left the room.

David, looking at Aurora, saw her eyes filled with that fierce determination he admired so, and she said, "Even the *Dark One* cannot tear us apart."

David smiled at her, and her expression instantly relaxed, and she beamed back at him. Then David said, "No *he* can't, not even Miles and Solidad's boys can do that."

She hit him again and said, "I'm going to get even with you if you keep it up," she said chuckling.

"I can't wait. All right, let's get out there."

BATTLE PLANS

David and Aurora entered the main room and saw two young men standing nervously near the door, looking expectantly in their direction. The others were sitting around the table, patiently waiting as the fire was roaring to life.

Eustus said to David, "These two men want to speak to you."

David and Aurora walked over to them, and David asked, "Can I help you?"

The older of the two, by perhaps a year or so, spoke first. "I'm William, and this is my brother Nathan. We are Miles and Solidad's sons, and we want to stand with you."

David felt Aurora's hand tighten on his, and resisted the urge to laugh. He said to them, "Why do you want to join us?"

William looked at Aurora and said, "We remember the day they came, and what they did to your parents. It still haunts our nightmares to this day. We want to stand for what is right so that no one else has to suffer the way you did."

David asked, "How old are you?"

William said, "I'll be 19 in two weeks."

Nathan said hopefully, "I'll be 18 in the spring."

David asked, "Will you do what you're asked without question?"

They both nodded and said, "Yes we will."

David asked, "Do your parents know you're here?"

William said, "Yes they do."

David turned to Aurora and asked her, "Do you think they should join us?" keeping his tone utterly devoid of any emotion.

She looked into their eyes as they pleaded with her to say yes. After a moment she said, "Alright, but so help me if you disobey a single order... I'll put you over my knee and spank you, just like I did when you poured honey down my back."

The two boys turned red but smiled, and David shook his head and laughed. Then he said, "I see you two are very brave."

They turned back to the table and took note of the serious faces before them. Meeting their gaze with unmistakable authority, David spoke, "Gentlemen, we scouted the city today, and I have a plan. If you all follow it, God willing, no one in this room should get hurt. But make no mistake; this will be extremely dangerous. If anyone is not entirely sure they want to go with us, they should leave now, and we will not think any less of them."

When no one moved, David went on. "Aurora and I will take the carriage into the city. We will be posing as emissaries from Southaven. Once inside the city, I will make my way to the council building and retrieve an artifact. After that, we will go to the barracks where the prisoners are kept and create a disturbance. When you hear the disturbance, you will ride in to help free the prisoners. Those that are well enough to fight will stand with us, and those who are not will be taken to safety. "

One of the men spoke. "I'm Micah. Please forgive me, but I don't understand. If we are only freeing the prisoners, then what about the troops?"

David answered, "Most of the troops will be inside the city, and they will be struck with such fear it will drive them insane. Whatever you do, you should not go into the city until morning. You and the prisoners will need to deal with any troops fleeing the city, and possibly a few guards at the Garrison."

Eustus said, "You made one mistake. I will be going with you to the council building."

"Eustus, you can just tell me where to retrieve the artifact."

"No, it's not that simple, and it will take you too long. I'm coming with you." The resolve in his voice was unshakable.

"Ok. Does anyone else have any questions?" After a moment of silence, David continued, "Tomorrow we'll have all day to prepare. You'll be arriving at the city after dark. Everyone should get some rest. We'll meet in the morning to organize the supplies we need."

The men all stood, and Jotham came to David and asked, "Is there anything I can do for you?"

"Yes, get a decent night sleep, and spend some time with your family. We'll have plenty to do tomorrow."

As the others were all leaving, David said to Eustus "Eustus, are you sure you want to come into the city with us? It'll be very dangerous."

"You said it yourself. It's time to take a stand. Yes, I'm coming with you."

"I'll protect you with my life."

"Let us hope that won't be necessary."

"Fair enough. I guess we ought to get some rest too."

"You can stay in this house if you like. Unfortunately, the family that lived here is gone now."

David turned to Aurora and said, "I wouldn't feel right taking so much space for just the two of us, with all those extra families out there ."

"Me too, Eustus. We'll find a place to sleep. Give this space to some of the others."

Eustus said, "As you wish." Then he turned and left.

David said to Aurora, "You're stuck with me again."

She smiled and hugged him, "I wouldn't have it any other way."

They left the house and headed to the wagon, planning to sleep there. Along the way they passed Aurora's childhood home. She pressed close to him, and he pulled his arm tight around her. He didn't say anything, feeling that if she wanted to talk about it, she would. As they approached the carriage, there was a couple with two small children milling around it.

David walked up to them and asked kindly, "Can we help you with something?"

The man said, "We were wondering who this carriage belonged to. We don't have anywhere to stay tonight and hoped we might sleep inside if no one else is using it."

"You're in luck. It's our carriage, and we're not going to sleep in it tonight, so you and your family can use it. There's some bedding inside, and if you draw the curtains, you should keep warm tonight."

"Thank you very much."

"We're just going to get a few things from the roof. Then you'll have it all to yourself. Tomorrow we can see about finding you someplace better."

"Come children, let's get you to sleep."

David and Aurora climbed on top of the carriage and found a small tent and extra blankets. They pulled them down and went to find a place to pitch their tent. They saw a grassy spot near a building that would get plenty of sun in the morning and set to work. In short order they had the tent up, and they climbed inside. They were thankful for the soft grass, even if the ground was cold.

Once they were settled under the blanket, Aurora said, "It's been a long day, but I have a feeling tomorrow will be even longer."

"I suppose you're right. I only hope I made the right decision. My heart breaks for these people, and I just couldn't bear the thought of leaving them to suffer any longer."

"I know. I couldn't have left either. I don't think you're wrong after what Eustus told us about the horn being made into a weapon. I think that's significant."

David said, "I thought so too, and we'll find out soon enough. Tomorrow will come quicker than we expect it."

Aurora said, "We'd better get some sleep then." She pulled him tight and kissed him on the cheek.

"Good night Aurora."

"Good night David."

They were asleep in no time, and soon found themselves back in the same place as the other night. They felt the warmth and peace of the light upon them. Then rolling in like a breeze over the water, they heard the Lord's voice again. "You have acted faithfully, and because of that I will be with you tomorrow. When you leave the council building, stand on the steps and call out My name, and I will purge the city of the evil that plagues it. Tell the people of Roktah that when the battle is over, they are to send two riders to every occupied city, stand at the front gates, and call out My name. If they remain faithful, they will be victorious."

Aurora and David said, "We will, Lord."

"Once Roktah falls, you are to take two horses and travel directly to Tartaros. I will be with you on your journey, hastening you along the way. At night, sleep under the canopy of an oak, and I will watch over you. Once you are in the valley of Tartaros, do not stray from the path or you will be lost."

They could feel His presence retreating, but this time they had no questions. They were on the final leg of their journey, and what would come, would come. They woke to find the sun warming them inside their tent. They lay there silently, still holding each other, knowing they had both heard the same thing. In spite of what lay ahead, they felt strangely at peace and were comforted by each other's embrace.

Finally David spoke, "As long as we're together, I'm ready."

Aurora pressed close to him, "So am I."

They got up, climbed out of the tent, and found their band of would-be warriors anxiously waiting for them.

Eustus stepped forward and asked, "Is everything all right?"

David said, "Yes, why?"

"When we came to see you, there was a white light coming from your tent, and we were afraid to come too close."

"I see. The Lord gave us instruction while we slept."

"Truly?"

"Yes, come let us tell the men."

The three of them walked over to the others. All nine of them stood, looking anxious. David said, "The Lord came to us last night and said He will be with us today." Their faces turned to a mixture of awe and joy. "He said that once Roktah falls, we are to send two riders to every city, and when they arrive, they are to shout His name, and He will deliver that city from the *Dark One*. These men must be faithful; are you men up to the task?"

They all stood straight, and with nods and an occasional "yes," affirmed their commitment. David then walked up to each one in turn, placing his hands on their shoulders, and said, "Lord, if I have found favor in Your eyes, please rest Your Spirit on this man and bless him."

When he finished, he said, "Now go, rest, and spend the day with your families. We have a long night ahead of us. We'll meet at the stables this afternoon to prepare the horses." The men all turned to leave, except for William, Nathan, and Eustus. "Eustus, I need to speak to you for a moment. William and Nathan, how can I help you?"

William said, "Our parents asked if you would like to come and join us for the midday meal."

"It would be a privilege. Please go and tell them we'll come as soon as we're finished here."

As the boys walked away, he turned to Eustus and said, "There's a family that had nowhere to sleep last night, so we let them sleep in the carriage. Can you please do me the favor of finding them somewhere to sleep tonight, since we'll be taking it with us?"

"Consider it done."

"After the city falls, Aurora and I have to leave immediately for Tartaros." He saw Eustus' face turn pale. "I would like you to take charge of the men and see that everything is done as instructed. From what I've been told, there's plenty of food in the city, and once it's safe, these people can join you there. We don't know how long we'll be gone or if we'll be coming back. Can I count on you to do that for me?"

Eustus looked at him for a moment with a mixture of admiration and sadness on his face, and said, "You can count on me, and I will stand in your place only until you return."

"Thank you, Eustus." David gave him a small smile, and Eustus walked off. Then he turned to Aurora and asked, "Are you ready?"

"Ready for what?"

"Miles, Solidad, and the boys," David said with a grin.

Aurora, giving him a stern look, said, "Don't you start with me," then let slip a small grin too.

"I wouldn't dream of it. I have a feeling they'll do it for me."

With a chuckle, Aurora said, "You're probably right."

They headed off arm in arm to see what lay in store for them.

***

Aurora, walking with David on their way to spend time with the people who were the closest thing she had to a family, suddenly felt light hearted. Here she was in her hometown with the man she loved. She could just as easily be taking him to meet her parents for the first time. She had long ago given up on such thoughts; not that she needed a man to feel complete, but he was different. He didn't act around her the way young men did. Either they had been intimidated by her or blustering trying to impress her, but he had a different kind of confidence. He didn't have to prove anything. She didn't intimidate him either. He lifted her up and made her feel special. He touched her heart in a way she couldn't put into words. Here they were in a life-and-death struggle, and they could still find moments of peace and happiness. How she wished her parents were here. But today that thought did not make her sad. She knew they were watching over her, and that they would be happy for her.

They arrived at Miles and Solidad's, and Aurora knocked at the door. From inside they heard the noise of people bustling over to meet them. The door swung open, and there stood Miles and Solidad, smiling broadly.

"Come in, come in," she said cheerfully. "Miles, step back. Let them inside."

"So good to see you both," Miles said, as he retreated into the house.

David and Aurora moved through the doorway as Solidad pushed the door shut behind them. "We were hoping you wouldn't be detained. The boys told us all about what is going on, and we thought you might not have time for us," Solidad said.

"What are we fighting for if not to spend time with the people we love?"

"Oh dear!" And she hugged Aurora. "Your parents would have been so proud of you. You have grown into such a magnificent woman."

"Thank you, Solidad."

Miles said, "Come in and sit down. It sounds like you've had a busy morning already."

David said, "Thank you, Sir."

Miles scoffed. "Sir, oh please, no need to call me sir. Just Miles."

"If you insist."

"Of course I insist. You are family now, and an important man."

David replied sincerely, "I would be honored to consider myself family, but I'm no more important than you and your family."

"But the Lord has blessed you."

"And He has blessed you too. You have a lovely wife and two fine sons. Who could ask for a better blessing than that?"

Solidad, blushing slightly, released Aurora from her hug. She turned and put her hand on David's arm. "Come on, dear. Let's go into the kitchen. Aurora where ever did you find this young man?"

"You might not believe me when I tell you."

As they moved toward the kitchen, they caught a glimpse of the boys. They had been listening by the door and were red in the face at the compliment.

The boys snapped to attention, and William said, "Commander, is there anything we can do for you?"

"Yes, there is."

Nathan asked, "What is it, Sir?"

"You can call me David."

They deflated a little and said, "Oh sure, ok."

"First, I'm a guest in your home, and secondly, I'm not actually a commander. I'm just a soldier like the two of you."

The boys stood a little taller and smiled, pleased to be labeled as equals.

Miles said, "All right, come on now everyone. Solidad has prepared a terrific meal for us. The smells have been driving me mad all morning."

Aurora said, "I can't wait." They had little to eat yesterday, and she was famished. "Is there anything I can do to help?"

Solidad answered "No thank you, dear. You two sit down. We want to hear all about what has been going on, and more importantly how you two met." Then she began putting their meal on the table.

Aurora asked, "Do you remember when I was a girl, I often talked about a boy who no one else could see?"

William said, "How could we forget? You used to go on about how the two of you would have adventures. Remember, Nathan?"

Nathan answered, "Yeah, she used to tell us that he was going to come and set us straight if we didn't stop bothering her."

William said, "That's right, and you would say that he was big and tall, and handsome." The boys were gleefully teasing her, and Aurora was turning scarlet with embarrassment.

Nathan, positively giddy now, added, "and you told us you were going to marry him one day, and he was going to take you away from here." At that they froze in mid laugh.

Aurora looked at them with an air of having just been proved right, and said, "This is him."

Solidad said, "That's incredible. Is it really him? I remember you speaking about him too, Dear. In fact, your mother and I used to think it was so sweet that you had come up this boy of your dreams."

David, in an effort to come to her rescue from all the embarrassment, said, "I have seen her my whole life too, mostly just flashes of her. I never dreamed it would be possible that we would meet, and in my whole life I never met a woman as enthralling who could drive her from my thoughts."

It didn't work. Now she was even more embarrassed.

Aurora said, "Ok, so on with the story;" anything to change the subject. She wasn't used to all this fuss. "After you helped me escape all those years ago, I traveled south. I found a group of people working to defeat the northern armies and joined them. I began going on special missions taking out supply lines and other disruptive activities. Several weeks ago I was given a special mission to retrieve a scroll from a monastery in the mountains about a prophecy that was supposed to help us change the tide of the war. On our way back we ran into trouble, and I was separated from my team. We had encountered some of the *Dark One's* special guards." Solidad let out a gasp, and the boys and Miles were rapt with attention. "They were tracking me, and a group of soldiers had me on the run. I was cornered and had to make a break for it through an open area. I was in real trouble when out of nowhere, David showed up and got me out of the way of one of their flaming catapult armaments. When he grabbed me, something happened, and we ended up in his world. It is somehow separated from ours, and we passed through a divide between them."

Miles said, "Aurora, we've never heard of such a thing."

Aurora said, "Neither had we, but there were servants there who knew about me, and what was going on, and they were aware of the prophecy too. They told us that we were the ones named in the prophecy. Also, David was able to use a Seal to commune with the Lord, and after that we have been traveling back to fulfill the prophecy. The Lord has come to us twice to give us instructions, and He told us to come here and help the people of Roktah. When we are finished here, we head to Tartaros."

The silence in the room was like a thick fog. Miles, Solidad, and the boys sat frozen as if the world had stopped turning.

Suddenly William blurted out, "but you can't go there. That's where they say the *Dark One* is, and no one who's ever gone there has been seen again."

Aurora said, "That's why we have to go there to face *him*. David and I have a special bond, forged since the day we were born, and that is our only hope. It's our destiny to stand and face *him*."

Solidad said, "But surely there has to be another way. How can two people stand and face *him*, and hope to survive? How can the two of you stop *him*?"

David said, "We can't stop *him* on our own. This is a matter of faith. We have to trust the Lord will deliver us."

Miles asked, "But how can you be sure? What if it is a trick to lure you to your deaths?"

"It doesn't matter. All along our journey we've met wonderful people and families like yours suffering terribly. We can't stand by while they suffer under the brutality and evil that plagues this land. If there is the slightest chance that we can put an end to it, even if it is a trick, then we have to try. As for me," He turned to Aurora and said, "I have never been happier since we met. If it is our destiny to die, I have no regrets in this life."

Aurora meeting his eyes said, "Neither do I."

Everyone sat in silence, looking somber.

David said in a jovial tone "Hey, we aren't dead yet."

Miles said, "No, of course not, we just uh…"

David said, "Now I have a very important question for all of you." Everyone looked at him stoically. "Can you tell me how much of a trouble maker Aurora was growing up?"

Aurora hit him on the arm and said, "I wasn't a trouble maker."

Solidad said, "I wouldn't exactly say that." And they all chuckled.

William said, "She probably didn't tell you why we poured honey down her back, did she?"

David said with a smile, "Now that sounds like a good story."

They spent the next couple of hours sharing stories of the boys and Aurora's antics growing up, and laughed until they all had tears in their eyes.

Around midafternoon David said, "As much fun as this has been, I'm afraid we have to get going. We need to prepare for tonight, and don't want to keep the others waiting. I can't thank you enough for your splendid hospitality."

They all stood, and Solidad came over and gave David and Aurora each a hug, saying "You two be careful, and promise you'll come back to see us again."

Miles said, "Yes, be careful out there."

David said, "We'll do our best to come and see you as soon as possible." He couldn't promise they would, because he didn't know what the outcome would be. "I want you to know that I'll watch over your sons as if they were my own today." Then turning to the boys, he added, "Why don't you stay a minute and give your parents a proper goodbye, and we'll meet you at the stables."

Aurora said, "Miles and Solidad, it's been wonderful seeing you again. Thank you."

Solidad said, "And it's been wonderful to see you too. We'll keep you in our prayers."

At that, they headed to the door. David and Aurora could hear Miles and Solidad admonishing their sons to be careful and telling them how proud they were as they walked out of the house.

Arm in arm, Aurora said to David, "Thank you for what you did there today."

David asked, "What did I do?"

Aurora answered, "You took away their fears and reminded us all what we are fighting for. I don't know how you do it. One minute I feel sad or frightened and the next at peace. You did the same thing for them too."

David said, "I didn't plan to do anything, I just don't dwell on what might be because whatever is coming will come, and how we face it will determine the outcome. I have hope, and I will not give up until my last breath. So between now and then, I'll savor every moment we have together so that if any one of them is our last, I won't have wasted it."

"You're right. I don't want to waste a minute we have together either. I just can't help but wonder what it would be like to be, well, regular people without all this responsibility."

David stopped and turned to face her, and then he lifted his hand to the side of her face, gently cradling it, and said, "God willing, someday we'll get the chance to find out." Then he gave her a tender kiss on the lips, lingering just long enough for the two of them to feel that tingle inside. Then he said, "Now let's go finish this thing so we can be free of it."

"That sounds good to me."

They arrived at the stables, where Jotham, Eustus, and the other six men were waiting.

Eustus said, "We took the liberty of packing up your tent. Your other things are all in the carriage too. I believe we're ready to go. Are the boys with you?"

Aurora said, "They're on their way."

Just then a man arrived. "I'm Micah. I had a vision that I should come with you. Will you have me join you?"

David stepped up to him and looked into his eyes. He saw only the light and said, "Yes, that makes us 13, a powerful number." He put his hands on Micah, and gave him his blessing just as he had with the others. At that moment the boys arrived. Turning to them, he added, "Good, we're ready to go."

Aurora said, "If we leave now we should arrive just before dark."

David turned to the group. "Men, we'll lead in the carriage. Before we get to the city, there is a ridge on the western side where you can wait for our signal. Once you hear it, ride down to the garrison and release the prisoners. If we run into anyone on our way, Aurora and I are posing as emissaries from Southaven, and you will be our escorts. Do any of you have questions?"

No one said anything. "OK, let's go," David said.

They all began mounting their horses. David, Aurora, and Eustus headed to the carriage. As they rode out of the village, a number of people lined the streets waving their goodbyes; women, children, elders, and Miles and Solidad. They rode at a comfortable pace, David and Aurora driving the carriage, having insisted that Eustus sit inside until they reached the city. David wanted to be out front so he could spy any trouble first, and Aurora was not about to leave his side.

It took them a couple of hours to reach the outskirts of the city. They only stopped a few times for water. David pulled the coach to a stop, and he and Aurora hopped down. The rest of the men pulled their horses up to meet them.

"You can take that trail up to the top of the ridge and wait for the signal. Stay inside the tree line until it is time. There is a path that winds its way down to the southern part of the city where the garrison is located. Remember, it is crucial that you do not come down until the signal is given; not one minute sooner."

William said firmly, "We won't."

"Good. We'll see you all inside the city," David said. Then he turned to Eustus. "Don't look anyone in the eye when we arrive. I'll talk to anyone we encounter. I don't want you taking any risks."

"I will do as you say."

"Then I guess we're ready."

David and Aurora climbed inside the carriage, and Eustus got into the driver's seat. As soon as they were settled, he set off. The moon was in the sky, and as they made their way around a bend, the city came into view. The sun was setting behind the trees to the west where they had been yesterday, casting an orange glow on the valley. The once grand city had an unkempt dirty look, surrounded by grounds trampled by men and horses with little regard for it. They passed the makeshift garrison outside the main city gate. The smell of men, sweat, rotten food, and poor sanitary conditions was like a slap in the face, only adding to the feeling of despair the city emanated. In front of the main gate was a shack of sorts for the city guards. Compared to the city architecture, it was like a trash can by the street.

They approached the guard post, and two guards stepped out, blocking their path. They appeared well fed, but looked as disheveled as the shack they came out of. Their hair and clothes were matted and splattered with dried mud and dust. The only items of note were the weapons at their sides. The one had a large battle-axe, and the other a sword. They were meant to intimidate anyone approaching. The moment Eustus pulled the carriage to a stop, David jumped out.

"Where do you think you're going?" The first guard asked in a gruff annoyed voice.

"My wife and I are emissaries from Southaven, and we need to see your commander immediately," David said with an air of authority, to show they did not intimidate him.

"Really, you want to see the commander?" The man said with mock concern, "Well he's a very busy man."

"I'm sure he is, but we have urgent business. We are on our way to Tartaros to negotiate a treaty and cannot be delayed."

At the mention of Tartaros, the man's bluster evaporated. "The commander doesn't like unexpected visitors."

"Since this is a secret mission, we couldn't very well send messengers ahead to alert him to our visit now, could we?"

"I suppose not. I guess you can go see him at your own peril," the man answered, looking them over. He walked over to the carriage to be sure it was just the three of them, "I'll warn you, he isn't as friendly as I am, and General Grog isn't known for his patience." He added with a smirk.

"I'm sure he'll want to hear what we have to say."

"All right, be on your way. He's in the council building at the north end of the city." The man said, then turned back to his post.

David quickly got back into the coach, and Eustus started off immediately. They rode down the main road through the center of the city, which was just as filthy. They passed one building after another with dimly lit windows. The glass only slightly muffled the sounds of the raucous eating and drinking of the men inside. Thankfully the smell wasn't as strong, but not by a lot. As they continued to the council building, they saw an occasional man staggering from one building to another, apparently having had too much to drink. They all had the same barbaric appearance as the guards at the gate, and all carried weapons.

Once they made it to the town square, they could see the council building. The square itself appeared to be the victim of a wild party of drunken men. Planters and statues had been lying on the ground for so long that weeds had grown up around them. The council building looked to be untouched by the madness that surrounded it. Only two of the windows had any light showing through them; one on the first floor and one on the second. Eustus drove the carriage around the square and pulled up in front of the main entrance to the building. David quickly got out of the carriage and made his way around to face the door. He wanted to be ready in case they weren't welcome.

The square was quiet. There weren't any soldiers on guard, which struck him as odd. This general didn't feel the need for any protection, which meant he was either foolish or extremely dangerous. Aurora joined David, and Eustus climbed down from the driver seat.

David's senses on high alert, he turned to Aurora and Eustus, and said, "Be very careful and stay close to me." Aurora gave him her warrior face, and Eustus looked terrified, indicating there was no way he was going anywhere without them. "Remember, Eustus, don't make eye contact with anyone." Eustus nodded, unable to speak.

David turned, took a step towards the door, and in mid-stride, it began to open. Appearing in the doorway was a small thin man whose stance gave him a rodent-like look. He was not as disheveled-looking as the troops but still had an unclean appearance.

He stepped out into the open and in a raspy voice asked, "Who are you?"

David took another step forward and said in a clear voice; "We are emissaries from Southaven on our way to Tartaros to negotiate a treaty with your master. We need to see the General."

The man hissed, "I see, then come this way."

David followed the man, with Aurora and Eustus close behind him. The inside of the building was dimly lit, and they were barely able to make out where they were headed. They could see an occasional side table or wall hanging, but the details were obscured by the darkness. They did notice that this building had not been ransacked like the rest of the town. They proceeded to a large staircase and climbed up to the second floor. They turned to their right and made their way towards the room they had seen lit from the outside.

The little man opened the door and said, "This way." They stepped inside the room. It was hot, and the thick air had a foul stench to it. The little man followed them in and shut the door behind him.

At the opposite side of the room sat a giant of a man. In the low light, it was hard to make out exactly what was strange about him, but it was clear he was not a normal man. His bald head had scars on either side, and his face was rugged with the bones of his cheeks and chin much larger than they should have been. He stood up as they approached. He was at least a foot taller than David and almost twice as broad. His meaty hands, pushing him up from the desk, were the size of David's head. As the man moved around from behind the desk, Eustus let out a slight gasp as the light washed over him. His skin was stretched taught and had a burned blackened appearance without a trace of hair on his head.

"Good evening General Grog., My wife and I are emissaries from Southaven on our way to Tartaros to negotiate a treaty. We apologize for disturbing you so late in the evening, but we needed a safe place to stay for the night," David said in a confident voice, not wanting to offer any doubt about their intentions.

The General moved in front of David and looked into his eyes. David met his gaze without blinking. He could see the darkness inside. It was pitch black, far more sinister than the others he had encountered.

The General paused for a moment, his face expressionless, then turned to look at Aurora's eyes. She too met his gaze unflinchingly. The general muttered, "So you say."

David said, "General, we have been traveling for weeks in secret, and will set out from here in the morning to meet your *master*."

The General looked back at David, raised a hairless eyebrow, and said, "Will you? Do you suppose *he* will grant you an audience?"

David asked, "Why wouldn't *he*?"

The General said, "There is only one man we are expecting to travel to Tartaros. There is only one man that my *master* wants to see. Are you that man?"

David realized they were on the verge of being exposed, and wanted to buy some time to come up with a plan. "I don't know what you mean, General. The land of Southaven wants a treaty with your *master* so that when *he* wins this war, we can have a place of honor under *his* rule."

The General asked, "Do you think my *master* needs you to win this war?"

David said, "I believe that your *master* wants the war to be over with *him* victorious, so *he* can establish *his* rule."

The General said, "Yes *he* does, but there are those of the light who would thwart *his* plans."

David knew he didn't have much time. Then the General moved past David's right to face Eustus. This was it; any second now their story was going to unravel, and he still didn't have a plan. The General wasn't looking at David. He was looking at Eustus, who was staring at the ground, trembling slightly. David took the opportunity to slip his hand inside his coat to find a knife.

"What are you getting at, General?" David asked contemptuously.

The General, ignoring David, reached out to Eustus with his left hand, his right casually moving towards his knife. Then tipping Eustus' head up, he looked into his eyes and saw the light. A small grin appeared on the General's face. Then David knew it was time to act. David pushed the General hard on his right shoulder saying, "Don't ignore me when I'm talking to you."

The shove and the indignant words surprised the General. His left arm still outstretched towards Eustus, he turned to face David with rage in his eyes. David didn't hesitate. The General stood before him, arms outstretched, exposed, and with all his strength, David drove the dagger into his heart.

David caught a glimpse out of the corner of his eye as he saw Aurora moving into action, but he couldn't afford to look at what she was doing. The General was now fully enraged and moved towards David. In an instant, David felt the air crack as the now familiar charge ran through him like a bolt of lightning. The General, in spite of being wounded and as large as he was, moved surprisingly quickly, but David was still able to duck under his massive fist. He slipped past him to his left, and stepped up onto a chair while drawing his short sword. Then with a mighty swing, spun around and cut off his head.

There was an unearthly scream that ripped through their ears like hot needles. As his bulk fell to the ground, he saw Aurora standing over the dead body of the little man. He had also pulled a knife, but was too slow for her. She looked up at David, her face set with grim determination. They stood still for a moment, and then Eustus fell to his knees.

The two of them went over to him, Aurora asking, "Are you alright, Eustus?"

Eustus looked up at them, pale as a sheet, and said, "Dear Lord."

David asked, "Are you hurt anywhere, Eustus?"

Eustus started to come back to himself. "I think I'm alright. I've never been so frightened in my life."

David and Aurora helped him to his feet.

David asked, "Eustus, are you well enough to find the artifact?"

Eustus, regaining some color in his, face said, "Yes, yes, I can, yes."

David grabbed a lamp off of the desk and said to Eustus, "Ok, then lead the way."

Eustus led them through a series of hallways downstairs through several rooms until they finally came to a small room that gave David the impression of a prayer chamber. In the corner was a niche. Eustus went over to it and removed a small statue. Behind the statue was a small seal. He placed his finger on it and began to pray. After a few moments, the back of the niche slid into the wall, exposing a hidden cubby. Eustus reached inside and withdrew the item wrapped in cloth. He turned to them and opened it. Inside were two golden daggers. He handed them to David and said, "May these help you in your final battle."

David took one and handed it to Aurora, then sheathed the other one. Aurora slipped hers inside her boot. Then David said, "We'd better get moving before someone shows up here."

They quickly made their way to the main entrance, with David telling them, "Stay behind me."

He walked out onto the landing and reached out, drawing on the Spirit. The air cracked and sizzled around him, and then he said in a loud clear voice, "I stand for Jehovah."

As the 'vah' sound left him, it exploded like a cannon. Even in the moonlight they could see the dust whipped up from the ground as it shot forth into the city. David knew the men waiting on the ridge would have heard it too. He turned to Aurora and Eustus, "Hurry, get into the carriage. We have to go meet the others."

David quickly climbed up onto the driver's bench, and Aurora joined him. Eustus got inside, and David set out immediately. He drove back down the main street. As they passed all the buildings where the men were, they could hear them inside. This time, the sounds were not of wild indulgence. This time the sounds were of brutal slaughter. Unholy screams of pain and suffering as the men turned on each other in a wild melee of killing.

Aurora was pressed up close to him as if seeking protection from the horrid sounds attacking them. They didn't stop. They kept a steady pace until they reached the garrison. They arrived just as their team rode up. They all looked a little pale and at the same time alert for any surprises.

"What happened?" Jotham asked a little breathless. "We heard a loud noise and felt the ground shake."

"The Lord delivered this city into your hands as He promised. Now you must go and free the prisoners. Then tomorrow you need to find two people of faith to replace Aurora and me. Eustus will take charge in my place, and he will send you out in pairs to all the cities of the land. You will ride up to the main gates of the city, stand tall, and proclaim 'I stand for Jehovah'. When you do, the Lord will liberate the city and cleanse it of evil." David said.

"We will do as you say." Jotham said, and the others agreed.

David turned to Eustus, placed his hands on him, and said, "Eustus I appoint you in my place to lead these men, and if it pleases the Lord may He rest my blessing upon you. Bless the two men you find tomorrow. You will know them when you see them. Arrange to get the food from the city to the surrounding villages, and let them know that the Lord has provided for them."

Eustus said, "I'm humbled, and will do what you say."

"Aurora and I must leave tonight, but fear not, because the Lord is with you."

"Will I see you again?"

David gave him a small smile and said, "I surely hope so."

Jotham and the others headed to the garrison, except for William and Nathan who walked over to the three of them.

"Aurora, please be careful. We don't want to lose you again," William said sadly.

"No one else ever got the best of us like you did," Nathan added with a sly grin.

Aurora placed a hand on each of their cheeks and said, "I have missed you both, too. Please give your parents my love, and stay out of trouble. If either of you get hurt, I will hunt you down and put you over my knee again." The boys hugged her.

"Eustus, we're going to grab our things and two horses. Then we'll head out." David said.

"I will do my best while you are gone. Come, you two, let's go help the others," Eustus said. Then he turned and walked off.

David and Aurora stood for a moment watching them leave. Then Aurora sighed, "Just us again."

David put an arm around her and replied, "That's all I need." She rested her head on his shoulder.

"I guess we'd better get a move on if we're going to find a place to sleep sometime tonight." Aurora said.

"I suppose so. Do you mind grabbing our things, and I'll get a couple of larger quarter horses?"

"Sure. How much food do you think we'll need?"

"3 days-worth should do it."

Aurora looked at him a little puzzled, and said, "But it's a 2 week journey."

"We can hunt along the way if we need to. These people are going to need every scrap of food they can get to make it through the winter."

Aurora still thought it wasn't enough, but she had learned to trust him. He seemed to know things without thinking about them. His confidence was always reassuring to her. She had gotten so used to having to rely solely on her own instincts and wits that it was a relief to share the burden of always having to decide. She was used to being in charge, and yet she found it so easy to follow him. It was like a big weight lifted from her shoulders.

She quickly gathered up their gear, food, tent, and weapons, and when David returned with the horses, she was ready. He walked up with two large strong horses in tow, the moonlight illuminating the area. They could hear the sound of the men being freed from their chains coming from the garrison. The men's rising voices, filled with relief, were coming even closer.

Standing there, looking in the direction of the garrison, David said, "We should leave before they come this way."

Aurora quickly helped him load up their gear and mounted her horse. As soon as they headed off, she asked, "Why didn't you want the men to see us?"

David paused thoughtfully and said to her, "Because we didn't free them. They need to reserve their thanks for God, and just as importantly, I need to remember that too."

"I understand. Do you know which way we're going?"

"I saw a trail leaving from the northeast end of the city when we scouted it the other day. What do you think?"

"I saw that too. I've never been beyond the northern border of the city. I only know what I've been told by others; I'm not sure what we'll encounter along the way."

"Sounds like loads of fun, doesn't it?" David said with a smirk.

"Oh I'm sure it will be," Aurora said with a small chuckle. "How long do you want to travel tonight?"

"Once we're beyond the city, we'll look for the first large oak, I guess. I don't think we should go too far at night since the visibility isn't good. We don't want one of the horses to trip."

"Or to run into anything unfriendly."

"Yeah we've had a few of those already."

As they made their way through the city, they could scarcely hear the sounds of the men they left behind. The rest of the city was as still and quiet as an empty field. There was a brisk breeze blowing that rattled an occasional shop sign or flag. The fading lights inside the buildings were unaccompanied by any sounds from within. Neither one of them spoke about what might be inside. They had heard the terrible deaths taking place, and did not want to imagine what was left behind.

They exited the northern end of the city and made their way to the trail through the forest. It was wide enough for them to ride side by side easily, and the tree canopy left enough room for the moonlight to guide them. The woods were damp and cold, and as they travelled along they began to feel the bite of the fall night on their skin. After a couple of hours, they saw the end of the tree line ahead of them and were relieved to be escaping its chilly grip. As they emerged from the woods, they entered a large meadow filled with grass and patches of fading wild flowers. A couple of hundred feet ahead, they spied a large oak with an enormous canopy.

"It looks as if we found our room for the night," Aurora said.

"And the neighborhood looks nice and quiet."

"No pesky neighbors. That sounds good to me," Aurora said with a smile.

As they approached the tree, they dismounted so they could easily walk under the branches. Stepping under the canopy, they felt warm air wash over them. They looked at each other with a smile.

"This beats sleeping out in the cold in a tent any day," David said.

"Look over here. There's a pool of water bubbling up from the ground."

They walked over to see some rocks with water springing up from between them, cascading down into the grass where a small pool of water had collected.

"God is good," David said, "I'll tie the horses over here so they can drink and graze, and we can fill our canteens in the morning before we head out. Where does it look most comfortable to sleep to you?"

Aurora walked around to the north side of the tree and said, "Here is a nice big mossy area that should be softer than the rest."

"Great. I'm ready for some sleep. How about you?"

"Definitely. This has been a long day, and I'm sure we're in for some long days to come."

David began unsaddling the horses as Aurora unpacked the blankets and bedroll. As soon as the horses were tied up and their bedding was in place, they took off their boots and traveling coats and laid down. David was lying on his back with Aurora on his right side, her shoulder tucked up under his arm, and her head on his chest. The moss was indeed soft, and lying there, they could see the stars off in the distance, peering at them under the branches. The canopy of the tree was thick like a thatched roof suspended in the air.

"Hmm, I could lie here forever," Aurora said.

"So could I," David said, "It would be nice someday, when all this is over, to go camping together when we won't have anywhere to go."

"It's a date. I love being outdoors."

"I know some great places we can go with beautiful lakes, spectacular sunsets, canoeing down the rapids, and hiking in the mountains. You'd love it."

"It sounds as if we might need some rest first."

David laughed and said, "I guess you're right. Perhaps we should take a vacation when we get back."

"What's a vacation?"

"Oh, a vacation is when you go somewhere and relax, like maybe stay at a beach or something. You don't cook, you eat out, and people come and clean your room. We could sit and do nothing all day or anything you like," David said a little weakly, not having gone on a vacation like that before.

"That sounds like a honeymoon," Aurora said shifting a little against him.

"Yes it does. Would you like that?" David asked tentatively.

Aurora squeezed him and said, "Yes I would. I've never gone anywhere, and just done nothing. I would love for us to have time together with nothing to do. I want to learn everything about you."

"I want to learn everything about you too, although I have to warn you, I'm not all that interesting, so I hope you won't be disappointed."

"Never."

They sat there quietly for a few moments. David noticed Aurora was still, and her breathing had slowed. She had drifted off to sleep. He smiled to himself, relishing the fact that this woman who was so strong and confident could find rest in his arms. It made him feel good about himself to know that she admired him as much as he admired her. He would do anything for her, and he knew that when the time came, the only sacrifice he was willing to make was his own life. He would never sacrifice her life for his, no matter what she said or did. He just prayed that there was a way they could have a future together. He thought about them having a real wedding, and how exquisite she would look in her gown, and with that image in his mind, he drifted off to sleep as well.

David awoke to Aurora stirring slightly in his arms. The sun was low in the sky and washed in under the tree canopy, signaling the start of another day. He was stiff from lying in the same position all night, but feeling Aurora still pressed up against him, he pushed the idea of moving out of his mind. He could see the horses out of the corner of his eye, and all was quiet. There was no rush to disturb her, and he enjoyed the feel of her next to him.

Lying there admiring her, breathing in her fresh outdoors scent, his thoughts finally pulled him back to the task at hand. Just as he was accepting that he would have to wake her, as if on cue, she turned up to look at him.

He said, "good morning," in a soft voice.

She gave him a small smile, "Good morning. I was trying to be still in case you were asleep."

"I was doing the same thing. Did you sleep well?" David asked as she sat up.

"Like a baby, and you?" she asked as she sat up too.

"One minute I was lying here thinking about... you," he said a little sheepishly, "then the next I was awake, and it was morning."

Aurora smiled, and asked, "How about something to eat? I'm starving."

"Sounds great." David said, "I'll fill our canteens." He got up and grabbed the canteens, taking them to the small pool on the other side of the tree. Then called out, "don't go crazy cooking a big fancy meal over there. I suppose we should try to cover as much ground during the day as we can."

"I hope you don't consider dried biscuits and dried meat fancy," Aurora laughed.

As David came back around to her, he said, "You really didn't have to go to so much trouble."

"Just don't think I'm going to slave over a meal like this all the time for you. I don't want you to get spoiled," Aurora gave him a sly grin.

"I wouldn't dream of it. I'll cook next time," David chuckled.

They sat down and ate the little bit that Aurora had rationed for them. Neither of them complained that it wasn't much. The unspoken truth was, in the end, it may not matter one way or the other. This may well be a one-way trip for the two of them, and how full their bellies were in that final hour seemed a small matter.

They quickly packed up their gear and saddled the horses. David checked the animals' hooves for stones. He didn't want to take any chances, not knowing how long this journey would be. After topping off their water supply one last time, they each took the reins of a horse and stepped out from under the tree canopy. The cold fall air was like a slap in the face. They had forgotten, under the comfort of their shelter, what was in store for them.

"I guess I don't need any coffee to wake up now," David said.

"No, me neither. I forgot how cold it was. Thankfully the horse will be warm."

They mounted their horses and started down the trail. "Hopefully the weather holds. The cold is bad enough, but I don't look forward to being wet too."

"At least today it looks as if we'll have clear skies."

"One day at a time then."

They travelled through rolling meadows without seeing any people or animals along the way. Except for the occasional bird overhead, it seemed that the land was utterly devoid of any life. After a few hours, they came to the top of a hill, and could see ahead the remains of what was once a forest. Unlike the previous forests they had passed through, these were sparse and littered with old tree stumps violently torn apart. Clearly this had been the scene of fierce fighting years ago, and a forest was trying to rise from the ashes. Climbing steadily higher, they passed through the woods, reaching the top of a plateau that overlooked a valley. Down below them they could see the remains of a small city that had been devastated in battle. Most of the buildings had been burned, and anything left standing appeared to be on the verge of collapse.

"Do you have any idea what this place is?" David asked Aurora.

"No, but it doesn't look like anyone lives here anymore, that's for sure. Do you think we should go around it?"

"It looks like the trail goes straight through and heads out again on the north side, so we'll lose a lot of time going around. Just keep an eye out, and we'll get out of there as quickly as we can."

They headed down the trail towards the city, keeping their pace steady. They didn't want to go too fast in case they came upon anything unexpected. Once they reached the outskirts of the city, they slowed to a walk, navigating their way through the rubble. As they reached the center of the city, David suddenly stopped and held up a hand for Aurora. Then he slipped down off of his horse, signaling her to do the same. He walked over to her and whispered, "Wait here. I heard something over there." She nodded her head in agreement.

Aurora stood looking around, all her senses alert. It still amazed her that he could hear things she didn't. She always prided herself on her keen senses. Yet on more than one occasion he had helped them avert disaster when she had not known anything was amiss. She wasn't worried now, because she felt that if he had sensed something dangerous, he wouldn't have left her alone.

Standing there waiting seemed like an eternity, even though she knew it was only a few minutes. Then she heard some noise in the direction he had gone, a small scuffle, and something knocked over. She froze, intently looking for any sign or sound that would indicate what was going on. She was just about to call out to him when he appeared around the other side of the ramshackle structure.

"David, is everything all right?"

David came fully into sight, much to her relief, and had a child, maybe 8 or 10 years old, in tow. The child was filthy with long hair and torn clothes. Aurora made her way towards them.

"Everything's fine. Meet Dylan. Dylan, this is Aurora. She's my wife."

"Hi, Dylan."

Dylan looked up at David, and said, almost pleading, "You said you had some food."

"Yes I do. I have to get it out of my pack." David said.

Aurora turned back to the horse, pulled out a biscuit and piece of dried meat, and handed it to Dylan. He attacked it with a ravenous hunger that broke their hearts. David and Aurora exchanged glances, not knowing what to do. They couldn't leave him here alone, or he would starve to death. He was frail and thin, without any shoes on his feet, and this place was death.

David knelt down in front of Dylan and asked, "Dylan, do you live here by yourself?"

Dylan shook his head and said, "No, my parents, sister, and I live nearby. I only came here trying to find some food. We take turns going out, but it's getting harder and harder to find anything." He finished sadly.

"Can you take us to your parents?"

Dylan looked at him suspiciously "Why?"

"Because maybe we can help."

Dylan gave him a curious look and asked, "Why would you help us? No one helps anyone around here."

"We aren't from around here."

Considering him for a minute, he asked, "Do you have any more food?"

David smiled and said, "Yes we do."

Dylan's eyes suddenly filled with fear, asked, "You wouldn't hurt us, would you?"

David, in a kind but firm tone, said, "I promise, I wouldn't do anything to hurt you or your family."

Looking relieved, he said, "Ok, come this way."

David and Aurora followed him out the eastern side of the city to a small wooded area. The trees were few and far between, but the underbrush was thick and tall. Dylan walked over to a particularly large patch of dense shrubs, got down on the ground, and crawled in through a small opening. David and Aurora could hear hushed voices, and a tone of slight panic.

David stepped a little closer, but leaving enough room not to frighten them, said, "Hello, my name is David. I promise we're not here to hurt you. If you come out, we have some food, and we'll try to see if we can help you."

The voices fell silent; David looked at Aurora and could see the heartbreak on her face. After a few moments, he heard a slight rustling sound. Someone was crawling out from under the makeshift shelter. David stood perfectly still, making sure he had a calm, patient look on his face, when he saw an eye spying on him through the branches. Then the man slowly pushed his way out from underneath, crouching like a rabbit ready to bolt.

"Who are you?" he asked in a meek voice.

"My name is David, and this is Aurora. We are travelers passing through this way. We found your son searching for food, and thought we could help you," David said kindly.

The man's eyes, darting back and forth between them and the surrounding area, eyed them suspiciously, "Why would you help us?"

"Because the Lord has put you in our path, and He wants us to deliver you from your suffering."

The man's face, a momentary mixture of shock and disbelief, quickly returned to his cynical gaze, and he said, "You are either a fool or very brave to say such things here."

David crouched down to meet his gaze, and asked, "Either way, what does it matter? You and your family are going to starve to death here if we don't help you."

The man lowered his head and nodded, saying, "You're right." Then he turned and called out, "It's all right. Come on out."

David stood and watched as the boy, a young girl, and a woman fought their way out from under the brush. All of them looked equally disheveled, dirty, and extremely thin. Aurora pulled a biscuit and piece of dried meat out of their pack for the man, his wife, and daughter, and an extra biscuit for the boy.

The man said, "Thank you." They all ate with the same ravenous hunger the boy had displayed. David turned to Aurora and took her hand. He could see the pain on her face at this family's desperation.

The man finally spoke. "My name is Milo, this is my wife Sheila, my Daughter Sandra, and you already met my son Dylan. I appreciate the food you gave us, but I don't understand how you're going to help us. There's nothing here, and there's nowhere for us to go."

David asked, "Do you have enough strength to travel on foot for a few days? We came from Roktah, and the city has been liberated. We have friends there that will help you."

"Roktah?" The man said, "That's a weeks' journey by horse. I'm afraid that we don't have the strength to travel that far on foot."

"But we just left there yesterday," Aurora said perplexed.

"I mean no disrespect, but that's impossible. I have traveled to Roktah many times, and it's a full weeks' journey."

David and Aurora exchanged curious glances. Deciding now was not the time to argue the point. David said to the man, "Very well, I saw a cart in the village. I imagine there aren't any more horses here so we'll have to give you one of ours."

The man, with a look of incredulity said, "You would do that for us?"

"We can't leave you and your family to die. Now gather anything you need, and let's go to the village."

"There is nothing here worth taking." Milo said, and they all turned and headed back.

Once there they found the cart that David had seen, he checked to see that it was sturdy enough to make the trip. David and Aurora rearranged their gear on one horse. David was able to fashion a harness from the cart to the other horse so that they could make the journey. David went into one of the buildings and found a canvas and a leather satchel. He pulled an extra blanket they had out of their things, and gathered the family in front of him and Aurora.

"I want you to all please listen to me very carefully. If you follow my instructions exactly, the Lord will provide for you. Do you understand?"

They all looked at him, in awe of his certainty, and nodded with agreement. David went on, "follow this road south, going up and over the ridge. Once you are through the forest, you will come to a large meadow. Along the road in the meadow you will find a large oak tree. You should be able to reach it by nightfall. Pull the horse and cart under the canopy of the tree, and you will be warm and safe when you sleep tonight. There is a small spring there where you and the horse can get water, and he can graze. I have placed some food inside this satchel. Do not look inside under any circumstances, but before you eat, say a prayer to the Lord, reach inside the satchel, and break what you find in half. Leave half of the food in the satchel and remove what is in your hand. Do that each time you need more, and you will have enough for the entire journey. The Lord will provide for you if you put your faith in Him. Each night when you stop, you must find a large oak to sleep under, and you will be safe until you reach Roktah. Do you all understand?"

They all nodded in agreement. Then Sheila spoke, "We have prayed for so long for the Lord to deliver us, but we almost gave up hope. Thank you for helping us."

David smiled at her and said, "It's our privilege to help. But don't thank us, give your thanks to the Lord, for it's your faith that will deliver you the rest of the way." He put his hands on Milo and Shelia's shoulders, and said, "Lord, if I have found favor with you, please bless this family, and watch over them on their journey."

With that, the four of them climbed into the cart and headed south out of the city. David and Aurora stood watching them in silence for a few minutes. Then David turned to Aurora, "I guess we should've brought some extra horses."

Aurora laughed, "You'd probably just end up giving them away too."

David laughed, "Indeed. Now you're going to have to ride with me. Do you think you can stand it?"

Aurora said, with a sly grin, "I think that was your plan all along."

"It worked, didn't it?"

David mounted the horse and reached down, taking Aurora's hand. She pulled herself up behind him and wrapped her arms tightly around his chest. "I would have done the same thing."

"I know. Just one of the many reasons I love you," he said, as he spurred the horse on.

"What do you think about Milo saying that we're over a week away from Roktah?"

"He did say He would speed us along the way."

"Yes, I just didn't take it literally."

"I was just as surprised as you, but I'm getting used to surprises these days," David said. "I hope the next ones are as pleasant."

"So do I," Aurora said, as she rested her head on his back, holding him tight.

They headed north out of the city, passing through yet another tortured forest filled with shattered trees and devoid of any life. The further they went, the more desolate the landscape became. It had been more than an hour since they had even seen a bird overhead. Steadily the grasses were replaced with rock and dirt, only allowing small patches of life to break through. The air was getting cold and crisp as the day wore on, and as dusk approached, they were chilled to the bone.

The moon was still bright enough to light their way as they kept a watchful eye for an oak tree where they could spend the night. The lack of trees gave them a clear view for a long way. Finally off in the distance they saw the dark shape of a tree that looked much like the oak they stayed under the night before.

"I think that may be our room for tonight," he said to Aurora.

"That would be nice. I'm ready to stretch my legs."

They arrived at the tree and dismounted. Walking under the canopy, they were not disappointed. Again they felt the warmth wash over their cold and aching bodies. A small pool of water on one side and a mossy bed on the other was a welcome relief. They began setting up their camp for the night. Aurora was about to open the satchel with their remaining food in it.

"Wait!" David said, startling her. "Don't open it."

Aurora said a little surprised, "All right. I just thought we'd eat something."

"I'm sorry I startled you, but just as I told Milo and Sheila, we can't look inside the bag now. Just reach in and break what you find in half."

"I meant to ask you about hat. Why did you tell them to do that?"

"That's a long story, but the short version is that when the Son of God, Jesus, was in our world, there were several occasions when he and his disciples were facing large crowds of followers. They didn't have enough food for all of them to eat. So Jesus blessed the food and told them to take the few loaves of bread and fish they had and pass it amongst the crowd. He had each person break it in half and pass it to the next person. By doing that, they fed thousands of people, and had more left over than when they started." David said, "Of course, I can't do what He did, but by not counting the food in the satchel, we are putting our faith in the Lord to provide for us. We are on a journey of faith. What the Lord has asked us to do, we can't do on our own. It's only with Him that we can succeed, so we have to put all of our trust in Him."

She reached into the satchel and pulled out half a biscuit and handed it to David; then she pulled out half a piece of meat. Smiling, she reached in and pulled out another half of each for herself. Then said, "I do trust in the Lord."

"I know you do. I have a feeling our faith will be tested far beyond how many biscuits we have."

"If Milo is right, and we traveled a week yesterday, and we travel another week today, then we may find ourselves at Tartaros tomorrow," Aurora said darkly.

"I was thinking the same thing," David said. "Thankfully we should be able to get a good night's rest tonight. I can't begin to imagine what we'll face once we get there."

"I've heard it described as a valley of death, and that is just from those who have passed near it. No one has ever returned who entered it," Aurora said solemnly.

They sat quietly for a moment, considering the implications of that statement, "no one has ever returned." Their journey that seemed so long and daunting may be over sooner than they thought.

David finally spoke, "I guess it wouldn't be a good place for our honeymoon then?" Then he gave Aurora a small smile.

She leaned over and put her arms around him, and he pulled her close to him. They sat there under the warmth of the big oak, surrounded by the night sky with only the sound of the small spring and the horse to keep them company. Could this be their last night together? Could all their hopes and dreams for a future end tomorrow?

"If tomorrow is the end of our journey and we don't get to go home, I just want you to know that I wouldn't trade the short time we've had for a lifetime without you."

Aurora pushed away from him and looked into his eyes, "Neither would I." Then she kissed him. The feel of her soft warm lips on his sent a wave of anticipation through his entire body. Her lips gently held his as she pulled back slowly, gazing at him with a longing look. Then, looking a little shy, she said, "I still hold out hope for us to have a future together."

"Nothing else would make me happier," David said, and then they laid down on their mossy bed, holding each other close.

"Tell me about somewhere we can go when all of this is over."

"Once when I was hiking in the mountains, I found the most beautiful waterfall. The water is crystal clear, coming from the melting snow above and runs down through the rocks. It falls at least 50 feet into a small pond surrounded by trees and a grassy meadow. The water is nice and cool on a hot summer day, perfect for a refreshing swim. Then we could relax in the sunshine, warming up while we have a picnic. There isn't anyone around for miles, and in the morning the sunrise glows a brilliant orange red, so we could camp there overnight."

Aurora said in a contented voice, "That does sound nice."

"There's a stream that carries the overflow water down the side of the mountain to a large lake. On the lake is an inn, and at night after we eat, we could dance."

Sounding a little groggy now, Aurora yawned, "I can't wait until we can dance together." Then she squeezed him tightly.

"I think you would like it there; the people are very friendly, the food is good, and we can sit by the large fireplace and look out over the lake as the sun sets."

Aurora didn't say anything. She had drifted off to sleep. David closed his eyes and imagined the two of them there without a care in the world. Then he too was asleep.

TARTAROS

When they awoke the sky was grey and cold. It was an ominous reminder of what lay ahead. They ate a small meal and sat quietly next to each other. They both knew today was the day. Even though they felt apprehensive, waiting weeks to make this last leg of their journey would have been worse. They hadn't had time to contemplate what they would face, but were resigned to the fact that whatever it was would come. They couldn't change it, but soon enough it would be over one way or the other.

They gathered their things and loaded the horse. David turned to Aurora, placing his hands gently on her arms. Then taking her hands in his, he said, "I just want you to know that no matter what happens, I love you with all my heart. In case I don't get to tell you again, please don't forget that."

Aurora wrapped her arms around him and melted into his embrace. "I love you too, and I've never been so happy."

David looked at her and smiled, "Are you ready then?"

"Yes I am."

They mounted the horse and headed out. Once out from under the canopy of the tree, the air was damp and cold, but they did not hesitate. They headed north along the road towards Tartaros. They rode through another war-torn forest, and found themselves entering a desolate plain. It was littered with small rocks and very little grass. The further on they went, life seemed to have abandoned the area completely. After a couple of hours, they reached the top of a barren plateau and could see their destination.

They looked down into the valley of Tartaros. It was smaller than they expected, and they saw in the center a rough-cut rock tower. This was not something forged by the hands of men. It looked as if it was forced up through the ground, like the head of a stone arrow. Jagged and uneven, its cold black color was anything but inviting. A swampy bog wrapped around it in a perfect circle, as if it grew out from the keep. The blackened landscape was darker at the center and became slightly lighter by degrees. It was spreading out like the rings of a tree until it met the desolate plateau above. The evil inside appeared to be poisoning the ground. It was devouring all life in its path and seeping ever farther outward from *his* lair, a stain spreading across the land. The road wound its way down the bowl of the valley to the bog, where a barely distinguishable land bridge provided a path to the center. At the edge of the bog, where the road pierced the ring, stood two enormous figures, its gatekeepers.

David turned to Aurora and said "I think we should go on foot from here. We'll let the horse go free. Bringing him down there can only mean his death." She nodded her agreement and dismounted. David followed her. They grabbed their packs and weapons, leaving the bedrolls and extra supplies. David removed the bit from the horse's mouth and turned him back in the direction they came from. Then he smacked him on the hindquarter, so he trotted off. They stood watching him go for a moment, then turned to face their destination.

"It looks horrible, like death itself," Aurora said.

"Or worse. When we get down there, don't do anything unless we're attacked. We don't know what to expect, so until we have some idea, it's probably best if we don't invite any extra trouble."

"Extra trouble; how much worse could it be?" Aurora asked nervously.

"I have no idea. Here," he reached up and took off the cross his father gave him, and placed it into Aurora's hand. "Just in case we get separated, please give this to my mother if you see her and tell her to put it on."

Aurora looked at him with fear in her eyes, "What do you mean, get separated? I'm not leaving your side."

David said, "Aurora, we are bound together, and no matter what happens, don't forget that. But one thing I would guess about what is coming, is that this will be a test of our faith and our wills, not a battle of swords and arrows. Together we are stronger than we are apart, so if it were me, I would separate us to try to find a way to weaken that bond."

"It won't work," Aurora said firmly.

"No it won't. Because you are in my heart, and whether you are next to me or 100 miles away, nothing can change that. But make no mistake; *he*'ll try."

"You are in my heart too, and no matter what happens, I'll never give up."

David pulled her into one final embrace and whispered into her ear, "I love you."

She whispered back, "I love you too."

Then, holding hands, they stepped onto the road together, standing tall and confident, ready to face what lay ahead. As soon as they crossed the unseen border, the air felt thick and warm like wading through water. It was oppressive and weighed heavy on their hearts. Breathing it in left a foul taste in their mouths, like something spoiled or rotten.

***

Aurora found herself remembering horrible things. It was as if each step she took pulled another dreadful memory to the surface. She could see the faces of men she had killed, and worse yet, men who fought by her side who had died.

"Do you feel it?" she asked David softly.

"Yes. Are you all right?"

She didn't answer. As clear as could be she saw a farmhouse. They had come upon it, finding the burned remains of the family that had lived there. The woman huddled in the corner of a room, unable to escape the blaze. The man was lying on the ground in front of the building, his arm reaching out for help that never arrived.

"Aurora, are you all right?" David asked, the sound of his voice penetrating her thoughts.

"Yes. It's just that this place is horrible."

As they passed into another darker ring of earth, she saw a family that had been brutalized. The man was beaten to death, bloodied, and his arms and legs broken, splayed out on the ground at odd angles. Inside his wife was on the bed, the look of torment still on her face at what they had done to her. She was covered in so much blood that it was clear her death had taken a long time.

The closer they got, the worse it became. She remembered too many children dying in her arms, women who had been tortured mercilessly, men who had been gutted like animals. Ten long years of the horrors of war flooding her memory, each one more terrible than the last. They were suffocating her.

***

David could feel the despair too, but he was lucky. His worst memories were those times of emptiness and loneliness, and of course when he thought he had lost his parents. As his memories flashed before him, he was able to find comfort knowing his father was home and safe. His mother was alive, and if there was any chance, he was going to save her. And he had Aurora by his side. It took all his concentration, but he was able to hold his negative thoughts at bay.

***

They were getting closer now, and Aurora was struggling desperately to keep moving forward. Then it came. Suddenly it was if she were standing in her childhood home. Before her eyes she saw the men burst through the door of their house. She watched as they beat her father, broke his cheekbone, and blood splattered across the room. She watched as they killed her mother, as she lay on the floor choking to death on her own blood, her throat slit wide open. Then as her father screamed in anguish over her death, they drove the sword into his heart. She was inside the cabinet, frozen with fear. Then she was kneeling next to their lifeless bodies, her hands covered in their blood. Sobbing uncontrollably at her loss, she tried desperately to stand, but her legs wouldn't move.

The vividness of her vision caused her to sway unsteadily. She felt as if she might vomit or collapse.

"Aurora... Aurora, are you alright?" David asked. He held her by the upper arm and giving her a slight shake, stared into her eyes.

The sound of his voice seemed to pull her back enough to allow her eyes to work again. She could see him standing there, the look of concern on his face.

She struggled to speak, "My parents."

David, having fought his visions, realized what she must have seen, and somehow her pain helped to clear his mind. She needed him, and that lit a spark in him. "Aurora, it wasn't real. Look at me. Try to breathe."

She looked at him, struggling to clear her mind. She took deep breaths and started to see their surroundings. She was not at her home. She was with him in this accursed place. That was not a comfort, but it allowed her to push the memory back. It was still gnawing at the edge of her thoughts, but it allowed her to regain herself enough to speak. "It ... It was so real, I..."

"I know. I'm sorry. We need to keep moving. Can you go on?"

"I think so," and they started forward again.

As they got closer to the bog, the damp musty air carried the smell of death. In spite of it, holding hands tightly, they moved ahead. The sentries were watching them, apparently unconcerned by their presence. They reminded them of General Grog. Gigantic man-like creatures with blackened skin stretched tightly over their skulls. Arms the size of David's waist and shoulders nearing four feet wide, they were an imposing sight. Both of them had large battle-axes on long poles at the ready, and they each bore the scars of battle. When they reached them, one asked in a growl, "What do you want?"

David mustering a confident voice, said, "We're here to see *him*."

The sentry grinned like an animal eyeing its prey, and said, "You must be the two *he*'s expecting."

"I thought *he'd* be expecting us."

"Yes," the sentry said, grinning even wider.

"I see then. I suppose we shouldn't delay."

The sentry laughed a little, and said, "I wouldn't be so anxious if I were you."

The sentry turned and headed down the path towards the tower. David and Aurora followed him in silence. The other sentry walked behind them, thankfully not too close. The smell of the bog was foul enough, but these two brutes had their own putrid odor. Combined with the bog, it was almost unbearable.

Thankfully the visions had stopped, and David and Aurora were able to think more clearly now. It was little consolation because it was obvious things were only going to get worse.

The stagnant water in the bog showed no signs of life, but David was sure he saw shadows dart past here and there. He knew without a doubt that he did not want to end up in it. At the base of the tower was a cave-like opening, tall enough that the sentries could walk through upright. It was pitch black, and he was wondering how they were going to see once inside.

***

Aurora was watching David in front of her, putting all of her focus on him and trying to block out everything else around them. She had made her up mind she would see this through to the end. Although she thought if he wasn't with her, she might not be able to go on. It was one thing to be brave in battle, but this took a different kind of bravery. Walking slowly into the belly of this horrible place was terrifying. She wondered how David even managed to speak. She didn't think she could utter a clear word right now. All the awful memories and visions she had seen had sapped her strength, and she was amazed her legs were propelling her forward at all.

Arriving at the entrance the sentry called out, "Festus. They're here."

The four of them stood there waiting. The sentries were motionless, unconcerned about what their 'guests' were doing. After a few minutes, there was a faint flicker of light dancing towards them. Then in a high pitched screeching voice they heard, "I'm coming. You better be right; otherwise *he* will be most displeased."

Appearing in the entrance was a small man-like creature standing maybe four feet tall, holding a torch. He was scrawny with razor-sharp teeth and nails. He too had the same burnt and blackened skin pulled taut over his emaciated frame. His eyes were wide, and his ears came to a small point, giving him a bat-like look. As he came out from the entrance, the two sentries instinctively took a step back. David thought it was odd that this creature would intimate these two giants, so there must be more to him than meets the eye.

Festus looked up at David and asked, "Who are you?"

David said, in a voice far more confident than he felt, "I'm David and this is Aurora, We're here to see *him*."

Festus looked into his eyes for a long moment and had a curious expression on his face. Then he walked over to Aurora and looked into her eyes, and gave the smallest of grins. "Follow me," Festus said.

The three of them walked into the entrance, leaving the sentries behind. They could feel warm air floating up to meet them as they snaked their way through a passage heading down into the keep. Up ahead there was a low light marking the end of the passageway, and when they stepped out, they found themselves in a small chamber. There were two hooded and cloaked figures standing waiting for them. A couple of torches on the wall lit the chamber enough for them to make out the rough rock walls. They could see that other than its inhabitants, it was empty. There were two passageways leading out of the chamber, one to the right and one to the left.

"Take the girl and put her with the other one. Remember, *he* wants her unharmed." Then with a devilish grin, he said in a hiss, "for now."

Aurora gave David a scared look, and he gave her a small nod, telling her not to resist. The hooded figures silently led her down the passageway to the right, and Festus went on to the left. David followed him. He watched Aurora heading into the passage, and she turned her head to give him one last look. He tried giving her a small smile of encouragement, but his muscles weren't working properly. It was clear she was barely holding herself together, and he wished he could say everything would be all right, but his confidence was waning.

***

David's heart broke for her, but he knew this was not the time or the place to fight. He had no idea what they were up against. He followed Festus, travelling deeper into the keep. He imagined they were well below ground now, and the heat emanating from the direction they were heading was becoming stifling. The passageway opened up into a massive chamber littered with stalactites and stalagmites. There was a large clear area on the ground that formed a semicircle against the back wall of the room. He could see that the ground dropped off before it reached the back wall and steam rose up from the chasm. Standing there, facing the wall and rising steam, was a man.

Festus led David over towards him and stopped short of the man, keeping his gaze on the ground. David stopped too, watching him. He was wearing a dark cape, and his long blonde hair ran down past his shoulders to the middle of his back. He appeared to be well over six feet tall with broad shoulders, and he stood perfectly motionless. There were torches around the room casting a soft orange glow on the walls and floors. David realized that coming up from the fissure against the wall was the red and orange light of fire, dancing on the stone.

Looking down still, Festus said, hesitantly, "*Master*, he is here."

David stood still watching the man, his apprehension building. He was trying to remain calm so he could think clearly, but his mind was racing. For all he knew, when the man turned, he could attack David or just strike him dead on the spot. Then what would happen to Aurora?

After what seemed like an eternity, the man began to turn. David saw his face, and he was momentarily stunned. He was handsome; even regal looking. If he met him on the street, David would never have thought he could have come from here. David looked up into his eyes and saw the darkness, pitch black, a cold lifeless void of light, and then he saw the man for who *he* was. What once was a handsome face now looked old and spotted, *his* expression showing *his* contempt and loathing at the man standing before him. David could feel the hate exuding out of *him* like waves of heat.

***

Aurora was taking calming breaths, trying to keep from passing out. Her anxiety was welling up inside her, and it took all of her control to keep it in check. The memories and visions she had walking into the keep were haunting her, the weight of it all making it hard to breath. She was afraid of what was going to happen to her, but even more so she hated that they had been separated. She came here knowing she could die, but if they were standing together when it happened, it would be one thing. The thought that perhaps something would happen to him before she saw him again was like a knife twisting inside her.

They arrived at a room where there was no one standing watch, and it didn't appear to have a lock. The robed man opened it and gestured to her to enter. She walked in, and the door was shut behind her. The room was bare except for a table, two chairs, and a pile of rags on the floor. Standing there not knowing what to do, Aurora was startled when the pile of rags began to move. She stood frozen, waiting to see what was there, fingering the knife on her belt, when a woman's face peered out from under them.

***

David stood there looking *him* in the eyes unflinchingly. This refusal to be intimidated was fueling *his* anger.

He said, in a soft hissing voice, "Bow down to me."

David heard himself speak, but didn't recognize his own voice, "Never."

With a mighty swing that came with such speed and force that David never saw coming, *he* slammed a fist into David's head. The blow was so forceful it lifted him off of his feet, throwing him to the ground. David wasn't sure of time after that. He could feel hot, sticky blood on the side of his face, and his head and ear throbbed bitterly. He managed to open his eyes and saw the Dark *One*'s feet standing in front of him. Using all his will, he pushed himself up on his hands and knees, and then with a mighty effort. stood up facing *him*.

David was unsteady on his feet, but still managed to meet *his* gaze. *He* was staring into David's eyes searching for something, and a curious expression came over his face. It was clear *he* was looking for something but could not find it. Then somewhat absentmindedly, *he* waved a hand and said to Festus, "Take him to the room. Show this young man the price of disobedience."

Festus, still looking down, with excitement in his voice said, "Right away, Master."

David didn't resist. He knew it would be futile anyway, but he didn't want show any fear. He was afraid. He knew that whatever this room was would be a torment he could not imagine, but that was not what frightened him. He was afraid for Aurora, and if he gave in, he knew she would be next.

***

Aurora knelt down to see the woman who was crawling out from under her makeshift blanket and asked her, "Are you all right?"

The woman said, "As good as can be expected. I never thought I'd see anyone else here." Then she turned to face Aurora, and a look of surprise came over her face. "I know you. I saw you a few weeks ago on my journey here. You were hiding from the troops."

"Dear God, you're David's mother."

David's mother looked at her with a mixture of shock and concern. "How did you know I have a son named David?"

"He came here with me. He gave me this to give you." She pulled out the cross necklace and handed it to her.

David's mother let out a horrible wail of pain. "Oh no, what's he doing here? Please, no, it can't be true." Then she began to sob.

Aurora put an arm around her and said, "Come sit with me, and I'll tell you."

His mother, sobbing, followed Aurora's instruction without knowing what she was doing. As soon as she sat in the chair, she asked, "Why, why would he come here? Are we all dead? Did he die too?"

Aurora, remembering what David said, put the cross around his mother's neck and said, "No, we aren't dead. David's here to fulfill a prophecy."

"So it's true?" David's mother said as her sobs started to slow. "I always hoped my husband was wrong about it."

"You mean Gabe?"

David's mother blinked. Hearing his name seemed to rally her. "Yes, did David tell you about him?"

Aurora smiled at her, happy to see her calming down, and said, "I met him. He is the one who gave us these crosses to wear for protection." Somehow his mother's distress had helped her rally her strength and set aside her own fears for the moment.

"Dear God! Gabe's alive!"

"Yes, he is. It's a long story, but he was being held by an evil spirit, and David rescued him." Aurora said, "How about if I tell you the story from the beginning. By the way, I'm Aurora."

"Oh yes, I'm Ruth. I've been gone so long and expecting to die every day since they took me. When they brought me here, I thought it was the end, I ... "she froze for a moment "Aurora, is it really you? They always thought you were the one. Forgive me my manners. I'm so happy to meet you."

"Don't worry about it. I'm so glad that we found you." Aurora was also relieved to have company. The waiting was going to be the hardest part, and being alone with her thoughts might be too much. Aurora pulled the second chair around so she could sit across from Ruth, and began to tell her first what she knew about the day of the accident, then everything else that had happened.

In spite of their predicament, Ruth smiled when she heard of her son's bravery in saving his father. She was relieved to know Gabe was going to be ok. She watched Aurora, how she spoke of her son with such admiration, and it raised her spirits to see how much Aurora cared for him.

Aurora left out the last part of the prophecy, just as David had at times, to spare her more concern than she already had. She also failed to mention that the two of them had been married, feeling that was something David should tell her.

When Aurora finished telling her story, Ruth said, "You love him, don't you?"

Aurora, even in this dark and horrible place, couldn't help but smile when she said, "Yes, I do."

"When he was a young boy he used to talk about you. His face would always light up when he told us he had seen you. Sometimes I would see him outside staring off at nothing, and I knew he was sitting there just hoping for a glimpse of you. I always knew when he had one of his visions, because he would walk around for hours with a special smile on his face."

***

Festus, positively giddy now, showed David the room, extending an arm to indicate he should enter. David walked in and saw it was empty. A single torch on the wall cast a dim light. He was about to turn to look at Festus when he was struck from behind. The blow to his upper back was so brutal that it knocked the wind out of him, and he dropped to his knees.

David could hear Festus chuckle with enjoyment as the whoosh of the staff hit him hard again and drove him face down on the floor. Festus knelt down next to David and said, "That was just a tiny taste of what is to come." Then he took one of his long sharp nails and drove it into David's side. This time it was not the force of the blow, but a searing pain that ran through his entire body, causing him to let out a scream of agony. It felt as if he was on fire. His skin burned over every inch of him. Worse yet, he experienced the same torment as when he pulled the spirit trying to kill his father into himself, only a hundred times stronger. His soul was on fire too, and it was a blinding, burning pain, far beyond anything he could have imagined.

He heard Festus laughing and felt himself falling, then landed on a cold hard slab of stone. The impact knocked the breath out of him and sent his head spinning wildly. He could barely see as he lay there trying to catch a breath. Then they came.

***

The two women sat there, the panic in them having eased. Somehow they felt there was hope, even though there was no reason for it. "Do you have any idea of what's going to happen?" Ruth asked Aurora.

"No. David always seemed to know what to do, but even he said he didn't know what to expect once we arrived. I'm so frightened for him."

Ruth put an arm around her this time, and said, "After these six long years, I thought I would never see my son again. I thought my husband was surely dead, and now anything seems possible. I'm afraid too. We're in the foulest place in the world, but there's still hope."

Aurora absentmindedly rubbed the cross between her fingers. "I do have hope, and I'm not worried for myself. I only want to know that he's all right."

***

He wasn't sure how many there were, but they were foul creatures. Black as pitch, carrying the rancid smell of death, they made a sucking sound with each horrible rattling breath they took. David couldn't see what they were doing until he saw the flash of steel. He suddenly realized he was naked, and had no idea how it happened, but he did not have time to ponder it. It seemed that Festus's touch had sent him from the room into the bowels of the *Dark One*'s kingdom, and he had no power here. He was unable to move, and felt the first blade pierce his skin. He let out a scream of utter torment as he felt the blade moving down the length of him, peeling away his skin in its wake. Shaking with the pain of it, he gasped for breath until one of the beasts poured something onto the wound. The burning of his raw flesh released another wave of agony worse than the first. David screamed and cried shamelessly. There was no escape, he could not move; he could only suffer.

Again and again they tortured him, only pausing long enough for him to stop screaming, filling him with the false hope that it would end. On and on it went. Time had no meaning. His entire existence had become an endless scream. He couldn't think anymore. He could only endure it.

***

Aurora and Ruth had been doing their best to keep each other company, but after some time there was little to say. The hours stretched out, and eventually they managed some sleep. Time had become elusive. There was no sunlight, only the dim flickering of the candles.

Their keepers brought a meal of something indiscernible in a bowl. They ate in silence as their thoughts eroded their confidence. Periodically Aurora paced the room, trying to clear her head. She thought about trying to venture out, but Ruth was too weak to fight anyone, and she wouldn't leave her.

Sitting together on the makeshift bedroll, they often held hands for comfort. When they spoke, their conversation always led them back to the situation at hand, and speculation that only fueled their doubts. After so many years as a prisoner, Ruth must have adapted to the endless uncertainty. She slept often. While Ruth was asleep, Aurora's thoughts were muddy and troubling. She fought against the memories their walk into the keep had brought to the surface, tortured by them again and again. When she was able to push them away, her fears for David and what was going to happen easily took over. The time spent here was turning into constant torment, robbing her of all her strength.

They'd had several meals and slept numerous times. She had no idea if they had been there for days or even weeks. She began to feel that her life had always been in this room, and everything else was a dream. Her feeling of helplessness was consuming her, eroding her confidence. In some distant corner of her mind, she knew she was a warrior. But with every passing moment, it seemed to be slipping further away.

***

After an eternity they stopped, and David lay there feeling half dead, unable to move. Then they dragged his father before him, his feet and legs bound. They forced him to kneel, and he uttered a single word "Son". Then it began; they beat him badly. David cried shamelessly with the anguish of being unable to move. He couldn't do anything to help him. While lying there on the floor, in a pool of his own blood, one of the beasts lifted his father's head and slit his throat. David wailed in torment, and before he could catch a breath, his mother was there.

She too was bound, a look of abject terror on her face. David cried out begging "No, no", but it did not matter. Every scream of his mother's cut him like a knife. It was all too terrible to witness, and then she was dead too. David was scarcely able to breathe, his eyes burned fiercely, and when he blinked to clear them, he was staring up at Aurora.

He spluttered out a choked, "I'm sorry I failed you." Her look of horror at seeing him and the terror on her face ripped through him like hot coals. They beat her endlessly. She was strong and fought hard, which made it all the worse. He wailed and screamed uncontrollably, trapped in a nightmare that seemed like it would never end. When her lifeless body finally fell face down on the floor, her beautiful face, horribly disfigured, stared at him unmoving. The light gone in her eyes, he lay there frozen in a silent scream. He thought the pain would rip him apart into so many shards that he would cease to exist.

Once again David was lying on the hard stone floor of the little room, wracked with pain in every part of his body. He didn't know how he had returned or if he had been there for hours or for days. He was clothed again and all alone, just lying there trying to find some rest in the break from his torment. Festus hadn't asked anything; none of them had asked anything. They just unleashed endless torment on David and cackled with laughter while they did it. He wasn't sure if the death of his parents and Aurora had been real, or if it had been a warning, but the pain of seeing it burned like hot coals.

David didn't ask why. He knew it didn't matter. He knew that it was coming no matter what. All he could do was suffer it. He held onto the memory of those he loved, looking for strength in the knowledge that somehow all this would be for their protection.

While he lay there, he heard footsteps. He couldn't tell who or what it was, and didn't care. As they entered the room, he didn't even try to see who it was. He was waiting for the pain to start again and was surprised to feel a cold wet cloth on his face.

As the blood and sweat was wiped from his eyes, he could make out a face in the dim light. "Aurora, is that you?"

"Shh, rest. I will tend to you."

"Are you alright?"

"I'm fine. Just relax while I clean you up."

"What did they do to you?"

"They haven't done anything to me yet."

"Did they say anything to you?"

"David, we are lost. You need to surrender. You have to bow down to *him* to save us."

"I can't. You know I can't."

"David, your mother is here. I can only imagine what they will do to the two of us if you don't," she said urgently.

David looked at her. He couldn't find the words to say what he was thinking. The pain had left him disoriented. "I… I can't."

She leaned in close to him and whispered into his ear "If you do what *he* asks, we can be together," she said in a husky voice as her hand ran down his chest to his stomach. She started to kiss him on his neck. "Wouldn't you like for us to be free?" Her hand was moving under his belt. "We could have whatever we want." Then she kissed him on the lips hard. Immediately he knew it wasn't her.

Suddenly he found some strength and pushed her off him. "Who are you?" he demanded as he sat up.

She flashed him a wicked grin, turning Aurora's beautiful face into something evil. "You know who I am. Don't you want me?" she said, as she started running her hands up her side towards her bust, writhing slightly.

"You aren't Aurora. Get away from me."

She hissed at him, flashing pointed teeth, and suddenly he could see her for the demon she was. She jumped to her feet and ran from the room. David shook his head a little to clear it, but immediately regretted it. The small shake sent a wave of pain through him. He rolled over onto his hands and knees and vomited. He took deep breaths to steady himself and slowly began to regain control again. Pushing himself up, he was relieved to see he could stand, and that he didn't have any broken bones.

He could just make out patches of blood on the floor telling him he had some wounds, but there wasn't enough for him to worry about now. It occurred to him that he must not have actually been skinned, because there would have been a lot more blood. He stumbled a little, walking over to the wall and leaned against it, giving himself a chance to catch his breath. He felt inside his traveling coat, and was amazed to find they had not taken away his weapons. Then it occurred to him that could mean only one thing. They were not a threat to the *Dark One*. Then he found the gold dagger they recovered from Roktah. He hoped that the *Dark One* did not know it was there, and that it could be used against *him*. His strength failing him, he slid down the wall and collapsed into a heap, desperately trying to hold onto consciousness. He cried out with what little breath he had, "Lord, help me."

***

Ruth and Aurora sat there in numb silence. Their anxiety had been steadily growing, and they both jumped slightly when the door swung open. In the doorway were the two hooded figures. They moved forward, each of them holding a small piece of rope. Behind them stood Festus. He looked at them with a contemptuous grin and said, "Put out your hands."

The two of them complied, and the hooded figures began binding their wrists. "Where's David?" Aurora asked, trying to clear her thoughts.

Festus's grin grew wider, exposing his ragged teeth. "Oh, you will see him soon enough. Now come with us."

They followed Festus down a series of corridors with the hooded figures behind them. With each step, their fear began to build. Aurora was wondering where David was, and struggling against the notion that he might already be dead. Everything about this place was pressing in on her, and it took all of her resolve to keep from collapsing. Finally, they entered a large chamber with a lone man standing facing a chasm against the back wall, with steam rising up from its depths. Festus stopped and said, "Master, they are here."

The *Dark One* turned to face them, and Aurora was struck at how handsome *his* face was, but *his* wicked smile sent a chill down her spine. She could feel Ruth shiver slightly next to her.

Somehow Aurora summoned her courage and said boldly, "What do you want from us, and where's David?"

The *Dark One's* smile broadened, "How sad! You stand here before me so bravely, concerned for young David, while he is off sampling the delights of real women."

"You lie!" she shouted angrily, a sudden fire burning inside of her.

He moved closer to her and said, "Look at you. All these years of battle have stripped you of your womanhood. You might as well be a boy fighting by his side." Ruth tried to speak, but he flicked a finger and her voice was gone.

Aurora looked at the *Dark One*, hatred for *him* rising up, churning her insides, and she croaked at *him*, "You're wrong. He loves me!"

"Did he tell you he loves you?" The *Dark One* said with a slight air of mock concern.

"Yes, he did," she said, struggling to maintain her composure. She was feeling too many emotions; fear at standing before *him*, anger at *his* words, and anxiety over *him* speaking her own doubts out loud. All her awful memories, every fear and doubt she had, still floated at the edge of her thoughts. They were pressing in on her, making her easy prey for *his* taunting.

"You must have had a long journey to come here. Did he seek solace in your embrace and enjoy the pleasures of your flesh?" *He* asked.

A tear ran down her face, and she said in a small voice, "He does love me," as she recalled in the carriage that night, how David had resisted her advances. She couldn't think clearly. Her thoughts swirled uncontrollably. He had said it was because he loved her, but was it because he did not find her desirable?

"Men have long used simple platitudes and professions of love to get what they want from women. What can you offer him as a man? What do you know of men? What can you do for him that a simple woods guide cannot?" *he* asked coldly.

"But I love him," she said in barely a whisper.

"Yes, I am sure you do. You, with your calloused, blood-stained hands. How many men have you killed without regret? What do you know of love? What do you know of the tenderness of a real woman?" *he* said, enjoying her anguish.

"I know what love is. I had wonderful parents until you took them from me," she said, tears streaming down her face as she tried to muster her failing strength.

"Ah yes. Your parents whom you let suffer. You showed great love for them as you abandoned them to die for you. How could David ever trust a love like that?"

Aurora, the pain inside her welling up, threatening to choke her, said in barely a whisper "I... I... didn't have a choice."

"Of course you did. My men were looking for you. I suspected you were the one in the prophecy, and all you had to do was come with them, and your parents would still be alive," *He* said, twisting the words into her like a knife, "and yet you sacrificed them. You wouldn't even lift a finger to save your own parents."

Aurora, desperately fighting the urge to vomit, struggled to think. The weight of her life felt like an avalanche crashing in on her. She struggled to breathe. The loathing and hatred she felt for *him* was turning in on her. She had always blamed herself for her parent's death. David had helped her to forgive herself. "David told me it wasn't my fault," she said desperately.

"Of course he did. He needed you to lead him here, and couldn't stand the thought of you whining about it endlessly. Do you think he would have left his parents to the same fate?" *he* said, grinning at her torment.

Like getting slapped in the face, *his* words stung bitterly. Without hesitation David had selflessly saved his father at considerable risk, and relentlessly traveled here with the hope of saving his mother. What must he think of her? She sat frozen, hiding, while before her eyes, her parents were slaughtered. Her knees buckled, and she fell to the ground, speechless. Ruth knelt beside her, and when she reached out, Aurora pushed her away. She didn't deserve to be consoled. Her grief was an inadequate punishment, and she sobbed, gasping for breath, unable to look at *him*.

Showing no mercy, *he* said, "So child. How can he possibly love you when there are so many other women with so much more to offer?"

She barely heard him turn and walk away, consumed by her grief. She tried desperately to catch her breath. She looked around frantically, trying to find something to console her. Out of the corner of her eye, she saw David enter the chamber. She saw his bruised face and bloodstained clothes, and then she gasped. He turned and saw her too. For a split second, her heart lifted at seeing him; then her hope faded. With a look of anger and disgust on his face, he looked away to face the *Dark One*. She went numb. Was it all true? Here they were facing their final moments, and he showed no sign of concern for her or even his mother.

David stopped, standing midway between Aurora and Ruth and the *Dark One*, with his back to them. Festus stood off to David's left, looking at the scene, waiting with an expression of glee on his face. Looking past David, she saw the *Dark One's* head with *his* long blonde hair tip up to sniff the air, like a beast searching for prey. Then *he* slowly turned to face David.

"Festus thought you would have needed more rest after enjoying the pleasures my servants had to offer you. I must admit your stamina surprises me."

"Perhaps they are not as practiced as you think," David said. Aurora, her ears ringing, thought to herself that he didn't deny it. How could she have been such a fool?

The *Dark One's* face was placid, almost contented-looking, and asked David, "Are you ready to bow down to me?"

David, standing tall, said in a firm clear voice, "No."

The *Dark One* took a deep breath and Aurora could see *he* was controlling his rage. Then with a smirk *he* said, "I thought as much. That is why I have brought our guests here so that perhaps they can persuade you to change your mind."

Aurora had lost all hope. She could feel Ruth sway against her.

David said, "I won't."

With a feigned look of concern, the *Dark One* asked, "You could stand by while they are tortured and killed in front of you? You would let them endure a slow and painful death, listening to all of their screams?"

Aurora was shocked as David let out a huge laugh, then said, "You're a fool."

The *Dark One's* face contorted, and she could see *him* swell with rage, and *he* said, barely controlling his voice, "Am I?"

David said, in a voice filled with contempt, "You think I care what you do to them?"

The words hit Aurora like a slap in the face, and she saw the *Dark One's* expression turn to confusion. David was confirming everything the *Dark One* had said.

David went on, "I came here for one reason alone. I came here for power."

Aurora's head was spinning. What was he talking about? She couldn't think clearly. It was all too much.

The *Dark One* asked, confused, "power?"

David went on, "That's right, I want power. I've had a taste of it, and I want more."

Aurora's ear started to fill with a buzzing sound, as if trying to block out what he was saying. Then she saw the *Dark One* begin to smile.

"My mother, what good is she to me? The old hag has served her purpose, and I have no more use for her."

With those words, Ruth began to sob. She was leaning against Aurora to keep from falling to the ground. Aurora couldn't believe what she heard, not from David. It was one thing if he didn't really love her. Still she had never known a kinder gentler man, and here he was saying such vile things. Had she been blinded by her loneliness?

The *Dark One* was looking at David, enjoying the pain that Ruth was feeling, barely holding *his* glee back.

David went on, "and the girl is a fool. I used her to make my way here. She is a stupid child, so desperate for love; she actually thinks I care for her. Festus showed me the error of my ways. He showed me that they only hold me back. They represent weakness."

Aurora thought she was going to vomit. Everything was crashing down around her. How could she have been so wrong about him? How could she not have seen this darkness in him? She was swaying too and realized that tears were streaming down her face again. She could hardly breathe.

The *Dark One* was positively giddy, enjoying their torment. *He* asked David, "And how do I know that is true?"

David pulled out the golden dagger, "Do you know what this is?"

The *Dark One* looked at it curiously and said, "No."

David said, "This is a dagger made from the horn of Gideon." Then he spun around to his left, and slashed Festus across the throat so hard it nearly took his head off.

Aurora bent over and vomited. It was all too much for her to bear. David then turned and reached out, offering the dagger to *him*. Even the *Dark One* was surprised as he reached out and took the dagger from David.

"A token of good faith," David said. Then he turned and walked over to Aurora. David reached down and grabbed her by the hair, pulling her head up.

Aurora looked up at David. His eyes filled with rage as he looked back at her, a look that might as well have been a knife to her heart. She saw past David. The *Dark One* was licking *his* lips with anticipation, relishing her suffering.

"I will show you what I think of her." David pulled a knife out from under his coat and brought it up past her hands. He grabbed her throat with his left hand and held the knife to it in his right.

Aurora felt as if she died already. He pulled the knife across her throat. She could feel the hot blood running down her neck. The pain from the knife was nothing compared to the torment of her soul. He had shredded it like a vicious beast. He pushed her down to the floor as she instinctively reached up and grabbed her throat. The warm sticky blood on her fingers confirmed the horrible reality of what had happened. Then David reached down, grabbed her leg, and dragged her towards *him*. She didn't have any fight left in her. She didn't care what he was doing. When he stopped, she lay there in a heap, not even trying to move. She saw the *Dark One* move towards her to inspect David's handiwork. *He* was positively beaming at what *he* had just witnessed.

As the *Dark One* stepped closer, David said, "Here a gift for you."

The *Dark One* was looking at Aurora with hunger in *his* eyes, savoring her last moments of suffering. He never saw it coming. David took the other Gold dagger he had pulled from inside Aurora's boot and drove it into the *Dark One's* heart, all the way up to the hilt. For a moment, *He* did not realize what happened. Then turning to David, *he* suddenly exploded with rage. *He* let out a scream of pain that shook the walls. She could see it was all David could do to hold onto the dagger.

The shock of the scream seemed to bring her to her senses. Then she saw that David's left arm was dripping with blood. She suddenly realized that under her hands, there was no cut on her throat. She placed her hands on the floor, and found he had cut the rope that bound them. Everything snapped back into place in an instant. He had not betrayed her nor would he ever betray her. Her anger at falling for the *Dark One's* lies exploded within her and propelled her into action.

She immediately jumped to her feet. David was struggling with *him*, but she also saw the two cloaked figures making their way towards Ruth. Ruth was completely defenseless. She had to help her. In an instant, she had pulled out a knife and plunged it into the heart of one of the cloaked figures. Then she leapt towards the other one, slashing it across the throat. She reached down and cut Ruth's bindings, then turned towards David.

David was holding the dagger in his right hand while keeping the *Dark One's* right arm at bay with his left. The *Dark One* was trying to pull David's hand off the dagger while *his* scream of rage and pain continued to echo through the chamber. Aurora didn't know what to do when she saw a dark black shape start to escape from where the knife penetrated *him*. It began to envelope David's arm, and he let out a scream of pain almost equal to that of the *Dark One*.

David was pushing the *Dark One* back, but his physical strength was waning, and the blackness was moving further up his arm. Checking once to see that Ruth was safe, Aurora ran forward. She grabbed David with one hand and the *Dark One's* arm with the other, trying to pull it away from the dagger. If *his* roar was horrible before, it was nothing compared to what came next. Stalactites started to fall from the ceiling, and *he* was convulsing under their touch.

Aurora noticed a white light starting to emanate from the two of them, causing the dark shape to recede from David's arm. *He* shook more violently with the pain as they stumbled further back towards the chasm. The moment the black shape had reentered its host, there was an explosion. The force of it knocked David and Aurora back and blasted the *Dark One* against the wall. *His* lifeless body hung there suspended momentarily. *His* dead eyes stared blankly beyond them before *he* fell like a limp doll into the pit.

Ruth ran over to them and was about to speak when a violent rushing wind entered the chamber. The three of them held onto one another as the roaring wind swept over them down into the pit after *him*. They saw Festus's lifeless body fly through the air, sucked down after his master. Then the cloaked figures followed. Soon enough the sentries outside the keep, arms flailing and screaming, went sailing overhead. The three of them laid there hunkered down as the vortex raged, seemingly pulling every vile thing that had been unleashed back to where it belonged.

There was no way for them to tell how long it had lasted, but it felt like an eternity when it abruptly stopped. The three of them lay there taking large breaths to purge their lungs of the foul air when the keep began to shake.

David said weakly, "You two have to go."

Aurora said, "We aren't leaving without you."

"I don't think I can make it. You don't have much time. Mom, I'm so happy to see you again. Please go so you can find your way home."

"David, I'm overjoyed to see you again too, and I'm not going to lose you. Now get up and we'll help you get out of here."

David looked pleadingly at Aurora, and she said, "I can't leave you. Please, if you don't get up, we'll all die together."

David drew what little strength he had left and rolled onto his hands and knees. Ruth and Aurora helped him to his feet. It was extremely dark, so they had to move slowly, and the ground was shaking violently. They made it to the passageway and found themselves in pitch darkness.

"I don't know which way to go," Aurora said.

Then David, hearing a slight whisper up ahead, said, "That way." They moved as quickly as they dared, occasionally bumping into the walls. At each juncture, David heard the whisper that guided them. Finally, they saw light up ahead and quickened their pace. The ground and the walls were shaking so violently now that they had trouble keeping their footing.

The moment they stepped outside into the fresh air and light, the ominous rock tower began to sink into the ground. The bog was gone, and they moved as far away as possible until David fell to his knees. Ruth and Aurora helped him down onto his back.

Looking at his left arm, Ruth said, "It looks as if he's lost a lot of blood." She began tearing some cloth off of her dress to wrap the deep cut on his wrist that supplied the blood for his ruse to save them.

Aurora, kneeling next to him, put a hand on his chest and head and closed her eyes. She let her power flow into him, drawing as much as she possibly could. She saw some color returning to his face.

She bent down to kiss him on the forehead, and said, "Please stay with us."

David managed a small smile. "I'll do my best."

Once Ruth finished bandaging his arm, he turned to get onto his feet again. Aurora and Ruth helped him up, and they slowly made their way towards the top of the valley. The darkness of the valley floor was gone now, but it left behind a barren sandy bottom that was no help to them in their escape. After a long and tortuous climb, they finally reached the top, the three of them exhausted from the effort. They sat on the edge of the plateau, David lying on his back again to rest.

"I'm so sorry I said those horrible things to the two of you. I was standing outside the chamber and heard everything *he* was saying to you. It was the only thing I could think of to throw *him* off. I hope you can forgive me. I hope you both know that I didn't mean a single word of it." Then looking into Aurora's eyes, he added, "He was wrong about everything. I do love you."

Ruth put a hand on his forehead and gently stroked his hair. "Don't worry, my son, we understand. Just rest. I've never been more proud in my life."

Aurora looked at him tenderly, took his hand, and said, "I know. Now do as your mother says. Close your eyes. We'll watch over you."

After a moment, David smiled, then sat up. The two of them looked at him, and Aurora asked, "What're you doing?"

"Our ride's here."

They turned to see the horse they left behind come trotting over to them. He walked right up and stopped where they sat. Aurora and Ruth beamed with relief as they helped David to his feet.

"If we take it slow, I think he can carry the three of us," David said.

Aurora went to the saddlebags and pulled out their water skins. She also reached into the satchel with their food, broke the biscuits and dried meat pieces in half, pulling out some for each of them. The little bit of food and water seemed to restore some of David's strength.

David began unsaddling the horse and said, "I want to take the extra weight off; it will give us more room to ride. We can put some blankets on his back. Let's take whatever supplies we have and carry them on our backs."

Aurora said, "We don't have much, but I'll organize it."

Ruth asked, "Are you sure he can carry all three of us? I can walk."

David looked at her kindly for her offer, but said in a firm tone "Mom, when was the last time you had a decent meal? I've never seen you look so thin. The saddle weighs more than you do. We're all going to ride together, and that's final."

Ruth said, in mock disapproval, "Don't you take that tone with me, young man." Then she wrapped her arms around him in a long overdue hug.

David hugged her back, and they stood lost in the realization that they were reunited again after all this time. David leaned back to see her face, with tears of joy running down it.

"Mom, everything's going to be all right."

"I know it is… I just never thought I'd see you again."

David reached out an arm and pulled Aurora to him. She had been standing there smiling affectionately at their reunion, and welcomed his invitation. She wrapped her arms around the two of them. The three of them could have stood there for hours holding each other, but they needed to move on.

"Come on. Let's go home so we can have a proper reunion," Aurora said.

David walked over to the horse, stroked the side of his head and neck, and said, "Thank you for coming back for us." Then he put the bit back in the horse's mouth, and once securely fashioned, he pulled the reins to one side while pulling his head down. The horse, understanding the cue, knelt down so they could climb onto him.

David had his mother sit in the front, he sat in the middle, and Aurora sat behind him. When the tension on the reins was released, the horse stood, and they headed back down the road that brought them here.

"Mom, a couple of hours down the road is a large oak tree that may provide us some shelter. In the meantime, if anything should happen, stay close to Aurora and me, no matter what."

"I will."

David said playfully, "Don't you forget that either, Aurora."

Aurora gave him a squeeze "I'm not going anywhere." Sitting there holding him, everything seemed right again. All the fears and doubts the *Dark One* had brought to the surface were gone as if *he* had taken them with *him*.

They made their way back through the war-torn forest, and finally found the familiar oak tree. They climbed down from the horse and stretched their legs before approaching it. David stood there for a moment looking at it, until he realized something was different.

Aurora had the water skin in her hand and was headed towards the canopy. "Wait," David said to her. She turned, and gave him a puzzled look.

"Something's different," He said, "Do you feel it in the air?"

Aurora, her senses dulled from the day's events, shook her head. Ruth looked at him questioningly. She didn't sense anything either.

"Hold on a moment," David said, then removed the bit from the horse's mouth.

"What are you doing?" Aurora asked.

"I'm not certain yet. Mom, please hold onto my arm, and whatever you do, don't let go." He reached out for Aurora to do the same. "I could be wrong, and it may be nothing, but just to be on the safe side, let's walk under the canopy together." They nodded in agreement.

The three of them walked forward. Aurora and Ruth were holding David tightly, and as they stepped under the canopy of the tree, there was a large boom. The air cracked and sizzled, and they were enveloped in a bright light. It wasn't as violent as before, and when the light faded they found themselves standing in the meadow on their family farm where they first crossed the divide.

David immediately recognized where they were. Then with a huge sigh, he said, "We're home."

Ruth clutched him tightly, and through a choked voice said, "Dear God! I never thought I'd live to see the day!"

Aurora looked up at him, beaming. "I can't believe it. A few hours ago I thought our lives were lost, and now they're just beginning."

David, exhilarated, said, "Come on, let's get back to the house."

They made their way as quickly as possible. David was still weak and in a lot of pain from his ordeal. It took them a while to get through the path in the woods where the Jeep waited for them. He helped his mother into the car, and when he turned the key, the engine roared to life.

"I don't think I've ever been happier to hear that sound," David said.

They headed back down the road to the house, and no sooner had he stopped the car than his father, Molly, and Michael burst through the front door, followed by Rusty, barking wildly. His mother pushed the door open and shouted "Gabe!"

Gabe shouted, "Dear God, Ruth! Is that really you?"

He rushed over to her door, and she jumped into his arms. David and Aurora climbed out of the car, walking over to see the two of them crying shamelessly with joy, kissing each other. They were holding onto each other tightly as if they were the only two people in the world. David put his arm around Aurora and pulled her close. They were speechless at the wonderful sight. Rusty was barking, wagging his whole hindquarters. David reached down and rubbed him behind the ears.

Molly went over to Ruth and Gabe, and Michael walked over to David and Aurora. Even he was choked up as he said, "I have no words to describe how happy I am to see all of you."

David said, "You have no idea how happy we are to be here. If you'd asked me this morning, I wouldn't have thought we were going to make it back."

"Then you must tell us all about it."

"First Michael, I want to thank you for staying here to look after my father. I can't tell you how much that means to me."

"Dear boy, it was a privilege, and besides we had a grand time. He's quite the story teller."

David chuckled, "Yes, he is."

Suddenly Gabe yanked David into a hug. "My boy, I'm so proud of you."

"Ouch! Thanks Dad."

Then Gabe let go of him and grabbed Aurora, who blushed a deep scarlet. "Dear girl, oh thank you for bringing my son and wife home to me. I'm so glad you're all right too."

Aurora, startled by the unexpected affection, said, "oh... uh.... Well you're welcome." She looked at David who was smiling at her, and then squeezed Gabe tightly, suddenly overwhelmed with emotion.

"Please tell me you'll stay with us for a while."

Aurora looked at David, pleading for help. David put his hand on his father's shoulder and said, "Dad, Aurora, and I are married."

Gabe broke away from Aurora's embrace and said, "What!"

Aurora suddenly went ashen-faced at the tone of displeasure in his voice.

Gabe exclaimed, "You got married! And didn't invite me! I won't hear of it!!"

David started to laugh. After a second, Aurora realizing what he was saying, laughed with them.

"Now that you mention it, if it's all right with you, Aurora, I'd like us to have a proper wedding."

Aurora turned hugged David tightly, and said, "Oh yes! I'd love that."

Molly screeched, "A wedding! Oh how wonderful!"

Gabe said, "On one condition. I get to give the bride away."

Aurora said, "That would be splendid."

Ruth said, "Gabe let's get them inside. David has a wound that needs to be tended, and I don't think I can handle any more excitement standing up."

Gabe put an arm around his wife and said, "Of course. Are you hungry?"

She smiled broadly, "We're all famished."

HOME

They made their way into the house and went straight to the kitchen. The prospect of a good meal was exciting, to say the least. Gabe immediately began getting things out of the refrigerator and piling food in front of them. Michael redressed David's arm under Molly's close supervision. After a week of very little to eat, David and Aurora almost didn't know what to do. Ruth had endured years getting barely enough to survive, so all she could handle were small bites.

After they had a few morsels, David asked, "Mom, what did they do to you all those years?" He had not wanted to imagine it, but needed to know. If it was horrible, he wanted to get it over with.

Ruth gave him a sad smile, "Thankfully nothing more than hold me prisoner in unpleasant conditions. I heard them say from time to time that *he* wanted me unharmed. That was the only thing that spared me the brutal treatment that I heard many of the other prisoners get." She lowered her eyes, trying to push the memories away.

"I'm sorry, Mom. I didn't mean to bring up painful memories."

"It's all right. I'm just glad it's all over." She paused a moment, then in a firm voice said, "Now what I want is to hear all about what happened to the two of you. Every detail of it, so don't leave anything out."

"Yes Mom," David replied and smiled.

Gabe said, "Yes, and start at the very beginning. I want to hear it again. You'll like it, Ruthie."

Ruth flashed Gabe a grin when he called her Ruthie. He was the only one who ever called her that.

Michael said, "Now you don't have to embellish it like your father. I'm sure it's a good story all on its own."

Gabe said, "What, me embellish?"

Ruth said, "Only when you're speaking, dear." And they all laughed.

They sat for hours recounting every detail of their journey. When they told them about their marriage ceremony, Molly said, "That just won't do. We'll have to have a proper wedding to welcome this wonderful young woman to our family." Aurora smiled brightly.

When they recounted their final battle, David said, "I lost track of the second dagger."

Aurora reached down to her boot, and pulled out the gold dagger, placing it on the table. "Do you mean this one?" she asked with a smile.

David looked at her with admiration. "Just another reason I love you."

Aurora smiled and said, "*He* dropped it when you stabbed *him*, and when we were blasted back before *he* fell into the chasm, I landed next to it. You have become fond of pulling knives out of my boot, so I thought I'd better put it back."

Gabe laughed, "The two of you make quite a pair I must say." Looking at the fatigue showing on their faces, he said, "I think we should let you get some sleep though. You all look like you desperately need it. And tomorrow we have to start planning a wedding!"

Molly said, "Oh that sounds wonderful."

David turned to Michael. "Will you stay for the wedding?"

"I wouldn't miss it."

Gabe said, "Good, we can talk about it all tomorrow. Michael is staying in the guest room. He's been a devoted friend and comfort. Now you three need to go to bed."

David said, "That sounds like a great idea. I'm exhausted."

Gabe said, "Come on Ruthie, I'll tuck you in."

Ruth turned to her son and gave him a kiss on the cheek, and a hug. "Good night my son, I love you so much. Goodnight, dear Aurora. I'm truly looking forward to spending more time together."

They all said goodnight to Ruth.

Gabe turned to them, "I'll be back in a little bit to clean up."

Molly replied "Don't worry, Gabe, I'll look after it."

Gabe gave her a look and said, "I'll be back. Ruth needs her sleep, not to have me talk her ear off." And they headed out of the room.

Molly and Michael stood up and started clearing the table. David said, "I'll give you a hand." As he stood up, he staggered a bit and had to lean on the table for support.

Aurora jumped to her feet to help him. "Are you all right?"

"Yeah. I guess I just sat too long. I'm still pretty sore from my visit with Festus."

Michael said, "We need to get you to bed. Let me help."

David straightened up and said, "Thank you, Michael. I think I can make it."

Molly placed a hand on him, and closing her eyes said, "Yes, he needs some rest."

Aurora, putting his arm around her shoulder, said, "Come on. Let's get you to bed."

Michael followed them to the living room just in case. Seeing they were going to make it, he said, "Good night, you two. Come get me if you need anything."

"Thank you Michael, good night."

When they entered the hallway, David stopped, and Aurora asked, "What is it?"

"I just realized… Since we haven't officially gotten married in "my" world, should I sleep on the couch, so you can have my room?"

Aurora pulled him forward and said, "Don't be stupid. I'm not leaving you alone tonight, and it isn't like we haven't been spending the night together."

"All right, I was just checking."

"I know. Now shut up and get in there."

David chuckled, "ok… ok."

David went in to wash up, and then lay down on the bed. Then Aurora went in to wash up, and when she came back, she pulled off his boots.

"Thank you."

Aurora pulled off her boots and lay down next to him, putting her arm around him. She reached up and kissed him on the cheek. "You're welcome. Now get some rest, and I'll see you in the morning."

David groggily said, "Good night. I love you Aurora."

Aurora said, "I love you too. Sleep well."

They were both asleep in a matter of moments. Again David and Aurora found themselves standing in the light. They could feel the warmth wash over them as the wave of sound approached from the distance.

"You have done well, and I am pleased with you. Your willingness to sacrifice everything has restored your houses. You honor me with your plans to marry, and I will bless you."

David said, "Thank you Lord. Has *he* been defeated?"

"No. You vanquished *him* from one world, and now *he* makes plans to corrupt the other."

Aurora asked, "Lord, what do we need to do?"

"I have given you each other in marriage. Honor me with your love for one another, and at the appointed time I will reveal my plans to you."

David said, "We will, Lord."

They felt His presence receding, and suddenly found themselves awake in bed with sunlight flooding the room.

Aurora rolled onto her back and said, "I guess we have more work to do."

"Yes, but not until after we get married."

Aurora rolled back and kissed his cheek. "Yes indeed. We aren't going to have to wait long, are we?"

"Not a chance. Besides, Aunt Molly is so excited that she may have gotten everything ready last night."

"I knew I liked her." Then she got up from the bed and asked, "How are you feeling this morning?"

David sat up and said, "Good. No more aches and pains." He felt his arm under the bandage, and noticed it didn't hurt at all. Then peeling the bandage back, he saw his arm was fully healed. "Look at that."

Aurora looked at his arm and said with a smile, "It's a good thing too. I don't want you to have any excuses not to dance at our wedding."

"I wouldn't dream of it." Aurora turned and headed to the bathroom. "If you want to take a shower, there should be towels and soap in there."

"That sounds like a grand idea," Aurora said, as she headed into the bath.

David was lying there considering what he had been told. What would they face next? He thought it was naïve of him to think they would defeat the *Dark One*. They vanquished *him* from that world, and now *he* was trying to corrupt this world. That was a worrisome prospect. He couldn't very well run around brandishing a sword here too easily.

Then he remembered that all would be revealed at the appropriate time. He wasn't going to waste whatever time they had between now and then worrying about what was to come. He was going to marry the woman he loved, and enjoy every moment they had together. Just then the bathroom door opened, and Aurora stuck her head out.

"David, I'm not sure how to turn the shower on," she said, a little embarrassed.

David hopped up, smiling, and said, "I'll be happy to show you."

He walked over, and Aurora stepped back out of the way to let him into the room. He went over to the shower faucet and leaned down as she watched him carefully.

"You turn this to make it warmer, this to add cold water, and then turn the one in the middle." As he turned it, the water shot out of the shower head, startling Aurora, and she laughed. "I think you know what that one does now."

Then as he stood up and turned, they were face to face in the small room. Aurora, looking into his eyes, said in a husky voice, "Thank you."

David suddenly felt extremely warm and said, "You're welcome."

Aurora placed her hand on his chest and said, "I suppose there are a lot of things you are going to have to teach me."

The gentle touch of her hand sent a tingling sensation running up his back. "I imagine you'll catch on very fast."

David leaned in towards her. He could feel her warm breath on his lips when a knock on the bedroom door startled the two of them. They looked at each other and laughed.

"I guess I'd better get the door."

"I'll come find you after I bathe."

"Coming!"

He made his way to the door, and when he pulled it open, his Dad was standing there with a big grin on his face.

"I hope I didn't wake you, but Michael told us you were a bit under the weather last night, and I wanted to make sure you were ok."

David held out his arm, "right as rain."

"How did you do that?"

"Come on, I'll tell you all about it. Aurora's taking a shower. I thought I'd give her some privacy."

Gabe put his arm around him and said, "Sure, come on. You must be hungry too. By the way, you could use a shower as well."

"Thanks Dad. Believe me, I'm well aware of that."

"Only a true friend will tell you that. You don't want to scare off that young lady, now do you?"

"No, I don't."

They made their way into the kitchen, and as he entered the room, he saw his mother looking worlds better, sitting with Molly and Michael at the table.

"Good morning. How are you feeling today, Mom?"

"Much better. I haven't had such a good night's sleep in ages."

"Good Morning, Aunt Molly and Michael."

"I see you're looking a lot better too. I have to admit I was a little worried about you last night," Michael said.

David held out his arm for them to see. "All better now."

Molly asked, "And where is your lovely young bride-to-be?"

"Taking a shower."

Molly whispered, "You might want to do that too, dear."

"Thanks. I knew that. It was a rather eventful journey, and not a lot of amenities."

"Of course, dear. Just thinking of that young lady, you know."

"David, come sit next to me. I could use some time with my son."

"Sure Mom, and I have to tell you all what happened last night."

Gabe exclaimed, "What! Something happened after you went to bed?"

"Yes, Aurora and I had another vision."

Suddenly everyone was silent. Then after David was seated, Michael said, "Another vision? That is extraordinary."

"The Lord came to us and told us He was pleased, and that our willingness to sacrifice ourselves has restored our houses. Then He told us that we honored Him with our plan to marry, and He would bless us. He also told us that even though we vanquished the *Dark One* from that world, *he* was working on corrupting this one. We asked Him what we needed to do, and He wants us to go ahead with our plans to marry, and He will reveal his plan to us at the appointed time."

They sat staring at him, their mouths all slightly open. Even Molly was speechless.

David said a little weakly, "It isn't all that bad." Then more confidently he added, "We're going to get married, and our family is all back together. So I'm not going to worry about it. In the meantime, I'm going to enjoy every minute of the time I spend with all of you. Then when the time comes, if we're called upon to act, we'll know the Lord is with us."

Michael cleared his throat and said, "Very wise indeed."

Gabe added, "That's right." He placed his hand on Ruth's shoulder. "Spending your days worrying about what might happen only prevents you from seeing the blessings that are right in front of you." Ruth lifted her hand to his, looked up at him and smiled.

David said, "So that leaves me with two questions. Is there anything for breakfast?"

Gabe said with a big smile on his face, "You bet."

"Second. Mom, Aunt Molly, how quickly can the two of you put a wedding together?"

Molly almost burst with excitement, and Ruth said, smiling, "I'm sure with Molly's help it will take no time at all."

"Oh yes!! Ruth, it will be so much fun."

David then turned to Michael and asked, "Can you perform the ceremony?"

Michael beamed at him. "It would be my honor."

Just then Aurora came walking into the room. Her hair was slightly wet, pulled back into a ponytail, and she was wearing a large button-down shirt of David's that barely came to the middle of her thighs. David jumped up from his chair at the site of her and almost tripped on his own feet.

Stammering a little, he said, "Aurora, I didn't hear you coming. Uh, we were just going to have some breakfast, and um, talking."

Aurora, looking a little embarrassed, said meekly, "I didn't have any clean clothes to wear, so I borrowed one of your shirts."

Ruth stood up and said, "Come on. Let's get you something out of my closet before David knocks the table over."

David went scarlet, and Aurora grinned at him, enjoying the fact that she had such an effect on him. Ruth went over and put an arm around her, and said, "I have some things that should look wonderful on you."

David sat back down, and Gabe came over with some food, chuckling. "What are you laughing at, Dad?"

Michael and Molly began to laugh a little too. "She's quite a beautiful young girl, David. I thought you might end up face down on the floor there for a minute."

David, beet red now, said, "Yes she is."

Molly said, "Oh young love. It's a marvelous thing. I can only imagine how beautiful she'll be in a wedding gown."

David, regaining his composure, said, "I was thinking of taking her into the city. We could do some clothes shopping, and I could get her a dress too."

Gabe said, "That's a grand idea."

"I was hoping we could spend today here with all of you. Then the two of us could head out in the morning tomorrow. If Aunt Molly can organize things, then we could get married the day after."

"Don't you worry about me, dear. I'll have everything ready. We could have a beautiful ceremony out in the garden."

Gabe said, "All things considered, there's no point in waiting. What do you want to do after the ceremony?"

"I was thinking of the Lodge, Tom's place up in the mountains. I promised Aurora that I'd show her the waterfall I found, and that we'd go dancing."

"That sounds splendid. I'll give Tom a call to see if we can't get you the honeymoon suite."

David flushed a little. "Thanks Dad."

Michael said, "It just occurred to me that Aurora isn't going to have a birth certificate, or any other identification for the marriage license. I have some friends who may be able to help us with that. Under the extraordinary circumstances, I think we need to bend the rules."

"I never thought of that, but you're right. If we have to travel somewhere by plane, it would be impossible without a driver's license or passport."

"My thinking exactly. But don't worry about it. If I need anything, I'll let you know."

"Thank you, Michael."

Just then Ruth and Aurora returned. Aurora was wearing a blue one-piece dress that showed off her beautiful figure. The cross necklace hanging around her neck was on display against her bare skin. David thought she looked magnificent.

"Everyone, what do you think?" Ruth said, "She wears it better than I ever did."

Aurora beamed, and Molly said, "Oh dear, she looks lovely."

Smiling, Gabe said, "Yes, like an angel, and so do you, Ruthie." Ruth gave him a smile.

David stood slowly this time, not wanting to trip again. "You look lovely, Aurora."

Aurora, completely embarrassed now, said, "Thank you everyone. I'm not used to wearing such splendid clothes."

"Speaking of that, I was hoping if it's all right with you, we could stay here with my family, OUR family today. Then tomorrow I'd like to take you shopping for clothes and a wedding dress. Would you like that?"

Aurora stepped up and threw her arms around him, saying "I would love that."

David said, "Aunt Molly and Mom can get everything ready for our wedding by the day after tomorrow, if you don't think that's too soon."

Aurora, her eyes glistening, smiled brightly and said, "That's perfect." Then she buried her head in his shoulder.

David gently stroked the back of her head while the others busied themselves with the dishes, so as not to intrude. After a minute or two, David said, "Why don't you have some breakfast while I go get dressed."

Aurora looked up at him and said, "That sounds good."

"I'm sure Mom and Aunt Molly will have loads of questions." Turning, he said, "Dad can you fix a plate for Aurora, please?"

"It would be my pleasure."

David left to get cleaned up, and Aurora sat down to join the rest of them. Gabe brought her a large plate of food, and Molly jumped right into the topic of the wedding. Her enthusiasm was contagious and put Aurora at ease. They talked about who should come, flowers, food, and Aurora was relieved when David came back. She had never been involved in a wedding, and was overwhelmed by all the things they came up with.

Seeing Aurora was looking like she might faint, trying to take it all in, David asked, "Aurora, is there anything in particular that you want at the wedding?" Everyone else stopped talking to hear what she had to say.

"I remember going to a wedding when I was a little girl. The bride had white flowers woven into a ring that she wore on her head and a pretty white dress. I thought she looked like an angel."

"Mom, I'll take her to get the dress. Can you arrange for the flowers?"

"I'm sure Molly and I can handle that request."

"Then if it's all right with you Aurora, how about if we let Mom and Molly worry about everything else?"

Aurora, looking relieved, said, "That would be wonderful."

David gave her a knowing smile, and said, "Great. Mom, Aunt Molly, you have carte blanche. You can surprise us with the rest."

Ruth, quickly catching on, said, "I think we can manage that."

Molly said, "Oh yes, dear, you won't be disappointed."

David stood and reached out a hand to Aurora, who immediately took it, and he pulled her to her feet. "I'd love to take a walk through the garden to stretch my legs. Would you like to come?" Aurora gave him a small nod.

Gabe jumped in and said, "Great idea. It'll give your mom and Molly some time to talk, and you two a little time to decompress."

"I'll help you clean up from breakfast when we get back."

"Don't worry about it. Now go on, you two."

David and Aurora went out the back door. The cool air felt refreshing, and the bright sun on them felt warm.

"I hope you didn't mind leaving for a few minutes. I thought you looked like you could use a break."

"Oh not at all. Everyone is being so nice, but I'm just not used to all the attention, and … I have no idea about things like wedding plans." She said as her voice trailed off.

"Don't worry, neither do I."

Aurora looked at him with a concerned expression. "David, how am I going to be a good wife for you? I don't know anything about it, or anything about this world." She looked surprisingly insecure. "I have spent my whole adult life fighting, and living with soldiers, and …"

David pulled her close to him and said in a tender voice, "I don't know anything about being a husband either. We're just going to have to learn together. The life you've lived has helped make you into the extraordinary person you are, and I wouldn't change a thing about you."

She held him tightly, and they stood quietly enjoying the sunlight. After a few moments, she said, "It's so beautiful here. Is this where we'll get married?"

"I think so. Mom and Aunt Molly will probably go overboard. I can tell they really like you."

"Oh, they've been so kind to me. They make me feel so welcome. Is it going to be difficult for us to get a dress? I don't have to have something fancy."

"There's a place that sells only wedding dresses, and we'll go there tomorrow."

"They only sell wedding dresses? How can that be? The only shops I ever saw sold clothes of any kind really, although I never bought anything from a shop before."

"The city we're going to is large and many people live there, so shops tend to specialize in one thing." They began walking around the garden while they were talking.

"How big is the city?"

"There are around 500,000 people who live in and around the city."

Aurora looked at him wide-eyed. "The city must be enormous."

"It is actually a fairly small city."

"I can't even imagine it. It must be exciting."

"I normally avoid going to the city, but I'm looking forward to taking you. It'll be an adventure for us, and hopefully one without people trying to attack us."

"That would be nice for a change. Of course, then we might not know what to do."

David said with a chuckle, "You have a point. I guess if we get too bored, we could always start a fight at a tavern."

"I think I'm ready for some boring."

"That's good to hear. I was thinking after we get married we could take a trip to that place I told you about with the waterfall in the mountains. Would you like that?"

"That sounds perfect."

They walked around the house arm in arm, David telling Aurora about all the various plants in the garden, the vegetables he grew, and the fruit trees. They picked a few fresh apples to bring inside to have with lunch. Then David said, "I suppose we ought to go back and find out what Aunt Molly and Mom have planned. I would imagine by now they have the whole event sorted out."

Aurora, with a broad grin on her face, said, "I bet it'll be wonderful."

They went inside through the kitchen and found it empty. So they set the apples on the counter and headed into the living room. They found the four of them sitting around the room. Molly and Ruth were still talking about the wedding, and Gabe was telling Michael a story, animating it with wild hand gestures.

"Oh, David, I was just telling Michael about the time we were camping, and that big bear showed up."

David chuckled a little, and asked, "Has it grown to 10 feet tall yet, Dad?"

Michael burst out laughing, and Gabe pointed a finger at him, and said, "Are you suggesting I would exaggerate? It was one big bear."

"Yes it was."

Aurora giggled a little, and the two of them sat down to join in the conversations. They had a grand time sharing stories and talking about the wedding. Gabe managed to embarrass David a few times, and Aurora told them all about her life before the war. They went from the living room to the kitchen and back again. Life seemed as if it had gone back to normal. David couldn't have been happier. His parents were home, and it felt almost like the last six years hadn't happened. His dad was doting after his mom, who was still regaining her strength, and it wasn't long after dinner that she decided to call it a night.

"I hope you can all forgive me, but if I have any chance of keeping up with Molly tomorrow, I'm going to need some rest."

"We can get started first thing in the morning. Don't you worry, Ruth, we'll have everything sorted out in no time."

They all said their goodnights and Gabe went back with Ruth to get her settled in for the night. When he came back, David asked, "How's Mom doing, Dad?"

"She's doing well. She cried a little last night. After all that time, she thought she'd never get home again. She seemed really good today though, and I barely had her tucked in under the covers, and she was asleep."

"I don't blame her for that. I never dreamed all of us would be sitting here together again. We aren't going to stay up too late either. I want to get an early start in the morning. I'm going to take Aurora to Bob Johnson's on our way into the city."

Gabe chuckled a little, and said, "Oh, I bet she'll like that."

Molly clicked her tongue and said, "Oh, you boys, really."

Aurora asked, "What is it."

David said, "It's a surprise for you. Trust me. You'll like it."

Aurora looked at Molly questioningly, and Molly said, "He's probably right, dear. It's just not my cup of tea."

Aurora, looking pleased, said, "Considering everything tomorrow will probably be a surprise. I'd better get used to it."

"Oh Dad, I just realized, we never talked about the farm. The day I first met Aurora, I had gone into the city and paid off the loan. So we are debt free and have enough reserves for a few seasons." David said. He was thinking about all the shopping to do. He had never been one to spend much money on himself. He wanted his dad to know he had been responsible with their finances, and that he wasn't going to compromise them by spending some money the next day.

"I never worried about it. I knew you could handle things. It sounds as if you've earned a good long vacation, and now you have a good reason for one."

"Thanks Dad. Now, that has me thinking. When we get back, I guess we should consider a place of our own to live."

Aurora said, with a look of surprise, "A place of our own? Really?"

Gabe said, "Of course you two are going to need your privacy. I haven't forgotten what it was like to be young and in love."

Aurora smiled at the words 'in love'. She still couldn't believe that she could be this happy after all these years. "I haven't had a place to call home for so long I never even considered it."

"Hey, Dad, what do you think temporarily, about the cabin out on the north ridge? The road isn't too bad, so it only takes about 20 minutes to get there. It needs a little sprucing up, but just until we sort things out, it might do."

"Oh dear. You two will be all alone out there, and that place is so small, and well... it isn't very fancy, and that's putting it mildly," Molly said.

Aurora said, "It sounds perfect."

Gabe laughed, "I don't think you two could be a better fit."

Michael said, "I have to agree with you on that, Gabe. I'm calling today their pre wedding counseling. I don't have any worries about these two getting along."

Molly turned to David, "At least get her some decent curtains for it. Would you, dear?"

David chuckled, "I promise, Aunt Molly. On that note, I guess we'd better call it a night. It sounds like we have more shopping to do tomorrow."

They all stood, exchanged hugs, and said goodnight. Then David and Aurora headed back to their room. David pulled the door shut behind them, and Aurora said, "I'm going to go use the bath. Can I wear one of your shirts to sleep in?"

"Of course. Anything you want."

While she was in the bathroom, David changed into some sweatpants and a t-shirt, and thought to himself that this is the first night he hadn't slept in his clothes since they left. Aurora came out, and David went in to wash up himself. When he got out, Aurora was in bed under the cover, lying there staring up at the ceiling. David walked over and saw a tear on her cheek.

He sat down next to her, "What's wrong?"

She pulled him down to lie next to her, and put her head on his chest, holding him tightly. Then she asked, "Is all this really happening? Please tell me it isn't just a dream."

David held her, gently stroked her hair, "It is a dream, it's a dream come true for me, and it's all real."

Aurora squeezed him, "It's a dream come true for me too. Promise you'll never leave me."

"I promise, never. You're stuck with me."

"That's OK with me."

"Do you promise you'll never leave me either?"

"Never."

David, lying still, stroking her hair, could feel her breathing slow until he realized she had fallen asleep. He closed his eyes and pictured the two-room cabin he and his dad had built years ago. His mother didn't like sleeping in a tent, so he and his dad built it so she would go hiking with them. Then if they got back late, they could stay there for the night. As much as he wanted to spend time with his parents, he thought they needed time too. After all these years apart it would take some time to figure out how to be a couple again.

He thought about what they could do to make the cabin nice. What it would be like waking up in the morning, just the two of them, in a real bed, not on the floor of a carriage, and then he too drifted off to sleep.

David woke as the sun started to enter the room. It was still early, but he was looking forward to the day. Aurora was still asleep with her arm and leg wrapped around him. He smiled to himself, enjoying the way she was still holding onto him as if to make sure she didn't lose him. He carefully slipped out from under her, and made sure to make as little noise as possible in the bathroom before he left the room.

David made his way to the kitchen. He could smell the fresh coffee and hear the sounds of his parents' voices. When he entered the room, he saw his mother and father standing by the counter near the stove.

"Go sit, Ruthie. I'll fix breakfast."

"I'm feeling much better, Gabe. I need to do normal things. Now stop spoiling me or I'm getting out the frying pan."

"I see you two are getting back to normal."

Ruth and Gabe turned to see David entering the kitchen. Ruth walked over to him, arms extended for a hug.

"Good morning, David. How are you today?"

David held her tightly. He had missed his mother's hugs. "Good, Mom. It's wonderful to see you looking so much better. I missed you something fierce."

"I do feel a lot better," she shot Gabe a sideways look, "and if I'm going to get my strength back, it won't be by sitting around all day."

Gabe said kindly, "Just don't push too hard, Ruthie."

"He's right, Mom."

She looked up at her son and said, "I won't. Now please sit down. I want to hear what you have planned for today."

David gave his dad an "I guess I can't argue with her look", and Gabe shrugged his shoulders slightly, shaking his head. David grabbed a cup of coffee and sat down. Gabe joined him.

"I thought we'd go to Bob Johnson's and get some gear for Aurora, so we can take a hike up to that waterfall I found. Then I was thinking we could go into the city to the wedding store so she could get a dress."

"Don't forget to get a suit too, dear."

"Oh yeah! I guess a flannel wouldn't do, would it."

Gabe said, "Molly might have a stroke."

"Then I was thinking of taking her clothes shopping. She doesn't have anything to wear except what she borrowed from you," David said, "After that, I was thinking about having dinner on the river."

"That would be nice. I can imagine it will all be a big shock for her. Things are so different in her world."

"I was thinking the same thing, but the day we went to get dad, I was really impressed at how unflappable she is." David said, "If it gets too late, we may just stay overnight and come home first thing in the morning."

Gabe said, "Just give us a call so we don't worry about you. And don't worry about tomorrow, Molly is organizing an army to help."

"Yes, when the two of you were outside yesterday, she made a few phone calls, and the reinforcements are coming this morning."

"Don't worry about a thing, Mom. Just have a good time. The two of you can do whatever you want. All we care about is that at the end of the day, we're married. So if Aunt Molly wants circus clowns, and you want a string quartet, get them both. If you want hot dogs on paper plates, that's OK too."

"I think we can find something in between hot dogs and caviar. Neither of us ever had a daughter of our own to fawn over, so we're very excited."

"Aurora. Good morning," Gabe said cheerfully. "How are you?" Aurora, standing in the doorway looking a little sleepy, was still wearing David's shirt as a nightdress.

"Good morning," she said as she walked into the room. "It smells good in here."

David asked, "Would you like a cup of coffee?"

"Yes, that sounds good."

Ruth said, "Sit down, dear. I'm making breakfast too."

"Thank you," Aurora said, "Can I help with anything?"

"I have it under control. You just relax. It sounds like you have a big day ahead of you."

"David said he had some surprises in mind for me."

"We won't spoil it then."

David asked, "Did you sleep well?"

"Like a rock."

"Mom, did Dad tell you about my idea about us staying in the cottage on the north ridge after the wedding?"

"Oh that would be nice and cozy, but we'll have to clean it up for you first. How long do you think you are going to be gone?"

"I hadn't thought about it. A few days at least, I suppose."

Gabe said, "That'll be plenty of time. We'll go up there and get it ready for you while you're on your honeymoon."

Aurora smiled at the mention of a honeymoon, and said, "You're all being so kind to me. I just don't know what to say."

Ruth walked over to her with a plate of food, and said, "After all we've been through together, you would be part of our family even if you weren't marrying David."

Aurora smiled at her, a little glassy eyed, and said, "Thank you so much."

"Thank you. You helped bring our family back together again."

David put his arm around her and kissed her cheek. "You should eat. Mom's right, we do have a big day ahead of us," he said to change the subject for her. Aurora nodded silently and took his advice.

Ruth served all of them breakfast then sat down to join them. "I imagine Molly and Michael should be up soon."

Gabe said, "They stayed up a while talking last night. But knowing Molly, she'll want to get an early start."

"I'm going to go shower and dress before we head out. Mom, can Aurora borrow some jeans and a shirt? I was thinking that would be more comfortable than a dress, since we'll be doing a fair amount of walking."

"Of course. I'll take her back to pick some things out while you're getting dressed."

As soon as they were done eating, David headed back to his room, and Ruth and Aurora went to get her an outfit. They passed Michael and Molly on their way into the kitchen. David came back to the kitchen carrying a small bag, so he was ready to stay the night in the city. Then Aurora headed back so she could shower and dress too.

Molly was already a bundle of energy "David, I was thinking we could use the grape arbor for Michael to give you your vows. What do you think?"

"Aunt Molly, that sounds perfect, and like I told Mom earlier, whatever the two of you decide will be fine with us as long as we're married at the end of the day. So have fun." David said.

Molly said, like a giddy young girl, "Oh, we will."

It wasn't long before Aurora came back to the kitchen, dressed and ready to go. She had on the jeans and boots they had picked out, and a flattering top exposing the cross necklace Gabe had given her. She had pulled her hair back into a braid again, and David was struck by how comfortable and confident she looked.

"I'm ready when you are."

"Great! Bob's will be open by the time we get there." David said. Then he stood and turned to the others. "Thank you so much, all of you. I have my cell phone with me so if you need us, just call. I put the number over by the telephone."

They all said goodbye, and Gabe walked the two of them out to the Jeep. "You two have a great time and don't rush."

David was holding the door for Aurora as she stepped up into the car. "Thanks Dad, you have a good time too. Don't let them work too hard."

"I won't. Call me later. I love you, Son."

"I love you too, Dad."

"Keep an eye on him, Aurora. Make sure he stays out of trouble."

"I will Gabe, but that's much easier said than done."

David hopped into the driver's seat, started the car, and said, "Alright, see you later, Dad."

Then he backed down the drive while Aurora gave him a self-satisfied grin. She enjoyed the way his family made her feel welcome and at ease. She was excited about them spending the day together alone while not on a dangerous journey. "How far is it to Bob Johnson's?"

"Not far, 15 or 20 minutes. He'll probably just be opening up when we get there. I've known him as long as I can remember. He can be a little colorful, so don't be too surprised by anything he says."

Aurora chuckled a little. "We do seem to meet interesting people together."

"Yes we do."

They drove down the drive and onto the highway. They passed through a number of fields; then David turned off the main road. Off to the right was a huge square building with a tin roof and sides, and a sign out front that said 'Bob Johnson's Sporting Goods'.

"What are sporting goods?"

"Oh, you'll see."

The dusty gravel parking lot crunched under the tires of the jeep as they pulled up in front of the building. There was only one truck in front, and David knew it would be Bob's. David and his dad had been coming here for as long as he could remember. They bought all their camping, hunting, riding, and fishing gear here, as well as work clothes for the farm.

The outside was plain and unassuming, but inside it was packed from one end to the other.

David got out and went to get the door for Aurora, offering her his hand to help her step down. They walked up to the front doors to find them locked. David could see Bob standing at the counter with his back to the door. He knocked a couple of times and saw Bob turn and squint in their direction. Once he recognized David, he waved and headed their way.

Bob unlocked the door, and pulling it open, said with a big smile, "David, it's good to see you. And who is this pretty young lady?"

David said, "This is Aurora. She and I are getting married tomorrow."

Bob said, "Well, I'll be!" as they entered the building. "I almost gave up on the idea. That's terrific news. I must say, Aurora, this young man has never brought a girl here before. When he was young, he and his friends would come, and the other boys brought their girls trying to impress them, but not David. It's very nice to meet you. You must be quite special."

"Thank you. It's nice to meet you, too."

"Here, let me get the lights."

When Bob flipped the switch, Aurora froze, staring at the enormity of it. There were tents set up on display, as well as racks of fishing poles, small boats, and it went on and on. She stared out at what looked like an endless sea of equipment that could supply an army. "What is this place?"

"The best sporting goods store in the world. Bob has everything anyone needs for hunting, fishing, hiking, and a whole lot more."

"If I don't have it, you don't need it."

"Except for a wedding dress."

Bob laughed, "True. I guess I had to draw the line somewhere." Then he added in a somber tone, "Oh, it is a shame your parents aren't here to see your wedding."

"Actually Bob, they are. Both of them are home, safe and sound."

"What! When … I thought your dad was still in the hospital, and…. Well, your mom?"

"It is a long and exciting story that I'd hate to deprive my dad the opportunity to tell you. Why don't you come over tomorrow for the wedding, and I'm sure he'll enjoy giving you all the gritty details."

"For that, I might even close the store. I imagine you're right. I'm sure he'd be disappointed if he didn't get to tell me. Along with a few embellishments, I imagine. I'll be there. Now what are you two here for, the day before your wedding?"

"We're going up to Tom's place in Blue Rock after the wedding, and plan to go hiking for a few days. We need some equipment, packs, a tent, and all-weather clothes for Aurora."

"I can fix you up with all that, no problem."

"Also, Aurora lost something very important to her, and we need to get a replacement."

Aurora looked at him with a puzzled expression and asked, "What?"

David asked Bob, "Do you remember Tommy Hicks?"

"Sure, how could I forget? He won every contest we had."

"He's an amateur compared to her."

Bob raised an eyebrow and asked, "Really?"

"I've never seen anything like it. Is everything set up in the back?"

"You bet. I'll lock the door until Ernie gets here. Ooh, this is going to be fun."

"What are you talking about?"

"Come on, I'll show you."

"I'm right behind you. Don't start without me."

David and Aurora headed toward the back of the building, weaving their way through a jungle of supplies. She was still mesmerized by the sheer volume of it, never mind all the things she'd never seen before. They arrived at a wall behind a large rack of hiking boots. It was about ten feet tall and didn't even go halfway up to the ceiling. David made his way to an archway. When they stepped through, she saw a short fence made of posts dividing a large open space with targets at the far end. To her right was a rack with dozens of bows.

Aurora smiled, walked straight over to the rack, and began inspecting them. She turned to see David watching her with a big grin on his face, "My bow never made it out of the tower."

"I know. I thought you might want a new one for our trip."

Aurora lifted her hand and gently touched a long bow, running her finger down the smooth surface. Hers had been handmade and had a rough texture to it after years of use. These were like polished pieces of art to her. Bob appeared through the doorway, looking excited at the prospect of a good demonstration.

"Yes that's a nice one, but I'm thinking this one over here might be a good place to start." Bob said as he walked over to the rack and pulled down a short bow; then grabbed an arrow for her.

Aurora took it as Bob handed it to her and said, "Go ahead, try it."

Aurora walked to the fence, nocked the arrow, and pulled back on the string. As she let it fly, she turned back and said, "I like more tension on the string."

Bob stood speechless as the arrow struck a perfect bull's-eye. Stammering, he said, "Well, I can't argue with that."

David chuckled a little but didn't say anything. Bob walked over and took a long bow off the rack. "Tell me if this one's too strong for you."

Aurora held the bow for a moment looking at the camouflage finish, feeling the weight. Taking another arrow, she nocked it, took aim, and fired. She turned smiling as the arrow found the target directly next to her first shot. "I like this one much better."

Bob hooted, "I'll be! You sure are something, young lady. Let's try a few more just for fun."

David stood and watched as Bob had her try every type of bow he had, giddy as she hit the targets dead center every time. Aurora had a grand time too. David imagined that trying all these bows would be like some women trying on dresses or shoes. Aurora had never had so many choices of anything before.

Finally, Bob said, "I have never seen anything like it before. David, I knew you weren't one to exaggerate, but I thought maybe you were blinded by love. Now I know you are, but I sure can understand why."

"Thanks Bob. Aurora did you find one you like?"

"I think I still like the long bow the best."

"Let's be sure then, shall we?" David said. Then he walked over and grabbed 6 arrows. He laid each of them on the counter about 6 feet back from the fence and about 4 feet apart. Then he said, "How fast do you think you can deliver these 6?"

Aurora gave him a wicked grin and sprang into action. She was fluid motion, spinning from one arrow to the next, nocking and releasing it before the previous had even reached the target. She was standing, bow in hand, smiling broadly at David, looking calm and relaxed as the last arrow struck. All 6 of her shots were bull's-eyes.

David stood smiling back at her as Bob exploded with laughter. "You two are quite something. Oh, I'm going to be at that wedding. In fact, this bow is my wedding gift."

"Bob, you don't have to do that."

"Are you kidding me? No one else can ever do that bow justice, especially after today. I insist."

Aurora walked over and gave Bob a kiss on the cheek. "Thank you so much. That's very kind of you."

Bob was blushing now. "We'd better get you two fixed up for your trip."

"Yes, we still have a wedding dress to buy."

The three of them walked through the store, with Bob's guidance, and got Aurora some hiking boots and clothes, the camping gear; everything they would need in record time. Bob knew where every item was, and which ones would be the best. Ernie had arrived, and was standing up front when they came up to check out. He looked at Bob with a strange expression, not used to seeing him so buoyant.

"Hi Ernie," David said, "How have you been?"

"I'm doing ok. What's up with Bob?"

"Ernie, you wouldn't believe me if I told you. Help me ring them up; they need to get a move on. The bow, arrows, and quiver are on me."

Ernie, eyes wide said, "Ok, if you say so."

With the gear all loaded in the car, they said goodbye, and as David and Aurora were pulling out, Bob shouted, "I'll see you two tomorrow."

David headed back to the highway, turned to Aurora, and asked, "What'd you think of Bob?"

"Oh, what a sweet man. That was so nice of him to give me the bow."

"I have known Bob almost my whole life. I've never seen him as excited as he was watching you hit all those targets."

"I've just always been good with a bow ever since I was a little girl," Aurora said. "Thank you for taking me there. I've never seen so many things in one place or bought so much from a shop before. Actually I rarely ever bought anything from a shop."

"You're welcome. Think of today as a wedding gift. I normally don't spend much money on myself so we can afford to splurge. Now that you're living in this world, you need to be able to blend in."

"Where are we going next?"

"To get your wedding gown. They may need to alter it. We can get you fitted, and come back later to pick it up."

Aurora couldn't help but sit there smiling. She was getting a wedding dress. She hadn't had a dress of her own since she was a little girl, and now she was going to have one fitted for her. Without realizing it, she reached over and put her hand on David's arm. He looked at her and smiled, but didn't say anything, so she could be alone with her thoughts.

She sat looking out the window, gazing at the plowed fields that had yielded their crops, and were now sitting idle until spring. Her thoughts were quiet, taking in the peaceful countryside. Everything looked so neat and cared for, unlike the war-torn land they had left. Something caught her attention; she looked forward and saw the buildings of the city rising up ahead of them.

In a voice filled with awe, she asked, "Is that the city? It's enormous. I've never seen such tall buildings."

"Yes it is. Actually it isn't very large, compared to some."

"Really? I can't even imagine," she said, her voice distant as she tried to soak it all in.

As they approached the city, the traffic started to build, and David could see Aurora looking back and forth as businesses and homes began to sprout up along the highway. It was a beautiful sunny day, and there were a lot of people out, going about their daily lives. She was startled when a big rig passed them, and the Jeep swayed a little from the wind.

"I don't see any horses. Do all these people use carriages like this to get around?"

"For the most part we only use horses on the farms." David said, "It's too dangerous for them to be around all these vehicles. That's something to remember when we're walking around the city. Not all drivers are safe."

"I'll keep that in mind."

"Here's our exit. The bridal shop is just up ahead."

Aurora was looking closely to see if she could spot it. As they turned the corner, she didn't have to look hard. There on the right, on the bottom floor of a big building, she saw it. There was one window after another of female mannequins, wearing wedding gowns standing with male ones wearing suits. Above the door was a sign that said 'Rene's Wedding Boutique'. David was fortunate enough to find a parking spot in front, and pulled the car to a stop.

Aurora sat frozen, staring at the windows. David waited a few minutes, then asked, "Would you like to go inside?"

"I've never seen anything so splendid in my life. Am I really going to get one of those dresses?"

David placed a hand on her arm, and said gently, "any one you like."

"Are you going to wear clothes like that too?"

"If I don't, I think my mother and Aunt Molly will kill me," he said with a slight chuckle.

She smiled and said, "Yes, I'm ready."

David got out of the car and went around to get her. She was still looking transfixed by the displays in the windows. They walked into the shop, barely noticing the people making their way up and down the streets. The moment they entered the door, a woman came bustling over.

"Good morning. How are you today? I'm Gwen. May I help you?"

David said with a smile, "Yes, Gwen. My fiancé needs a wedding dress, and I need to get a tuxedo. We're getting married tomorrow, so is there any way we can get the alterations done today?"

"You're in luck. We're a little slow this week, so it shouldn't be a problem, but there is an express fee."

"That's fine."

Gwen smiled broadly. She worked on commission, so she was happy to see it would be an easy sale. Then she asked, "Do you have a budget?"

Aurora gave David a look of uncertainty. She had never had any money of her own, and she imagined these dresses had to be terribly expensive.

David said in a kind but firm tone, "She can have any dress she wants. I only ask that you please make sure it's ready today."

Aurora took David's arm and gave him an affectionate look. Gwen almost jumped with excitement and said, "You can count on it." Then she turned and waved to one of her coworkers, and another young lady came over.

"Yes, Gwen."

"Stephanie, this young man needs a tux and needs it altered today. Can you please help him while I take his bride back to pick out a dress?"

Aurora looked at David and asked, "Aren't you coming with me?"

"It's bad luck for the groom to see the bride in her dress before the wedding."

Aurora, looking a little concerned, said, "But I want to make sure I get one you like."

Gwen stepped in, "Don't you worry about a thing, dear. You'll be irresistible when we finish."

David smiled at her and said, "I'm sure I'll love whatever you pick out. Go and have fun. I'll be waiting for you when you're finished."

Gwen took Aurora's arm and began to lead her away. Stephanie grabbed David to do the same. For an instant, Aurora flashed a look at the young girl touching the man she loved. Then she saw the expression on his face as he watched her walk off. He only had eyes for her, and his warm, encouraging smile lifted her heart.

"So, dear, what's your name?"

"Aurora."

"Aurora, that's one nice young man you have there. What's his name?"

"David. And yes he is," she said, regaining her smile.

Gwen was an expert at reading people and noticing the little things, which is what made her so adept at her job. "Don't worry about Stephanie. She's a good girl, and besides, your David couldn't keep his eyes off of you. Every woman should be so lucky."

Aurora blushed. "I feel like the luckiest woman in the world."

Gwen, satisfied now that Aurora would not be distracted, said, "How about we get you something to drink, and start trying on some dresses?"

"That sounds nice. Thank you."

They walked into a bright white room with several mannequins wearing a variety of different styles of dresses. There was a platform surrounded by mirrors on 3 sides. It would allow someone trying on a dress, to see themselves all the way around. Across from the platform was a plush couch, and behind the couch were several doors. A young woman was in the room primping the dresses on the mannequins.

"Sharon, would you please bring Aurora here something to drink? What would you like, dear?"

"Some water would be nice, thank you."

"Water, please, Sharon."

"Do you like sparkling or regular water, Miss?" Sharon asked Aurora.

Aurora, not quite sure what sparkling water was, said, "Regular please."

Gwen led her over to the dresses and said, "Now, dear, you look at these, and tell me which ones you think you'd like best so we can find a place to start."

Aurora walked back and forth, studying each of the dresses. Some were enormous with billowing fabric, and she immediately passed them by. Others had so much lace they were too busy for her taste. She suddenly found herself standing in front of one dress made of the whitest fabric she had ever seen. It appeared to shimmer slightly as she looked at it. It had a small V neckline that would allow the cross David's father had given her to show. The sleeves were narrow with a slight flair at the end, forming a shape like a lily. The dress ran all the way to the floor with a slit running up the right side to above the knee. The way it tapered in from the shoulders to the waist was gentle and graceful. She found her hand reaching out to touch it in slow motion.

"Go ahead, dear. You can touch it," Gwen said. Aurora jumped a little. She hadn't even realized Gwen was hovering there behind her.

She touched the dress, and it was so smooth and soft she could hardly believe it. "This is magnificent. I've never seen such beautiful fabric before."

"Yes, that's a truly special dress. Not any woman could wear it, but with your figure, it would look lovely. Would you like to see more like this one?"

"No, this is the one I want."

"How about you try it on, just to make sure you don't change your mind." Gwen said, "Sharon, can you please come give me a hand with this?"

The two ladies carefully removed the dress from the mannequin, and Sharon escorted Aurora to the dressing room. "I'll go check on your young man, Dear, and come right back."

Inside the dressing room there was a screen, and Sharon said, "You can change behind here, and I'll be waiting to help get the dress on if you need it."

"You're very kind."

"Oh, it's my pleasure. I have admired that dress for a long time. I think you'll look wonderful wearing it."

Aurora quickly slipped off her clothes; then stepped into the dress. The smooth fabric caressed her skin as she pulled it up around her. After slipping her arms into the sleeves, she reached back for the zipper, but was nervous about damaging the dress. In a meek voice, she called out, "Sharon, are you still there?"

"Yes. Do you need any help?"

"I'm having a little trouble fastening the back."

Sharon immediately stepped behind the curtain with her and said, "That's no trouble. Let me help you." Sharon pulled the zipper up, drawing the loose fabric close around her.

"Thank you, I was afraid I'd damage the dress. I'm not familiar with those fasteners."

Sharon said, a little confused, "You mean zippers?"

"Is that what they're called? I have a small one on my pants, but I could see that one."

Sharon said in a kind voice, "It's all set now. Turn around and let me see you," Aurora turned to face her, and Sharon gave her a big smile. "Oh, yes. This dress was made for you. Come outside to the mirror and see for yourself."

Aurora, beaming with excitement, walked out with Sharon, who was holding the bottom of the dress off the floor for her. She made her way to the platform, trying not to look at herself yet. She was nervous about how she was going to look. She carefully climbed up onto the platform and closed her eyes, gathering her courage. Sharon primped the dress at the bottom as she had been doing with the mannequins when they walked in.

When she had stopped arranging the extra length of fabric, Sharon said, "You can open your eyes now."

Aurora stood there for a moment, taking steadying breaths, when Gwen walked into the room. "Oh my Lord!" Gwen exclaimed when she saw Aurora standing there.

Aurora held her eyes shut tightly and asked, "What's wrong? Do I look terrible?"

Gwen, in a suddenly gentle voice, said, "On the contrary. You look like an angel."

Aurora opened her eyes and looked in the mirror. She stared at herself and saw staring back at her a woman. The dress gently caressed her, showing off her figure in a way she had never seen before. She had never thought of herself as pretty, but here she was, looking elegant and like a lady. Staring at her reflection, she saw tears running down her face.

"Sharon, can you please grab some tissues? Aurora, it's all right. A lot of women cry when they put their wedding dress on for the first time."

Aurora nodded, and Sharon handed her some tissues. "Here, wipe your eyes. You don't want to stain your new dress."

Aurora nodded again as she wiped away her tears. "Do you want to try on any other dresses?"

"Oh no. I like this one. I've never had anything so beautiful to wear before."

"I just spoke to that young man of yours, and I imagine this may just be the beginning for you, dear. Sharon, would you mind asking Stella to come in so we can get her to pin it up for the adjustments?" Turning back to Aurora, she said, "We'll have our seamstress take care of your fitting."

In moments, Sharon was back with Stella. She was an older stout woman who looked a little harried. With a pin pad, chalk, and cloth measuring tape, her slight frown, glasses, and random hairs sticking out at odd places gave her a stern, no-nonsense look. She tugged here and there on the dress, stuck pins in a few places, pulled the extra fabric up off of the floor, and had Aurora put on some shoes. "That ought to do it, dear. When's your wedding?"

"They're getting married tomorrow. Stella, how quickly can you get it done? These are VIP customers." Then she winked at Aurora.

Stella said with a sigh, "You're in luck, Dear. I just finished another dress when Sharon came to get me, and since you need so few changes, I can do it right now. I should be done in a few hours."

"Perfect. Have they given you her fiancé's tux yet?"

"Oh is that his? It just came back a few minutes ago. Mary is working on it now. She should be done before me."

"Excellent. Stella you're the best."

"Yes, yes, no need to flatter me, but let's get her out of this dress so I can get started."

They hurried Aurora back to the dressing room and helped her out of the dress. She changed back into her clothes, and when she was finished, Gwen was outside the room waiting for her.

"I was thinking. Should we take a look at some shoes to match your dress?"

"Oh I suppose so. I don't have any."

"Not to worry. We have just what you need."

As they reached the door to leave, Aurora turned to Sharon, and said, "Thank you so very much for your kindness."

"You're welcome. I'll be here when you come back to check the fit."

Gwen led Aurora to another room. When they entered she could see, along one wall, beautiful glass shelves arranged against a mirrored background. The shelves displayed a dizzying number of shoes. Some with long, pointy heels, wide flat heels, open toes, closed toes, short tall, all of them looking decidedly impractical. Aurora thought that probably didn't matter since she wasn't planning on traipsing through the woods on their wedding day. She stood there speechless, having no idea where to start.

"It can be a little overwhelming, but I'll help you narrow it down, dear. Let's see, your young man isn't that much taller than you. I don't think you want a heel that's too tall. It's fall, so probably not an open toe. Do you know what size you wear dear?"

Aurora looked at her blankly, and said, "No, I don't suppose I do."

"Not to worry. I have an eye for that. Here is a pair of stockings to use while we try them on." Gwen had walked over to the wall looking at the shoes, periodically reached into a cabinet underneath and pulled out a box. Once she had 4 boxes picked out, she came back to Aurora and said, "Here we go. Let's try these on."

The first pair she pulled out had a square toe and large clunky heel; Aurora didn't even try it on before she said, "No thank you. I don't like that one."

Gwen pulled out the next pair; it had a tall, pointy heel. Aurora shook her head, wondering how anyone could stand in something like that. The third pair was better. The toe was pointed, and the heel was thicker. Aurora wasn't thrilled about it, but tried it on. The shoe was amazingly comfortable as she stood up. The leather sides came up around her foot and drew a straight line across the top, giving the appearance of a rectangle.

"What do you think of that one?"

"It is very comfortable, but I'm just not sure I like it."

"Well, I did save the best for last. I always like you to have something to compare it to."

She pulled the last pair out of the box. The toe was rounded, and the inside of the shoe matched the shape. The heel was short but wide so she wouldn't have to worry about tipping over. As she slipped it on, the soft, supple leather gently hugged the sides of her feet just above the heel line. She could just see where her toes started on the inner curve, and the inside cushion felt like standing on a silk pillow.

Aurora smiled at her and said, "Yes, these will do nicely."

Gwen smiled back, "I thought so too. Now, if you put your boots back on, we can go find your young man."

Gwen put the shoes back in the box and made some notations in a ledger. Then she stood by the doorway, smiling as Aurora came over. Aurora let out a little sigh as she and Gwen headed out into the hallway. "Is everything all right, dear?"

"Oh yes. It's just that where I come from… I've never seen such luxury. I feel guilty. I've been thinking about the many people I know who are struggling to get by."

Gwen, in a kind voice with an insight that surprised Aurora, said, "The Lord blesses us all in different ways. It's what we do with those blessings that defines who we are."

"You're right. I hadn't thought of it that way."

Gwen took her arm and led her to the front. "I hope you're happy with everything today?"

Aurora turned and gave Gwen a hug. "Oh yes, very happy. Thank you so much, Gwen."

Gwen, flustered by the sudden show of affection, said, "You're welcome. I just hope that I helped make your day a little more special."

"You have."

Up ahead they saw David waiting patiently, and the minute they came into view, he turned to face them. From across the room she saw him burst into a big smile, and she smiled broadly back at him. She felt the urge to run, but managed to contain herself.

David started walking towards her, and in a matter of moments they were face to face. He pulled her into a hug, slightly lifting her off of her feet. She held onto him tightly, totally lost in his embrace.

"I missed you."

"I missed you, too."

"Did you enjoy yourself?"

"Oh yes, Gwen and the others were just lovely."

David let go of Aurora and gave Gwen a hug too. "Thank you, Gwen, for taking good care of her."

"The two of you. If every customer that walked through theses doors was such a pleasure to deal with, my job would be a whole lot easier."

"We'll come back this afternoon to pick them up."

They turned and both said goodbye. "I realized while I was waiting for you that this was the longest we've been apart since we met."

"Except for that dreadful tower," Aurora said, suddenly quiet.

"Yes, I suppose so, but that's behind us," David said brightly as they got into the car.

Aurora gave him a small smile, "Yes, thankfully, but I feel guilty."

David asked in a concerned voice, "Why?"

"You spent lavishly on me, and all those people we left behind were struggling to survive," Aurora said softly.

"I see. I have something that might help." He reached down and started the car.

"Please don't think badly of me. I'm so excited about our wedding, and I had a wonderful time today."

"I would never think badly of you, and I understand what you're feeling. I have been very blessed in my life to live comfortably. I used to feel guilty about having more than others. Then I came to understand that it if we're good stewards of what we're given, then we're better able to help those who need it. As for all the people we left behind, the Lord is watching over them. He delivered the city into their hands so they could reclaim their food and not starve during the winter. When the spring comes, they will be ready to rebuild their lives. They have seen first-hand the Lord's love for them, and that is something that so many people in this world are blinded to. They may have more comforts here, but the people of Roktah have received a far greater gift."

"You're right. I'm being silly."

David said firmly, "No, you're not being silly. It isn't silly that you are so compassionate and caring. In fact, it's one of the things I love most about you."

"Then, in that case I won't argue with you."

"I wasn't planning on taking you here today," he said as they pulled to a stop in front of an older two-story building, "because this place isn't about me. I don't want you to get the wrong idea."

Aurora looked at him a little confused. "All right, I'll keep an open mind."

"That isn't actually what I meant. There are a lot of fine people here who work really hard. I only help in a small way."

Aurora, more confused now, said, "Ok?"

David got out of the car and made his way around to get Aurora. As she was watching him, she realized the area they were visiting wasn't nearly as nice as the place where the wedding salon was. David opened the door and helped her down from her seat.

They walked up to the doors, and Aurora noticed a small sign that said "Safe Haven". David opened the door for her, and they walked into a large room filled with people. Mostly women and children, but also a few men were all sitting at tables having lunch. They stood near the door for a minute, and then a woman from the other side of the room waved and headed toward them. Noticing her, a number of other people turned and began waving. Apparently David was well known here.

Suddenly out of nowhere a young boy came running up and launched himself at David, who picked him up in his arms. The boy couldn't have been more than five or six, and he was bubbling with excitement.

"Hi there Charlie! How are you today? Did you eat your lunch already?"

"Momma said I could come say hi," Charlie said, as David gave a woman sitting at one of the tables a wave, and she smiled and waved back.

"Charlie, I want you to meet someone very important to me. Her name is Aurora," David said, as he turned so Charlie was looking at her.

"Hello, Charlie. It's nice to meet you," Aurora said with a big smile.

Charlie, looking a little awe struck, asked David in a soft voice, "Is she an angel?"

David gave him a big smile and said, "Sometimes I think so. She and I are going to get married. What do you think about that?"

"Wow," Charlie said. "Will you still come visit me on Saturdays when you're married?"

"Of course I will."

"I missed you this Saturday. I thought you forgot. No one else had time to read to me."

"I'm sorry Charlie, but I promise I didn't forget. I was travelling, and I couldn't make it back in time. Do you forgive me?"

Charlie gave him a hug and said, "ok."

"David I'm so glad to see you." The young woman from the other side of the room had finally made her way over. "I was worried when we didn't see you Saturday."

"Sorry, Rebecca. It was unavoidable."

"He was travelling Miss Rebecca."

"That's right. Rebecca, I'd like to introduce you to Aurora. She and I are getting married tomorrow."

Rebecca, with a look of surprise and shock said, "oh… uh… that's wonderful. It's so nice to meet you. I thought he would never get married."

"It's nice to meet you too."

Rebecca then turned to David. "Now why haven't you told me about her before, David? That's just like you. He almost never talks about himself."

"We've known each other since we were children, but we only met a little over a week ago."

"Really? You are going to have to tell me the whole story whether you like it or not."

"I'll be happy to, but we won't have time today." David said, "Charlie, your mom looks as if she wants you to come back and finish your lunch. I'll come and find you before we leave, ok?"

Charlie slid down from David's arms and said, "Ok" as he ran back to his mother. David watched him as he sat down and began eating.

"Charlie was asking about you all day Saturday."

"I'm sorry. I won't be here this Saturday either, but I'll tell him before we leave."

Aurora asked, "What is this place?"

Rebecca looked at David and said, "You haven't told her."

"It just never came up." And with a nod he told her to explain.

Rebecca turned to Aurora and said, "This is a mission, so to speak. We give out free meals to the poor and homeless. Upstairs we have rooms where woman who are in trouble can come and stay with their children until they can get on their feet, like Charlie and his mom."

Aurora, starting to understand why they were there, said "Oh, that's so very kind of you."

Rebecca smiled kindly and said, "Thank you, but if it wasn't for David, there wouldn't be a mission."

Aurora, looking a little confused, said, "I don't understand."

"David is one of our largest donors. We get donations of food, clothes, and money from a lot of other people and businesses, but David helped us get started and is always here for us." The look of admiration and affection on her face was unmistakable.

Aurora, with a look of surprise on her face, said, "Really? I had no idea."

"That was the easy part. Rebecca and her staff do all the hard work."

"Don't you believe that, Aurora. He worked as hard as anyone to help get the doors open, and he comes every week to help out."

Aurora turned to David and reached up, tenderly placing a hand on his face, and said, "I should've known. He's the kindest man I've ever met." Aurora saw out of the corner of her eye, Rebecca wiping a single tear from her face, but she pretended not to notice.

"That's enough, you two." David said, even though the look of admiration on Aurora's face could have held him on that spot all day. "I'm not a saint or anything. Rebecca is the real heart of this place. It was all her idea. I only helped her get started."

Rebecca had regained herself, and said, "Typical. I've given up arguing with him about it. So what brings you here today?"

"To invite you to the wedding tomorrow, of course."

Rebecca stammered a little and said, "Tomorrow? That's such short notice."

Aurora, sensing her dilemma, said tenderly, "Yes, we'd love to have you come."

Rebecca said, flustered, "I'm not sure. I have to make sure someone can watch the place for me, and find a dress to wear." Her face was a little pale, and her eyes shone brightly.

David, picking up that something else was going on, said, "Rebecca, I'd love to have you there, but if you can't make it, I'll understand. I'm going to go say goodbye to Charlie. I'll be right back."

David walked off, leaving Rebecca and Aurora standing alone together. Aurora watched Rebecca, seeing her gazing at David sadly.

Rebecca said in a faraway voice "I'm so happy for you. David's such a wonderful man."

Aurora smiled at her and said, "Thank you. I never thought I'd meet him, and I never thought I'd find love. I'm sorry."

Rebecca asked, slightly surprised, "Sorry for what?"

Aurora said in a kind voice, "I spent most of the past 10 years of my life alone, and even when I was with people, I felt alone. I don't know anything about men or marriage, but since I met David, now I know what love is. I'm sorry because I can see that you love him, and he's marrying me."

Rebecca stood frozen, staring at Aurora until another tear ran down her cheek. She reached up, wiped it away, and asked "Is it that obvious?"

"I don't know. I just saw a reflection in your eyes of what I feel when I'm around him. I can tell you that David sees something special in you too, and if he can, then someone else will. I wouldn't have thought that before I met him, but now I'm sure of it."

Rebecca asked, a little choked up, "Do you truly think so?"

"Yes I do."

"Thank you."

Just then David returned and gave Rebecca a big hug. "We have to get going. If I don't see you at the wedding, I'll see you a week from Saturday. I'm going to stop by the bank this afternoon and make sure you have enough in the account to carry through."

David let go of Rebecca and turned to Aurora, taking her arm. Rebecca said, "Good bye. I hope you have a good time."

"Goodbye Rebecca. It was very nice meeting you."

They walked out into the bright sun and went straight to the car. Once inside, David turned to Aurora and asked, "Did Rebecca say anything? She didn't quite seem herself. I hope she's all right."

"She will be."

David looked at her with a quizzical expression on his face and asked, "What do you mean?"

Aurora looked back at the building, then turned and said, "Let's go, and I'll tell you."

David started the car, and they pulled out onto the street. Once the building was out of view, Aurora turned to him and said, "Rebecca loves you."

"I love her too. She's a wonderful person. She's so giving. She works tirelessly, helping all those people."

"I don't think you understand. She's in love with you. I don't know much about having a relationship, but I could see it in the way she looks at you."

"I think you must be mistaken. I've known her since we went to school together. We're just friends."

"Just be sensitive to her. That's all I ask."

"I will. So what did you think about the mission?"

"I feel more foolish now. I've seen time and time again how generous you are, and how you put the needs of others ahead of yours. I was just overwhelmed by everything this morning, and didn't feel as if I deserved it."

"You're not being foolish, and don't get carried away now. I'm not that special. It's just if I can help someone, I do. The Lord has given me everything I have, so I need to honor Him with what I do with it. You and Rebecca are the only people who know that I help with the mission because I don't want praise for His generosity. But that's not why I brought you there. Were the ladies at the boutique kind to you today?"

"Oh yes, very."

"Well, the money we spent there today will help to feed their families. Just as much as the money I put into the mission helps the families there too. If I hoarded the wealth I've been blessed with, what good would that do? By the same token, if I squandered it or gave it all away, I would not be able to make sure that the good work that Rebecca does can continue." David said, "To put it another way, I have been blessed with the ability to earn money, and Rebecca has been given the gift to help change or even save those people's lives. So by growing my wealth, I can do more good through people like Rebecca than I can myself."

"I didn't realize you were so wise too. How did you learn all these things?"

David laughed, "by making a lot of mistakes, and by reading the Bible, although I don't feel all that wise most of the time."

"Where are we going now?"

"Lunch, I don't know about you, but I'm starving."

"Me too. The food at the mission smelled delicious."

"We could've eaten there, but I wanted us to have some privacy. I thought we could go to a place I know on the river. The view is pretty, and the food is good."

"Privacy sounds good."

David made his way through what felt to Aurora like a maze of streets between buildings that seemed impossibly tall. It was beyond her how anyone could build something so high, and yet there was one after another. She watched the people walking the streets, completely unaffected by the grandeur of the place. Before she realized it, David was pulling the car up underneath one of the tallest buildings she had seen yet.

She looked at the massive stone columns holding the building up above their heads, and as large as they were, they seemed too small. She felt a little nervous contemplating what was above them. David maneuvered between rows of cars and up ramps until he found an opening. He pulled the car in and shut it off.

"Here we go. There's a restaurant on the top floor that will give us a magnificent view."

"How long will it take to climb to the top?" Aurora asked, looking a little dismayed.

"Don't worry. There's an elevator that will carry us to the top."

"Aurora gave him an 'if you say so" look that made him chuckle a little. He walked around and helped her from the car, then locked the doors. They walked across a row of cars, holding hands until they came to a glass wall that made a small room. When they went inside, he walked over to the wall and pushed the button; then he stepped back, taking her hand again.

"These are the express elevators. We can take them all the way to the top."

They heard a ding, and then the doors on the right opened. David led Aurora to the elevator, and she inspected the jamb to see where the doors went. When they used the elevators at the nursing facility she was too distracted by what was going on to pay much attention to them, but today was different. She was so absorbed that it took her a moment to realize the back of the elevator was glass, and they could see out onto the river.

She was a little surprised and said, "Oh, look out there. I can see the river."

David reached over, hit the button for the top floor, and said, "I know. Wait until you see it from the top."

The doors slid shut, and the elevator started to rise. Aurora quickly stepped back from the glass wall and bumped into David, who put an arm around her to keep her from tripping.

"Are we going to be able to see all the way up to the top?"

"Yes. I thought you'd like to get a good look at everything."

She leaned forward to look out and down as they moved quickly up the side of the building, but stayed back from the edge. "I feel as if I could fall off."

"I remember the first time I went up in this elevator. I was scared to death. I held onto my father's leg as if my life depended on it."

By the time they got to the top, Aurora had backed him up almost to the door. When the doors opened and they stepped out into the lobby, he could feel her muscles relax. They walked towards the opposite end of the lobby where a man stood behind a wooden podium. Aurora was admiring the polished stone floors of deep green and the smooth wood walls with decorative trim. Past the man at the podium, she could see into a large room, and at the far end, light was coming in from a tremendous window that she imagined looked out over the city.

When they reached the man he said, "Welcome to the Rooftop. Lunch for two?"

"Yes, please."

The man asked, "Would you like a seat by the window?"

David looked to Aurora, who gave a slight shake of the head and then he replied, "No, I think we'd prefer something away from the window today. Something quiet, where we can talk, would be nice."

"Very good, come this way, please."

Aurora gave David a slight squeeze to say thank you. She wasn't sure she could sit through an entire meal looking out the window from this high up. They stepped through the archway of the lobby into a huge room with people sitting at tables all around the perimeter. They were all very nicely dressed. Some were talking quietly, and others were laughing and joking. The atmosphere was relaxed, and Aurora didn't see one person carrying a weapon.

"Is this table acceptable, sir?"

The table was close enough to the window to see off in the distance, but far enough back to feel as though they were on steady ground. David looked to Aurora, and she nodded her approval.

"Yes, that'll be fine, thank you."

"Very good. Your server will be along shortly," the man said as he walked off.

Almost immediately a young man showed up with a pitcher, and asked, "Would you like some water?"

"Yes, please."

"And you, Sir?"

"Yes, thank you."

"I'll be right back with some bread."

David said, "Thank you," as he hurried off.

David was just about to say something when a young woman came up to the table and said, "Hello. I'm Darlene, and I'll be taking care of you today. May I get you something to drink?"

"Hello Darlene. Aurora would you like something else to drink besides water? They have tea, coffee, juices, milk, and what we call soft drinks, which are sweet."

"I'd like some tea, if it isn't too much trouble."

Darlene said, "No, that isn't any trouble."

"I'll have some tea too, please. Do you have any specials today?"

"Yes sir. We have 2 soups today, French onion and vegetable beef, we have broiled cod fish with a lemon butter sauce served over rice, a bacon bleu cheese burger, and shrimp with tomato basil served over angel hair."

"Aurora, would you like some soup while we're deciding on our meal?"

"That sounds good. I like onion soup."

"Darlene, could we have 2 cups of the French onion soup while we look over the menu?"

"I'll get them right away."

"Thank you."

As Darlene walked off, Aurora leaned in to David and said, "I really don't know what those other dishes she said were."

"I didn't expect you to. That's why I thought soup might be good. This way we can look at the menu together." Then David stood up.

Aurora looked up questioningly as he grabbed a chair and pulled it around next to her. The table was too narrow for them to sit side by side, so David sat caddy corner and leaned in, picking up the menu. He held the menu up and opened it for them to look at together.

Aurora smiled at him and said, "I like this better." Then she put her arm on his back and rested her head against his shoulder.

"Hmm, I like it better too. So what are you in the mood to eat? They have fish, beef, chicken, pasta, and salads… "

"I don't know," she said in a husky voice. "Why don't you tell me what sounds good?" Then she slid her hand up his neck, running her fingers under his hair.

"Uh… Ok."

Aurora turned and gave him a kiss on the cheek. Her lips felt full and warm, and lingered on his skin. David turned to look at her, and then leaned in as she closed her eyes. She felt his skin brush against her cheek, and he whispered in her ear, "You realize we're surrounded by people, don't you?"

At those words, Aurora sat bolt upright, her face flush, "I forgot, I just well … "

David said with a smile, "I didn't mind at all, but I'm afraid if I kiss you, I won't be able to stop."

Aurora gave him a pleased smile, "I hope so."

"Excuse me, but I have your soup." Darlene said, standing there looking at them with a little smirk of her own.

Aurora, completely red in the face, said, "Oh I'm sorry."

"Don't be. Most of the people who come in here are too stiff."

David got up and went back to his seat as Darlene set the soup cups down on the table. Then he said, "Thank you, Darlene."

"You're welcome. I'll be right back with that tea."

Aurora gave David an embarrassed little smile. Then David said, "don't worry about it; it doesn't matter to me what anyone else thinks. I love you, and I would be proud if the whole world knew it."

"I love you too, and I'm looking forward to us being alone together."

"So am I, and in one more day we'll have a real wedding ceremony, and then you'll be stuck with me forever."

"I can't wait. Perhaps you should just order something for us," she said with a grin.

David chuckled a little and said, "I can do that. I have a really nice place in mind for dinner, so I'll order us a small lunch. Do you like fish?"

"Yes I do."

"Then fish it is. After lunch, we need to stop at the bank for Rebecca, and go to a few shops to get you some more clothes. Things you can wear every day. How does that sound?"

"Ok, although I don't know how many more shops I can handle today." Aurora said then took a taste of her soup. "Mmm. This is good. Horatio could learn a thing or two."

David chuckled. "Horatio would have a grand time here, I suppose."

They spent the rest of their lunch talking about many of the people they had met together over the past week or so, and how different their two worlds were. When they were done, they braved the glass elevator again, and Aurora liked it even less the second time. The other reason David had picked this place for lunch was so that they could walk to the bank and the shops, and Aurora could see the city up close. She marveled at things like streetlights and crossings. There were so many people moving about, and all the traffic was incredible to her. They made 3 trips back to the car with packages, and had gone to pick up her dress and his tuxedo. She had no clothing of her own to wear, so they had to get her some of everything. David waited patiently in one shop while Aurora tried on a variety of undergarments, and by the time she finished she was looking flustered.

Walking around, David reveled in the fact that for the first time, in a long time, he didn't feel alone in the crowd. She was what had been missing in his life. As much as his parents' return meant to him, being with her was different. She ignited a spark in him that made everything feel as new and fresh for him as it was for her.

By the time they finished shopping, the two of them needed a break from it. "There's a small park over by the river. Would you like to go sit for a little while before we have dinner?"

"That sounds like a good idea. I don't think I could handle looking at another piece of clothing without my eyes crossing."

They wound their way through several streets alongside high-rise office buildings until they came out by the river. A little ways down they could see a small park with neatly manicured grounds. Several groupings of trees and benches were arranged around a jogging path. Even this late in the day, the park was alive with people enjoying the beautiful weather. The sunlight was warm on their skin and made the fall air feel refreshing. They made their way to a bench overlooking the river and sat down as pedestrians, bicyclists, skateboarders, and joggers all passed by. Since it was shortly after 5 P.M., many of the office workers were passing through to begin their journey home.

There were ships on the river, some docked and some slowly making their way up or down stream. Aurora asked questions about everything. There were so many new things she hadn't seen before. They sat until it was getting dark, and David was taken by her enthusiasm, not just for the things she saw, but also because of all the possibilities they represented. She was filled with life, with hope. She had always been a fighter, but now she saw the endless opportunities that lay before them. Together they could do anything, and as much as the world had changed for her, it was the fact that she would never be alone again that made dreams possible.

Basking in her joy, David could have sat there all night. She inspired him in a way that he hadn't thought was possible. He had a good life, but he had gone through the motions, doing what was right, making friends, being successful, all because it was in his nature and because he loved The Lord. But now here with her, he wanted to be more. He never wanted to lose the looks of admiration, of affection, of love and longing that she gave him.

"I suppose we should make our way to dinner. The sun is setting, and I don't want you to get cold."

"You'll just have to hold me and keep me warm then," Aurora flashed him a grin.

"That I can do," David said, and he stood up offering her his hand. As she pulled herself up, David gave a little extra tug, and he caught her in his arms. "How's that?"

"Much better," she said, and then rested her head on his chest.

They stood for a few moments, unconcerned about the people passing by until, without a word, they started walking down the path. David put his arm around Aurora, holding her close. They slowly started down the sidewalk that ran along the river's edge, as the water on their right reflected the orange glow of the setting sun. On their left, they passed a number of buildings with restaurants or shops busy with patrons. Up ahead, a few blocks down, was a glass dome. From inside it they could see the flicker of a number of gas lanterns.

"Do you see that glass building up ahead? That's where I thought we could go. In the evening, we should be able to see the stars through the roof, and watch the boats passing by on the river, and more importantly, it's on the ground."

Aurora laughed. "Thank goodness. I don't think I have it in me to take another ride up in that glass room today."

David chuckled, "I thought as much."

They made their way to the entrance, and when they walked inside, the hot air in the building wrapped around them like a warm blanket. They hadn't realized how cold it was until then, and were happy to be inside now. The hostess greeted them and found them a table on the river side. David knew if it had been a weekend, they probably would have ended up by the kitchen.

The dining room was circular and lit by a ring of gas lanterns and candles on the tables. There were plants all around, and the furnishings had a garden feel to them to complete the outdoor atmosphere. The sun was almost below the horizon, and the last of the orange glow glinted off the river. The boats with their lights on floated lazily along the dark water.

The sky was clear, and the stars were starting to shine brightly overhead. In the center of the room was a platform with a piano on it. They had scarcely finished ordering their meal when the piano player began serenading the room.

"This place is lovely."

"I thought it would be a good way to end the day." David said, "I've had a couple of lunch meetings here, and always imagined it would be even nicer at night."

Gazing affectionately at David, Aurora said, "I almost don't want this day ever to end."

"It isn't over yet." David said with a sly grin. "I have one more surprise for you."

"You've done too much for me today. As much as I appreciate everything, please tell me we aren't doing any more shopping."

David laughed. "No, that would be cruel. In fact, I have to admit I've never done so much shopping at one time in my life."

Just then the waitress brought bread and salad. They enjoyed a leisurely dinner, talking about their day. David ordered some coffee. They were both too full to entertain any dessert. After a couple of sips of coffee, David said abruptly, "Excuse me one minute." Then he stood up and left the table.

Aurora watched him walk off, thinking it was a little odd that he didn't say where he was going. He was so sensitive to the fact that she didn't know her way around. All day he made sure to reassure her that he was always there if she needed him. He never made her feel as if he thought she wasn't capable; just that she wasn't alone.

She was staring out of the window when David appeared at her side. She looked up at him smiling down at her, and he reached out a hand. She took it without question and stood. He led her to the middle of the room over by the piano, put an arm around her waist, and held her hand up in his. Then the music started.

"This is a song by a musician I like. His name is Billy Joel." David, staring directly into her eyes, began to move with her to the music.

The piano player started to sing, "She's got a way about her, I don't know what it is, but I know that I can't live without her."

Aurora's face beamed as she listened to the words.

"She's got a smile that heals me."

David held her close as they danced slowly with the music, still looking into her eyes.

"But I have to laugh when she reveals me."

She was lost in his gaze, feeling the words and sounds. It was different from any kind of music she had heard before, and filled her with emotion.

"She's got a way of talking, I don't know why it is, but it lifts me up when we are walking anywhere. She comes to me when I'm feeling down; inspires me without a sound."

"She's got a way of showing how I make her feel, and I find the strength to keep on going."

"She's got a light around her, and everywhere she goes a million dreams of love surround her everywhere."

The piano player sang the last line, "but I know that I can't live without her anyway."

Then the music stopped. They stood still staring at each other for a moment. Aurora was speechless. Then suddenly to her surprise, David got down on one knee. She didn't know what he was doing; still holding her hand, he reached into his pocket with the other one and pulled out a ring.

"Aurora, will you marry me?"

She knelt down in front of him, and said through tears, "Oh yes, of course I will", and David slipped the ring on her finger.

Aurora, surprised enough already, couldn't believe it when all of the people in the restaurant started clapping. She looked around stunned. She had all but forgotten where they were. Then she threw her arms around David and kissed him. The watching crowd made noises that neither one of them could hear. They were lost in their kiss.

They leaned back, beaming at one another, then stood and headed back to their table. A few of the other patrons clapped again or said encouraging things, and David gave them a small wave.

Once they sat down again, Aurora said with a broad smile, "It is a good thing that's your last surprise. I don't know that I could handle another one."

"Since you said yes, did I save the best for last?"

"Yes, yes, yes." Aurora said, "And where did you get this ring. It's beautiful?"

"It was my grandmother's on my mother's side. My mom wanted you to have it. She's very fond of you."

"I like her so much. She makes me feel truly welcome. I can't tell you how it feels to be part of a family again."

David reached across the table, taking her hand, and said, "You'll never be alone again."

Aurora lifted his hand up to her cheek and held it tightly as a single tear ran down her face. "If it's all right with you, I think I'm ready to go home," she said softly.

"Me too," David said. "I just need to pay the bill, and we can be on our way."

David signaled their waitress, and she hurried over. The place had begun emptying, and she was waiting for her last customers to leave. She quickly took David's credit card, returned with the receipt, and wished them luck as they headed out. The night air was even colder now, so they huddled close as they made their way the last couple of blocks to the building where the car was parked. Aurora was used to being outside all the time, so the cold didn't bother her too much, but she was thankful when the car's heater started producing warm air.

Driving out of the city on the dimly lit streets, there wasn't much to see, so Aurora didn't have many questions. Soon she was curiously quiet, and David realized she had fallen asleep. He was careful to avoid bumps and not take any turns too fast, so he didn't wake her. He was tired too, but his satisfaction with how the day turned out sustained him. He was impressed at how well she adapted to so many new things and situations. It was an emotional day for her, but it would have been for anyone.

When he arrived at the farm, he went especially slowly up the road to the house. She was clearly out cold, but tomorrow was going to be a big day, and he wanted her to get as much rest as possible. When he pulled the car to a stop, his dad and Rusty came out the front door. David got out of the car and pushed the door closed as quietly as he could.

"David, is everything okay? You drove up so slowly."

"Everything's fine, Dad. Aurora's asleep, so I was trying not to wake her. Can you get the doors for me please, while I carry her inside?"

"Sure thing," Gabe said as he headed up to the front door of the house.

"You be quiet now, Rusty," David said, as he scratched the dog behind the ears.

David went around to the passenger door and opened it slowly, unbuckled Aurora. Then taking her right arm and putting it around his neck, he rolled her out into his arms. She instinctively nuzzled her head into the crook of his neck but remained asleep. David carried her up to the house and carefully maneuvered his way back to the bedroom. He gently laid her down and pulled a blanket up over her. He would try to slip her boots off when he came to bed, but for now she was still fast asleep.

He walked back outside with his dad to shut the car door. "That's one tired little lady."

"She sure is, and I'm exhausted too. Where's everyone else?"

"They all went to bed a little while ago. I was waiting up to hear from you."

"Sorry I didn't call earlier. I didn't think of it until Aurora had fallen asleep, and I was trying not to wake her."

"That's alright. I didn't start worrying yet. You're a grown man, and have certainly shown you can take care of yourself. Did you two have a good time today?"

"Oh yeah. I'm really proud of Aurora, too. It was a lot for her to take in, and she handled it all so well."

Gabe mused, "There is no doubt she's a special girl. I'm so happy for you, son."

"Thanks Dad," David said. "So how's Mom holding up?"

Gabe gave a little laugh. "Your mom is tough as nails. She was tired at the end of the day, but if you didn't know her as well as I do, you'd never have guessed all that she's been through."

"I'm so glad. As much as I want Aurora and me to have time alone, I think moving to the cabin will give you and mom time to catch up too."

"Don't worry, Son. Your mom and I love each other very much, and we're going to be fine."

"You don't think I'm being selfish planning this wedding so soon do you?"

"Definitely not. A wedding is a joyous event, and after all we've been through, it is a terrific way to focus on something good."

"You did always teach me to plan for the future, but live in the moment."

"And I thought you didn't listen to me," Gabe said with a chuckle. "I suppose we should get to bed. Tomorrow will be a busy day."

David gave his father a hug and squeezed him tightly. "Thanks Dad, for everything. I missed you terribly all those years. Thanks for coming home. I had a small taste of what you must have gone through. I can only imagine how hard it was to hold on."

"I wouldn't have made it without you. Your faithfulness coming to see me all the time gave me the strength I needed. I am so proud of the man you've become." Gabe said, "Now If we stay up too late, your mom will have our heads."

They headed towards the bedrooms. "I hope she isn't stressed over things."

"Not at all. She and Molly are enjoying themselves, and I'm just doing what they tell me."

"That's terrific. Goodnight Dad, I'll see you in the morning."

"Goodnight, Son. Sleep well."

"You too, Dad."

David quietly pushed open the door to the bedroom to find Aurora sleeping exactly as he had left her. After a quick trip to the bathroom, he gently slipped her boots off and fixed the cover; then he carefully lay down next to her. He closed his eyes and lay there, listening to her soft rhythmic breathing, and before he knew it, he was asleep too.

***

David found himself standing in an office. It was large with a glass wall that looked out over a city he didn't recognize. The décor was dark and cold, and he didn't like being there. Something was wrong, and his mind was racing, trying to figure out what his options were, when trouble started. He knew trouble was coming; he just wasn't sure how and when yet. He walked over to the desk where a man sat with his back to him. He was staring out the glass, apparently completely unconcerned by David's entrance.

As David drew nearer, it felt as if alarm bells were going off inside every inch of him. He stopped a few feet back from the desk. Without turning, the man spoke. "It is so nice to see you again."

Then he slowly turned around in his chair, his hands steepled in front of him, his elbows resting on the arms of the chair. He was calm and relaxed. David's eyes went wide when he saw *his* face. It was *him*, the *Dark One*.

Seeing David's look of surprise, *he* let out a horrible cackling laugh. David woke a little panicked and sat up looking around. The room was bathed in sunlight. Morning had come.

"I'm sorry, did I startle you?"

David turned to see Aurora next to him, then laid back down. She laid down too, putting her arm around him and said, "I was thinking about getting up, but didn't want to wake you." She was smiling.

"No, you didn't wake me," he said kindly. "I had a strange dream, that's all. How are you? Did you sleep ok?" David asked, not wanting to put a damper on the day by telling her about the dream.

"Really! Was I in your dream?" Aurora asked with a coy smile. "You were in mine."

"What were we doing?"

"Hmm, I'll show you," she said as she leaned in and gave him a soft sensuous kiss. Then with a little smirk she added, "I guess I better get out of bed. We can't miss our own wedding." She gently stroked the side of his face, leaving him breathless, and hopped out of bed.

He watched her walk to the bathroom, turn, and give him a shy little grin as she stepped out of view. She had completely pushed the dream from his thoughts, so he got up and went to the kitchen. Everyone else was already up and finished with breakfast. He was greeted by all their smiling faces, and his mother rushed over, giving him a big hug.

"Good morning, dear. Come and have some breakfast. Your father said you two had a good day yesterday. We want to hear all about it."

"Good morning, Mom. Hi Aunt Molly, Michael, Dad; how are all of you?" David asked as he took a seat at the table.

"Good. And where is your lovely bride?" Aunt Molly asked.

"Good morning, everyone," Aurora said as she appeared in the doorway. She immediately went over to Ruth and hugged her. "I can't tell you how much it means that you gave David your mother's ring for me."

Ruth, a little surprised at first, squeezed Aurora tightly. "I couldn't be happier for you both, and after all we've been through, I'm proud to have you as part of our family."

David looked at the two of them and felt a rush of emotion. He felt very fortunate. All too often mothers and daughter-in-law don't get along so well, and it's a constant source of tension.

"Thank God we dodged that bullet," Gabe said, half whispering to David. "Your grandmother never liked me."

"Gabe, you stop that!" Ruth demanded as she and Aurora let go of each other. "She liked you just fine except for that one thing you did."

"Dad, what did you do?" David asked, as Aurora sat down next to him.

"Your father was a bit of a jokester when he was younger."

"You see, your mom wanted to make me dinner, and she was going to roast a chicken. She told me she was very worried about overcooking it, so...."

"What did you do, Dad?"

"I pretended to go to the car for some things, and sneaked around to the kitchen, and...."

"He took the bird out of the oven before it even got warm, and put a live chicken in there." Ruth said.

"Unfortunately your grandmother decided to go check on it for your mom. You can imagine her surprise when she opened the door and a very unhappy chicken came out squawking at her," Gabe said, trying not to laugh.

Everyone else started laughing, and Ruth said, "Mom wasn't too pleased, and we heard her screaming in the other room."

"It took us 30 minutes to catch the darn thing, and it made a huge mess in the kitchen," Gabe said, laughing now too.

"And you still married him, Mom?" David asked through a laugh.

"I have to admit I thought it was funny too. Then after we finally caught the chicken, he looked my mother in the eye, pretending he was innocent, and said 'I guess she didn't overcook it.' I thought your grandmother was going to hit him with a frying pan," Ruth said.

"With that thick skull of his, it probably wouldn't have hurt him," Aunt Molly said.

Aurora, laughing, turned to David and said, "You better not get any ideas."

"I wouldn't dream of it."

Michael declared, "A wise man."

"So tell us about your day yesterday. Bob Johnson called over here all in a twitter. He's coming to the wedding, by the way," Gabe said.

"Oh that's good. I hope you don't mind that I invited him. He was so excited to hear the two of you were home, and I didn't want to take the time to tell him the story. I'm not sure exactly what I would've told him."

"Tell us what the two of you did to him. He was downright giddy," Gabe said.

"Aurora tried out every bow he had, and I encouraged her to show off a little. She hit a bull's-eye every time."

"Wow! You did?" Gabe asked.

"It wasn't that hard." Aurora said, "The targets weren't moving or anything."

"Bob was so excited watching her shoot, he gave her a bow as a wedding present."

"I don't think Bob has even given as much as a pack of waterproof matches away before. You must have really impressed him."

"You've never seen anything like it. She barely has to look at the target, and off the arrow flies… bull's-eye. Bob was practically jumping up and down."

"That's all very interesting boys, but tell us dear, did you find a dress?" Aunt Molly asked.

"Oh, yes! It's the most beautiful gown I've ever seen," Aurora said, her eyes a little misty just thinking about it.

"You didn't see her in it did you, David?" Ruth asked.

"No, Mom. I got fitted for a tux while she picked it out."

"It's nice to know one of my boys listens to me."

"I listen sometimes. I just have a different idea about things than you do, Ruthie," Gabe said mischievously.

Ruth gave him an exasperated look and then said, "After breakfast, let's take a look at it. I can't wait to see it. Now what else did you do?"

"David took me to the mission. Then lunch on top of this frightfully tall building."

"What mission?" Michael asked.

"Safe Haven. They feed poor people and provide shelter for women and children. Didn't David tell any of you about it?" Aurora said, giving David a quizzical look.

David looking a little embarrassed said, "No, I haven't."

"I've heard of it. They do remarkable work there. The young woman, Rebecca, who runs it is well regarded," Michael said.

"That's right. Without her, there wouldn't be a mission," David said.

"What is it, son? What aren't you telling us?" Gabe asked knowingly.

David sat looking at his coffee cup, and Aurora put a hand on his arm, beaming at him with pride, and said, "David is the one who helped start it and provides money for it, but he doesn't want anyone to know. But you shouldn't keep something like that from your parents."

"I wasn't keeping it from them I just… "David said weakly.

"Son, we're very proud of you. Don't worry, your secret's safe with us," Gabe said.

"He's always been generous," Aunt Molly said.

"Full of surprises too. You are wise beyond your years, David." Michael said, "Matthew 6: Thus, when you give to the needy, sound no trumpet before you as the hypocrites do in the synagogues, and in the streets that they may be praised by others. Truly, I say to you, they have received their reward. But when you give to the needy, do not let your left hand know what your right hand is doing so that your giving may be in secret. And your Father who sees in secret will reward you."

Ruth, noticing David's embarrassment at all the attention, jumped in to change the subject. "So tell us, what else did you two do?"

David looked up at his mother with an expression of relief, and said, "I took Aurora to the rooftop for lunch, but she didn't care for the elevator too much."

"Honestly, I was terrified," Aurora said with a chuckle. "It was amazing to look out at the city, but standing in that glass room sliding up the side of the building was too much for me."

"If it makes you feel any better, it took David years to get over it too," Gabe said.

"He told me, but I have to admit I was very happy to get back on the ground again."

"I don't blame you, Dear. I still don't like it," Molly said. "Where else did you go?"

"We walked around the city, and David took me clothes shopping, so I don't have to keep borrowing yours," Aurora said, looking at Ruth. "Then we went to a park by the river and sat for a while."

"That must have been nice. The weather was perfect for it," Ruth said.

"He took me to this lovely place for dinner, and had the piano player play a song for us so we could dance. Then right in the middle of the place with everyone watching, he got down on his knee, and asked me to marry him," Aurora said smiling brightly at the memory.

"Oh! So romantic!" Molly said, and David noticed the slightest tick of her eye as she glanced at Michael.

"Thankfully she said yes," David said with a sly grin.

"Of course I did. I can't resist you," Aurora said playfully.

"So Aunt Molly, what about you and Michael? Are you two going to get married?" David said with a cat that ate the canary grin.

Michael choked on a sip of coffee, at which Molly hit him on the arm. Red in the face, Molly said, "I don't know what you're talking about."

"Aunt Molly, it's written all over you two."

Michael and Molly looked at each other dumbfounded, and Ruth exclaimed "Is it true? Oh how wonderful."

Michael said, in an embarrassed stutter, "We have been spending a lot of time together, and..."

Molly, taking on an air of defiance, added, "We are very fond of each other, yes."

"That's great news. Now, I don't have to worry about you becoming the old cat lady anymore," Gabe said.

"Ha, ha," Molly said without a hint of laughter. "I don't even like cats."

"I'm truly happy for both of you," Gabe said earnestly "Michael is one of the finest men I've ever known."

Molly, trying to hide her pleasure at his words said, "Thank you Gabe."

David stood up and said, "Before I get into any more trouble, I'm going to go unpack the car."

"I'll give you a hand," Gabe said. "It might help keep me out of trouble too."

"Not likely," Ruth said.

"I'll come too," Aurora said.

"I think I need some fresh air," Michael said, "I'll come too."

"You can put Aurora's dress in our room so she can get ready in private later," Ruth said.

Gabe waved at her as he, Michael, and David headed out of the door. Aurora stopped to talk to Ruth and Molly. "Would the two of you please help me get ready later? I've never actually gotten dressed up before, and …"

"I would love to."

Molly added, "Oh yes! I can't wait to see you in your dress. We'll have you sparkling like a jewel."

Aurora smiled. "Thank you so much. I guess I'd better go help." Then she turned and headed out to the car.

First they unloaded all the clothes, and then they uncovered the camping equipment. David pulled out the bow and quiver and handed it to Aurora. "Would you like to show Dad and Michael a little of what got Bob so excited yesterday?"

"Oh, they don't want to see me show off."

"Oh yes we do!" Gabe said with a big grin.

"Just once, I don't want to keep your mom waiting. Choose a target for me."

"How about that fence post down at the end of the drive?" David asked. "It's further than Bob's targets, but I'm sure you can do it."

Giving him a sly grin, she said, "All right."

David handed Gabe and Michael each an arrow. He took one, positioning each of them a full 4 feet apart. Then he nodded to Aurora. She walked over to Michael who was on the opposite end of David, smiled, then took the arrow, and spun. She let the arrow fly, turned and grabbed Gabe's, then turned again and grabbed the one from David. While they were all still in the air, she handed him the bow and gave him a kiss.

"See you later," she said as she walked off.

Each arrow hit the post clustered together. Gabe and Michael stood speechless for a second, then Gabe said, "Wow! That was something."

"Yeah," David said a little breathlessly, still tasting her lips on his as he watched her walk off.

"You'd better not get on her bad side," Michael said.

The three of them laughed, then walked down the drive to retrieve the arrows and inspect her precision. "You should see her when she's fighting.

Fluid motion. I've never seen anyone like her." David said, "I couldn't have made the journey without her."

Gabe knelt down to look where the arrows struck "Look at that, almost no wood between the tips. I thought Bob was exaggerating."

"I never saw Bob giddy before." David said, "I guess I should get back and organize our gear for the trip. I'm hoping to make it to Tom's before midnight."

"I'll give you a hand," Gabe said.

"I've got her ID and the marriage license at the house. I'll get it for you," Michael said.

***

Aurora walked into the kitchen and found Molly and Ruth. "Do you need help with anything?" she asked.

"We're all done," Ruth said. "Did the boys bring all of your clothes inside?"

"Yes, they put them in your room."

"Oh good, I can't wait to see. You're going to be such a beautiful bride." Molly said excitedly; then taking Aurora's arm, led her out of the room.

Aurora gave Ruth a quick glance, and she said, "I'm right behind you. I don't want to miss a thing."

They walked into the room to see the wedding dress, which was hanging on the closet door carefully wrapped in a white plastic bag. Stacked in another corner were bags of clothes and shoeboxes waiting to be unpacked.

Molly, letting go of Aurora, hurried over to the dress and stood staring at it, as if trying to see through the plastic wrapping. "I see they wrapped it well enough to keep David from getting a look at it before the wedding," she said a little absentmindedly.

Aurora gave Ruth a smile and said, "Aunt Molly, would you like to open it up?"

Molly flushed a little and said, "Oh dear, that's alright. I'm sure you…"

Aurora said, "Please. I'm afraid I might mess it up. I really don't know about these things."

"If you insist, Dear." Molly said, and quickly turned to the wrapping.

Ruth placed a hand on Aurora and smiled at her as Molly meticulously began unzipping the plastic bag. Then with a deep breath she pulled it off the dress. Aurora felt a gush of excitement when she saw the dress again that was amplified by the ooing and ahhing from Molly and Ruth.

Molly, positively beaming, said, "It's magnificent. So elegant, and look at this fabric. You will look like an angel."

"Oh yes. It's magnificent. No one will be able to keep their eyes off of you."

"I was a bit nervous. Most of the other dresses had so much lace and fabric, I was afraid I might have made a poor choice."

"Not at all." Ruth said, "This dress is perfect for you; elegant and pure just like you. You don't need all that extra stuff to show how beautiful you are."

Aurora flushed, "I've never thought of myself as beautiful. I just hope David likes it."

Molly said, "You might have to revive him after he sees you in it." Then she chuckled.

"If you don't mind, can I show you what else I got, so you can help me decide what to bring on our trip?"

The three of them went through each of the packages as Molly and Ruth helped her sort the clothes into groups for occasions; day to day wear, evening wear, etc. They put a selection together of enough variety for her to wear while they were gone. When they got to the last 2 bags, Aurora said, a bit embarrassed, "Oh, these are undergarments."

"Let's see what you have. Did you get something special for tonight?"

"Molly!" Ruth said in a slightly exasperated tone, "You are going to embarrass the girl to death."

"Thank you, Ruth, but the truth is I don't know anything about well … a wedding night. What if I'm terrible, and do everything wrong?" Aurora said in a rush, then looked down to hide her eyes, hoping they wouldn't think badly of her.

Ruth put a comforting arm around her and said, "I was terrified on my wedding night too, but Gabe and I loved each other very much, just the way you and David do, and nothing will change that. You'll know what to do. Intimacy between a husband and wife is an extension of that love. It brings you closer together because it's something you only share with each other. I'm sure David is just as nervous, because he's never been with anyone either."

Aurora looked up at her, tears in her eyes, and said, "Since my Mother couldn't be here on this day, I'm so thankful to have you here in her place."

Ruth hugged Aurora tightly, and Molly let out a wail. "Oh that's lovely. I want the two of you with me on my wedding day, too."

At that Aurora and Ruth chuckled a little, and Ruth said, "I wouldn't miss it."

"Neither would I."

Molly threw her arms around the two of them so forcefully she almost knocked them over. "I never thought at my age that I might meet someone. I just didn't want to make a big thing out of it because it's your special day."

"It's wonderful, and only adds to the occasion. I'm so very happy for you. I never thought I'd meet someone either."

The three of them were startled by a knock at the door, and all giggled a little. "Who is it?" Ruth asked.

Through the door, they heard David. "I was just thinking of getting in the shower, and wanted to know if Aurora needed anything from our room."

Aurora looked at Molly and Ruth and smiled, then said, "I have everything I need." The other two beamed back at her.

"Ok then, I'll see you in a little while."

"Oh my, look at the time!" Ruth exclaimed, "I guess we'd better start getting ready. Why don't you use our bath to shower dear, and Molly and I will go check on things and come back in a bit to help you finish getting ready."

"All right, a hot bath does sound nice."

"I'll grab Gabe's suit, and if Molly can take your bag for the trip, he can put it in the car for you, so we don't forget later."

"Thank you for everything."

"You're welcome," Ruth said as she and Molly left the room.

Ruth put Gabe's suit in Michael's room, and the two of them headed out into the living room where they found Gabe coming in the front door.

"Gabe, here's Aurora's bag. Can you please put it in the car?" Molly said.

"Of course. The cavalry's here in full force, getting everything set up in the garden. How's the bride?"

"She's taking a shower, so we're going to check on things, then go back and help her get ready." Ruth said, "I put your suit in Michael's room so you can change when you're ready."

"That's my Ruthie. Always on top of things," Gabe said, as he gave her a kiss on the cheek, "David's getting dressed so we can greet the guests. Is there anything else you need us to do?"

"Just behave yourself," Ruth said with a grin.

"Scouts honor," Gabe said.

"You were never a scout," Molly interjected.

"Oh, don't be so picky." Gabe said, "I'll go get dressed, and help usher everyone to the garden after I put this bag in the car."

"Thank you, Dear," Ruth said as he walked off.

The two women headed back to the kitchen and found it alive with people getting dishes of food together. The entire council had come the day before and were back today to help with all the preparations. They were greeted by a number of people, and said their thanks for all the help. Everyone was pleased to be participating in the event. All of them knew what had transpired over the past couple of weeks.

They walked out through the kitchen door, to the garden, to find even more people organizing a buffet, and all the chairs and tables for the reception. It hadn't been difficult to keep David and Aurora from going outside since they came back so late and were busy this morning. They wanted them to see it for the first time after everything was in place.

They used a grape arbor at the edge of the garden as the backdrop for the wedding vows. Rows of neatly-placed white chairs were lined up for all the guests, with a number of floral arrangements of red and white roses running along the perimeter.

Off to the left was a large tent with tables and chairs for the reception where the buffet was being set up. From the looks of it, enough food was being put out to feed a small army. The tables were all set with linen tablecloths and napkins, and a few people were placing the last of the silverware.

"It's amazing what you can get done on short notice with 50 people helping," Ruth said.

"Especially 50 motivated people. If you'd been here that first night before they set out to find you, Ruth, they're all so proud of what these two have accomplished."

"So am I."

"Molly," Michael said. Ruth and Molly turned to see Michael approaching with a woman and a young man.

"Michael, it looks as if everything is coming together nicely."

"Yes it does. I want you to meet someone. This is my sister Abigail, and my Nephew Charles."

"Oh, it's very nice to meet you," Molly said. "Michael has told me so much about you."

"It is very nice to meet you too." Abigail said, "Unfortunately Michael hasn't told me anything about you." Then she gave him a reproachful look.

"I just haven't had the opportunity, Abbey," Michael said weakly.

"We'll just have to sit together then," Molly said. "I'm sure there are loads of things he hasn't told me either."

Michael, in an exasperated tone, said, "I guess I'll go get ready now."

"So, Charles, is there anyone special in your life?" Molly asked.

"No, Ma'am. I just got back from overseas."

"Really, and what were you doing overseas?"

"Charles has been running a mission in Guatemala for the homeless, abused women and children for the past few years. I'm so proud of him." Abigail said, "but I have to admit I'm very happy to have him home for a while."

"It was so lovely meeting you, but I have to check on a few things and get back to the bride. I hope we get to spend time together before you leave," Ruth said.

"Yes, so do I., Please sit with me after the ceremony," Molly said.

"You can count on it. I need to find out what my brother has been up to lately."

"Nice meeting you both," Charles said.

Ruth and Molly hurried off to take a quick walk around the garden. "Either we did a really good job organizing everything, or they don't need us," Ruth said.

"Who cares? It just gives us more time with the bride," Molly said, huddling in close to Ruth.

"I'm not complaining." Ruth said, "After all the things that young girl has been through, and she's still so kind and sweet. I'm so happy for David."

"Let's go then. I can't wait to see her in that dress," Molly said, and giggled a little.

The two of them headed back into the house, and upon entering the living room, saw David coming from the other end wearing his tuxedo.

Molly squealed a little, and Ruth said, "David you look so handsome." And she walked up and gave him a big hug.

"Thanks, Mom. How's Aurora doing?"

"We're taking good care of her, don't you worry." Molly said.

"Thank you, Aunt Molly."

"We're just on our way back to help her get dressed," Ruth said, "Why don't you help your father greet the guests while we finish getting ready. By the way, Michael's nephew Charles is here. He just got back from running a mission overseas for the homeless and battered women and children. You might have something in common."

"You didn't tell him about the mission, did you?"

"No, of course not dear," Molly said. "Have a little faith in us."

"Just asking, Aunt Molly. I know you get excited sometimes," David said with a smile.

"I have plenty of other things to be excited about today."

"I'll see you both outside," David said as he walked off, and Molly and Ruth headed back to the bedroom.

David went out the front door, deciding to avoid the crowds in the kitchen. As he walked out onto the porch, Rebecca was coming up the drive. He waved and walked down to meet her.

She had a slightly stunned look on her face as she saw him dressed in his tuxedo. Remembering what Aurora had told him, he tried to lighten the conversation. "I know I look strange in a suit."

She gave him a brave smile and said, "You look dashing. I just never expected to see you dressed up ever."

"Thank you. I'm so glad you came. Hopefully the mission can survive without you for the afternoon."

"Sam and Doris are there, and they'll keep everything in order."

"Come on. I'll escort you to the back. I haven't seen what they've done yet so I may need a shoulder to lean on if it's too much."

As they walked back to the garden, Rebecca was unusually quiet, but he didn't press her. When they turned the corner, they both let out a breath.

"Wow! It looks incredible back here."

"It sure does. She's one lucky girl," Rebecca said softly.

David spotted Michael and pulled Rebecca along with him. "I want you to meet someone," he said as he felt her move woodenly under his guidance.

"David, I see you're dressed."

Michael was wearing his robes for officiating the ceremony. "I see you're ready, too. I'd like you to meet someone. This is Rebecca, who runs the Safe Haven mission."

"What a pleasure to meet you, young lady. I've been following your exceptional work for a long time," Michael said as he reached out a hand.

Rebecca, stepping out from under David's arm, took Michael's hand, and said, "thank you," her confidence buoyed by the compliment.

"Oh yes, I've read a number of articles about all the marvelous work you do, and was thrilled to hear David knew you. I really must come down sometime soon to see the place."

"I'd love to have you come and visit."

"The only thing I worry about is that Rebecca works too hard." David said, "I just wish I knew someone as dedicated who could help her." He looked at Michael.

"David, you know I love my work," Rebecca said, enjoying his praise. "I don't feel overworked."

Michael, looking at David, suddenly caught on and smiled. "I'd like you two to meet my sister." He turned and waved at Abigail and Charles, who immediately came walking over.

"David and Rebecca, this is my sister Abigail and my Nephew Charles."

"It's very nice to meet you David. Michael has had such lovely things to say about you. Thank you for inviting us to your wedding," Abigail said.

"Thank you for coming. Michael has been a tremendous friend, and I'm so pleased to meet his family," David replied. Charles was standing quietly, staring at Rebecca, and David extended a hand to him, which he absentmindedly took. "Nice to meet you too, Charles."

"Yes, nice to meet you." Charles said, "Rebecca, do you run the mission downtown?"

Rebecca, a little flustered by his intense look, said, "Yes I do, how did you know?"

"I just got back, and was reading some articles my uncle had saved about your mission. There was a picture, but you are much more beautiful in person. I mean, you know, newspaper photos aren't very... Well," Charles spluttered, as he and Rebecca both turned red.

"Thank you, Charles. I never like when they put my picture in those articles. Unfortunately, the press is good for our mission, so I have to do the interviews."

"Charles just got back from running a mission for the homeless and battered women in South America for the past few years," Michael said.

"Really?" Rebecca said smiling broadly.

Charles, looking even more embarrassed, said, "Yes, but it was nothing as impressive as what you've been doing."

Rebecca, slightly embarrassed said, "I do the best I can."

"Charles, would you please do me a favor?" David asked. "Could you escort Rebecca to a seat? I have to go and greet more guests."

Charles excitedly said, "It would be my pleasure."

Rebecca gave him a grin, and they headed off. Abigail asked, "What are you two up to?"

Michael said with a small chuckle, "You have some of your Aunt Molly's blood in you, David."

David said with a sly grin, "I only introduced her to you."

Michael gave a big laugh. "Yes, that's true. So you're a lot more subtle than she is."

Abigail interrupted. "You two are playing matchmaker! Now I've seen everything. At least she seems like a nice girl, and I've read those articles too. She certainly does do exceptional work, but don't think you are off the hook if anything goes wrong."

"Yes ma'am" David said. "I better get back to work."

David made it back out front in time to meet Bob Johnson coming up the drive. He told him about the morning's demonstration for his father and Michael, and Bob just laughed. David met a number of neighbors and a variety of people he didn't know, who evidentially were friends or relatives of council members. He was just happy to be busy, and was enjoying being outside on such a beautiful fall day.

As he made his way back to the garden, his dad came over and said, "It is just about time, Son. Are you ready?"

"Oh, I lost track of the time. What do I need to do?"

"Wait up by the arbor with Michael. Here is her wedding band." Gabe handed him the ring, "and I have yours. I'll walk her up when the music starts, and just remember, when Michael asks you if you take her as your bride to say yes." Gabe gave him a grin.

"I think I can handle that," David said, then gave his dad a hug.

"All right, I'll go get the girls. Tell Michael he has 15 minutes to get everyone in their seats," Gabe said as he walked off.

David found himself walking towards Michael, not quite sure if he was directing his legs or not. He hadn't taken any time to contemplate that they were actually about to be married. So much had happened in the past two weeks that it almost felt like a lifetime had passed, and yet it suddenly felt like the blink of an eye. He reached Michael and managed the words, "It's time."

Michael said, "Very well." Then in a big booming voice David had never heard from him before, he spoke to the crowd. "Everyone, can you please take your seats? We are about to get started."

Without hesitation, the group began quickly filing into the rows of chairs before them. As David stood there watching, he felt as if he were looking at the scene from a distance, the sounds were muted; people seemed to be moving in slow motion. Then before he realized it, everyone was seated, and he heard music start to play. He turned mechanically to see a string quartet, and wondered where they had come from.

From a distance, he heard Michael say, "Relax David, everything's going to be fine."

David turned to look at him, but found he didn't know what to say. He turned back, looking towards the house, and watched intently as the music played on. After what seemed like an eternity, the door finally began to open as his father made his way through. He looked dapper in his best suit, and once across the threshold, he stepped aside to reveal Aurora. The sight of her hit David like a bucket of ice water. Suddenly all of his sense snapped back into place. He took a deep, steadying breath. She looked more beautiful than he could describe.

Her hair had been pulled back, exposing her face and neck, and on her head was the delicate white braided flower wreath she had requested. Her face was alight with a mixture of nervousness and joy. Even from this distance, he thought he could make out a twinkle in her eyes. He admired the way her neck gracefully sloped down to her shoulders, framed by a small collar on the dress that stood up like the petal of a flower.

The front of the dress was cut just low enough to show the cross pendant resting gently in the center of her chest. The dress gently caressed her, showing off her exquisite figure, still leaving more to the imagination. Her long legs and curves were unmistakably feminine, and the soft, shimmering fabric made her graceful movements seem almost ethereal. As he watched her walking down the steps, her right leg teased him through the slit running up the side.

Her eyes found his, and he felt himself smiling like a schoolboy. In return, her smile lost its nervousness, leaving only the look of joy on her face. With his father to guide her up the aisle, she didn't even bother looking at anything but David. As their gazes locked on one another, they were entirely unaware of anything or anyone else around them.

When she stepped next to him, he reached out to take her hand, and said, "You look stunning."

She gave him a shy little smile, and said, "You look so handsome."

Michael cleared his throat, and the two of them were startled a little, looking slightly embarrassed. They had almost forgotten where they were. "Are the two of you ready?" he asked with a smile.

They nodded, and he said, "Let's get started, then shall we? I promise I won't take all day."

They gave each other a quick glance, then turned back to Michael.

"Ladies and gentlemen, brothers and sisters in faith, we have gathered here today to witness the joining of these two in holy matrimony, and to celebrate their love for each other and for our Lord. Although they only met recently, they have known each other all their lives. Those of us of faith understand that the Lord works in our lives, guiding us in ways we do not see or understand, but that by trusting in Him, we receive His good gifts in their proper time. As it is written in Galatians 5:22-23, but the fruit of the Spirit is love, joy, peace, patience, kindness, goodness, faithfulness, gentleness, self-control; against such things there is no law."

"I say to you that a union forged through the Spirit cannot be broken. So let anyone who opposes this marriage, speak now or forever hold their peace." Michael looked over the crowd, then continued. "David, do you take this woman to be your wife in holy union, in sickness and health, for richer or poorer, until death do you part?"

"I do," David said, then he took out the ring his father had given him and placed it on her finger.

"Aurora, do you take this man to be your husband in holy union, in sickness and health, for richer or poorer, until death do you part?"

"I do," Aurora said. Then Gabe handed her the other ring, and she placed it on David's finger.

"Then by the authority vested in me, by the Lord as His servant, I pronounce you man and wife. Let no one tear apart what the Lord has brought together. You may now kiss the bride."

David stepped forward and put an arm around her waist, pulling her close. She put her arm around him, and he reached up, gently cupping her cheek and neck. Pulling her to him, her full soft lips slightly parted with anticipation, he kissed her. He felt that familiar charge course through him, the hairs on the back of his neck standing up. His heart was pounding as a warm breeze washed over them. He could feel her body pressed up against his; then a rush of emotion as she pulled him even closer.

As he slowly leaned back, their lips gently held on, not wanting to let go. He opened his eyes to see her gazing at him longingly, the light behind her dark eyes glowing brightly. It took them a moment to realize the guests were still there, and that they were all murmuring in hushed tones. They stood up straight, and looked at Michael, who had a slight look of surprise on his face.

"I'm sorry. Did we do something wrong?" David asked.

"No, no, come let's sit down," Michael said.

"Come this way, Son," Gabe said as he led them to the tent for the reception.

Ruth and Molly hurried over to them as they made their way to the head table. Once they were seated, Michael asked, "Did you notice anything unusual?"

"What do you mean?" Aurora asked.

"When the two of you affirmed your vows with that kiss, there was a glow of white light around you." Michael said, "I've never seen anything like it."

"Oh," David said, "that happened to us before when we took our vows in Aurora's world too."

"Really? That's extraordinary," Gabe said.

"Why?"

"Just another way the two of you seem to break the rules. But we have a wedding to celebrate. It's certainly nothing to worry about," Gabe said.

"That's right," Ruth said, "It was a beautiful sight; a good sign. So enjoy yourselves."

David and Aurora looked at the four of them smiling, and silently agreed. Then David said, "I believe you owe me a dance."

Aurora smiled as David stood and offered her his hand. "Excellent!" Molly said, "I'll tell the musicians."

Once they started dancing, others began joining them. Neither one of them knew much about dancing, but they didn't care. Several people, including Gabe and Michael, asked for a dance with Aurora; even Bob Johnson wanted a turn. David took the opportunity to dance with his mother and Aunt Molly. Everyone was enjoying themselves, and they didn't bother with the traditional formality of toasts and speeches.

David and Aurora were dancing to a slow number amongst a thinning crowd when Aurora said to David in a hushed tone, "Look! Rebecca is dancing with that young man over there."

"His name is Charles. He's Michael's nephew, and they've been together dancing all afternoon."

"Do you know him? Is he a nice man?"

"I only met him today, but he seemed very nice, and he knew all about Rebecca from newspaper articles. He just got back recently from overseas where he ran a similar mission. They have a lot in common."

"That's wonderful. She looks so happy."

David leaned forward and dipped her down. "Not as happy as I am," he said. Then he stood her up, and pulled her into a slow spin.

"I thought you didn't know how to dance."

"That's it. I've exhausted everything I know." He said, "I don't know about you, but I'm ready to change clothes and start our trip."

"I'd like that."

As they made their way to the house, they greeted guests along the way and thanked them for coming. Once inside, they had to navigate through a number of people in the kitchen, who were replenishing food dishes for the guests. Finally they made their way to the bedroom hallway, and Aurora asked, "Can you undo the back of my dress please?"

David moved her hair to the side and slowly ran the zipper down to her lower back. Then he leaned in and kissed her on the back of the neck. Aurora gave a little titter, and said, "Don't start something you can't finish." Then she opened the door to his parents' room.

"I wouldn't dream of it."

She gave him a mischievous smile over her shoulder as she stepped through the door, and said, "I'll meet you back outside," closing it behind her.

David went to his room and quickly got dressed, meticulously hanging his tuxedo up in the closet. He had already packed his bag and put it in the car. All that was left was for them to say their goodbyes, and they could be on their way. As David was making his way outside, he ran into Rebecca heading into the house.

"Hi! I see you changed. Are the two of you getting ready to leave?" Rebecca asked.

"Yes. We have a bit of a drive ahead of us."

"Is Aurora inside? I wanted to talk to her before you left."

"Yes. If you go through the kitchen to the living room and then head back to the bedroom, she should be on her way out any minute."

Rebecca reached up and gave David an affectionate kiss on the cheek. "I'm so very happy for you. Have a wonderful time, and I'll see you a week from Saturday," she said with a big smile.

David looked at her warmly, and said, "You can count on it."

Then Rebecca headed into the house. David turned, spotted his parents, and made his way to them. They were sitting at a table with Michael, Molly, and Abigail. As soon as he got close, his dad said, "I see you're getting ready to skip out on us."

Stepping up to the table, David said, "I can't thank you all enough. We had a terrific time, and it looks as if everyone else is enjoying the party too."

"We may end up with everyone dancing under the moonlight at this rate," Gabe said.

Michael nudged Abigail, and said, "I don't think Charles and Rebecca would mind that."

Abigail said, "You might be right about that."

David smiled and said, "That's great. So they're hitting it off then?"

Molly said, "This is the first time since the music started that I haven't seen them together. I'm a little put out that you two think you can encroach on my territory," she added with a grin.

"We wouldn't dream of it, Molly. It was purely accidental," Michael said.

"HA," Abigail said, "accidental, my foot!"

***

Aurora came out of the bedroom to find Rebecca waiting in the living room. "Hi Rebecca. Is everything all right?"

"Yes, everything's fine. I just wanted to see you. I hope you don't mind. I know we only met yesterday, but honestly I didn't know who else to talk to."

"I don't mind at all," Aurora said with a comforting smile, then sat on the couch, and Rebecca joined her.

"Yesterday when you came to the mission, you were right. I thought I loved David for years, and after you left, I cried all night long."

"I'm so sorry."

"Don't be. It took that for me to realize that I was in love with something that wasn't there. David is so kind and generous, and he's always been there for the mission and me. It took me seeing the two of you together to realize that, in my mind, I had created an image of him that wasn't real. It was easy because he is such an incredible person. So I came today to see your wedding, hoping to have closure and then move on. Don't get me wrong. I'll always love David, but just not in that way. Then here I am getting over my imaginary love, and I end up meeting someone."

With a knowing smile, Aurora said, "I saw you with him all afternoon."

"It's uncanny. He ran a mission like mine overseas, and we have so much in common. He has a gentle spirit and seems so, well, perfect. I can hardly believe it."

"I'm so happy for you."

"He even wants to come and volunteer at the mission tomorrow. I'm just nervous. I don't know what to do. How did you know David was really the one for you?"

"I have to tell you that I don't have any experience in relationships, so I can only tell you about David."

"Please."

"From the first moment I met him, he was kind and gentle, and at the same time strong and self-assured. He made me feel safe. He treated me with respect and as an equal, and didn't try to impress me with silly boasting or theatrics. And when we stood close or if I placed a hand on him, I felt weak inside, and longed for him to kiss me. I never had any of those feelings before, and I was frightened at first. As we spent time together, though, I knew without a doubt that not only would he never harm a hair on my head, but that he would never break my heart. The first time I heard him say he loved me, I was overcome with joy, and all my fears washed away," Aurora said, her face alight with happiness.

"Thank you so much for sharing that with me. I feel a lot of those same things with Charles, and it scares me." She gave Aurora a hug. "I guess you'd better get to your husband."

"I know David thinks so highly of you, and it would be great if we can be friends too."

"I'm sure we will," Rebecca said, and the two of them stood and headed to the back.

The moment they stepped out of the house, David turned. He could feel Aurora's presence like a charge in the air. He smiled when he saw she and Rebecca were walking arm in arm, talking like old friends. Charles was sitting next to David, facing the door, and saw them too. When Rebecca noticed him watching her, she giggled a little and said something in private to Aurora.

David thought to himself that he couldn't ever remember seeing Rebecca giggle before. Laugh yes, but giggle like a schoolgirl, never. He leaned over and whispered to Charles, "She must really like you."

Charles flushed a little and asked, "Do you really think so? I think she's amazing."

"I'm sure of it, and yes, she is an amazing woman," David said, then stood, and so did Charles.

"Rebecca, would you like to join us?" Charles asked as they approached.

David moved, freeing up the chair next to Charles, and said, "I suppose we're going to get going."

Charles took the cue, offered Rebecca the chair, and she sat down to join the rest of them. Aurora walked over, taking David's arm, and said, "I'm ready when you are."

Gabe, Ruth, Michael, and Molly all stood, and David and Aurora gave them all a hug, expressed their thanks again, and said their goodbyes.

"It was nice meeting you, Abigail," David said.

Abigail, giving him a stern look, glanced to see that Charles and Rebecca were too involved to notice, and said, "You remember what I said, young man." Then she smiled a little as she saw how happy Charles was.

"Absolutely. I'll check on it as soon as we get back," David said with a wink.

"All right, you two. I guess you'd better get going so you aren't on the road too late," Gabe said.

"I'll give you a call tomorrow to let you know we arrived ok."

"Goodbye everyone," Aurora said as she and David made their way to the car. Saying goodbye to a few of the guests they ran into along the way, they finally found themselves alone in front of the house.

"I really enjoyed everything, but I'm ready for some alone time. How about you?" David asked.

"Yes, everyone was so nice to me, but I have to admit I'm happy we're leaving."

PROMISES KEPT

David opened the car door for Aurora, and she climbed inside. David moved quickly around to the driver's side and hopped in. He turned to look at her, paused, taking her in with his eyes, and asked, "are you ready?"

"Yes." She said with a smile. "So where are you taking me?"

David started the car and began to turn it around. "We're going to the lodge up in the mountains that I mentioned. In the winter, a lot of people go there for skiing, and in the fall a lot of hunters go there. During the spring and summer months, people mostly go hiking and swimming in the lake. It's really beautiful country, and the lodge itself is very nice." Heading down the drive, David added, "I thought we could hike up to the waterfall I told you about. It's spectacular this time of year. We'll have a view of the mountains for miles."

"Hiking in the mountains without a band of soldiers trying to kill me, or on a secret mission, I won't know what to do."

"Hopefully it isn't too boring for you."

"Boring sounds good, but I'm sure we'll be able to find something to keep us busy," she said with a sheepish smile, and a little red in the face. "We do have a lot to learn about each other. It is our honeymoon."

"Oh," David said, stumbling a little for words. "I guess you are right, I ... Uh well... I have to admit I'm a little nervous. I hope you won't be disappointed. I'm afraid I won't be any good," his voice failing as he avoided looking at her. He turned onto the main road and was struck by a raven sitting perched on the fence. It flew into the air as they passed, and he quickly forgot about it.

"I'm nervous too. I don't know anything about what to do either, but someone very special told me that when two people love each other, they'll figure it out."

Driving down the highway, David gave her a quick glance and said, "There's one more thing. I've been told that the first time for a woman can hurt, and the idea of hurting you ..."

"I know, but I've been stabbed in the side, shot in the shoulder with an arrow, hit with a club in the back, punched in the head by a very large man, just to mention a few painful experiences, so I think I can handle it," she said reassuringly.

David reached out, took her hand, and said, "I have no doubts about how tough you are. Just please promise me that if it is bad, you'll tell me."

"I promise. Now it is my turn to tell you not to worry. In fact, I don't think I have seen you worry about anything else."

"I guess getting tortured or killed isn't as scary as disappointing you," he said light heartedly.

"Good. Let's keep it that way, so I don't have to hit you with a frying pan for giving me any trouble," she said with a laugh.

"I'll make sure we don't have any cast iron pans then."

"That reminds me. Please tell me more about the cabin we're going to live in."

"Yes, the cabin. It isn't much. Dad and I built it years ago so my mom would come with us when we went hunting. It has a main room with the kitchen at the back, two bedrooms, and a bath. We put in a well for water, and were able to get electricity to it. The only heat is a wood stove, but it warms up the place nicely. There's a dirt road that runs up from the house, and it's remote with a great view of the valley."

"Considering that I spent the better part of the past 10 years sleeping in tents and under bushes, it sounds luxurious."

"We haven't stayed there in a long time. I've checked on it a few times, but it's going to need to be cleaned up. Hopefully you don't change your mind when we get there."

"I think I can handle a little dirt. The idea of having a place where we can live alone together; I just never thought I would have a home again."

It was dark now, and David couldn't see her face clearly. He reached out and took her hand. They sat in silence for a while, accompanied only by the sound of the car and the wheels on the road. Sitting there alone, they felt as if they didn't have a care in the world.

"Will we have a garden of our own?" Aurora suddenly asked.

"If you want, we can plant one in the spring."

"I think I'd like that, but I've never planted anything before."

"I can teach you if you'd like. Technically, I am a farmer."

"I don't know anything about a garden, or keeping a house, or … or … or being a wife... I... I..." She stammered.

"It's all right," David said tenderly. "Gardening and keeping a house, those are easy things. I don't know anything about being a husband either, but we're going to find out together what being married means."

"I just don't want to be useless. It seems my whole life I've only been a soldier; I don't know anything else. How will that serve us, living in a house, gardening, farming… having children," she blurted out. "What kind of mother can I be?" she said, sounding a little panicked.

"Aurora, do you know anything about horses?" David asked calmly.

A little surprised by the question, she replied, "Yes, I rode horses all the time, and tended them."

"We have horses. I have to care for them. Do you think you could help me with that?"

"Yes, I can help with the horses."

"Do you know how to hunt?"

"Yes, I can hunt; I had to live off the land most of the time."

"I go hunting so we can store food. Will you go hunting with me?"

"Yes, of course I will," she said, realizing what he was doing.

"Those are important parts of living on a farm. We have to tend to the animals; we hunt for meat and prepare our catch. There are lots of things that you'll know how to do, and I'm sure are good at. Nobody's good at everything."

"I suppose you're right. Everything has changed, and it's a little scary."

"Do you know why I love you?"

"Please tell me," she said with a slight pleading in her voice.

"You are the strongest, bravest, smartest woman I've ever known. You are so filled with life. Just being in your presence, I feel more alive than I ever dreamed possible. You have a kind and generous spirit, and as fierce as you can be, you are also gentle and passionate. Who could ask for a better role model than that?" David said, "When the time comes for us to have children, you'll be a wonderful mother."

"Do you really think so?"

"I'm sure of it."

"Can you tell me again why you love me?"

David laughed a little, and said, "Until you're sick of hearing it, if you want."

"I won't get sick of hearing it." She said, "But I'm ready to get out of this carriage so you can tell me while I'm holding you."

"Unfortunately, we still have a ways to go." David said, "Why don't you tell me what else you like to do for fun, besides impressing old … and young men with your archery skills?"

She chuckled. "I did enjoy the looks on their faces. I don't normally like to show off because so many men get upset when they're bested by a woman."

"I suppose that's true, but they were very impressed."

"And what about you? Were you impressed or unsettled?"

"Both, but not unsettled in the way you think."

"Oh, and how did I make you feel unsettled?"

"I find your confidence very attractive."

"I'll have to remember that," she said playfully.

"I think you already knew that. You too easily take my breath away."

"I guess that puts us on an even footing then."

David laughed. "I have a feeling you'll always have an advantage over me."

"I like the sound of that," she cooed.

"Now you haven't told me what else you like to do for fun."

Aurora told him about the little time she had in between missions, and how she would spend it with various supporters. She welcomed the time she got to spend with their children. They would follow her around, and she would teach them things about life outdoors, finding hiding places, telling them stories about fierce battles. She explained that spending time with them, basking in their innocence, and reveling in how full of life they were, made the battles and the missions bearable. To know that she struggled and faced evil, so they didn't have to, gave her the strength to face whatever challenges arose.

They talked effortlessly for hours, sharing thoughts and feelings they hadn't spoken aloud before. They both knew, without a doubt, that they could bare their souls to one another without fear or risk. They each knew that the safest place for their heart was with the other. They had both been guarded, protecting their secrets and their feelings their whole lives. Finally, being able to let that guard down was liberating.

When David finally said, "This is our last turn; the lodge is just ahead a couple of miles," it was almost disappointing that the moment would end. But they had days to spend with nothing to do, and their whole life together.

"I lost track of the time, we were talking so much."

"So did I. To be honest, I almost missed the turn."

They pulled up in front of the lodge and parked the car. David turned to Aurora, and asked, "Are you hungry?"

A little sheepishly she replied, "Actually, yes I am. I hardly got to eat anything at the wedding reception."

"Neither did I. Would you like a quick bite to eat before we go upstairs?"

With a grin, she said, "I think we'd better. You're going to need your strength."

David chuckled, "I'd be a fool to argue with you about that."

He got out of the car and walked around to her door. As he helped her step down to the ground, he pulled her into his arms and looked into her eyes. He reached up gently, brushing a stray hair back from her face, and said, "I didn't think I couldn't possibly love you any more than I already did, but tonight you touched my heart in ways I never imagined. I love you so much, and I know that I will spend the rest of my life loving you more every day."

Aurora looking up at him, her eyes glistening in the moonlight said, "I never thought I could be so in love either. From the moment I met you, I knew you would protect me, and that I was safe with you. What I didn't fully realize is that everything that I am is safe with you. You lift me up in every way and fill my heart with joy. I can't imagine my life without you." Then she kissed him, and he kissed her back.

It was a slow, tender kiss, and time lost all meaning. They were lost in each other's embrace. When suddenly the sound of people and a car door brought them back, they looked at each other, and grinned. "I suppose we should go inside."

They turned and went to the back of the Jeep, grabbed their packs, bags, and of course Aurora's bow, and headed inside. The Lodge was a huge log structure with a steep roof and a handful of dormers offering a view of the rooms inside. There was a large porch across the entire front that turned the corner on either side. It had numerous tables and chairs for guests to enjoy the view, but was empty of people this time of night.

As they made their way up the stairs, the heavy timbers were as solid as stone under their feet. The entrance doors were glass, and light flooded out onto the dimly lit porch, inviting them to enter. Crossing the porch in several strides, David pulled the door open, and a welcoming gust of warm air beckoned them inside.

The lobby was not all that different from most hotels except that everything was made of heavy timber, well kept, polished, and smooth.

They were in a variety of colors that all blended perfectly, giving it a warm rich feeling. To their right was a counter, and David made his way over with Aurora following him.

The clerk behind the counter, seeing them enter, said, "Hello. Welcome to 'The Lodge'. How can I help you tonight?"

David stepped up to the counter, noticed the clerk taking stock of the two of them, and said, "Hello. How are you tonight? I believe we have a reservation. I'm..."

The clerk cut him off, and said, "Oh yes, we've been expecting you. Tom insisted I get him the moment you walked through the door. Please excuse me. I'll be right back." Then he turned and hurried through a door behind him.

David turned to Aurora, "I wonder what my dad told them that he knew it was us right away?"

"Of the little I know of your father, it could've been anything," Aurora said with a grin.

"He does keep me on my toes," David said fondly.

"David!" A booming voice came from behind them through a set of doors opposite the entrance. As Tom walked through the lobby to greet them with his arms held out wide, he exclaimed, "It's great to see you after all this time. You haven't been up here in years."

"Tom, it's great to see you too," David replied as he stepped towards Tom and shook his large hand. Tom was a big man, and stood a full six inches taller than David. He was powerfully built and did not give any sign of being twenty years David's senior.

Tom, in a softer voice, said, "I was so thrilled to hear from your father. It's such a blessing to have him and your mother back, and your news too."

"Thank you so much, Tom." David said, then turning to Aurora, "This is my wife Aurora."

"It is so nice to meet you, young lady. For once in his life Gabe didn't exaggerate. He said you were stunningly beautiful."

Aurora, going flush, said, "Why thank you. It's nice to meet you too."

"What else did my father say, Tom? We were wondering how the desk clerk knew it was us right away."

"He said you were coming with your beautiful bride, and she would be carrying a longbow, and not to cross her because she knows how to use it," Tom said with a laugh.

"That sounds like Dad. Is the kitchen still open? We're starving."

"You're just in time. Leave your things here. Charlie, please take these up to their room for them, and then bring their key to the dining room for me. Come with me, and we'll get you something to eat."

"I can take the things up to the room. It's no trouble."

"Nonsense! It's your honeymoon. You get the royal treatment this week."

"Thank you, Charlie."

"No trouble at all, sir," Charlie said with a smile.

Tom led them back through the door he came from into the center of the lodge. As they passed through the doorway, Aurora was amazed at how large the building was. The center was open all the way to the roof, and there were four rows of balconies, one above the other, lining the perimeter. She could see the doors and windows facing the center of the building, and guessed they were all guest rooms.

In the center was a dance floor that was surrounded by tables and chairs. Tom led them across the room to a corner that was raised up above the main area, and offered a more private setting. They sat caddy corner so they both could look out over the room. There were couples and small groups scattered throughout the hall, all talking and enjoying the end of their day.

The perimeter was lined with planters, creating an outdoors feel, and separating it from the guest rooms that ran along the front and back walls. There were lanterns here and there, creating a low warm light, and hanging from the rafters were large wrought iron chandeliers that had an old world feel to them. At this time of the night, they were turned off, apparently so the guests in the adjacent rooms could get some sleep.

"Would you like to try our house special for two? its prime rib of beef, and it's delicious tonight," Tom asked.

David looked at Aurora, who gave a nod of approval, and he turned to Tom. "That sounds delicious. Could we have some tea and water too?"

Tom turned to the waitress who had appeared at his side. "Did you get that, Addie?"

"Yes sir. I'll take care of it right away," she said, and hurried off.

"No champagne to celebrate?"

"I don't think I want any, but if you'd like some Aurora." David looked at her questioningly. She gave him a quizzical look, to which he answered. "It's like wine with bubbles."

"No thank you, not tonight."

"Very well then, I'll give you some time to yourselves, but if you need anything at all, just tell Addie to come get me."

"Thank you so much, Tom. I really appreciate you taking such good care of us."

"Not at all." Then he turned to Aurora and said, "I've known this young man since he was a little boy, and his father and I go way back. In fact, I might not be here today if it weren't for Gabe. This family is one of the finest I know. I'm so proud that you chose to come here for such a special occasion."

"I couldn't think of anywhere better."

"Ah, there's your father coming out in you. All right, you two. Just remember, anything at all." Tom said, then turned and headed towards the kitchen.

"What a nice man."

"Yes, he's a really nice guy. But when I was a kid, he terrified me. If he caught me running along the balconies, all he had to do was give me a look, and I froze on the spot."

"I can see that. He looks like a small mountain."

"Back then, he looked like a big mountain," David said, with a chuckle. "I suppose that's one of the reasons this place is so successful. Even if some of the guests have too much to drink, no one ever causes trouble with Tom around."

Suddenly Addie was standing there with their tea and water, some fresh bread, and two small salads. "Here we go. This should tide you over until your dinner is ready. I understand that the two of you were married today. How exciting!" Addie was a young girl of no more than 18 or 19, attractive, with a warm smile. "If you need anything else, please let me know, I should be back with your meals shortly." She gave them both a grin as she walked off.

"Thank you, Addie." David said.

"Did you come often when you were a child?" Aurora asked.

"We usually came twice a year. Once in the summer and once in the fall. The farm is a lot of work, and it isn't always easy to get away. But after a long hot summer, my dad would try to work it out so we could come up here and swim in the lake. It was a lot of fun, and there are always a lot of people here. Then in the fall we'd come up and do some hunting while my mother relaxed here at the lodge."

"And did you get into trouble a lot with Tom?" she asked with a suspicious grin.

With a laugh, David said, "You bet. Tom, seemed to be everywhere."

David went on to tell her stories about accidentally letting a number of frogs lose in the dining hall during dinner, the time he thought a skunk was a cat, and on and on while they enjoyed their dinner. A few times he had her laughing so hard she almost spat her tea all over the table.

About the time the two of them had given up on finishing the enormous meals Addie had brought them, Tom showed up. "How are you two doing? Did you enjoy your meals?"

"I don't think I can eat another bite, and I can't remember having a better prime rib, Tom. Thank you," David said.

"How about you, Dear?" Tom asked Aurora.

"Oh, it was fabulous. It was the best piece of beef I've ever had." Aurora said, "So tender and juicy. I've never tasted anything like it before."

"I'm so glad you enjoyed it. That's my own special recipe," Tom said beaming with pride.

"David was telling me stories about some of the trouble he caused you growing up," Aurora said, giving David a sly grin.

"Oh yes, he was a handful. One of the most curious kids I've ever seen, and he wasn't afraid of anything. He used to scare the heck out of me. It was practically a full time job keeping an eye on him. The funny thing about it is he never got a scratch. Did he tell you about the time with the skunk?"

"Yes he did," she said, smirking.

"Did he tell you that four of us got sprayed getting the thing out of here, and he didn't get a drop on him?" Tom asked with a chuckle.

"You guys scared him."

"Luckiest kid I ever knew. I think he was four years old, and his dad was helping me fix a leak on the back roof. Next thing we know, there stands David on the ladder with a jug of water. He says, "Momma was afraid you were thirsty." His dad and I were so startled we almost fell off the roof." Tom said, "Meanwhile his mother was frantic, looking for him."

"So this is what I have to look forward to?" Aurora said teasingly. "Are you going to scare me to death too?"

"I'll try not to, but I can't make any promises there."

"Don't worry too much. He mostly grew out of it. Mostly," Tom said with a grin. "All right, you don't need me intruding on your evening anymore. I'll leave you alone now."

"It's been such a pleasure meeting you, Tom. Thank you for all your hospitality."

"My pleasure. Your room is ready. Did Charlie bring the key over?"

"Yes, he did. Room 501."

"Best room in the place. I save it for special occasions."

"Thank you so much, Tom."

"You enjoy the rest of your evening, and I'll see you tomorrow." Tom said as he turned and walked off.

David turned to Aurora, and asked, "Would you like anything else?"

"I couldn't eat another thing."

"How about a dance before we call it a night?"

"I'd like that, but I don't hear any music."

"Come with me, and I'll show you."

They made their way down to the dance floor, and in the corner was an old jukebox. David pulled out a quarter and put it in the slot. "Is a slow number, all right with you?"

"I think I'm too full for a fast one."

David picked an instrumental track. He didn't want some else's words intruding on his thoughts, and pushed the buttons. When the music started to play, Aurora said, "That's amazing. It's going to take me some time to get used to all of the machines you have."

She turned from the jukebox and gave him a smile. They walked onto the dance floor and held each other closely. Swaying slowly to the music, they became lost in each other's movements.

"Did you enjoy our wedding day?"

"Every moment. Did you?"

"Yes, I married you."

"Yes, you did. It almost seems like a dream."

"Then let's never wake up."

She squeezed him tightly. "Never."

The feel of her pressed against him, breathing in her scent, the warmth of her body, was bliss. David could have stood there forever. Then he realized, "The music has stopped. Should I play another song?"

In a soft husky voice, she said, "No, let's go upstairs."

Without a word, they headed back to the table. David gave Addie a small wave, and she moved quickly to meet them. "Would you like something else?"

"No, thank you, Addie. Just our check, please."

"There is no check, sir. Tom said tonight was on him."

David reached into his pocket pulled out a large tip, and discretely put it into Addie's hand. "That was very thoughtful of him. Thank you for taking such good care of us tonight. Hopefully we'll see you again. Please tell Tom I said thank you for dinner."

Addie glanced down at her hand, her eyes going wide, and she said, "Oh, thank you very much, sir. Yes, I'll be here all weekend."

David put his arm around Aurora as they turned to walk off, pulling her close to his side. They moved slowly across the hall to where David knew the elevators were. Time had seemed to stop. They were in no rush at all. They arrived at the elevator, and when David pushed the button, Aurora gave him a look.

"Don't worry, you won't mind this one," he said reassuringly.

"If you say so," she said skeptically. The doors opened, and she was relieved to see wood paneled walls and no windows. "This is much better."

They stepped inside, and David pressed the number 5 button for the top floor. Aurora put her arm around him and rested her head on his chest.

He kissed the top of her head, and then rested his head gently against hers. The door opened, and they walked out onto the balcony. There was a small sign indicating which rooms were on either side. They turned to their left. The room was on the front side of the building at the far end. They could see the gentle flickering of the lanterns below and hear the sounds of the remaining guests floating up to them.

Reaching the corner, they turned to the right. The 5th floor was quiet and still as they made their way down to the last room on the end. There were fewer doors here, due to the large size of the suites. At once it seemed so far to the end, then suddenly they were there. David pulled out the key, unlocked the door, turned the knob, and pushed it open. The lights were on, inviting them inside.

He placed a hand on Aurora's arm to stop her from entering, and she turned to look at him. "There's a tradition," he said, and he scooped her up in his arms. "I'm supposed to carry you over the threshold."

She smiled at him and tucked her head against his neck. He could feel her warm breath on his skin, and it sent a tingle through him. Once inside, he pushed the door shut and gently lowered her to her feet. Then he reached back and locked the door.

Aurora turned to look at the room, standing silent for a moment, taking it all in. To her right was a large bed with a number of pillows on a thick soft looking comforter, a dresser with their bags sitting on top. Next to it, their camping packs were carefully placed against the wall with her bow. On the opposite side, she could see the open door to a large bath and a closet. To her left was a sitting area with 2 sofas, tables, a counter with a sink and cooktop. Across the room was an enormous set of windows with a table and chairs for dining while enjoying the view. The table was covered with a platter of fruits and a variety of bottles and glasses. The décor was nothing like the rustic look of the lodge. It was elegant and welcoming at the same time. The rich green and earth tones were warm and comforting.

She turned to David to see him looking at her affectionately, waiting to hear her reaction. "Oh, David, this is splendid," she said, as she stepped closer to him.

"I have to say that I can't take credit for it. My dad made the arrangements."

"I'll have to remember to thank him when we get home," she said as she placed her hand on his chest, standing very close to him. He felt that breathless weakness again at her touch. "In the meantime I'm going to change. I have something for you, too." Then she gave him a small kiss on the lips that lingered only briefly, but it was enough for him to feel himself flush. "I'll be right back," she said, then retrieved her bag and headed to the bathroom. She turned to give him a last smile before she shut the door behind her.

David stood looking out the window. Even in the dark with a crescent moon, the view was still impressive. He was nervous and excited about the next step in their journey together. It was one of the things he hadn't

thought about; hadn't planned. He wanted her to want him as much as he

wanted her. He didn't know if most men felt this way, but he hoped she

would feel the same thrill, same excitement, same longing that he did. He

knew that was not something he could manufacture, that having just the

right table setting or sheets or any other contrivance could create. When

she touched him, kissed him, every inch of him tingled with excitement,

and he hoped she would feel that too.

David walked over to the table and absentmindedly poured a couple

of glasses of ice water "David," he heard Aurora say, sounding far away.

He turned, holding up the two glasses, and said, "I was…" Then stood

frozen on the spot. The sight of her took his breath away. She had undone

her hair, and it fell in waves over her shoulders, shimmering ever so

slightly. She wore a thin white robe that ran down to the middle of her

hips, exposing her long shapely legs. She hadn't tied it closed, offering a

glimpse of a lacy white bra, small white matching pantie, and her smooth

lean stomach.

She started walking towards him, but stopped at his sudden silence.

Looking embarrassed, she asked, "Do I look foolish? The woman at the

shop said I should wear this."

David, struggling to regain control of his wits, said, "Oh no… you

look"… she looked up at him hopefully, and he rallied. With a clear confident voice he said, "Exquisite! I have never seen anyone more beautiful."

Beaming with confidence again, she moved towards him, taking slow measured steps. "Have you seen many woman dressed like this before?" She asked, her expression now one of a huntress eyeing her prey.

David's heart pounded in his ears as he stammered a little, saying, "Only in pictures."

She was very close to him now. "Hmm, that's good, because this is for your eyes only." She reached out, taking a glass of water from him, placed it to her lips and took a small sip. When she drew the glass away, her lips were wet, and the tip of her tongue came out and slowly caressed them dry.

David took a drink to steady himself as she reached around him, saying, "What's this?" She had to lean forward slightly to reach, and was as close as she could be without touching him. When she leaned back, she held up a strawberry covered in chocolate. David set down the glass, afraid he might drop it.

"A chocolate covered strawberry. Have you ever had one?"

"No, are they sweet?"

"Yes, and juicy."

She lifted the fruit up to her lips and took a bite. As she closed her mouth down on the fruit, her eyes shut, and she uttered "Mmm" from deep in her throat. As she pulled the remaining piece away, a small amount of juice trickled down the side of her mouth. Instinctively, David reached up and wiped the juice off of her chin with his finger.

She opened her eyes at his touch, took his hand, and pulled it to her mouth, taking his finger in and rolled her tongue around it, licking off the juice. "That was delicious," she said. "Would you like a taste?"

Without waiting for a reply, she placed the fruit to his lips, and he also took a bite. She placed the top of the strawberry on the table behind him, and as he swallowed, he reached out, placing a hand on the side of her face. Her eyes closed as she leaned into his touch. He leaned forward and placed his lips on hers. They were full and soft and welcomed his kiss. Her arms slid around him as his other hand found the small of her back, pulling her closer.

Suddenly his mind snapped back. He regained control of himself as he felt her pressed close to him. He felt strong and alive with her warm body against his. Every part of him was screaming with the desire he felt for her. The passion of their kiss grew, the taste of her mouth, the feel of her soft flesh under his hand, ignited an inferno inside him he had never felt before. Both his hands on the bare skin of her waist now, slowly, firmly moved up her back. He felt her leaning into his touch as she tilted her head back; eyes closed, exposing the nape of her neck. David leaned in and began kissing the small curve where her shoulder and neck met. She moaned slightly, her hands groping at his shirt, and she began to pull it out of his waistband. Her hands found his skin, as she slid them up along his sides.

Her hands on him created a fresh wave of excitement. The feel of the firm caressing of his muscles moving inch-by-inch up his body was intoxicating. Her hands inspecting him like a treasured possession was the affirmation he desperately yearned for, to know that she wanted him the way he wanted her. In that moment, every doubt, fear, or worry he had ever had was entirely stripped away, and he felt invincible.

***

Aurora could feel his strong muscles and broad shoulders under her hands. She had never considered men this way before; never felt desire for a man before. Something about him had awoken a part of her that had been smoldering inside, desperate to escape. He was gently kissing, tasting her neck, shoulders, and the top of her chest. His strong hands on her bare skin were warm and comforting. She was lost in sensations she had never experienced before, and didn't want them to end. She managed to push her arms up, lifting his shirt, forcing him to let go and tip his head up. As he pulled his arms out of the sleeves, she saw what he had seen, and was drawn in to kiss and taste him. Her lips touching his neck, she felt him sway slightly as he gasped with pleasure. Her excitement grew, hearing and feeling the effect she had on him.

Her hands were exploring his chest. He was well built from hard work, and she could feel the strength of his chiseled muscles under her hands and lips. She felt his fingers gently lift the top of her robe as his hand found her bare shoulders. He pushed the robe back and down off her arms. She felt the soft fabric slide down her back to land gently at her feet. Her arms wrapped around him, pulling him close so she could feel his bare skin against hers. As she pressed up against him, he let out a soft moan of pleasure, and she responded with one of her own.

Suddenly his knees bent, and she was slightly startled, thinking he was collapsing. To her surprise, his arms wrapped around her waist, pulling her tight to him as he stood up, lifting her off the ground. She threw her head back, letting out a small laugh as she instinctively wrapped her legs around his waist. He began kissing her neck and chest again as she squeezed him tightly. He effortlessly carried her to the bed. She found his strength exhilarating.

He stopped at the edge of the bed, and she dropped her legs down to stand before him. He cupped her face with his hands and kissed her. She reached in between them and unbuckled his belt, then after opening the front of his pants, she ran her hands around his waist and pushed them down over his underpants. Once past his hips, they fell to the floor. He reached his right arm around her waist, pulled her close, then leaned forward and lowered her onto the bed. She looked him in the eye, then gave him a playful inviting smile as she scurried backwards up to the top of the bed.

A couple of hours later, they were thankful for the food and drinks that had been left in their room. They were both feeling a satisfied exhaustion from several passion-filled workouts. Laying there holding each other, David said, "I suppose it is a good thing we don't have to get up early."

Aurora said in a sleepy voice, "I don't think you could drag me out of bed at sunrise."

"You won't have to worry about that."

"Mmmm," she cooed.

David sat quietly, and in a moment she was asleep. He pulled the blanket up over them with his free hand, and the moment he closed his eyes, he was asleep too.

THE WATERFALL

David awoke, feeling Aurora lying next to him with sunshine filling the room. His senses coming back to him more slowly than normal, it took a minute to realize they were naked under the cover. He smiled, remembering the night before, and that they were finally fully husband and wife. He turned to find the clock, and saw it was ten a.m. Six hours of sleep wasn't too bad, he thought. He slipped out from under Aurora and went to the bathroom.

When he came out, he found his pants and pulled them on. He went to the far side of the room to use the other guest phone, and called down to room service. In a hushed voice, he asked, "Is it too late to get breakfast?"

The woman on the other end of the phone asked, "Room 501, Sir?"

"Yes."

"No, Sir. We have special instructions to get you whatever you want."

"That's very kind of you. I don't want to be any trouble."

"No trouble at all, Sir. What would you like?"

"Bacon and eggs, toast, fruit, juice, and a big pot of coffee would be great."

"We'll have it up there in 30 minutes for you, Sir."

"Thank you. That'll be great."

"You're welcome," she said and hung up.

David found his shirt and went over to the table by the window to sit down and wait. He gazed out at the valley below them. The fall colors were fading, but the majesty of their surroundings was not diminished. Off to his left, rolling hills cascaded down to the sprawling lake. On his right, he could see the mountain stream winding its way down to feed it, and at the far end he could just make out a tributary draining off the excess water in the distance.

The sun was bright and warm and shimmered off the water. It appeared that most of the birds had already migrated for the season, as he hadn't seen any movement in the trees that blanketed the surroundings. The only activity he saw was a handful of people milling about, as the water was undoubtedly too cold to swim in this time of year. He smiled absentmindedly as images of their night together danced in and out of his thoughts. As much as he enjoyed losing himself completely in his desire for her, he was glad to find his mind clear this morning. The world was still a dangerous place, especially for them. He needed to be aware of his surroundings in order to protect her.

"Hi. Did you sleep well?" he asked without turning around.

"I see you got your hearing back."

David turned to see her standing there in her little robe and nothing else. "Not disappointed, are you?"

She sat sideways in his lap, looked into his eyes, and said, "No, but I did enjoy having a little advantage over you last night."

"Hmm, I think you know that you always have a big advantage over me. You're irresistible," he said, and gave her a long soft kiss.

"Mmm, good morning."

"Good morning," he said. "I ordered us some breakfast. It should be here any minute."

She smiled "Wonderful. I'm starving."

"I thought you might be. I am too. We had quite a workout," he said, grinning.

"You can say that again. I'd better put some clothes on if someone is coming." She got up and headed to the bath, where she had left her suitcase the night before.

David watched her walking off, admiring her figure, her grace, and her confident stride; she stopped and turned to look at him before stepping out of view. "What are you looking at?"

"You," he said with a grin.

"Good," she said with a self-satisfied smile and disappeared into the bath.

David chuckled a little out loud. He was sure that she would keep him on his toes the rest of his life, and looked forward to it. Just then he heard a soft knock at the door. Getting to his feet, he made his way over and opened the door. Addie stood in the doorway with the room service cart filled with covered dishes and pitchers.

"Hi, Addie I didn't expect to see you again so soon," David said inviting her in.

"I'm covering for one of the other girls, and since breakfast is over, the normal room service staff is changing shifts. When I heard it was your order, I volunteered to bring it up. I hope you don't mind."

"Of course not. I'm happy to see you."

"I hope I thought of everything. I don't normally do room service," she said, then proceeded to show David all of the dishes, condiments, coffee, juice, etc. She asked, "Did I forget anything?"

"Not a thing! It's perfect. Thank you," David said, as Aurora came out wearing the outfit from the night before.

"Good morning, Miss, how are you today?"

"Wonderful," she said with a smile "and how are you?"

"I'm fine, thank you. I normally work nights and have a double shift today, so I'll be tired later, but I can always use the extra work."

David signed the ticket and handed it back to Addie. He reached into his pocket to retrieve some money, and she said, "Oh, please you don't have to do that. You were so generous last night there's no need."

David took her hand, placed the money in it, and said, "I insist. It was very nice of you to make the extra effort to look after us this morning. Besides, when we come for dinner tonight, I want to make sure you don't mind taking care of us again."

"Oh no, Sir, it would be my pleasure."

"Great! It's Friday, isn't it? What time is good to come for dinner?"

"If you want to eat early, you want to come around six. There is a lull then in between the families and the hunting crowd. If you want a late dinner, come after eight. The dance floor starts to get busy around nine."

"Will there be a lot of people dancing?" Aurora asked, a glimmer of excitement in her voice.

"Yes Miss, we get a lot of people from all around who come on Friday and Saturday for the music. The band that's playing is extremely popular."

Aurora turned to David, "Are we going to go?"

"I thought you might like to. That's one of the reasons I wanted to come here."

"Oh, that sounds like fun," Aurora said with a hint of the little girl in her showing.

"I should get back." Addie said, "Otherwise they might think I'm goofing off. But if you need anything at all, please let me know, and thank you for your generosity."

"You're welcome. We'll ask for you when we come tonight then. Have a good day, and don't work too hard," David said as Addie left the room.

The two of them were feeling ravenous now. They quickly set the food and drinks on the table and sat down to eat. Aurora, finally getting a good look at the view, said, "What a beautiful valley. Are we high up in the mountains?"

David explained that the Lodge was in the foothills and the mountain went up for miles behind it. That not far from where they were was a ski resort, a village, and further down into the valley was farmland.

"If you'd like, we could take a drive after we eat, and I could show you around. The village is very charming, and there are lots of shops to see. I think you'd enjoy it."

"That does sound nice."

Once he finished eating, David said, "I should take a shower and clean up if we're going out." He stood up and walked over, giving her a kiss. "I won't take too long. Do you need anything before I go?"

"No, I'll be fine."

David walked over and grabbed his bag, then made his way to the bathroom. Before entering, he looked back at Aurora to find her watching him." What are you looking at?" he asked teasingly.

Caught in her own trap, she giggled, and said, "You."

"Good," he said smiling broadly.

The bathroom was long and large. Opposite the door was a counter with two sinks. To his right were two racks. One held an assortment of towels and Aurora's bag, so he set his down on the other one. Past the racks were two private water closets, on the left an extra-large shower, and at the far end, a tub large enough for two.

David turned on the water so it could warm up and placed the towel on a hook by the shower door. By the time he was undressed the water was just right, so he stepped inside under the spray. The hot water running down his body felt invigorating, and he stood there letting the warmth wash over him. Then he heard the door slide open. He turned to see Aurora standing there, her clothes discarded. With a slightly sheepish expression, she said, "I thought I should take a bath too. Do you mind if I join you?"

David reached out a hand to her. She smiled as she took it, stepped in, and shut the door. "Here, stand under the water. It's nice and warm."

She tipped her head back to let the water run through her hair. He watched as the water cascaded down her body, droplets forming on all of her curves. His heart started to pound, and he didn't need the warm water to fight off the cool air. She lifted her head straight again, and saw him gazing at her. She stepped forward, putting her hands on his chest, and in a husky voice asked, "Are you all right?"

As he pulled her close and kissed her, she melted in his arms. The feel of her wet body was a whole new sensation. After freeing her arms, she squeezed him tight and kissed him back with equal passion.

They never left the room that day, and around 4:30 the phone rang. David reached over to the bedside table and picked up the receiver. "Hello."

"Sir I'm sorry to bother you, but this is housekeeping, and we wanted to know if you would like the room cleaned today before our staff goes home."

"The room is fine, thank you. I think it can wait until tomorrow."

"Very good, Sir. If you could please just put the room service cart outside in the hall, someone will be by to pick it up later."

"Thank you. I will. Have a good evening."

"You too, Sir."

"Who was that?"

"Housekeeping. They wanted to know if they should clean our room." David said, "I guess they didn't expect us to be here all day."

"Hmm, I didn't mind."

"Neither did I. Are you still up for going dancing tonight?"

"Oh, yes! That sounds like fun."

"It's too early to go down to dinner now. How would you like to take a walk to the lake? When we get back, it should be about time for us to go to dinner."

"That does sound good. Some outdoor air would be nice."

David leaned over and gave her a kiss. "I'm going to get up and get dressed then." Then he rolled out of bed.

"I think I'll wait here until you are done this time."

"That's probably a good idea," David said, flashing her a grin as he shut the door.

While Aurora was getting dressed, David gathered up the room service items and organized them on the cart, wheeling it out into the hallway. He was used to keeping busy, and in spite of, or maybe because of, the day's activities, he was filled with restless energy. He walked around the room straightening up a bit, and then saw their camping packs. He knelt down beside his and retrieved a few precautionary items. He thought he'd rather be prepared, even though he didn't expect anything other than a nice walk.

As he was getting to his feet, Aurora came out and asked, "What are you doing?"

"Just taking some precautions."

"Should I bring my bow?"

"No, I think that would be a bit too conspicuous, and I'm sure there's no need. I just don't want to get too complacent."

She trusted him and said, unconcerned, "All right."

David held her jacket for her as she put it on, then grabbing his, they set out. They headed down to the lobby, saying a quick hello and goodbye to Charlie at the front desk. The sun was low in the sky as they made their way down to the lake. They held hands, strolling along completely relaxed. David began to point out various trails and activity areas, relating them to stories he had told her or sharing new ones. The sun was almost down when they reached the lake, and there were a few other people enjoying an evening walk too. The setting sun was a dark orange, and the light dancing on the lake was soothing. Once they made it to the end of the trail, the cool air was starting to bite their exposed skin. David put his arm around Aurora as they began the walk back.

Even though the cold was setting in, they still weren't in any rush to get back. Aurora mused how, if David had grown up in her village, that

William and Nathan would have been his partners in crime, and she might have had to set him straight too. She wondered how Miles and Solidad were doing, and what was happening to all the people they left behind. David also hoped they were all well, and that with the fall of the *Dark One*, chaos did not ensue.

It was completely dark out when they returned, and the moon was just about gone. Thankfully the path was lit, so they had no trouble making their way. They were happy to enter the warm lobby. Lost in conversation, they hadn't realized how cold they were. It was still a little early to go to dinner, so they decided to go back to their room and warm up first before heading to the dining hall.

Back at the room, David fixed some tea and they relaxed on the couch while they waited. "You told me you'd show me what that is on the wall. Do we have time now?"

"Sure. It's called a TV." David said, "It shows moving pictures." David found the remote and turned it on. It was a large screen and was set to a local news channel.

"That's incredible," Aurora said walking over to it. "They look like real people, not pictures."

"They are real people; a camera records them and sends it here. This show is live. These people are actually doing what you see as we speak."

"Really," she said, as she inspected it, looking all around the screen. After a few moments, she sat back down next to David and picked up her tea. "What kind of show is this?"

"This is the news where people find out what is going on around them," David said. Then he flipped through a few channels, showing her examples of other programs. Aurora was amused by some singing and dancing, startled by explosions and gunfire, baffled by a strange cartoon, and captivated by a nature show filmed flying over various landscapes.

"How do they do all that?"

"That's a long story. Since it's almost eight o'clock, how about we go down and talk about it at dinner?"

"I think that's a great idea, since I'm starving again."

David stood and reached out a hand. Aurora took it and got to her feet. Having warmed up, they left their jackets and headed straight down to the dining room. When they arrived, David saw Tom, who came over to welcome them.

"Hello there. I was wondering when I was going to see you two again. How's your room?"

"Fantastic, Tom! I can't thank you enough."

"Do you have everything you need?" he asked, looking at Aurora.

"Yes, I've never enjoyed such splendor before."

"Great. Are you going to enjoy some dinner and dancing tonight? The band that's playing is extremely popular."

"You bet."

"Good. I'll get you a table."

"Can you sit us in Addie's section?" David asked, "We really enjoyed her, and she brought us our breakfast this morning so we wouldn't have to wait."

"Sure thing. She's a good girl. I wish I had more people like her working for me. Come this way."

Tom wound his way through the hall with David and Aurora in tow. He brought them up to the same area where they sat the night before and invited them to sit down.

"Here you go. I'll let Addie know you are here. I'll be running around tonight, but if you need me, just tell Addie."

"Don't worry about us. I'm sure we'll be just fine."

"You enjoy, and I'll stop back by later," Tom said, then hurried off.

There was a lot more noise in the room tonight, and they were happy to be out of the way, so they could hear each other easily. The room was very busy, and almost all of the tables were occupied. Addie hadn't exaggerated. David could see more people coming in from the lobby doors.

"Do you need any help with the menu?" David asked Aurora.

She picked it up and began looking it over, "I don't know."

Before she could finish her thought, a bus boy arrived with some bread and water. They could see the steam rising from the hot bread, and it pushed all thoughts of looking at the menu out of their minds for the moment.

"Thank you," David said.

"Yes, that bread looks delicious," Aurora said.

"You're welcome. Addie will be along in a minute to take your order," the bus boy said, and he hurried away.

They each helped themselves to some bread in the hope it would take the edge off their ravenous hunger.

"Mmm, this is delicious," Aurora said.

"It sure is. Suddenly I'm so hungry I could eat the basket."

Aurora chuckled, "Me too!"

Addie arrived, beaming at them. "Hi, how are you doing tonight? I'm so glad you asked for me."

"Of course. You're our guardian angel," David smiled back.

"And thank you for saying such nice things to Tom about me."

"He thinks very highly of you already," Aurora said.

"Are you two hungry?"

"Ravenous. We haven't eaten since the breakfast you brought us," Aurora replied.

"Oh my, you must be hungry! Do you know what you want to eat?"

"We haven't actually looked yet. Can you recommend anything?" David asked.

"I know just the thing. Do you like pasta and seafood?"

David looked at Aurora, and she said, "That sounds good to me."

"We're in your hands, Addie. Whatever you think is best."

"Don't worry about a thing. I'll take care of you. Tea to drink again tonight, or would you like wine?"

"Just tea I think," Aurora said. "I want to do some dancing after dinner."

"Tea for me too."

"Ok, I'll get you some salad so you don't starve to death, and be right back." Addie said and hurried off.

"She's such a sweet girl."

"Yes she is," David said, looking at Aurora affectionately.

She looked at him and asked sheepishly, "Why are you looking at me like that?"

"I'm just so in love with you. I love that you're so confident and secure. So many women would find a pretty young girl like her threatening, but not you. Your kindness to her and everyone we meet is so precious to me."

Aurora reached over, taking his hand in hers, pulling it to her cheek. She leaned against him and said, "You always make me feel special apart from anyone else. There's no room for doubt in my heart."

"I hope I'm not interrupting," Addie appeared, standing there with two salads. "I hurried since you were so hungry."

They sat up straight, making room for her to set the plates down. "Not at all, Aurora was just saying how much she liked you."

"Thank you. Aurora. That's such a pretty name, and fitting for such a beautiful woman," Addie said. "Just let me know if you need anything." Then she left them to eat.

The sight of food reminded them of their hunger, and they both began eating. They did their best to pace themselves, and thoroughly enjoyed their meal. Addie's suggestion was delicious and filling. They enjoyed watching the crowd of people and discussed the prospect of hiking the next day.

"It's a few hours' hike to the spot I want to show you. I'm surprised more people haven't found it, but no one else I've talked to has ever seen it. I think you'll enjoy it."

"I'd like that."

Before they realized it, nine o'clock rolled around, and the band began to play. They were a country music group, and the crowd became excited when they started.

Addie came over and asked, "Would you like me to hold your table while you dance? Then when you need a break, you can come and sit down."

"Are you sure that wouldn't be too much trouble?"

"No. We aren't likely to get many more dinner guests. Go, enjoy yourselves."

David stood and asked Aurora, "Would you like to dance?"

"Yes I would."

They had both been watching the other patrons, and once on the dance floor, tried to follow their example of how to dance. They were sure they probably looked silly, as they had no idea what they were doing, but they didn't care. They had fun and only had eyes for each other. By the time they made it back to the table, it was already 10 o'clock. The time had flown by.

They slumped into their chairs and Aurora said, "I had so much fun. I felt like a little girl again."

"I was really happy I didn't step on anyone," David said. "I had no idea what I was doing."

"Neither did I!"

Addie appeared at the table and said, "It looked like you had a good out there. Would you like a drink to cool down?"

"I'd like some more water, please."

"That sounds good to me too."

"Coming right up," Addie said, then left.

"I think you wore me out today," Aurora said to David with a grin. "Would you be disappointed if we go upstairs?"

"Not at all. I think I wore myself out too," David said. "Would you like to take some dessert up with us?"

"I don't think I can eat another bite."

"Neither could I."

"Here's your water."

"Addie, can we please have our check? I think we're finished for tonight."

"Sure. I'll be right back."

They both had several drinks of water before Addie returned.

"Are you working tomorrow, Addie?"

"Yes Sir. Sunday, and Monday too."

"Good, then we'll see you again. I hope you don't have to work much longer tonight."

"No, you're my last table, so I'm heading home. Thankfully I get to sleep in tomorrow."

"Be careful going home, and thank you again for taking care of us."

"Goodnight Addie," Aurora said.

"Goodnight. Have fun tomorrow." Addie said as the two of them left.

As they made their way across the hall, they saw Tom towering over two young men with a scowl on his face. They appeared terrified, and David chuckled at the sight he knew all too well. Tom caught a glimpse of them out of the corner of his eye, and turned and waved. David and Aurora waved back, and Tom immediately returned to his quarry.

This time the slow pace back to the room was caused both by the fatigue they felt, and the heavy meal they ate. Arriving at the room, Aurora turned to David with heavy eyes. "I'm going to use the bath. I'll be right back."

"Ok, take your time."

David walked over and sat on the couch, regretting it almost immediately. It was very comfortable, and he was afraid if he sat too long he might doze off. He tried weakly to convince himself to get up, but lost the argument to his tired muscles. In an effort to stay awake, he started

digging through his memory for the exact route to find the waterfall the

next day, and before he knew it, Aurora was emerging from the bath.

He looked over to see her striding towards him, smiling and wearing

only her shirt, which barely covered her hips. "Hi there."

She sat on the couch and leaned across his lap, putting her arms

around him. "I had a wonderful time tonight," she said, and then she

kissed him slowly.

"Hmm, so did I," David said, "but can you please hold that thought

while I run to the bathroom?"

"I suppose I can wait," she said with a smile.

David got up from the couch, and Aurora stretched out, giving him an

alluring look. "Don't keep me waiting."

"I won't," he replied, and quickly went to the bathroom. Although he

was only gone for a few minutes, he wasn't surprised to find her asleep

when he returned. He gazed affectionately at her for a moment, pulled

down the bed covers, turned off the lights, and got undressed. Returning to

the couch, he scooped her up in his arms, carefully carried her over and

laid her down on the bed. He slid into the bed, doing his best not to wake

her, and pulled the cover up over the two of them. As soon as he was lying

down, she rolled over, wrapping an arm around him, still fast asleep. He closed his eyes, taking in her scent, enjoying the comfort of her against him, and in moments he was asleep too.

Sunlight began filling the room, and it was a gentle reminder to David to wake up. He was used to getting up at sunrise, and when he opened his eyes, he knew it was later than that. Looking at the clock, he saw it was nearly eight am. It had been many years since he slept that long. He lay there for a time, trying to gather his thoughts, when Aurora stirred. Lifting her head, up she looked at him, and he said, "Hi."

She smiled and said, "Hi," then looking around a little, she asked, "How did I end up here? I don't remember coming to bed."

"You fell asleep on the couch, and I carried you over."

She put her head on his chest and said, "I'm sorry."

"Don't be. I was asleep the minute my head hit the pillow. I guess we wore each other out," David said. "Did you sleep well?"

"Like a rock. And you?"

"Me too. How about I order us some coffee and breakfast?"

David sat up and looked at Aurora more seriously, and said, "While I was lying here waking up, I got a feeling that we need to go on our hike today; that somehow it's necessary, and we should head out early. I hope you don't mind."

Aurora looked at him and said affectionately, "You know I'll always follow you anywhere. I trust you without question, and if you think we need to go, then I'll be at your side."

David smiled and then kissed her. He felt such affection for her that it brought a lump to his throat. When he sat up again, she said with a mock admonition, "Don't start anything you aren't prepared to finish."

He laughed and said, "I'll make it up to you when we get back."

"I'll hold you to that," she said teasingly.

David got up, strode over to the phone, and called down to room service. He ordered their breakfast and some sandwiches for later, as well as bottles of water. Then he encouraged Aurora to shower and get dressed while he waited for the meal to arrive. He put on his clothes from the night before and walked to the window. Staring out at the landscape, he tried to retrieve the feeling that had come to him. He didn't think there was any danger, but he did feel a sense of urgency that the sooner they left, the better.

When room service arrived, he told the young lady they were going out for the day, and asked if she could please arrange for housekeeping.

Aurora came out of the bathroom dressed and ready to go. She had pulled her hair back into a braid, and wore some of the hiking pants they bought, a button down top with t-shirt underneath, and hiking boots. Yet she moved as gracefully as ever.

"Breakfast is here. Are you hungry?"

"Yes, and I'd especially like some coffee."

They sat at the table and ate. David told her about the hike ahead of them and some of the things they would see along the way. He wasn't nervous, but he was a little anxious, and as soon as he finished eating, he got up to go get himself dressed.

He took a quick shower, and just as she had, he put on hiking clothes and boots with a layered top. Back in the room, he found her relaxing by the window and walked over to retrieve the sandwiches and water bottles. "See anything interesting out there?"

"Nothing in particular, although it's beautiful. I do get to bring my bow, right?" she said firmly.

"Absolutely," then he knelt in front of her and said, "I don't think we're in any danger. I don't exactly know what to think, but I don't want you to worry."

"I'm not worried," she said with a smile. "I'll be with you, but just like you, I always like to be prepared."

David leaned in, kissed her, and said, "and I love that about you." Then he stood and offered her his hand.

They walked over to their camping packs, and David put a few bottles of water in each pack, and the sandwiches in his. For their size, they were exceptionally lightweight, which was one of the reasons David had chosen them. They headed out the door without looking back.

Once downstairs, David went to the lobby to see the desk clerk. "Good morning. We're in room 501. Can you please leave Tom a message for me?"

The young lady behind the desk said, "Hold on. He's in the office. I'll ask him to come out." Then she went through the door behind her, and a minute later Tom appeared.

"Good morning. I didn't expect to see you so early today," Tom said in a jovial tone.

"Good Morning, Tom. We're going hiking up past Bucks Gorge. I remembered I forgot to call my father when we got here. Would you do a big favor for me and call him?"

Tom let out a hearty laugh. "Are you kidding me? He called the night you arrived to check on you."

David smiled. "I should have known. We should be back for dinner, but just in case we don't make it, we're prepared, so don't go calling out the search and rescue."

"All right, but I probably should call your dad; otherwise he might. Have a safe trip, and be sure to let me know when you get back."

"We will," David said, as he and Aurora headed out the door.

They stepped out into the brisk morning air. They had their traveling coats in their packs, knowing once on the other side of the lodge, the sun would warm them. They walked the length of the building, and at the far end took the path that led around back. As large as the Lodge felt on the inside, it felt even bigger walking around the outside of it. Soon enough, they were behind the building heading north up a well-worn trail into the mountains.

The lodge sat on a relatively flat spot on the side of the mountain, and the grassy area behind it slowly rose for a couple of hundred yards until it began a steeper incline to meet the tree line. David explained that there were two trails, one that wound slowly back and forth, and another that was more direct, but harder climbing. Aurora knew he wanted to take the direct route, and told him she was up for it. They made their way across the meadow at a brisk pace. Even though he knew they weren't in danger, he didn't like being exposed.

Once they entered the tree line, he felt more relaxed and paced himself. Aurora was no stranger to hiking, and keeping up wasn't any trouble for her. They began talking about the wildlife they saw, other places they'd been, the lodge, even about TV and how it worked, and in no time they were enjoying a relaxing hike through the woods.

The weather was chilly but felt good, due to the exertion of the climb. The sun filtered down through the tree canopy from time to time, warming their bare skin. A couple of hours into their hike, David left the trail, heading up a steep rock formation. Once on top, they entered another clearing that was pristine from the lack of any other visitors.

"We're getting close now. We should be there before noon. We can stop to eat if you're hungry, or we can wait until we get to the falls."

"I'm fine. Let's keep going."

David led her across the meadow and back into the woods on the other side. They climbed up another couple of miles until they came to a small gorge. The gorge looked as if a giant axe had split the ground into an enormous V. They walked through the center where the ground was littered with loose rocks, and when they emerged on the other side, there was a dense pocket of trees and brush. Looking up, it was clear the mountain continued, but the forest ahead was so thick it was impossible to see the grade that lay beyond.

David entered the thicket through an opening that was so obscured that Aurora thought it was no surprise no one else had been here. This was no easy place to find. "How did you find this place the first time?"

"Oh, I don't know. Just by accident I suppose."

"It's so secluded that it's no wonder no one else seems to know about it."

Once clear of the heavy brush, they made their way around an outcropping, and there before them was a small pond cupped into the side of the mountain. Grass lined the bank where they were standing. Tall trees whose canopies reached almost completely across the water surrounded the area. On the opposite side was a small stream funneling off the excess water and carrying it down the mountainside. On the other side of the stream was the waterfall, meandering back and forth as it made its way into the pond. It had to be at least 50 feet tall, and the last 10 feet or so dropped straight down, creating a curtain of water.

Small rainbows, fed by the sunlight streaming in through the opening above, illuminated the churning water at the bottom of the fall. The sun also created a trail through the middle of the pond that shimmered with the movement of the water, splitting it in two. The banks on either side leading back to the falls were barely passable, as the earth and rock went almost straight up. The moss and small plants that thrived in the bowl would have made climbing down nearly impossible, but at the same time gave the scene a warm earthy feel that was peaceful and comforting.

They stood for a few moments in silence until David asked, "What do you think?"

"I think it's incredible. It's the most beautiful place I've ever been."

"I was hoping you'd enjoy it. There's something about being here that has always made me feel renewed." He said, "I came here a lot after my parent's accident, when I thought I'd lost them both."

"I feel it too. There's something more here than just beautiful scenery."

"Why don't we sit down, have our lunch, and relax a bit?"

"I'd like that."

They took off their packs and were getting the supplies out when David stood and turned. There, standing behind them, was a man. He was a tall and powerful looking man, yet at the same time, he was handsome, and wore a kindly expression. David placed a hand on Aurora, who had instinctively reached for her bow, telling her to wait. The man was standing in a patch of sunlight shining down on him, and it gave him an ethereal look. He wore simple robes, and clearly did not just climb the mountain to get here.

"Hello. I hope I didn't frighten you."

David said, "No, I just didn't hear you approach, and wasn't expecting to see anyone here."

"Weren't you?" the man asked, "Isn't that why you've come?"

"I knew I needed to come, but I wasn't sure why," David said. Then he asked, "Who are you?"

"I'm Asis, and I have come to meet you, David and Aurora."

David felt Aurora stir next to him at the mention of their names. "I see. What can we do for you?"

Asis looked at them appraisingly, then after a moment's pause, said patiently, "You have found favor with the Lord, and He has chosen you to lead the battles that are to come. I was sent here to tell you certain things you need to know."

David sighed, then turned to Aurora. He knew that Asis was telling the truth, and told her with a look. She nodded slightly to indicate she understood. He could see what he felt in her eyes too. Why? Why did it have to be so soon? They had been through so much, and just when their own happiness seemed within reach, couldn't they have had a little more time?

Then David turned back to Asis, and said, "We were about to sit down for a meal. Would you please join us?"

Asis stepped forward to meet them, and tipped his head saying, "Thank you."

David returned to his pack and retrieved a blanket, then handed it to Aurora and asked, "Would you please spread this out for us to sit on?"

She gave him a small smile and said, "of course."

David rummaged through the packs, pulling out a few bottles of water, the food they had brought, and a knife to cut the sandwiches. They all sat down, and David handed Asis and Aurora each a water bottle. Then he began to divide up the sandwiches and placed some fruit in the center for them to share. He gave thanks for their meal, and then encouraged Asis and Aurora to eat.

"Why did we meet here?"

"This place is not actually part of your world. It lies in between yours and mine, and is protected. Only those who are uniquely gifted can find it. It allows us to speak freely, without concern for those who will seek to deter you from your path."

"Are we being followed?" Aurora asked.

"The *Dark One*'s minions are all around. You must always remain vigilant. Events are beginning to unfold, and you will be drawn into them whether you are ready or not."

"What events are unfolding?" David asked.

"The *Dark One's* physical being was trapped in Tartaros. That limited *his* influence on your world. When you defeated *him* there, you also freed *him*. Now *he* has a physical presence here."

"But we were sent to defeat *him*," David said with a slight air of pleading, even though he already knew they hadn't. The Lord had told them the *Dark One* was already making plans to corrupt their world. David had only hoped they had more time, but then he remembered his dream the night before the wedding. The truth was, he knew it had already started.

"Even trapped in Tartaros, *his* darkness was spreading like a plague. *He* must be brought out into the light and exposed, so that the final battle lines can be drawn."

"Are you referring to the end times?"

"Yes and no." Asis said, "No one knows when those days will come. Only our Father knows that. But before they do come, the *Dark One* must rise to *his* full power so that all *his* servants will be revealed. Then the chaff can be separated from the wheat."

"Are you saying *he*'s more powerful than before, and will rise-up here?" Aurora asked.

"No, *he* is constrained here just as *he* was in Tartaros, and must be freed. Once *he* is released from the form that binds *him*, *he* will begin preparing for the final battle. Until then, *he* will work to poison this world as *he* did the other, corrupting as many as *he* can in advance of *his* return. *He* knows that if not for the final battle, even the elect would fall. *He* will try to avert the prophecy by claiming everyone first."

"Does that mean that we have to destroy *him* again?" David asked.

"Yes, but it will not be as easy as it was before."

"That was easy?" Aurora said, half to herself. David put a comforting hand on her, and she looked up at him and said, "You almost died," her eyes bright.

"Almost, but I had you to save me, remember?" David said with a reassuring smile. She nodded a little but said nothing.

"The difficulties lie along a different path than before. This world is more corrupt, and *he* has been sowing the seeds for *his* arrival for a long time. *He* will not directly control an army as *he* did before, not that you should underestimate how dangerous *he* is; *he* will use others already in positions of power to do *his* bidding. *He* will seek to attract followers with false promises, and prey on their fears and vanity."

"Then what do we need to do to defeat *him*?" David asked, resigning himself to the fact that they had known this was coming, and fighting it would only waste precious time.

"You must expose *him* for what *he* is, and reveal *his* true identity. Be warned though. In doing that *he* will become enraged, and you will be in considerable danger."

"I tricked *him* the first time, but I would imagine *he* will not be so easily fooled again," David said thinking out loud.

"*He* will not be easily fooled, but *his* arrogance knows no boundaries, and you must use that against *him*."

"Pride comes before a fall," David said absentmindedly. "What are you suggesting?"

"*He* will believe that you cannot defeat *him* again, and *he* will be prepared against any direct attack, such as the daggers you used last time. You are going to have to travel to Aurora's home and retrieve something that will help you."

"What is it?" Aurora asked.

"I don't know; you will have to find that out for yourselves. I do know that when *he* fell from grace, *he* roamed those lands until *he* was banished to Tartaros. You need to learn about *his* time before *his* exile, to find what you need."

"We'll probably need to travel to the temple," Aurora said. "That's where I obtained the scroll about the prophecy. The priests there are wise and have scrolls thousands of years old. It was an extremely difficult and dangerous journey. I had to travel through territory controlled by *his* army. That was when I saw your mother."

"I remember. You told me about it. With any luck, the tide of the battle has turned since we left."

"There is still a formidable army of evil, corrupt men, and you will be best served if you seek help from those you liberated."

"I guess we're going to Roktah," David said to Aurora. "It wasn't part of my honeymoon plans, but as long as we're together."

"As long as we're together," Aurora said with a smile.

David took her hand and gently kissed it, his love for her welled up inside him. She reached out and tenderly placed a hand on the side of his face, looking into his eyes. Without question, she would be by his side no matter what happened, without complaint, and suddenly it didn't matter where they were going or what they had to do. His doubts fell away. The gift they had been given was so precious to him that this burden was a small price to pay.

Asis, looking pleased said, "You have a unique bond, and it protects both of you. Through your union, your bond has been strengthened, and David's gift of anonymity has been passed to you Aurora, just as your gift of healing has passed to him. Therefore, the *Dark One* will not know where you have gone, so you must be extremely cautious when revealing your intentions."

"I understand," David said, turning back to Asis. "I presume we need to leave right away?"

"You should return home and make your preparations. Although I said you could not simply use the daggers alone to defeat *him*, you would be wise to keep them with you." Asis said, "You face a long journey, and must be ready for anything. You will have much work to do along the way. You have another advantage in that *his* attention is on this world. *He* disregards the other world, underestimating the importance of *his* loss there."

"What kind of work are you referring to?" Aurora asked.

"The people there must be united and restore the balance, destroying *his* armies, and sending *his* minions back to where they belong."

"That sounds as if it will take some time. What will happen here while we're gone?" David asked.

"*He* will begin gathering supporters, corrupting as many as *he* can," Asis said. "*He* will not take any overt action until *he* has established a large enough following to overwhelm any that oppose *him*."

"In order to defeat *him* we have to go, but we need to do whatever it is we have to do as quickly as we can so that *he* doesn't get too powerful while we're gone."

"That is right."

"What do you think?" David asked Aurora.

"It will take us at least 3 weeks to travel to the temple, and if we arrive where we did before, we have another week to get to Roktah. Travel is much slower in my world than it is here. I can't imagine we'll make it back in less than 2 months. It may take even longer, depending on what we find out," she said as if she was planning another in a long line of missions.

"I was thinking the same thing. Do we have that much time?"

"Your journey will take as long as it takes. The question is, what will you come back to, and that I cannot answer. I do not know how quickly or what *he* will do while you are gone, but every day *he* will grow stronger. I would suggest that you must be sure you have accomplished what you need to before you return. If you are unprepared when you face *him*, you will fail."

"Like I said, do it, and do it quickly," David said. "Aurora, do you have any thoughts?"

"I don't think it will be hard to rally our supporters. The cities that were trying to remain neutral should fall in line with us too. Since *his* defeat, they will want to be on the winning side. When we left, there was still a massive force to the south of Roktah. Defeating them will be no small task. We should have the advantage that they will be in disarray without leadership. Then there is the matter of our journey to the temple. We'll need to be well supplied, but I think I can arrange it. We may need a small team of trusted men to accompany us," she said, and David could see her mind running through the calculations. He smiled at her unintentionally. "What, did I say something wrong?" She added, looking fiercely ready to defend her position.

"Not at all. I was just thinking how fortunate I am that we're going together. I couldn't do it without you," David said proudly.

Aurora smiled and said, "And don't you forget it."

"Not on my life." Then David asked, "Is there anything else you can tell us that will help, Asis?"

"I will tell you two things. I see why you have found such favor from the Lord. You follow Him faithfully without question, and because of that He will be with you always. Remember that, even in your darkest hour. As you know, the *Dark One*'s skill for fostering distrust and betrayal are unmatched. *He* will seek to prey on what you fear most, and try to fill your thoughts with lies. It will be the strength of your bond, your love for each other, that will protect you from *his* deceptions."

"I trust David with my life and my heart without question."

"I have no doubts child. I only warn you so you can be prepared. And now it is time for me to depart your company," Asis said, then stood. David and Aurora stood as well, and he reached out and placed a hand on each of them. "May the Lord's blessings be on you both. Should you return to this place, and the Lord is willing, I will come to you."

"Thank you, Asis," David said.

"Till we meet again," Asis said, as he turned and headed towards the beam of sunlight that was breaking through the treetops. As he walked into it, he became extremely bright again, and as he moved closer, the light became almost blinding, and then he was gone.

David and Aurora reached for each other's hands and stood quietly for a moment. Then turning to face one another, they came together in a comforting embrace. David, gently stroking the back of Aurora's head, said, "at least we had a few ordinary days together."

"No."

"What do you mean?"

"They were extraordinary, and the happiest days of my life." she said, nuzzling her head against him.

"When this is over, we'll pick up where we left off."

"Do you promise?"

"Yes, I promise," he said softly. "I'm sorry we didn't have more time. I'm sorry we don't have a normal life."

"I'm sorry too. I've never been happier since the day we met. But I know that neither of us would be satisfied sitting by while so many others suffered. And that is one of the reasons I love you."

They stood quietly for a while, holding each other and holding onto the moment. They both knew that as soon as it was over, they would start a new journey filled with uncertainty, and they were savoring their last fleeting moments of peace.

Finally David said, "We should probably start heading back."

"I know," Aurora said without moving.

"We can get back to the lodge for dinner, stay there tonight, and head back in the morning. If that's all right with you?"

"I'd like that," she said, as she relaxed her hold and leaned back.

David kissed her tenderly, then looked at her and said, "Hmm, we had better get going. Otherwise, we might end up here all night."

"I wouldn't mind, but you're right, we should get going." Then they cleaned up the remnants of their lunch and put everything away in their packs, leaving the area as if they had never been there.

With their gear stowed and their packs on their backs, they took one more look at the sanctuary they were leaving. David turned to Aurora and said, "We'll come back someday, but in the meantime, as long as we're together, I'm happy."

"As long as we're together," Aurora said with a smile, and they set off without looking back.

On the hike down they replayed their conversation with Asis over and over, trying to think through what it all meant. Ultimately they came to the conclusion that they actually had no idea what to think, and that they would have to wait and see what they found when they got to Roktah. They finally reached the path that led to the meadow behind the lodge, and when they came out in the open, it was a welcome sight. They were both tired now after such a long hike there and back.

"Would you like to eat before we head upstairs, or do you want a late dinner and dancing?"

With a chuckle, she said, "I think if we go dancing, you'll have to carry me upstairs. Why don't we have dinner first? I don't know about you, but I'm hungry. That was a quite a workout."

"I was hoping you'd say that," David said, and then he stopped abruptly.

"What is it?" she asked.

"Something seems wrong," he said quietly. Looking as if he was trying to reach out for something that wasn't there, he added urgently, "Let's get inside."

They quickly made their way down the path, and the closer they got to The Lodge, the more apprehensive he felt. David pushed open the front doors of the lodge, staying a step ahead of Aurora, prepared to shield her from anything unexpected. Stepping inside the lobby, he quickly scanned the room, seeing there was no one else there except Charlie behind the counter. He began removing his backpack. Aurora followed his lead, taking hers off too.

"Charlie, how are you tonight? Would you mind if we leave our packs here with you while we go to the dining hall?"

"No problem, Sir." Charlie said, as David was already making his way to the dining hall. David patted his belt to assure himself that he was still armed, not knowing what to expect. He pulled the door open, trying to act as normal as possible, hoping not to draw any extra attention to himself. As the two of them walked towards the podium, David was rapidly cataloging the various groups in the room. It was early, so the full dinner crowd hadn't arrived yet, and he was thankful for that. Nothing jumped out at him, but his senses were on full alert.

"Can we please have a table in Addie's section?" David asked the hostess.

"Certainly. Come with me."

Aurora leaned close to him, and asked in a hushed voice, "Do you see anything wrong?"

"Nothing," he said, sounding disappointed. He would rather know what they were up against.

As they made their way across the room, Addie saw them, waved, and they waved back. She turned to come and meet them. They had just about reached the steps to the upper level when Addie caught up with them.

"Hi Terry. I'll take them to their table," Addie said excitedly.

"Thanks Addie," Terry said, and headed back in the other direction.

"A friend of yours is here to see you. He's such a nice man," Addie said, and started up the stairs.

David tried to ask her, "Who?" but she hurried off as if it was a big treat.

David and Aurora gave each other a questioning look and followed her. Addie made a beeline to the far corner where a lone man sat. David's ears began to ring slightly, and he felt the heat and anxiety rise in him. He hesitated, and then pushed his fears aside. He needed his wits about him. In two strides he had regained his composure and cleared his mind. He was not one to panic; that only led to mistakes. He reached out and took Aurora's hand. Her grip was firm, and he looked to see her warrior face too.

The sight of it all was surreal, Addie standing there beaming next to *him*, the *Dark One*.

"David and Aurora, congratulations," *He* said in a silky voice as *he* stood to greet them. "Dear Addie here has been telling me what a happy couple you are."

Addie looked at their expressions, and nervously said, "I hope it's all right. *He* said you were old friends."

"Of course we are," *he* said. "Why don't the two of sit and you join me?"

David turned to Addie and gave her a reassuring smile. "its fine, Addie. Thank you. Can you please get us some tea?"

Addie, looking relieved said, "Of course; right away." Then she hurried off.

David pulled out a chair for Aurora to sit, and gave her a slight nod telling her it was all right. The *Dark One* was dressed in an expensive dark suit with a black turtleneck. *His* polished looks and relaxed demeanor told David *he* was not there to exact *his* vengeance, at least not by trying to kill them, yet anyway.

The three of them sat, and David asked casually, "Why are you here?"

"I came to congratulate you on your wedding. I do owe the two of you a tremendous debt." *He* said.

"And what might that be?" Aurora asked, in a "as matter of fact" tone she could muster.

"You see when the two of you, shall we say, evicted me from that tower, it freed me to come here. This world offers so many opportunities I was denied there that I have only begun to sample," *he* said as he leered at Addie, who arrived with their drinks.

"Here you go; do you want anything else?" Addie asked.

"Not yet, Addie," David said kindly. "Can you give us a little bit to catch up?"

"Sure, just let me know," Addie said as she left them.

"What a sweet girl; so innocent and ripe," *he* said, watching her walk away, with a sickening emphasis on the word ripe.

"What do you want?" David asked firmly to draw *his* attention from Addie.

He turned his attention back to David. "What do I want," *he* said in a distant voice, as if *he* was considering the question.

"Yes, you didn't come here to congratulate us, so what do you want?"

"I want what everyone wants. I want to be free; I want to choose my own destiny. I want what has been denied to me, my rightful place of honor. You see, I once found His favor. Then I made the unforgivable mistake of defying Him, and for that I was cast out," *he* said, *his* voice rising slightly "I was left trapped in darkness, consigned to the shadows. Oh, men's evil hearts gave me glimpses of the world, but it was not enough. Then the two of you came along, and now here I sit, free. Free to bask in the light, free to enjoy the many pleasures this world has to offer," *his* gaze glancing at Addie and back, a sick smile growing on his face, "free to claim what is rightfully mine. You ask me what I want. I'm here to ask you to join me. Don't be fools doing His bidding; I can give you so much more. I can make you king and queen. You can have anything you want. He offers you a lifetime of servitude; I offer you a lifetime of rule. Imagine servants at your beck and call, spending your days indulging yourselves in whatever you want. And what does He offer you? Perilous journeys and hardship! You must have had quite a time coming to find me, while He denied you the solace of each other's touch didn't He? He would have sent you to your death, never knowing each other fully. I would never do such a thing. You deserve the rewards of your conquests, and I would give you that, and so much more."

David looked at him in silence for a moment; the hungry expression on *his* face, the burning hatred behind *his* eyes. As handsome as *he* was, it was a thin veneer over something truly foul. "I'm afraid the answer is no," David said. He could see the anger bubbling in *him* just below the surface. Now was not the time to stoke that fire.

"I see, yet you did not even consider what I have to offer."

"We don't have to," Aurora said, through a mask of false calm. "We've seen what you offer your followers and what they become. They are the vilest creatures in our world."

"They are that way to begin with. What they do with their freedom is not my fault. You could change that. You two could establish peace in my name."

"You have nothing we want. The Lord has blessed us with everything we need, and much more. Our faith rests in Him, and He has proven time and time again to be true. His way is light, life, and joy. Yours is death, destruction, and sorrow. We won't be tempted," David said, and he could see the anger burning in *his* eyes despite his calm exterior.

"Very well then. You have chosen, and when His kingdom falls and mine rises, do not expect to be afforded the opportunity for such honor. In the meantime, do not cross my path again or I will set my sights on all that you hold dear, and the pain and suffering I will inflict upon you will be unimaginable," *he* said with a steely gaze of controlled fury.

David looked at *him* and smiled, "And here I thought you wanted to be friends."

He looked at David curiously. It troubled *him* that *he* could not 'see' what was behind his eyes. "I underestimated you during our last encounter, but I will not make that mistake again. My time has come. As my influence grows in the world, His rule will diminish, and you will be left alone and wanting. Then you will come crawling to me and beg for my mercy."

"I see. Then you have nothing to worry about, do you?" David said.

Suddenly *he* laughed a cold chilling laugh. "No I do not, but I do enjoy your lack of concern. Perhaps I have overestimated you. Perhaps you just got lucky in our last encounter." *His* voice turned deadly. "Make no mistake. If you interfere with my plans again, you and your bride will not be so lucky this time. In the meantime, I want you to watch as I ascend, knowing there is nothing you can do about it."

He stood, and so did David and Aurora. They were standing there casually, but both were ready to act, as *he* looked them up and down. Just then Addie arrived.

"Do you need something?" Addie asked.

"Not yet. Our friend was just leaving," David said.

"Yes," *he* said in a snakelike hiss; then turned, and stared intently at Addie. She seemed slightly mesmerized, as if held fast in a trance as *he* asked, "and how would you like to join me?" Then *he* reached up to stroke her face, but in a flash, David had grabbed *his* wrist stopping *him*.

Addie seemed to snap out of her daze, and she saw the *Dark One's* face contorted into an ugly rage. They both felt a searing pain at each other's touch, but David held fast.

"Oh I can't, I have to work I... I... " Addie said, in a frightened voice as she scurried off, clutching her arms around herself, a look of horror on her face.

David let go of *him,* pushing away the pain, and said to *him* in a clear voice, "Good night then, until we meet again."

"Until we meet again," *he* said as *he* stepped out from behind the table; then added in a deadly voice, "Remember what I said." And *he* walked off.

David and Aurora stood watching *him* make *his* way across the room and out the doors. They turned to face each other, and David pulled her into his arms. She melted into his embrace, and he could feel her shaking slightly. "It's all right," he said. "*He*'s gone now." David knew *he* had left. He could not feel *his* presence anymore.

"He's so evil," Aurora said, "and I was afraid *he* was going to hurt poor Addie. Then when you grabbed *him*... I," She stopped not sure what to say.

"I'm sorry. I couldn't let *him* hurt her."

"I know. That's one of the reasons I love you, but I didn't know what to do."

"You did the right thing. This wasn't the time for us to act. Anything more and things could have gotten out of hand. Then who knows what would have happened."

"What's going on?" Tom said, suddenly standing there with Addie.

David and Aurora let go of each other, and David said, "Everything's okay, Tom. Addie, are you alright?"

Addie, looking frightened, said, "I am so sorry. *He* said you were old acquaintances, and he seemed so charming before, but he was so frightening, I ..." Then she burst into tears.

David looked at Tom and encouraged Addie to sit down. Then he and Aurora joined her. "Tom, would it be Ok if Addie sat with us for a little bit?"

"I'll get the other girls to cover her tables. I'll be back in a minute."

"Here Addie, drink some water," Aurora said, placing a reassuring hand on her arm.

"Who was *he*? When *he* looked into my eyes, I felt like *he* was violating me, and I was frozen, unable to move. Then the look on *his* face when you grabbed *his* arm; I've never been so frightened in my life."

"You might not believe me if I told you, but *he's* gone now," David said. "Did *he* say how *he* knew we were going to be here?"

"Yes. He said a birdie told him," she said, in a nervous laugh at the absurdity of it.

David considered it for a moment, but Tom interrupted his thoughts. "The other girls have everything covered. Now, tell me what's going on," Tom said in an authoritative voice.

"Putting it mildly, that was a very dangerous man, and we aren't on his good side."

"This doesn't have anything to do with that trip you took before the wedding, does it?"

"You know about that?" Aurora asked, still comforting Addie.

"Yes, Gabe told me all about it."

"So you know about everything?" David asked.

"Of course. I told you your father and I go way back. I'm on the council too. I would've come that first night, but I was out searching for some lost guests and missed the call."

"I see. Then I should tell you that it was *him*," David said.

"You don't mean the *Dark One*, do you?"

"Yes I do," David said, as Addie began to cry again.

"But I thought the two of you finished *him* off?"

"So did we, but evidentially by destroying *him* there we freed *him* to come here," Aurora said.

Tom, in a resigned voice, said, "Addie, I think it may be time to join the others."

"What do you mean?" David asked.

"We knew this time would come. We've been making preparations for a long time. I'm sorry I kept it from you two. It's just a habit, but Addie is my daughter, and now that *he* knows she's here, it won't be safe for her. We'll pack and leave tomorrow."

"What about the lodge?" David asked.

"I'll leave Charlie in charge. It really doesn't matter. Addie is more precious to me than anything. She's the light of my life," Tom said, smiling at her with the deepest affection.

She jumped up and hugged him. "Oh daddy, I love you so much."

"Of course, that was a silly question," David said. "We're leaving tomorrow too, but we can wait until you're ready to make sure you get off safely. Where are you headed?"

"The same place as you, I believe. We're supposed to meet at your parents' place, then head out from there to a sanctuary we have."

"I'll give him a call, and let him know we're coming. Where are the two of you staying tonight? I'm sure *he's* gone, but we shouldn't take anything for granted."

"Addie can stay here with me. We'll be fine." Tom said, "Why don't we get the two of you something to eat so we can all get an early night, and head out first thing."

"That sounds like a good idea. Would you and Addie like to join us?" David asked.

"My stomach is all in knots," Addie said.

"Mine too," Aurora said reassuringly. "But we need to keep our strength up. I learned a long time ago, if anything does happen, you can only go for so long on an empty stomach."

"I have just the thing," Tom said. "I'll go tell the kitchen and be right back."

Tom left, and Addie sat down. "*He* seemed so charming when *he* arrived. I can't believe what a fool I was," Addie said.

"Don't blame yourself," Aurora said. "He's fooled many people older and wiser."

"Why did *he* come here?"

"*He* claimed to want to offer us a place under *his* rule, but I don't think that was it," David said.

"What do you think *he* really wanted?" Aurora asked.

"I think *he* wanted to see what *he* was up against; if we're a threat to *him* here, too," David said thoughtfully.

Tom appeared and sat down to join them. "Dinner will be here shortly. Perhaps you should tell us what happened up until now. It would be helpful for me to catch up, and besides, according to your dad, it's quite a story even without his embellishments," Tom said with a smile.

"I can only imagine what my dad could do with the story," David said with a small chuckle. "Since we have some time, I suppose we should start at the beginning."

While they ate, David went on to tell them how he and Aurora had seen each other through glimpses their whole lives. As they told them of how they were drawn together, how they saved his father, of their bond, how it helped save his mother and defeat the *Dark One*, their moods lifted. Their story gave them hope, knowing that even when all seemed lost, there was still a way. David and Aurora looked at each other with only love in their hearts, and it made Addie blush.

"I only hope I find someone who loves me like that someday," Addie mused.

"Be careful what you say. David is a secret matchmaker," Aurora said with a smile.

"That's enough of that. I can only handle so much change at once," Tom said with a laugh.

"I have a feeling I'm going to be a bit tied up in the near future anyway, so don't worry too much," David said. "As for tonight I think we should go pack, and I need to call dad and fill him in."

"Yes, I need to go get with Charlie on a few things, and then get ready too. Why don't you come with me, Addie, and we can give each other a hand," Tom said. He clearly had no intention of letting her out of his sight.

"In other words, you are going to chaperone me tonight, Dad?" Addie said slyly.

"Smart girl, isn't she?"

"This time I won't complain."

Tom and Addie stood, and David and Aurora followed their lead. "Why don't we meet down here for breakfast?" Tom said.

"That sounds like a good plan to me. Get some rest, and if you need us, just ring our room, and we'll come right down," David said.

David fished some money out of his pocket and put it on the table. "What are you doing?" Tom asked.

"For the waitress," David said.

"All right, see you in the morning" Tom said, and he and Addie left.

David put an arm around Aurora, and they walked towards the elevators. "I'm sorry again our honeymoon was cut short."

"What we had was wonderful. Besides, it isn't over yet," Aurora said with a grin.

"I'd better get my dad off of the phone quickly then."

"Yes, you had."

They arrived at their room, to find Charlie had brought up their backpacks, and housekeeping had cleaned it. It looked just like the night they arrived. "I'll call dad," David said as he made his way to the sitting area.

"I'm going to change," Aurora said as she headed to the bathroom.

David dialed the house, and considered what he was going to say while the phone rang. He didn't have to wait long until his father answered, "Hello."

"Hi, Dad."

"It's a good thing Tom called. Otherwise, I would've started to worry about you. Are you two having a good time?"

"We had a terrific time, but we're coming home tomorrow. Something has come up."

"What's wrong?"

"I'll fill you in on everything when we get home, but *he* was here tonight."

"*He* who? What are you talking about?"

"The *Dark One*," David said. The line was silent for a moment until David asked, "Dad are you still there?"

"Is everyone all right?"

"Everyone is fine. Tom and his daughter are coming with us. We're leaving first thing in the morning."

"Are you saying *he* just showed up there?" Gabe asked, "How would *he* know where you were?"

"I'm not sure, but I think I have an idea," David said. "*He* was sitting in the dining hall waiting for us to get back from our hike, and we talked to *him*."

"You just sat down and talked to the *Dark One*?" Gabe asked incredulously.

"Yes. I promise I'll tell you everything when we get home. There's too much for me to tell you now, but I want you to please alert everyone and be on the lookout. I don't think *he*'s going to bother you, but please don't take any chances."

"Son, you promise me YOU won't take any chances. I'll get the word out, and we'll be safe here inside the seal. Don't worry about us. You just get back here safely."

"We're going to be fine, Dad. How are you and Mom doing?"

"Your mom's fine. She's been telling me not to worry about you. She is starting to feel like herself again, so I'm having trouble getting away with anything."

"Good. You need her to keep you out of trouble."

"Hey, look who's talking!"

Aurora stepped out of the bath, wearing her small robe. It was hanging open, revealing a little of her bare body underneath. David took a breath at the sight. She began walking towards him with a seductive gaze.

"Dad, please tell Mom I love her, and that we'll be there tomorrow, Ok?"

"What do you mean that's it, you tell me that you sat down for a chit chat with the *Dark One*, and that's all you're going to say?"

Aurora leaned towards him, her robe falling open leaving him breathless, and she whispered in his ear, "I drew a bath for us." Then she stood up and sauntered back to the bath.

"Sorry Dad, Aurora…. Needs me." David said, forcing his voice not to betray him "I promise I'll tell you everything tomorrow."

"All right son, please be careful. I can't tell you how much your mother and I love you, and if anything were to happen…" Gabe said, words failing him.

"Dad, I promise, we'll be there tomorrow, and I love you both too. Give Mom an extra hug and kiss for me, and tell her not to worry."

Regaining himself, Gabe said, "You owe me. I'm going to get an earful for not finding out more. Goodnight, son, see you tomorrow."

"Goodnight, Dad." David hung up, and immediately headed to the bath.

HOME AGAIN

If they hadn't been so tired from their long hike to the waterfall and back, they might have been up all night. Lost in each other, the troubles that lay before them seemed like a distant memory, but their fatigue won out, and they fell asleep in each other's arms. The light of the morning woke them, and they quickly dressed and brought their bags down to breakfast. Tom and Addie were waiting, and the four of them talked about their trip. They decided it would be best to stay together, much to David's relief. There was no doubt Tom was not easily intimidated, and David was afraid Tom would not like the idea of them watching over him and Addie. It seemed that Tom's concern for his daughter was too strong for him to take any unnecessary risks.

The four of them made their way to the cars and began loading the bags, when David felt a slight tingle. He casually turned around, pretending to check the bags on the ground when he spotted it. Turning back to the car, he whispered to Aurora, "act naturally, but behind me across the road on a fence post is a raven. Do you think you can hit it with an arrow? You'll have to be very quick."

Aurora dropped her bag, making it look like an accident, and when she leaned down to pick it up, caught sight of the bird. Then she whispered back, "I think so."

"You'll only get one shot, so don't rush."

David shielded her from view, and she retrieved her bow from inside the car and got an arrow ready. With an imperceptible nod, she signaled to David, who stepped aside. She turned and let the arrow fly. The bird barely spread its wings to take flight when the arrow hit it. It fell to the ground, letting out a horrible screeching sound and flopped around violently.

"What are you two doing?" Tom asked. "We need to get going."

David and Aurora ran over to where the bird was in the throes of death. Tom and Addie followed close behind. The bird was looking at them, screeching angry hate-filled sounds. Then it fell still. A moment later, an unearthly scream erupted from it and a dark shadow burst forth and shattered in the sunlight.

"What was that?" Tom asked.

"I think that's how *he* knew where we were," David said. "I saw a raven when we were leaving and thought it was odd, especially the size of it." Then he added, "We should get going."

David grabbed the arrow, pulled it from the dead bird, and then pushed its carcass into the tall grass off the road. They all walked back to the lodge where he broke the arrow and tossed it into a trash bin. They got into their cars and left without pause. David felt sad leaving this place that had always represented peace, beauty, and fond memories. It had been tainted by '*his*' presence. He thought to himself that this was a foreshadowing of things to come. Everything *he* touched would be tainted, and *his* taint would spread like a disease over the world. He only hoped they could find what they needed quickly enough to prevent *him* from gaining too much ground. Then it occurred to him that even if they did succeed, what came next would likely be even worse.

On their last journey, he thought they would end it, and that thought made it bearable. This time would be different. David would be setting in motion a dreadful chain of events. It would require more courage and greater faith to do what must be done. Then a comforting thought came to him. He saw the wisdom in how it had all unfolded. On their first mission, they had been told what they needed to know, and their faith had delivered them. If they had known then what they know now, they may not have made the right choices. This time was no different. It didn't matter what he thought the outcome would be; he had to have faith and trust that the Lord's plan was the best one.

"You're awfully quiet. Are you Ok?" Aurora asked.

"I'm sorry. I was lost in thought, but I had a kind of revelation about us."

"Is it a good one, I hope?" Aurora asked lightheartedly.

"Actually it is. I think our last mission was more than just about accomplishing a task. I think it was also a lesson for us."

"What do you mean?"

"When we walked into that tower, we were both prepared to die, and it seemed hopeless."

"That's right."

"Yet, even though it seemed as if there was no hope, we did not lose our faith. Because of that, we were delivered," David said. "What we're about to do is going to make things worse before they can get better. How could we do that, if we had not seen for ourselves that if we are faithful to the end, there's still hope?"

"So you think we can't fail?"

"No, we could still fail, or still die, but no matter what happens to us, if we're faithful to the very end, the Lord will not abandon us, and there will be hope."

"I believe that. Not only did He deliver us, but He also has blessed me with more than I ever dreamed. I will follow whatever path He sets us on, but I wouldn't complain if we knew where we were going."

"If we had been told what the outcome was going to be, would we have made the right choices? I don't know."

"I see what you mean. At least we don't have to worry about that, because I have no idea what we are going to do," Aurora said with a smile.

David chuckled. "Neither do I, but I don't mind as long as you come with me. "

"To the very end."

"I'm a lucky man. By the way, that was a terrific shot back there."

"Thanks, but I hope you aren't going to throw away every arrow I use. We won't be able to go to Bob's any time we want and get more where we're going."

"Sorry about that. I just didn't want to waste time cleaning it. We can go tomorrow and get some more for our trip."

They spent the rest of the drive making their plans for their upcoming journey, discussing the kinds of weather and terrain they would encounter so they would know what to bring with them. They had to be prepared, but since they would have to carry everything they took on their backs, they didn't want to take anything they didn't need.

As they were getting close to home, David said, "I was thinking about what Asis said. We should discuss who we're going to tell about our mission, and what we're going to tell everyone else."

"Yes, I suppose you're right. Of course, I think we should tell your parents, Molly, and Michael. Is there anyone else you think should know?"

"As soon as we get home, we're going to have to talk to them before the council arrives. I'm thinking that if Tom and Addie are with us, it should be ok if they know. What do you think?"

"I trust your judgment and will follow your lead when the time comes, so whatever you decide, I'll back you up."

"Thank you. As for the rest of the council, I think we should tell them that we have a mission we can't discuss. I don't want to lie, but I think the less we say, the better."

"I agree. Lies are some of the poison *he* uses."

"Absolutely, and if we fight this battle playing by *his* rules, we'll surely fail."

They turned off the highway, and David was relieved to see the road up to the house. Tom and Addie were close behind. Making their way up the drive, David's heart leapt at the sight of his parents, Molly, Michael, and Rusty coming out to meet them, their waves of encouragement welcoming them home. David turned to look at Aurora, and she was beaming with pleasure too. Having lost her family, it meant a lot to her being so warmly accepted into his.

David was hardly out of the car when his father gave him a strong hug. David looked to see his mother embracing Aurora.

"You had me so worried, Son. I'm glad you're back," Gabe said. Then letting go, they walked to the other side of the car, and when Aurora and his mom let go of each other, Gabe said, "Come here, you", and took Aurora into his arms. David saw her smiling brightly. "I'm so happy to see you, too. Thank you for keeping him out of trouble."

"Your father has been pacing all morning," His mother said, as she gave her son a hug.

"I'm sorry you were worried. I didn't want to say too much last night. We were followed to the Lodge, and I wasn't sure by who or what."

"Followed? What do you mean?" Gabe asked.

"A raven was host to something dark. I didn't make the connection until this morning; I saw it when we left, and it was waiting for us again this morning," David said. "Aurora killed it."

"You should have seen that too," Tom said. "She shot that thing from 50 yards dead center, so fast I couldn't believe it."

Gabe and Michael chuckled. "Yes, we've seen her handiwork," Michael said.

"Why don't all of you come inside? We have lunch ready, and you must be hungry after that long drive. Then you can tell us everything," Ruth said.

David felt at ease being back as they walked up the steps. It may have been the seal or the company, or both, but he was happy for the relief. It would allow him to think clearly. The house was warm and inviting. Once inside, David pulled Aurora close. She looked up and smiled at him. He could see she felt the same sense of peace he did at being home. Wafting in from the kitchen were the smells of his mother's handiwork. He guessed while his dad was pacing, she was cooking.

"I baked some fresh bread and put a pie in the oven. I hope you're all hungry," Ruth said.

They sat down, and after giving thanks, Gabe asked impatiently, "Are you ready to tell us what's going on?"

"Gabe, let him eat," Ruth said.

"It's ok, Mom, I want to talk about it. We have a lot to do and the sooner we get started the better." David said, "I trust all of you without question." He gave a nod to Tom and Addie, letting him know they were included "What I'm about to tell you must remain between us. You must under no circumstances talk to anyone else about it. If any of you don't want that burden, I would understand." He looked again at Tom and Addie.

"You can count on me," Tom said, "what about you, Addie?"

"I saw up close what we're up against. I want to help." Addie said confidently.

"As you know we had planned to go to the waterfall I found years ago. Yesterday when I woke up something told me we had to go right away. When we arrived we were visited be an emissary of the Lord." Addie gasped slightly "He came to tell us about what is coming."

David and Aurora relayed to them, word for word, what Asis had said. "So tomorrow we're planning to leave on our mission and no one may know where we have gone."

"Of course you can count on us. What do you plan on telling the council they'll be here tonight?" Michael asked.

"The truth. We're going on a mission, and we can't tell them where. We're also going to tell them that you must all be prepared for what's coming."

"They'll want to know more, I'm sure." Gabe said.

"They must have faith."

They all sat quietly for a moment, then Molly asked, "What happened when you got back to the lodge? Gabe said you saw 'Him'."

"He asked us to join Him, and take a place of honor in His kingdom. He wasn't too happy when we turned *him* down. After that, *he* set his sights on Addie. I grabbed *his* arm to keep *him* from touching her, and it was excruciating for both of us. I think *he* was surprised. *He* must have thought that *he* was no longer at risk from us after *he* got here," David said. "But after that, Addie would have been in danger if she had stayed. I'm sure of it."

"What do you think *he*'s going to do?" Michael asked.

"*He*'s going to corrupt as many people as *he* can, and spread *his* evil like a plague. Anyone who gets in *his* way will suffer," Aurora said.

David saw his mother looking like she might be sick. "Are you alright, Mom?" he asked, and Aurora, sitting next to her, put an arm around Ruth to comfort her.

Ruth welcomed her embrace, and said, "I'm just afraid for both of you. I was there too. Remember, it almost killed you." She finished weakly, a tear running down her cheek.

"I'm sorry, Mom. I know it's dangerous, but so many people are going to suffer. Look at what happened to you and to dad. We can't sit by and let *him* have free reign. We have to do what we can. We need to have faith that whatever happens, good or bad, if we trust in the Lord, He will deliver us," David said gently.

"We know, Son, and we're both very proud of the two of you," Gabe said. "We lost so many years together, we'd just hoped we'd have more time to spend together first. We knew this was coming; just not so soon."

"I know, Dad. It breaks my heart to leave you, too."

"David, we have a long journey ahead of us. I don't think one more day would hurt. Maybe we could stay tomorrow, and leave the next day instead," Aurora said.

David looked at her quietly for a moment then said, "You're right, and preparing our hearts is just as important as preparing our gear."

The mood lightened with the prospect of another day together, even as they talked about what Asis had said, and what it might all mean. After lunch they unloaded the cars, then sat together to relax until the rest of the council members arrived. It didn't take long until Gabe and Tom were entertaining them with stories, each one more fanciful than the other, and they enjoyed every minute of it.

Before they knew it, the council members began arriving. The house was overflowing with people and buzzing with conversation. Once everyone was there, they gathered into the living room, with several people overflowing into the hallways. The mood was solemn as Michael called order to the group. They immediately stopped talking to listen, in hopes of finding out what was going on.

"Thank you, everyone, for coming on such short notice. We have much to discuss, but first let us pray. Father, we thank You for all the blessings You have bestowed upon us, for bringing us all together here tonight in Your name. We ask that You would grant us wisdom and discernment in these trying times, that we would follow Your will, and help to further Your kingdom. Amen," Michael said.

The group echoed, "Amen."

"David and Aurora have some important news to share with us, so I will ask them to speak to you," Michael said; then nodded at David encouragingly.

David stepped into the center of the room in front of the fire. "I hope you'll all forgive me. I'm not an eloquent speaker, so if I'm blunt, I mean no disrespect. While we were on our trip, we went hiking to a special

place in the mountains and were visited by an emissary of the Lord."
There were several whispers from the crowd. "He explained to us that
when we faced the *Dark One* and vanquished *him* from the other world, *he*
was freed from its hold, and has come here to ours." There were several
gasps, and many hushed whispers at this. "He told us that this was a
necessary step towards the final battle. As difficult as this is to hear, *he*
walks among us now and will spread *his* poison like a plague on our
world. We know this to be true because *he* came to us in person." The
crowd erupted in chatter, and David calmly waited for them to settle
down.

One of the men asked, "How can you be sure it was *him*?"

"We sat down at a table and talked to *him*. *He* asked us to join *him*,
and of course we refused," David said, and the crowd became silent. "You
should also know *he* threatened us, saying that if we crossed *his* path, *he*
would come after us, our friends, and our family. So you must all take
precautions, stay together, and if possible, avoid any direct confrontations
with *his* followers. Your work should be to protect and strengthen those
who are vulnerable so they may not fall to *him*. Aurora and I have been
tasked with a mission, and I apologize that I can't share with you what it
is, but when we return, we hope to know what to do next."

"Are you saying that we're approaching the end times?" Another man
asked.

"No, we don't know when those days will arrive. *His* time here must pass before that is to come. That's all we know," David said. "But *he*'ll do *his* best to gain strength now for *his* return."

Everyone stood in silence, looking at him, and waiting for something more. David didn't know what to say. Then he looked at Aurora standing by his side, confident and sure, and it came to him.

"After all that we've been through the past few weeks, the most valuable lesson we learned was we ventured out with only our faith, we had no idea what to expect, but that was all that we needed. Putting our trust in the Lord, even when there seemed to be no hope, is what delivered us. Remember that it is the only true protection we have," David said, and looking across the faces staring at him, he saw people beginning to smile. "Remember Gideon. He was asked to stand before overwhelming odds; it was not up to him to defeat the Midionites. No, he had to trust in the Lord, and the Lord destroyed their army before his eyes." Everyone was nodding in agreement, and their mood lifted. "What we face is a battle of faith. In a battle of force we will lose, but in a battle of faith, we can surely be victorious."

"What should we do in the meantime while we wait for your return?" a man asked.

David reached out and took Aurora's hand, pulling her close to him. "Stand united. You must strengthen your bonds with all those in our family of faith. Those bonds are the best protection against the poison *he* spreads; *his* lies. *He* fosters mistrust and plays on people's fears and desires, seeking to draw you to *him* of your own will. Alone we are easy targets, but together our combined strength can prevail." David paused, seeing the nods of agreement. "Don't travel alone. Tom mentioned a sanctuary. That sounds like a good idea. We need places we can meet in safety, but we cannot cut ourselves off from the world. We must continue to do the Lord's work. We must reach out to all the believers we can. We must make it as difficult for *him* to corrupt them as possible. *He* already has the nonbelievers, so *he* will not waste *his* efforts there. I would suggest you avoid direct conflict with *his* followers. It will only make you a target, and force you to go into hiding."

"When will you be back?" a woman asked.

David suddenly realized they were looking at him as their leader. "Honestly, we don't know, but you all know Michael and my father, and there are no two men I trust more to speak for me in my absence."

Many of the people looked at Michael and Gabe, nodding their agreement. David looked at them for reassurance, and their expressions told him he hadn't overstepped his bounds. "I'm sorry I don't have all the answers, but I realized something significant today. The Lord tells us what we need to know, not necessarily what we want to know. Just as nonbelievers fail to understand, the Bible is not meant to be a how-to guide to salvation. It is a story of faith, and what it means to be faithful. We must not fall into the same trap. When Aurora and I set out on our last journey, we knew what we needed to know. We walked into that pit, fully expecting to sacrifice everything, and just as when Abraham acted faithfully as he prepared to sacrifice Isaac, the Lord delivered us. In doing so, He showed us that no matter how desperate the situation might be, through Him there is always a way. We all need to remember that, because what lies before us is far beyond what we can accomplish or understand on our own. We must all remember that the Lord even uses tragedies and pain for good, and most importantly, if we seek His will in all things, He will not take us where his grace cannot sustain us."

"I would remind you of Matthew 24:42. Therefore, stay awake, for you do not know on what day your Lord is coming."

"Remember, no one knows when the end days will come; only our Father. There will be many false prophets and people who perform miraculous things in order to trick us. Be sure to seek the truth in all things, and look to the fellowship of the faithful to sustain you."

They all stood in silence, considering what he said. "From what I understand, there is a plenty of food. Why don't we all share this meal in fellowship? Remember what Michael said, 'where two or more gather in my name I am with them.' Today is the beginning of our journey. The Lord has brought us together, and what the Lord has brought together, let no man or beast tear asunder. The *Dark One* can't break our bonds; only we can." Then David said kindly, "I'll be here all night if any of you should want to ask me any questions."

He turned and led Aurora over to his father and Michael. "I apologize, Michael. I didn't mean to take over. It just sort of happened."

Michael looked at David with admiration, and said, "David, you were chosen to lead, and I follow you willingly. There is nothing for you to apologize for."

"Thank you, Michael. That means a lot to me."

Ruth put her hand on Gabe's shoulder, and said, "Our boy has grown into quite a man while we were away."

"I'm happy to take full credit if you want," Gabe said, and Ruth hit him squarely on the arm. "Ouch!"

They all chuckled a little, and David said, "Thanks Mom. I'm only trying to do the best I can."

"We'd better get something to eat. I have a feeling you're going to be quite busy," Aunt Molly said, eyeing a group of people looking their way.

They started to move towards the kitchen, and David caught Michael. "Any word on Charles and Rebecca since we've been gone?"

Michael chuckled, "Oh yes. They're like peas in a pod. We aren't off the hook yet though, so keep praying it all works out. I might rather face the *Dark One* if it doesn't."

"I may be with you on that."

"What about you and Molly?" Aurora said, teasing him. "Another wedding would be a lovely treat."

"Well, I…. Uh…. " Michael sputtered.

"And you gave me a hard time about being a matchmaker," David chided Aurora.

"I guess you are rubbing off on me," she said mischievously.

"All right you two. Don't spoil the surprise, but I have been walking around with the ring in my pocket for a week now. I just hadn't found the right moment to ask her," Michael blushed. Then pausing a moment, added, "But considering the latest events, I'm not going to wait any longer." He pulled his shoulders back, pushed his way forward, and put his hand on Molly's arm.

David and Aurora looked at each other dumbfounded. Molly turned and looked at Michael curiously, and when Michael suddenly dropped to one knee, pulling out the ring in his pocket, her hands flew up to cover her mouth.

"Molly, I don't want to wait another minute. I want to spend the rest of my life with you. Will you marry me?"

For the first time in his life, David saw Molly speechless. Her hands dropped from her mouth, her jaw moved, and yet no sound came out. Everyone left in the room stood and stared in shocked silence. Michael, always so calm and even keel, acting so impulsively, was almost as shocking as proposing this way.

"Molly, if you're going to turn me down, please do it quickly while I can still get back up without your help," Michael said with a grin.

"You old fool, of course I'll marry you," Molly said as she grabbed his shirt with both hands, pulling him in to kiss her as he rose. He wrapped his arms around her as everyone in the room began to applaud.

"Well I'll be," David said, "I didn't see that coming."

From behind them Gabe asked, "What did you two do?"

"We just gave him a little nudge," Aurora said gleefully.

"Dad, I just remembered I may need you to take care of some business for the mission while I'm gone. I also need Rebecca to get a message to little Charlie telling him I won't be there. I'll leave you all of the instructions."

"I'll take care of it."

They tried to make their way through the crowd, but people kept stopping David to talk to him. He encouraged his parents to go on without him, but Aurora stayed by his side. After a while, she decided he would never get to eat unless she went and got his food and brought it back to him. Between bites, he and Aurora sat for the next several hours, meeting individually with each and every one of the guests. It seemed they all needed to make a connection with him. They all needed to share their plans, their hopes and fears, looking to David to assuage their doubts.

David didn't mind. These were the same people who dropped everything to help with their wedding on a minutes notice, and more importantly, look after his father while he was gone. Their desire to talk to him was like giving him their vote of confidence. He was humbled by it all, and at the same time determined not to let them down.

The last of the guests had left, and the eight of them were relaxing in the living room. It had been a long evening. "David, I think you broke the record for the longest council meeting yet," Michael said.

"I'm pretty sure we talked to everyone one on one, and a few people twice," David said. "If you don't mind, I think I need a little fresh air before I call it a night, if anyone wants to join me."

"That sounds like a great idea," Tom said.

"I'll go," Gabe said.

"I'm coming," Michael said.

David stood and looked at Aurora. "I think I'm going to stay here with the girls," Aurora said.

David leaned down and kissed her on the cheek. "Ok, I won't be too long," and the four of them walked out onto the front porch. The night was crisp and the sky was clear. Through the opening in the trees, they could see countless stars. The moon was gone now, so the darkness on the ground was like a wall around them. David didn't sense anything out of place, so he stretched and breathed in the night air.

"The two of you are headed into some cold weather. We'd better make sure you have all the right gear tomorrow," Gabe said.

"Sure, Dad. Maybe we can go to Bob's together. I need to pick up a couple of things."

"What's it like in the other world?" Tom asked.

"It's like going back in time hundreds of years. The only metalworking I saw was for weapons or cooking," David said.

"How dangerous do you think this is going to be?" Michael asked.

"Honestly," David said, then paused a moment and looked at his dad, "more dangerous than last time. Although we won't have *him* to contend with, which is an enormous plus." They all stood silently, then David added, "This time I'm going to be better prepared. A few attention getters might go a long way in preventing some of the fighting. These people aren't particularly sophisticated, so loud noises and bright flashes could prove extremely helpful."

"I like it," Gabe said.

"Almost makes me want to come with you," Tom said.

"Maybe you and my dad can find something to blow up while I'm gone. Someone has to keep him out of trouble."

"Hey now," Gabe said, "These days I have to worry more about getting into trouble with your mom than anything else."

"That's too dangerous for me," Tom said with a laugh.

"I think Michael's in the most danger of us all," David said, and they all laughed.

When the men walked back inside, they found the women huddled together on the couch. They immediately stopped talking as they entered the room, and Addie and Molly were both a little red in the face.

"What are you four up to?" Gabe asked suspiciously.

"Never mind, Gabe," Ruth said.

"I think Michael is in more trouble than we thought" Gabe said, and they all laughed as Michael and Molly shone bright red in the face.

"Gabriel, you watch out," Molly said half amused.

Aurora stood up, and walked to David "I told Aunt Molly not to wait for us to get back for the wedding. I hope that's all right with you."

"Definitely. Aunt Molly, we have no idea how long we're going to be, and you two shouldn't wait to start your lives together."

Molly looked around at everyone, and seeing no objection finally said, "Ok."

"Besides," Gabe said mischievously "If you wait too long Michael may change his mind."

"Gabriel I warned you," Molly said with a little laugh, and stood as if she were going to hit him.

Michael stepped in, and taking Molly in his arms said, "Don't give it a thought. I'm not changing my mind."

She smiled at him, and reached around and pinched her brother. "Ouch!" Gabe exclaimed.

Everyone laughed, "I don't know about the rest of you, but I'm going to call it a night before I get dragged into this." David said.

"Smart boy," Tom said.

"Smarter than his father," Ruth said.

"Hey now, brothers and sisters are supposed to give each other a hard time," Gabe said.

"Good night everyone," David said as he and Aurora moved towards the hallway. He bent down and gave his mother a kiss on the cheek. Addie was sitting next to her on the couch, and he said, "Be careful Addie, once they get started …"

"I will. They aren't getting me in the middle."

"Goodnight everyone," Aurora said and gave Ruth a hug. Ruth looked up at her, and gently placed a hand on Aurora's cheek smiling.

Once inside the room they began changing for bed. David said, "My dad and I are going to sort through our gear in the morning, and then go to Bob's to pick up a few things. Would you like to come with us?"

"If you don't need me, I might just stay here with your mom."

"That's fine. I'm so happy you two get along so well."

"Yes, I truly like her. I know this isn't actually our home, but I feel so at home here."

"Of course it's our home. This is where our family is."

They climbed in under the covers, the room was chilly, and the sheets felt icy against their skin. David was lying on his back, and Aurora pressed up close against him her arm and leg draped over him as much for warmth as comfort. She was holding him tightly, and he could sense the slight melancholy in her mood. His arm wrapped around her, he pulled her close to him.

"Are you all right?"

"Yes. As happy as I am, I would love to have had my parents here to meet you."

"I would've liked that."

"I wish we didn't have to leave. It would be wonderful to stay here with our family longer, and be normal for a change."

"It sure would, but I have to tell you, you aren't normal."

In an uncertain voice, Aurora asked, "What do you mean?"

"You are exceptional, and if we never get to live 'normal lives' it's a small price to pay to be together." David kissed her on the top of her head.

She squeezed him tightly, "That it is." He could feel her smiling against his chest.

They sat quietly for a little while then David realized she had drifted off to sleep. He closed his eyes and joined her.

The next morning they woke with the sun, and found the kitchen buzzing with activity. His parents, Tom, Michael, and Molly were all busy getting breakfast ready and talking. David and Aurora joined them, and a little while later Addie appeared. David assumed with her nighttime schedule working at the restaurant she wasn't used to getting up so early.

They had an enjoyable breakfast filled with lively conversations. With the exception of Aurora and Addie everyone had known each other a long time, so there was plenty to talk about. As soon as breakfast was done Aurora and Addie volunteered to help clean up while Tom went with Gabe and David to begin reviewing all of their gear, and help them round out what they needed for the trip. The three of them were all expert woodsmen, and by the time they finished they felt they had everything covered. A couple of hours later, and a trip to Bob's, they all felt David and Aurora would be ready for anything.

When they returned, David was happy to find the girls and Michael all engaged in conversation. Michael had opted to stay with his bride-to-be since he wasn't much of a woodsman anyway. Aurora, seeing David enter the room, rushed over to give him a quick hug and kiss. Then she hurried back to where his mother was teaching her how to make a pie. They put it in the oven just before lunch, and the smell of it baking made them all anxious for it to finish.

They decided to leave right after breakfast in the morning. Gabe and Ruth were going to drive them up to the clearing so they could bring the car back. They didn't want any signs indicating where they had gone. During the afternoon plans for the sanctuary were discussed. Years ago, they had begun building a small village in a remote part of the property that David was surprised to find out about. It was one of the few places he hadn't explored; primarily because once he was managing the farm by himself he just didn't have the time.

No one had been there in years, but seals protected it, and they were hopeful that they could get it into shape without too much trouble. The good news was that they had many hands with all the council members and their families. Once they had finished a long dinner, cleaned the kitchen, and enjoyed the pie Ruth and Aurora made, David was ready for some fresh air. He and Aurora decided to sit outside for a while before calling it a night.

Sitting on the same bench, where David had saved her from an assassin's arrow, all was calm tonight. "I think it's a good thing we're going to be on foot for a couple of days. I need to work off all the food we ate today." David mused.

Aurora ran her hand around his middle, "you still feel good to me."

"I think you're delirious from too much food too. It was great spending the day with everyone. I'm glad you suggested it."

"I'm not delirious, and I had a really good day too."

The fresh air felt refreshing, but it was cold with a slight breeze. They pressed close against each other for warmth. "I suppose we shouldn't stay up too late so we can get an early start tomorrow."

"And this may be the last night we get to sleep in a bed for a while."

"Hmm maybe we should take advantage of the bed then?"

Aurora giggled a little, "then what are we doing out here?"

They got up, and went inside, said their goodnights to everyone, and made their way back to their room. The minute the door was shut David kissed her, his gentle sensual lingering lips sent waves of sensation rippling through her whole body. His strong hands on her waist pulling her close to him made her feel weak in the knees. She cooed her approval as her hands began roaming over his strong frame. His heart was pounding, and feeling her body pressed against him was intoxicating.

Hours later they laid there breathless, wrapped around each other, lost in the closeness they felt. Neither one of them spoke not wanting to disturb their peaceful contentment. At that moment nothing else existed for them, they didn't have a mission. There was no journey ahead of them. It was just the two of them, lost in each other. Lying there, holding onto the moment as long as possible, they both drifted off to sleep.

Finally, the morning sunlight drifting into their room woke them. They looked at each other and smiled, as if they had just lain down. "Hi," Aurora said.

"Hi."

"I guess we have to get up."

"I guess we do."

Reluctantly they got up showered, dressed, and straightened up the room. They weren't going to be back here for a while. They put all the things away they weren't taking with them, then turned and looked one last time on their way out the door. As they made their way to the kitchen, they could smell the enticing aroma of breakfast.

The morning's conversation was upbeat, but subdued. They all felt the weight of David and Aurora's impending departure. They weren't just leaving; their voyage marked the beginning of what was to come. Their lives were all going to change and no one had any idea of what to expect. After they had eaten Michael, Molly, Tom, and Addie insisted they would clean up, and that Gabe and Ruth should take David and Aurora so they could have some time to themselves to say goodbye.

David assured them all that they would be back. He quietly asked Michael and Tom to look after his parents for him while he was gone, and of course they agreed. Even though they had regained a lot of their strength, they both still had a way to go after their long ordeals. Then the four of them set out for the clearing where they expected to make their way back to Aurora's world. It was a short drive to the wooded path, and once out of the car they donned their backpacks. Aurora looked at the sword on one side of David's pack, and a weapon she hadn't seen before on the other. She wasn't sure what it was, but thought they had plenty of time for her to ask later. He also had extra arrows for her bow, adding to the large supply she had on her pack.

Gabe and Ruth walked with them through the woods to the edge of the clearing. Gabe turned to David, "Son be careful, I'm going to miss you terribly, and want you back here in one piece."

David hugged his dad, "I will Dad. You be careful too. I expect you and Mom to be safe when I return. Don't take any unnecessary risks while I'm gone."

"I'll have my hands full with your mom, and the wedding, remember? So don't you worry about us."

David saw Aurora and his mother hugging and smiled. Then he walked over and gave his mom a hug too. "Hurry back, Son."

"We'll do our best Mom," David wiped a tear from her cheek "try not to worry; I promise we'll be back."

David and Aurora took each other's hands and headed into the field. Gabe and Ruth stood and watched as the air began to crackle. Then with an explosion of light they were gone. The two of them stood staring at the spot they last were; Gabe put his arm around Ruth who began to sob quietly into his chest. He didn't say anything. He had to be strong for her, and the lump in his throat told him his voice would betray him. In silence, they turned and headed back.

Coming soon. David and Aurora continue their journey in "Seal of the King into the Heart of Darkness".

David and Aurora, head back to her homeland to rally the people. They have to prevail in the final battle against the Dark One's army before they can continue their quest. Outnumbered and facing monstrous demons, it will require all of their skills and faith to survive.

If they succeed, they face a far greater challenge. They must travel to the temple, and into the heart of darkness to discover the Dark One's secret. To make matters worse, every day they are gone His influence on our world will grow.

Thank you for taking time to read Seal of the King. If you enjoyed it, please consider telling your friends or posting a short review. Word of mouth is an author's best friend and much appreciated.

Made in the USA
Charleston, SC
15 December 2014